To Love Again

TO LOVE AGAIN

A Novel by

Bertrice Small

Ballantine Books

New York

ISBN: 0-345-37391-X

Cover design by James R. Harris
Cover painting by Elaine Duillo

Manufactured in the United States of America

To my friend, Judy Walker, of Aston, Pa.,
who has twice given up a career
in publishing.

To Love Again

Prologue

BRITAIN

A.D. 44–406

T*he Celtic warrior*, a Catuvellauni by tribe, lay facedown in the mud upon the smoking earth. His naked body, battered and broken, was painted a vibrant shade of blue. Around him a thousand more of his kind lay dead or dying while Roman legionaries moved methodically over the battlefield administering the coup de grace to those unfortunate enough to still be clinging to life. He could hear the calls of the carrion birds gathering, and a shudder ran through him.

Nearby, a party of Roman officers stood watching. Turning his head slightly, he viewed them through slitted eyelids, recognizing to his amazement the emperor himself. The warrior moved his hand stealthily toward his javelin. Slowly, his fingers closed about its shaft, feeling the comfortable familiarity of the smooth ashwood. He was barely breathing, but it did not matter. Breathing hurt too much now.

With superhuman effort, he pulled himself stiffly to his feet. Then howling like a demon, he hurled his weapon directly at the

Roman emperor, exhausting every bit of his remaining strength. To the warrior's deep disappointment, a tall, young tribune standing in the group reacted far more swiftly than he would have thought possible and flung himself in front of the emperor, taking the full brunt of the javelin in his kneecap.

The Catuvellauni warrior had no time to admire the young man's bravery. He was already dead; his head severed from his neck by a second tribune who had leapt forward in his own defense of the emperor. The head, its long hair bloody and matted, rolled across the ground, stopping at the feet of the emperor.

Claudius looked down and sighed deeply. He recognized the head as belonging to one of the personal bodyguards of the Catuvellauni war chief. He had noticed the boy when the Catuvellauni had come to talk peace, even as they were treacherously massing their forces in an attempt to drive the Romans from Britain. The young man had a smallish, but very distinct birthmark upon his left cheekbone. Claudius, physically impaired himself, was quick to notice others with impairments of any kind. He shook his head sadly. He did not like war. So many young lives like this one wasted. Young men fought wars, but it was the old men like himself who planned those wars.

He turned away from the severed head, giving his attention now to the tribune who had shielded him from certain death. "How is he?" the emperor asked the surgeon who was kneeling by the tribune's side, staunching the copious flow of blood.

"He'll live," came the dour reply, "but there will be no more soldiering for this one, Caesar. The javelin, by the grace of the gods, missed the artery to his heart. It has chipped the knee bone, and damaged the tendons. The boy will walk with a marked limp the rest of his days."

Claudius nodded, and then he asked the injured young man, "What is your name, tribune?"

"Flavius Drusus, Caesar."

"Are we related, then?" the emperor wondered aloud, for he was Claudius Drusus Nero.

"Distantly, Caesar."

"Who is your father?"

"Titus Drusus, Caesar, and my brother is also Titus."

"Yes," the emperor said thoughtfully. "Your father is in the senate. He is a just man, as I recall."

"He is, Caesar."

"You are the Tribunus Laticlavius of the Fourteenth," the emperor said, noting the young man's uniform. "You will have to go home now, I fear, Flavius Drusus."

"Yes, Caesar," came the dutiful answer, but Claudius heard more than just disappointment in the young man's voice.

"You do not want to go home?" he asked. "Is there no young sweetheart or wife eagerly awaiting your return, then? How long have you been with the Fourteenth, Flavius Drusus?"

"Almost three years, Caesar. I had hoped to make a career in the army. I am the youngest son of Titus Drusus. There are three older than I am. My eldest brother will follow in our father's footsteps, of course; and Gaius and Lucius are both magistrates. Another magistrate from the Drusus family, and we could easily be accused of a monopoly," Flavius Drusus finished with a small smile. Then he winced, and grew pale as the javelin was drawn from his leg.

Claudius almost groaned in sympathy with the young man's obvious pain. Although the titular second-in-command of his legion, a Tribunus Laticlavius was really an honorary post. There were six tribunes in each legion, and five of them were usually battle-hardened veterans. The Tribunus Laticlavius was always a youngster in his teens from a noble family, sent to spend two or three years with the army to shape him up, or get him out of trouble, or away from bad companions. Usually at the end of his term the Tribunus Laticlavius went home to a magistrate's position, and a rich wife.

The emperor turned to the legionary commander. "Is he a good soldier, Aulus Majesta?"

The legionary commander nodded. "The best, Caesar. He came to us like they all do—green, and wet behind the ears—but unlike the others I've had to put up with in my career, Flavius Drusus has been eager to learn. He was to stay on until one of my other tribunes retired in another year. Then I planned to move him up in the ranks." He looked down at the young man, pale with his injury. "What a pity, Caesar. He's a good officer, but I can't have a tribune with a gimpy leg, now can I." It wasn't a question.

Claudius was tempted to ask Aulus Majesta what a man's gait had to do with his ability to make good military decisions, but he refrained from it. His own limp, and stammering speech, had made him a laughingstock his whole life. He had been considered unfit for anything, even by his own family. But when his dreadful nephew, Caligula, had been murdered and deposed, the army had turned to him to rule Rome. Claudius was more aware than most of the disadvantage Flavius Drusus faced. Prejudice of any kind was difficult to overcome.

"You must be rewarded for saving my life," he said firmly.

"I but did my duty, Caesar!" the young tribune protested.

"And in doing so you have lost your military career," the emperor replied. "What will happen to you when you return home? You have nothing, being a younger son. In saving my life you have, in a sense, lost yours, Flavius Drusus. I would be unworthy of the noble tradition of the Caesars if I allowed such a thing. I offer you one of two choices. Think carefully before choosing. Return to Rome with honor, if you desire. I will give you both a noble wife and a pension for all of your days. *Or*, remain here in Britain. I will give you lands that will be yours and your descendants' forever. I will also settle a sum of money upon you that you may build a home."

Flavius Drusus thought a long moment. If he returned to Rome, noble wife or not, he would be forced to live in his father's house, which would one day be his eldest brother's house. His pension would probably not be enough for him to buy his own home. The noble wife would be some younger daughter with little of her own. How would they dower daughters, or successfully launch their sons' careers? If he remained in Britain, however, he would have his own lands. He would not be beholden to anyone. He would found a new branch of his family, and with hard work become a rich man in his own right.

"I will stay in Britain, Caesar," he said, knowing that he had made the right decision.

❧⚜❧

A *nd that,*" Titus Drusus Corinium told his children in the summer of A.D. 406, "is how our family came to this land some three hundred and sixty-two years ago. The first Flavius Drusus was still alive when Queen Bodicea revolted against Rome. Though the town of Corinium, where he had settled, was not touched by the revolt, he realized then that perhaps our family would be better served by making alliances with the local Celtic tribes rather than by sending for Roman wives. So his sons married into the Dobunni tribe, and the sons and daughters who came after that have intermarried with both Celts and Roman Britons until this day."

"And now Rome is leaving Britain," Titus's wife, Julia, said.

"Good riddance!" her husband answered. "Rome is finished. The Romans just don't have the good sense to realize it. Once Rome was a great and noble power that ruled the world. Today it is corrupt and venal. Even the Caesars are not what they once were. The Julians died out long ago, and in their place have come a succession of soldier-emperors, each backed by a different set of legions. You children know that in your own short lifetimes the empire has been split, with Britain and Gaul being broken away, and then patched back again. There is even an eastern empire now, in a place called Byzantium. Better we Britons be rid of Rome once and for all that we might chart our own destinies. If we do not, the Saxons immigrating from northern Gaul and the Rhineland onto our southeast coast will push inland, and overwhelm us altogether."

The young people grinned mischievously at each other. Their father was forever preaching gloom.

"Oh, Titus," his wife chided. "The Saxons are only peasant farmers. We are far too civilized to be overcome by them."

"Too civilized, aye," he agreed. "Perhaps that is why I am afraid for Britain." He picked up his younger son, Gaius, who had been playing quietly on the floor. "When a people becomes so civilized that it does not fear the barbarians at the gates, then the danger is the greatest. Little Gaius and his children will be the ones forced to live with our folly, I fear."

CAILIN

BRITAIN, A.D. 452–454

Chapter

1

"*Oh, Gaius, how could you!*" Kyna Benigna asked her husband irritably. She was a tall, handsome woman of pure Celtic descent. Her dark red hair was woven in a series of intricate braids about her head. "I cannot believe you sent to Rome seeking a husband for Cailin. She will be furious with you when she finds out." Kyna Benigna's long, soft yellow wool tunic swung gracefully as she paced the hall.

"It is time for her to marry," Gaius Drusus Corinium defended himself, "and there is no one here who seems to suit her."

"Cailin will be just fourteen next month, Gaius," his wife reminded him. "This is not the time of the Julians, when little girls were married off the moment their flow began! And as for finding no young man to suit her, I am not surprised by that. You adore your daughter, and she you. You have kept her so close she has not really had a chance to meet suitable young men. Even if she did, none would match her darling father, Gaius. Cailin has but to socialize like a normal young girl, and she will find the young man of her dreams."

"That is impossible now, and you know it," Gaius Drusus Corinium told her. "It is a dangerous world in which we live, Kyna. When was the last time we dared venture the road to Corinium? There are bandits everywhere. Only by remaining within the safety of our own estate are we relatively safe. Besides, the town is not what it once was. I think if someone will buy it, I shall sell our house there. We have not lived there since the first year of our marriage, and it has been closed up since my parents died three years ago."

"Perhaps you are right, Gaius. Yes, I think we should sell the house. Whomever Cailin marries one day, she will want to remain here in the country. She has never liked the town. Now tell me. Who is this young man who will come from Rome? Will he stay in Britain, or will he want to return to his own homeland? Have you considered that, my husband?"

"He is a younger son of our family in Rome, my dear."

Kyna Benigna shook her head again. "Your family has not been back to Rome in over two centuries, Gaius. I will allow that the two branches of the family have never lost touch, but your dealings have been on a business level, not a personal one. We know nothing of these people you propose to give your daughter to, Gaius. How could you even consider such a thing? Cailin will not like it, I warn you. You will not twist her about your little finger in this matter."

"The Roman branch of our family have always treated us honorably, Kyna," Gaius said. "They are yet of good character. I have chosen to give this younger son an opportunity because, like the younger son who was my ancestor, he has more to gain by remaining in Britain than by returning to Rome. Cailin shall have Hilltop Villa and its lands for her dowry that she may remain near us. It will all work out quite well. I have done the right thing, Kyna, I assure you," he concluded.

"What is this young man's name, Gaius?" she asked him, not at all certain that he was right.

"Quintus Drusus," he told her. "He is the youngest son of my cousin, Manius Drusus, who is the head of the Drusus family in

Rome. Manius had four sons and two daughters by his first wife. This boy is one of two sons and a daughter produced by Manius's second wife. The mother dotes on him, Manius writes, but she is willing to let him go because here in Britain he will be a respected man with lands of his own."

"And what if Cailin does not like him, Gaius?" Kyna Benigna demanded. "You have not considered that, have you? Will not your cousins in Rome be offended if you send their son back home to them after they have sent him here to us with such high hopes?"

"Certainly Cailin will like him," Gaius insisted, with perhaps a bit more assurance than he was feeling.

"I will not allow you to force her to the marriage bed if she is not content to make this match," Kyna Benigna said fiercely; and Gaius Drusus Corinium was reminded suddenly of why he had fallen in love with this daughter of a hill country Dobunni chieftain, instead of another girl from a Romano-British family. Kyna was every bit as strong as she was beautiful, and their daughter was like her.

"If she truly cannot be happy with him, Kyna," he promised, "I will not force Cailin. You know I adore her. If Quintus displeases her, I will give the boy some land, and I will find him a proper wife. He will still be far better off than if he had remained in Rome with his family. Are you satisfied now?" He smiled at her.

"I am," she murmured, the sound more like a cat's purr.

He has the most winning smile, she thought, remembering the first time she had seen him. She had been fourteen, Cailin's age. He had come to her father's village with his father to barter for the fine brooches her people made. She had fallen in love then and there. She quickly learned he was a childless widower, and seemingly in no hurry to remarry. His father, however, was quite desperate that he do so.

Gaius Drusus Corinium was the last of a long line of a family of Roman Britons. His elder brother, Flavius, had died in Gaul with the legions when he was eighteen. His sister, Drusilla, had perished in childbirth at sixteen. His first wife had died after half a dozen miscarriages.

Kyna, the daughter of Berikos, knew she had found the only man with whom she could be happy. Shamelessly she set about to entrap him.

To her surprise, it took little effort. Gaius Drusus Corinium was as hot-blooded as the Celtic girl herself. His proper first wife had bored him. So had all the eligible women and girls who had attempted to entice him after Albinia's tragic death. Once Kyna had gotten him to notice her, he could scarce take his eyes from her. She was as slender as a sapling, but her high, full young breasts spoke of delights he dared not even contemplate. She mocked him silently with her sapphire-blue eyes and a toss of her long red hair, flirting mischievously with him until he could bear no more. He wanted her as he had never wanted anything in his life, and so he told his father.

Kyna was beautiful, strong, healthy, and intelligent. Her blood mixed with theirs could but strengthen their family. Titus Drusus Corinium was as relieved as he was delighted.

Berikos, chieftain of the hill Dobunni, was not. "We have never mixed our blood with that of the Romans, as so many other tribes have," he said grimly. "I will barter with you, Titus Drusus Corinium, but I will not give your son my daughter for a wife." His blue eyes were as cold as stone.

"I am every bit as much a Briton as you are," Titus told him indignantly. "My family have lived in this land for three centuries. Our blood has been mixed with that of the Catuvellauni, the Iceni, even as your family has mixed its blood with those and other tribes."

"But never with the Romans," came the stubborn reply.

"The legions are long gone, Berikos. We live as one people now. Let my son, Gaius, have your daughter Kyna to wife. She wants him every bit as much as he wants her."

"Is this so?" Berikos demanded of his daughter, his long mustache quivering furiously. This was the child of his heart. Her betrayal of their proud heritage was painful.

"It is," she answered defiantly. "I will have Gaius Drusus Corinium for my husband, and no other."

"Very well," Berikos replied angrily, "but know that if you take this man for your mate, you do so without my blessing. I will never look upon your face again. You will be as one dead to me," he told her harshly, hoping his words would frighten her into changing her mind.

"So be it, my father," Kyna said with equal firmness.

She had left her Dobunni village that day and had never looked back. Though she missed the freedom of her hill country, her in-laws were loving and kind to her. Julia, her mother-in-law, had wisely insisted the marriage be postponed six months so that Kyna could learn more civilized ways. Then, a year after their marriage was celebrated, she and Gaius had left the house in Corinium for the family villa some fifteen miles from town. She was not yet with child, and it was thought the serenity of the countryside would aid the young couple in their attempts. Sure enough, when Kyna was in her seventeenth year, their twin sons, Titus and Flavius, were born. Cailin came two years later. After that there were no more children, but Kyna and Gaius did not care. The three the gods had blessed them with were healthy, strong, beautiful, and intelligent, even as their mother was.

Berikos, however, had never forgiven Kyna for her marriage. She sent him word of the birth of her sons, and another message when Cailin had been born, but true to his word, the Dobunni chieftain behaved as if she did not exist. Kyna's mother, however, came from their village after Cailin's birth. She immediately announced that she would remain with her daughter and son-in-law. Her name was Brenna, and she was Berikos's third wife. Kyna was her only child.

"*He* does not need me. He has the others," was all Brenna would say by way of explanation. So she had stayed, appreciating perhaps even more than her daughter the civilized ways of the Romanized Britons.

The villa in which Brenna now lived with her daughter, son-in-law, and grandchildren was small but comfortable. Its porticoed entrance with four white marble pillars was impressive in direct contrast to the informal, charming atrium it led to. The atrium was planted with Damascus roses, which had a longer blooming season than most, due mainly to their sheltered location. In the atrium's center was a little square pool in which water lilies grew in season and small colored fishes lived year-round. The villa contained five bedchambers, a library for Gaius Drusus, a kitchen, and a round dining room with beautiful plaster walls decorated with paintings of the gods' adventures among the mortals. The two best features of the house, as far as Brenna was concerned, were the tiled baths and the hypocaust system that heated the villa in the damp, chilly weather. Beyond the entrance there was nothing grand about the house, which was constructed mostly of wood with a red tile roof, but it was a warm and cozy dwelling, and its residents were happy.

They had been a close family, and if Kyna had one regret, it was that her in-laws insisted upon remaining in Corinium. They liked the town with all its bustle, and Titus had his place on the council. For them life at the villa was dull. As the years passed, and the roads became more dangerous to travel, their visits grew less frequent.

Although neither Kyna nor her husband remembered the days when the legions had overflowed their homeland, keeping Britain's four provinces and their roads inviolate, their elders did. Julia bemoaned the legions' loss, for without them civil authority outside the towns was hard to maintain. A plea to Rome several years after the withdrawal of the armies had been answered curtly by the emperor. The Britons would have to fend for themselves. Rome had troubles of its own.

Then suddenly, three years ago, Gaius and Kyna had been sent word that Julia was ill. Gaius had taken a party of armed men and hurried to Corinium. His mother had died the day after his arrival. To his surprise and even deeper sorrow, his father, unable to cope with the loss of the wife who had been with him for most of his adult life, pined away, dying less than a week later. Gaius had seen to their burial. Then he had returned home, and the remaining family had drawn in even closer.

Now, Kyna Benigna left her husband to his accounts and hurried off to find her mother. Brenna was in the herb garden transplanting young plants into the warm spring soil.

"Gaius has sent to his family in Rome for a husband for Cailin," Kyna said without any preamble.

Brenna climbed slowly to her feet, brushing the dirt from her blue tunic as she did so. She was an older version of her daughter, but her braids were prematurely snow-white, providing a startling contrast to her bright blue eyes. "What in the name of all the gods possessed him to do a silly thing like that?" she said. "Cailin will certainly accept no husband unless she herself does the choosing. I am surprised that Gaius could be so foolish. Did he not consult with you beforehand, Kyna?"

Kyna laughed ruefully. "Gaius rarely consults with me when he plans to do something he knows I will disapprove of, Mother."

Brenna shook her head. "Aye," she answered. "It is the way of men. Then we women are left to repair the damage done, and to clean up the mess. Men, I fear, are worse than children. Children know no better. Men do, and yet they will have their way. When are we to expect this proposed *bridegroom?*"

Kyna clapped a hand to her mouth. "I was so distressed by Gaius's news that I forgot to ask him. It must be soon, or he wouldn't have said anything. Cailin's birthday is in a few weeks. Perhaps Quintus Drusus will arrive by then. I expect that Gaius has been dealing in this perfidy since last summer. He knows the young man's name, and even his history." Her blue eyes grew angry. "Indeed, I am beginning to suspect this plot was hatched some time ago!"

"We will have to tell Cailin," Brenna said. "She should be aware of her father's actions. I know Gaius will not force her to marry this Quintus if she does not like him. That is not his way, Kyna. He is a just man."

"Aye, he is," Kyna admitted. "He has agreed that if Cailin refuses his choice, he will find Quintus Drusus another wife, and give him some land. Still, I wonder, Mother, will these Roman relations be content if their son marries another girl when they have been promised our daughter? There are no young girls of our acquaintance whose families can equal or even come near Cailin's dowry. Times are very hard, Mother. Only my husband's prudence has allowed Cailin the advantages of an heiress's wealth."

Brenna took her daughter's hand in hers and patted it comfortingly. "Let us not seek out difficulties, or see them where none yet exist," she said wisely. "Perhaps this Quintus Drusus will be the perfect husband for Cailin."

"*Husband?* What is this talk of a husband, Grandmother?"

The two older women started guiltily and, swinging about, came face to face with the main object of their discussion, a tall, slender young girl with wide violet-colored eyes and an unruly mop of auburn curls.

"Mother? Grandmother? *Who is Quintus Drusus?*" Cailin demanded. "I want no husband chosen for me; nor am I yet even ready to wed."

"Then you had best tell your father that, my daughter," Kyna said bluntly. Although she had worried about broaching this problem with Cailin, it was not her way to beat about the bush. Plain speech was best, particularly in a difficult situation like this. "Your father has sent to his family in Rome for a prospective husband for you. He thinks it is time you were married. Quintus Drusus is the young man's name, and he is, I surmise, expected at any minute."

"I will certainly not marry this Quintus Drusus," Cailin said, with stony finality in her tone. "How could Father do such a thing? Why should I be married off before Flavius and Titus, or has he sent to Rome for brides to wed my brothers too? If he has, he will find they are no more eager than I am!"

Brenna could not help but laugh. "There is far more Celt than Roman in you, my child," she said, chuckling. "Do not worry about this Quintus Drusus. Your father has said if you do not like him, you do not have to have him; but perhaps he will turn out to be the man of your dreams, Cailin. It is possible."

"I cannot imagine why Father thinks I need a husband," Cailin grumbled. "It is too ridiculous to even contemplate. I would much rather stay at home with my family. If I marry, then I must take charge of a household and have babies. I am not ready for all of that. I have had little enough freedom to do anything I really find interesting, for I am deemed too young, but suddenly I am old enough to wed. How absurd! Poor Antonia Porcius was married two years ago when she was just fourteen. Now look at her! She has two babies. She has grown fat, and she always looks tired. Is that what Father thinks will make me happy? And as for Antonia's husband, well! I hear he has taken a very pretty Egyptian slave girl to his bed. That shall not happen to me, I assure you. When the time comes, I will choose my own husband, and he will never stray from my side, *or I will kill him!*"

"Cailin!" Kyna reproved her. "Where did you ever hear such salacious gossip about Antonia Porcius? I am surprised at your repeating it."

"Ohh, Mother, everyone knows. Antonia complains about her husband at every turn. She feels put upon, and she very well may be, though I think it her own fault. The last time I saw her at the Saturnalia, she was unable to stop talking about all her woes. She pinned me in a corner for close to an hour chattering.

"It's all her father's fault, you know. He chose a husband for her. How smug she was at the time, too! She loved lording it over us other girls when we met at the festivals. Sextus Scipio was so handsome, she bragged. Handsomer than any husbands we'd ever get. Why, there wasn't a man in all of Britain as handsome as he was. He was rich, too. Richer than any husbands we'd ever get. By the gods, how she carried on! She's still carrying on, I fear, but now 'tis a different tune she sings. Well, that's not for me! I will pick my own husband. He will be a man of character, and of honor."

Brenna nodded. "Then you will choose wisely when the time comes, my child."

"Like I chose," Kyna said softly, and her companions smiled in their agreement.

When they came together that evening for their meal, Cailin teased her father. "I hear you have sent to Rome for a *very special* birthday gift for me, Father," she said. Her large violet eyes twinkled with humor. She had had the afternoon to cool her temper. Now Cailin thought it very funny that her father believed her ready to marry. She had only begun her moon cycles a few months ago.

Gaius Drusus flushed nervously and eyed his daughter. "You are not angry?" Cailin had a fierce temper. Even he could be cowed by it. Her Celtic blood was far hotter than that of her twin brothers.

"I am not ready for marriage," Cailin said, looking her father directly in the eye.

"*Marriage? Cailin?*" Her brother Flavius hooted with laughter.

"The gods pity the poor fellow," said his twin, Titus. "Who is this sacrificial offering on the altar of matrimony to be?"

"He comes from Rome," Cailin told them. "One Quintus Drusus, by name. I believe he is escorting the maidens chosen to be your wives, dear brothers. Yes, I am certain he is. We're to have a triple wedding. 'Twill save our parents a fortune in these hard times. Now, what did Mother say the brides' names were? Majesta and Octavia? No, I think it was Horatia and Lavinia."

The two sixteen-year-olds paled, only realizing it was a jest when their entire family burst out laughing. Their relief was comical.

"You see, Father," Cailin said. "The thought of anyone choosing their spouses is abhorrent to my brothers. It is even more abhorrent to me. Is there no way you can stop this Quintus Drusus from coming? His trip will be a wasted one. I will not marry him."

"Quintus Drusus will be here in two days' time," Gaius said, looking distinctly uncomfortable.

"*Two days!*" Kyna glared at her husband, outraged. "*You did not tell me until this man was but two days from our villa?* Ohh, Gaius! This is really too intolerable of you! Every servant is needed in the fields for the spring planting. I have no time to prepare for an unexpected guest from Rome." She glowered fiercely at him.

"He is family," Gaius replied weakly. "Besides, our home is always pristine, Kyna. You well know it."

"The guest chamber must be cleaned and aired. It hasn't been used in months. The mice always take up residence there when it is shut up. The bed needs a new mattress. The old one is filled with lumps. Do you know how long it takes to make a new mattress, Gaius? No, of course you do not!"

"Let him have the old mattress, Mother," Cailin said. "He will leave all the quicker if he is uncomfortable."

"He will not leave," Gaius Drusus said, recovering his equilibrium, and his dignity as head of this household. "I have promised his father that Quintus will have a future in Britain. There is nothing for him in Rome. My cousin, Manius, begged me to find a place for the boy. I have given my word, Kyna."

"You did not approach him first with this silly scheme to marry Cailin off?" she demanded. She was beginning to see the issue in a different light now.

"No. Manius Drusus wrote to me two years ago," said Gaius. "Quintus is the youngest of his children. If he had been a girl it would have been easier, for they could have married off a girl with a modest dowry; but he is not a girl. There is simply no place for Quintus in Rome. The sons of Manius's first marriage are all grown with children of their own. Manius parceled off his lands to them as each married. His daughters were well dowered, and wed as well.

"Then, after having been widowed for several years, he suddenly fell in love. His new wife, Livia, bore him first a daughter, and Manius was rich enough that there was enough for her dowry. Then Livia bore Manius a son. My cousin determined that the boy would inherit their house in Rome. His wife agreed that there must be no more children, but . . ."

Kyna laughed. "Cousin Manius dipped his wick one final time, and Quintus was born of their indiscretion," she finished for her husband.

He nodded. "Aye. My cousin hoped to make another small fortune for this last child, but you know, Kyna, how bad Rome's economy has been over these past years. The government is constantly spending more than it has to spend. The legions must be paid. Taxes have risen threefold. The coinage is so debased now as to be worth nothing. My cousin could but support his family. There was nothing to give young Quintus. So, Manius Drusus appealed to me to help him. He offered Quintus as a husband for our daughter. It seemed to me a good idea at the time."

"It was not," his wife said dryly, "and you really should have discussed it with me first."

"I will not marry this Quintus Drusus," Cailin said again.

"You have already told us that several times, my daughter," Kyna said soothingly. "I am certain that your father accepts your decision in this matter, even as I do. The problem remains, however, of what we must do. Quintus Drusus has traveled hundreds of leagues from Rome to come to a new and better life. We cannot send him back to his old one. Your father's honor—indeed, the honor of the whole family, is involved." She furrowed her brow for a moment, and then she brightened. "Gaius, I believe I may have the answer. How old is Quintus Drusus?"

"Twenty-one," he told her.

"We will tell him that we have decided Cailin is too young to marry at this time," Kyna said. "We will imply his father misunderstood you. That all you offered was to give Quintus a start in Britain. If Cailin eventually fell in love with him, then a marriage could certainly take place. You did not actually make a marriage contract with Manius Drusus, Gaius, did you?" She looked anxiously at her husband.

"Nay, I did not."

"Then we will have no problems," Kyna said, relieved. "We will give young Quintus that little villa with its lands by the river, the one you purchased several years ago from the estate of Septimus Agricola. It's fertile and has a fine apple orchard. We'll supply him with slaves, and with hard work he can make it quite prosperous."

Gaius Drusus smiled for the first time that day. "It is the perfect solution," he agreed with her. "I could not manage without you, my dear, I fear."

"Indeed, Gaius, I am most certainly of the same opinion," Kyna replied.

The rest of the family laughed.

When they had recovered from their mirth, Cailin said, "But do not make a new mattress, Mother. We want Quintus Drusus gone from this house as quickly as possible, remember."

There was more laughter. This time Gaius Drusus joined in, relieved that a potentially difficult situation had been resolved by his beautiful, clever wife. He had not made a mistake all those years ago when he had married Kyna, the daughter of Berikos.

⊰⊱

T*wo days later*, exactly as predicted, Quintus Drusus arrived at the villa of his cousin. He came astride a fine redbrown stallion that his father had gifted him with when he departed Rome. Quintus Drusus's sharp black eyes took in the rich, newly turned soil of his cousin's farmland; the well-pruned trees in the orchards; the fine repair of the buildings; the good health of the slaves who were working outdoors in the spring sunlight. He was well-pleased by what he saw, for he had not been overly happy with the plans his father had made for him.

"You have no choice but to go to Britain," his father had told him angrily when he had protested the decision. His mother, Livia, was weeping softly. "There is *nothing* for you here in Rome, Quintus. Everything I have is distributed among your siblings. You know this is to be true. It is unfortunate that you are my youngest child, and I can offer you neither land nor monies.

"Gaius Drusus Corinium is a very wealthy man with much land in Britain. Though he has two sons, he will dower his only daughter very well. She will have lands, a villa, gold! It can all be yours, my son, but you must pay the price for it, and the price is that you exile yourself from Rome. You must remain in Britain, work those lands you receive. If you do, you will be happy and comfortable all your days. Britain is most fertile, I have been told. It will be a good life, I promise you, Quintus," his father had finished.

He had obeyed his parents, although he was not happy with the decision they had made for him. Britain was at the end of the earth, and its climate was foul. Everyone knew that. Still, he could not stay in Rome, at least not right now. Armilla Cicero was becoming most demanding. She had told him last night that she was pregnant, and that they would have to marry. Her father was very powerful; Quintus Drusus knew that he could make life most un-

comfortable for any man he thought had made his daughter unhappy. It was better to leave Rome.

Armilla would have an abortion, as she had had on a number of
occasions. He was not the first man she had cast her nets for, nor
would he be the last. It was really quite a shame, Quintus thought,
for Senator Cicero was a wealthy man, but his two other sons-in-
law lived unhappily beneath his thumb. That was not the kind of
life Quintus Drusus envisioned for himself. He would be his own
man.

Nor, it occurred to him as he approached the villa of his cousin,
Gaius Drusus Corinium, did he have in mind a lifetime spent
farming in Britain. Still, for now there was nothing else he could
do. Eventually he would think of a plan, and he would be gone,
back to Rome, with a pocket full of gold coin that would keep him
comfortable all of his days.

He saw a handful of people come out of the villa to greet him,
and forced a smile upon his extremely handsome face. The man,
tall, with dark brown hair and light eyes, was like no Drusus he
had ever seen, but was obviously his cousin Gaius. The woman,
tall, with a fine, high bosom and dark red hair, must be his cousin's
wife. The older woman with white hair was her mother, no doubt.
His father had told him that their cousin Gaius's Celtic mother-in-
law lived with them. The two almost-grown boys were images of
their father. They were sixteen; close to manhood really. *And there
was a girl.*

Quintus Drusus was close enough now to see her quite clearly.
She was tall like the rest of her family, taller, he thought irritably,
than he was himself. He did not like tall women. Her hair was a
rich auburn, a long, curly mass of untidy ringlets that suggested an
untamed nature. She was very fair of skin with excellent features;
straight nose, large eyes, a rosebud of a mouth. She was actually
one of the most beautiful females he had ever seen, but he disliked her on sight.

"Welcome to Britain, Quintus Drusus," Gaius said as the young
man drew his horse to a stop before them and dismounted.

"I thank you, cousin," Quintus Drusus replied, and then politely

greeted each of the others as they were introduced. To his amazement, he sensed that his proposed bride disliked him even as he
did her. Still, a man did not have to like a woman to wed her, and
get a proper number of children on her. Cailin Drusus was a
wealthy young woman who represented his future. He didn't intend to let her get away.

For the next few days he waited for his cousin, Gaius, to broach
the matter of the marriage contract and set a wedding date. Cailin
avoided him as if he were a carrier of the plague. Finally, after ten
days, Gaius took him aside one morning.

"I promised your father that because of the bonds of blood binding our two families," the older man began, "I would give you the
opportunity to make a new life for yourself here in Britain. I have
therefore signed over to you a fine villa and farm with a producing
orchard by the river. It has all been done quite legally and filed
properly with the magistrate in Corinium. You will have the slaves
you need to work your lands. You should do quite well, Quintus."

"But I know nothing about farming!" Quintus Drusus burst out.

Gaius smiled. "I am aware of that, my boy. How could a fine fellow like yourself, brought up in Rome, know anything about the
land? But we will teach you, and help you to learn."

Quintus Drusus told himself he must not lose his temper. Perhaps he could sell this farm and its villa and escape back to Rome.
But Gaius's next words dashed all his hopes in that direction.

"I bought the river farm from the estate of old Septimus
Agricola several years back. It has lain fallow since then. I was fortunate to get it cheap from the heirs who live in Glevum. Property
values are down even further now for those wishing to sell, but
they are an excellent value for those wishing to buy."

There was no quick escape, then, Quintus Drusus thought
gloomily, but once his marriage to Cailin was settled, they would
at least be monied. "When," he asked his cousin, "do you propose
to celebrate the marriage between your daughter and myself?"

"*Marriage?* Between you and Cailin?" Gaius Drusus wore a puzzled face.

"My father said there would be a marriage between your daugh-

ter and myself, cousin. I thought I came to Britain to be a bridegroom, to unite our two branches of the family once again." Quintus Drusus's handsome face showed his barely restrained anger.

"I am so sorry, Quintus. Your father must have misunderstood
me, my boy," Gaius said. "I but offered you an opportunity here
in Britain where there was none for you in Rome. I felt it my duty
because of our blood ties. Now if you and Cailin should fall in love
one day, I should certainly not object to your marrying my daughter, but there was no contract for a marriage enacted between our
two families. I regret your confusion." He smiled warmly, and patted the younger man's arm. "Cailin is still just half grown. If I were
you, my boy, I should seek a strong, healthy woman from amongst
our neighbors' daughters. We are celebrating the festival of manhood, the Liberalia, for our twin sons in a few days. Many of our
neighbors and their families will be attending. It will be a good
time for you to look over the local maidens. You are a good catch,
Quintus. Remember, you are a man of property now!"

No marriage. No marriage. The words burned in his brain. Quintus Drusus had not been privy to the correspondence between his
father and his cousin Gaius, but he had been quite certain his father believed a marriage was to take place between himself and
Cailin Drusus. Had his father misunderstood? He was not a young
man by any means, being some twenty years older than Gaius
Drusus.

Or had his father known all along that there would be no marriage? Had Manius Drusus tricked him into leaving Rome because
Gaius was willing to offer him lands of his own? Did Manius
Drusus dangle a rich marriage before his youngest child because
he knew that he would not go otherwise? It was the only explanation Quintus Drusus could come up with. His cousin Gaius
seemed an honest man in all respects. Not at all like that sly old
Roman fox, his father.

Quintus Drusus almost groaned aloud with frustration, running a
hand through his black hair. He was marooned at the end of the
earth in Britain. *He was to be a farmer.* He shuddered with distaste,
seeing a long, dull life filled with goats and chickens stretching

ahead of him. There would be no more glorious gladiatorial battles at the Colosseum to watch; or chariot racing along the Appian Way. No summers on Capri, with its warm blue waters and endless sunshine, or visits to some of the most incredible brothels in the world, with their magnificent women who catered to all tastes.

Perhaps if he could get that little bitch Cailin to fall in love with him . . . No. That would take a miracle. He did not believe in miracles. Miracles were for religious fanatics like the Christians. Cailin Drusus had made her dislike plain from the moment they laid eyes on one another. She was barely civil when they were in the presence of their elders, and ignored him when they found themselves alone. He certainly did not want a wife as outspoken and unbridled as this girl was. Women with Celtic blood seemed to be that way. His cousin's wife and mother-in-law were also outspoken and independent.

Quintus Drusus made an effort to swallow his disappointment. He was alone in a strange land, hundreds of leagues from Rome. He needed the goodwill and the influence of Gaius Drusus and his family. He had nothing, not even the means to return home. If he could not have Cailin, and the fat dowry her father would undoubtedly settle on her one day, there would be another girl with another fat dowry. He now needed Cailin's friendship, and the friendship of her mother, Kyna, if he was to find a rich wife.

Quintus's young cousins, Flavius and Titus, would be celebrating their sixteenth birthdays on the twentieth of March. The Liberalia fell on March 17. The manhood ceremony was always celebrated on the festival nearest a boy's birthday—although which birthday was up to the discretion of the parents.

On that special day, a boy put aside the red-edged toga of his childhood, receiving in its place the white toga of manhood. Here in Britain it would be a mostly symbolic affair, for the men did not normally wear togas. The climate was too harsh, as Quintus had discovered. He had quickly adopted the warm, light wool tunic and cross-gartered braccos of the Romano-Britons.

Still, the old customs of the Roman family were kept, if for no other reason than they made wonderful excuses to get together

with one's neighbors. It was at these gatherings that matches were
made, as well as arrangements to crossbreed livestock. They gave
friends a chance to meet once again, for unnecessary travel on a
regular basis was simply no longer possible. Each party setting out
for the villa of Gaius Drusus Corinium made burnt offerings and
prayers to their gods that they would arrive safely, and return home
in safety.

On the morning of the Liberalia, Quintus Drusus said to Kyna
in Cailin's presence, "You will have to introduce me to all the eligible women and maidens today, my lady. Now that my cousin
Gaius has so generously made me a man of property, I will be
seeking a wife to share my good fortune with me. I rely on your
wisdom in this matter, even as I would rely on my own sweet
mother, Livia."

"I am certain," Kyna told him, "that such a handsome young
man as yourself will have no trouble finding a wife." She turned to
her daughter. "What think you, Cailin? Who would best please our
cousin? There are so many pretty girls among our acquaintances
ready to wed."

Cailin looked at her cousin. "You will want a wife with a good
dowry, will you not, Quintus? Or will you simply settle for virtue,"
she said wickedly. "No, I do not think you will settle for just virtue."

He forced a laugh. "You are too clever by far, little cousin. With
such a sharp tongue, I wonder if you will ever find a husband for
yourself. A man likes a little honey with his speech."

"There will be honey aplenty for the right man," Cailin said
pertly, smiling with false sweetness at him.

Earlier that morning Titus and Flavius had removed the golden
bullae that they had worn around their necks since their twin
births. The bullae, amulets for protection against evil, were then
laid upon the altar of the family gods. A sacrifice was made, and
the bullae were hung up, never to be worn again unless their owners found themselves in danger of the envy of their fellow men, or
of the gods.

The twins next dressed themselves in white tunics, which, according to custom, their father carefully adjusted. Since they descended from the noble class, the tunics donned by Titus and Flavius Drusus had two wide crimson stripes. Finally, over each of their tunics was draped the snow-white toga virilis, the garment of a man considered grown.

Had they lived in Rome, a procession consisting of family, friends, freedmen, and slaves would have wound its way in joyful parade to the Forum, where the names of the two sons of Gaius Drusus would have been added to the list of citizens. It had been the custom since the time of the emperor Aurelian that all births be registered within thirty days in Rome, or with the official provincial authorities; but only when a boy formally became a man was his name entered in the rolls as a citizen. It was a proud moment. The names of Titus and Flavius Drusus Corinium would be entered in the list kept in the town of Corinium, and an offering would be made to the god Liber at that time.

Just as their neighbors and friends began to arrive for the family celebration, Cailin took her brothers aside. "Cousin Quintus would like us to introduce him to prospective wives," she said, her eyes twinkling. "I think we should help him. He will be gone all the sooner. I can barely remain civil in his presence."

"Why do you dislike him so, Cailin?" Flavius asked her. "He has done nothing to you. Once Father told him there would be no marriage between you, you should have felt more at ease. Instead you take every opportunity to snipe at him. I do not understand."

"He seems a good fellow to me," Titus agreed with his twin. "His manners are flawless, and he rides well. I think Father was correct when he told Quintus that you were too young for marriage."

"I am not too young for marriage should the right man come along," Cailin responded. "As for Quintus Drusus, there is something about him that my voice within warns me of, but I know not what it is. I simply think he is a danger to us all. The sooner he is gone to the river villa and settled with a wife, the happier I will be! Now, what girls do you feel would suit him? *Think!* You two know every eligible, respectable, and not so respectable maiden for miles around."

They laughed in unison, rolling their eyes at one another, for if there was one thing Cailin's brothers liked, it was the ladies—so much so that Gaius Drusus was declaring his sons men in order to find them wives and marry them off before they caused a scandal by impregnating some man's daughter or, worse, being caught debauching some man's wife.

"There is Barbara Julius," Flavius said thoughtfully. "She is a handsome girl with nice big breasts. Good for babies."

"And Elysia Octavius, or Nona Claudius," Titus volunteered.

Cailin nodded. "Yes, they would all be suitable. I like none of them so well that I would warn them off our cousin, Quintus."

The families from the surrounding estates were arriving. The twins made their suggestions to their mother, and Kyna dutifully made the proper introductions. Quintus Drusus's handsome face, coupled with his lands, made him more than eligible.

"He needs three arms," Cailin said dryly to her grandmother, "for Barbara, Nona, and Elysia will certainly end up in a cat fight trying to hold on to him. Will I have to simper like that to gain a man's attention and devotion? It's disgusting!"

Brenna chuckled. "They are simply flirting with Quintus," she said. "One of them must gain ascendancy over the others if they are to capture your cousin's heart. Men and women have flirted for centuries. Someday a man will come along who appeals to you so strongly that you will flirt with him, my Cailin. Trust me in that."

Perhaps, Cailin thought, but she still felt that the three girls being dangled before Quintus were silly creatures. She wandered through the crowd of her neighbors filling the gardens of the villa. No one was paying a great deal of attention to her, for this was not her day, but rather her brothers'. Cailin could smell spring in the air at long last. The ground was warm again, and the breeze mild, even if the day was not as bright as they might have wished. Then she saw Antonia Porcius, but before she might turn in another direction, Antonia was hailing her noisily, and there was no avoiding her.

"How are you, Antonia?" Cailin inquired politely, bracing for the flood of words to come, for Antonia Porcius could not answer the simplest query without going into great detail.

"I have divorced Sextus," Antonia announced dramatically.

"*What?*" Cailin was astounded. This was the first she had heard of it.

Antonia put her arm through Cailin's and said in confidential tones, "Well, actually, he ran away with that little Egyptian slave girl of mine. Father was furious. He said I must not remain married to Sextus Scipio under those circumstances. Then he granted me a divorce!" She giggled. "Sometimes having the chief magistrate of Corinium for a father isn't such a bad thing. I got everything, of course, because Sextus wronged me publicly. Father says no honest magistrate would allow a good wife and her children to suffer under those circumstances. If Sextus ever comes back, he will find he has come back to nothing, but I hear they took flight for Gaul. Imagine! He said he was in love with her! How silly of him."

Her blue eyes narrowed a moment. "I hear your cousin has come from Rome, and that your father has given him the old Agricola estate. I hear that he is divinely handsome. My estates match those lands, you know. My father wanted to buy them for me, but your father got to the heirs in Glevum first. What is his name? Your cousin's, I mean. Will you introduce me, Cailin? The gossip is that he is looking for a wife. A rich woman such as myself would not be a bad match now, would it?" She giggled again. "Wouldn't it be nice if we were cousins, Cailin? I've always liked you, you know. You don't say cruel things about me to the other girls behind my back. I think you must be the only friend I have, Cailin Drusus!"

Cailin was astounded. They were hardly friends; at seventeen, Antonia was her senior, and had rarely given her the time of day. *Until today.*

Why, the silly cow, Cailin thought. She really wants to meet Quintus! I suppose snatching him from beneath the noses of the others would give her a double victory of sorts. She would best those who spoke unkindly of her, *and* she would prove to the world that she was still a very desirable woman; that Sextus Scipio was a cad, and a fool.

"How kind you are, dear Antonia," Cailin heard herself saying as her mind raced with delicious possibilities. Antonia might be plump, but she was more than just pretty. By marrying her, Quintus would gain a wife rich in both lands and money. She was her father's only child, and she would inherit everything he owned one day.

She was also foolish, and selfish. Sextus Scipio must have been absolutely miserable with her to have left everything his family had built up over the last few hundred years. Antonia Porcius certainly deserved her cousin, and most assuredly Quintus Drusus deserved the daughter of the chief magistrate of Corinium.

"Of course I will introduce you to my cousin Quintus, Antonia. You must promise me, however, that you will not swoon," Cailin teased her companion. "He is as handsome as a god, I vow! I only wish he found me attractive, but alas, he does not. It would be exciting indeed if you and I became cousins." She pulled Antonia about and said, "Come along now! My mother has already begun introducing him to every eligible girl in the province. You do not want them to steal a march on you. But I think, mayhap, when Quintus sees you, dear Antonia, both your lives will change. Ohh, wouldn't it be wonderful!"

Quintus Drusus was very much in his element, surrounded by attractive, nubile girls who were all fawning over him. He saw Cailin's approach with a plump little blond, but he waited until she spoke to him before acknowledging her.

"Cousin Quintus, this is my good friend, Antonia Porcius." Cailin pulled the simpering woman forward. "Antonia, this is my big cousin from Rome. I'm certain that you two have much in common. Antonia is the only child of the chief magistrate in Corinium, Quintus."

Well, well, well, he thought. Little cousin Cailin is being most helpful indeed. I wonder what mischief she is up to now? Yet, he was curious. She had quite clearly signaled him that the blond girl was the daughter of a powerful man, *and* an heiress to boot. He couldn't understand why Cailin would want to do him a favor. She had made no secret of her dislike of him since they had first laid eyes upon one another. Her candidate for his hand must have a flaw of some sorts. Then he gazed into Antonia's limpid blue eyes, and decided whatever that flaw was, he would certainly enjoy ferreting it out.

His hand went to his heart, and he said, "The sight of you, my lady Antonia, gives me comprehension at long last of why Britain's women are so famed for their beauty. I prostrate myself at your feet."

Antonia's mouth made a small round O of delight, while the other girls pressing in on Quintus Drusus gaped with surprise. Then the handsome young Roman took Antonia Porcius by the arm and requested that she show him the gardens. The couple walked slowly from the group, seemingly enraptured by each other's company, while those left behind stared in amazement.

"Is there madness in your family, Cailin Drusus?" Nona Claudius asked, her tone one of a young lady most put out.

"Whatever possessed you to introduce Antonia Porcius to such an eligible man?" demanded Barbara Julius.

"And whatever does he see in her?" Elysia Octavius wondered aloud. "We are younger and prettier by far."

"I did not mean to distress you," Cailin said innocently. "I simply felt sorry for poor Antonia. I just learned that she is divorced. Sextus, her husband, ran off with a slave girl. I but sought to cheer her up by introducing her to my cousin. I certainly never thought he would be attracted to her. She is older than all of us, and you are correct, Elysia, when you observed that we are all prettier." Cailin shrugged. "There is no accounting for men's taste in women. Perhaps Quintus will quickly become bored with her and come back to you all."

"If your villa were not the most remote of all of our homes from Corinium, Cailin, you would have known about Antonia's divorce," Barbara told her irritably. "Frankly, none of us blames poor Sextus Scipio. Antonia is selfish beyond bearing. Whatever she sees and desires, she must have. Sextus claimed he was being driven to poverty by her. If he denied her anything, her father would upbraid him. She is not a good mother, and she is cruel to her slaves, my father says. Ohh, she is sweet and charming when she gets her own way, but when she doesn't, beware! She wanted Sextus Scipio because he was the most handsome and the richest man about. Once she had lured him into her trap, however, she became once more what she really is, a spoilt little bitch. You should really warn your cousin."

"I hear," Nona Claudius said, lowering her voice so the other girls were forced to lean forward, "that although Antonia got her husband's estate, his goods, and chattel, that Sextus Scipio and his little mistress escaped with much gold and other coin. My father was his banker, you know. He says that Sextus Scipio had been transferring funds abroad for months now. Antonia's not telling anyone that. She's put it right from her mind. The thought of her husband getting away to live happily ever after in comfort is frankly more than she can bear."

"She is obviously casting her nets for a new husband," Barbara said in annoyed tones, "and once again it is the most handsome man in the province. I suppose he is rich, too. I don't know why Antonia has all the luck!"

"He's not rich at all," Cailin told them, hoping to frighten them off and further Antonia's cause. "He is the youngest son of my father's cousin in Rome. It is a very big family. There was nothing left for poor Quintus. Father felt sorry for him, and asked his cousin Manius to send Quintus to us. Then he gave him the river villa along with all its lands. Of course, he will loan him slaves to work the lands and keep the orchard, but my cousin Quintus has very little but his handsome face to recommend him."

"Antonia's lands match those of the river villa," Nona said. "When your gorgeous cousin learns that, he will be even more intrigued by her. Antonia's a rich woman. Frankly, Quintus Drusus would be a fool not to have her. There is no hope for us, I fear."

"Do you really think so?" Cailin said. "Oh, dear!"

Brenna joined her granddaughter as the other girls drifted away. "You scheme like a Druid, Cailin Drusus," she murmured.

"The sooner he is married off," Cailin said, "the safer I will be. Thanks be to the gods that he did not like me on sight. There is something about him, Grandmother. I cannot put my finger on it, but I feel Quintus Drusus is a danger to me, to us all. I hope he weds Antonia Porcius for her wealth, and her connections. I will not be content until he is gone from our home." She looked into Brenna's kindly face. "You do not think me foolish to feel so strongly?"

"No," Brenna said. "I have always said you were more Celt than your brothers. The voice within calls to you, warns you about Quintus Drusus. Listen to it, my child. That voice will never play you false. It is when we do not listen to that voice that we make errors in judgment. Always trust your instincts, Cailin," her grandmother counseled.

Chapter

2

With so many lovely girls in the province to choose from, why on earth did Quintus marry Antonia Porcius?" Kyna wondered aloud to her husband and family.

Their cousin's very lavish wedding had been celebrated the morning prior in Corinium. They were now traveling back to their own villa, which was some eighteen miles from the town; a good day's travel. Gaius and his sons were astride their horses. The three women rode in an open cart. They journeyed with a large party of families from nearby villas. The neighbors had banded together to employ a strong troop of men-at-arms for their protection along the road.

"Antonia is a very attractive woman," Gaius answered his wife.

"That is not what I mean," Kyna said sharply, "and you well know it, Gaius! Quintus might have chosen a virgin of good family. Instead he decided upon a divorced woman with two children, and a father who cannot let his daughter be. Anthony Porcius will not be an easy father-in-law, as poor Sextus Scipio found to his dismay."

"Come now, my dear," Gaius Drusus told her, "you know as well as I do that Quintus fixed his sights on Antonia for several reasons. She is rich. Her lands match the lands I gave him. There is little mystery to it, Kyna. Quintus was promised land and a wife if he came to Britain. Of course, I had intended that wife to be Cailin; but since Cailin would not have him—and indeed, if I must be honest, she and Quintus would have been a bad match—Quintus chose wisely in Antonia. He is strong enough to control her. It will be a good marriage."

"I thought they made a most handsome couple," Cailin ventured.

Her mother laughed. "You would have thought Quintus and Hecate made a good couple if it would save you from marrying him, my daughter. Now what will you do for a mate?"

"When the right man comes along, Mother, I shall know it," Cailin replied confidently.

"Why is it," Flavius asked, "that Antonia and Quintus chose you to be one of their witnesses, little sister?"

Cailin smiled with false sweetness. "Why, Flavius, did you not know? I introduced our cousin Quintus to my dear friend Antonia. I suppose they believe that having played Cupid, I am responsible, in part, for the great happiness they have found in each other."

"*Cailin!*" her mother exclaimed. "You introduced Quintus and Antonia to each other? You never told me this before. I wondered how they met that day."

"Did I not mention it, Mother? I suppose it slipped my mind because I thought it of no import," Cailin answered. "Yes, I did introduce them. It was at the Liberalia, when my brothers became men."

"You plot like a Druid!" her mother said.

"Grandmother said the same thing," Cailin admitted mischievously.

"I certainly did," Brenna agreed. "Of your three whelps, she is most like a Dobunni Celt. Berikos would approve of her."

"Mother," Cailin asked, "why did Berikos disapprove of your marriage to Father?" She never thought of her mother's paternal parent as *Grandfather*. He was rarely mentioned in her household, and she had never even once laid eyes on him. He was as big a mystery to Cailin as she would have been to him.

"My father is a proud man," Kyna said. "Perhaps overproud. The Dobunni were once members of the powerful Catuvellauni Celts. A son of their great ruler Commius, one Tincommius by name, brought a group of followers to this region many years ago. They became the Dobunni. Your grandfather descends from Tincommius. He is proud of his line, and prouder yet of the fact that none of his family until me ever married into the Roman race. He has always hated the Romans, although for no real reason that he ever shared with any of us.

"When I saw your father, and fell in love with him, Berikos was quite displeased with me. He had already chosen a husband for me, a man named Carvilius. But I would not have Carvilius. I would only have your father, and so Berikos disowned me. I had shamed him. I had shamed the Dobunni."

"He is a fool, and ever was," Brenna muttered. "When word was brought to him of the twins' births, a smile split his face for the briefest moment, and then he grew somber, saying, 'I have no daughter.' His other wives, Ceara, Bryna, and that little fool Maeve, were all preening and bragging over their grandchildren, but with my one child exiled, I was forbidden to say a word. Indeed, what could I have said? I hadn't ever even seen the boys."

"But," Cailin questioned Brenna, "if Berikos had three other wives, and other children, why was he so angry at Mother for having followed her heart? Didn't he want her to be happy?"

"Berikos has sired ten sons on his other wives, but my child was his only daughter. Kyna was her father's favorite, which is why he let her go, *and* why he could never forgive her for turning her back on her heritage," Brenna sadly explained.

"When you were born, however, I told Berikos that if he could not forgive your mother for marrying a Romano-Briton, I must leave the tribe to be with my daughter. He had other grandchildren, but I had only your mother's children. It was not fair that he rob me of a place by my daughter's fire, or the right to dandle my grandchildren upon my knee. That was fourteen years ago. I have never regretted my decision. I am far happier with my daughter and her family than I ever was with Berikos, and his killing pride."

Kyna took her mother's hand in hers and squeezed it hard as the two women smiled at each other. Then Brenna reached out with her other hand and patted Cailin's cheek lovingly.

⊰⊱

Q*uintus's marriage had* been celebrated on the Kalends of June. To everyone's surprise, including his own, he was a most proficient manager of his estates, including his wife's vast portion. The river villa he deemed in too poor repair, and had it demolished. The fields belonging to the estate now bloomed with ripening grain. The orchards thrived. Quintus, comfortable in his wife's lavish villa, put on weight. His devotion to Antonia was astounding. Though it was his right to take any slave who caught his fancy to his bed, he did not do so. His stepsons feared and respected him, as should the children of any respectable man. His slaves found nothing to gossip about their master. And as for Antonia, by early autumn she was pregnant.

"It is astounding," Gaius said to his wife. "Poor Honoria Porcius in all her years of marriage could get but one child; but her daughter ripens like a melon each time a husband comes through the door. Well, I must admit that Cailin's matchmaking was a good thing. My cousin Manius should be most grateful to me for his son's luck."

Quintus Drusus, however, was not quite the man he seemed. His good fortune had but given him an appetite for more. The civil government was crumbling with the towns themselves. He could see that soon there would be no central government left. When that happened, it would be the rich and the powerful who controlled Britain. Quintus Drusus had decided that he would be the richest and most powerful man in Corinium and the surrounding countryside when that time came. He looked covetously at the estates of his cousin, Gaius Drusus Corinium.

Antonia had been recently chattering to him about possible matches to be made for his cousins, Titus and Flavius. They were already disporting themselves among the slave girls in their father's house. The rumor was that one of them—and no one was certain which, for they were identical in features—had gotten a young slave girl with child. Their marriages could quickly mean children; another generation of heirs to the estate of Gaius Drusus Corinium.

And then there was Cailin. Her parents would soon be seeking a husband for her. She would also celebrate a birthday in the spring. At fifteen she was certainly more than old enough to marry. A powerful husband allied with his cousin Gaius—the thought did not please Quintus Drusus. He wanted the lands belonging to his benefactor, and the quicker he got them, the fewer complications he would have to deal with. The only question remaining in his mind was how to attain his goal without being caught.

Gaius and his family would have to be disposed of, but how was he to do it? He must not be suspected himself. *No.* He would be the greatest mourner at the funerals of Gaius Drusus Corinium and his family—*and the only one left to inherit his cousin's estates.* Quintus smiled to himself. In the end he would have far more wealth than any of his brothers in Rome. He thought of how he had resisted the idea of coming to Britain, yet had he not come, he would have lost the greatest opportunity of his life.

"You look so happy, my love," Antonia said, smiling at him as they lay abed.

"How could I not be happy, my dear," Quintus Drusus answered his wife. "I have you, and so much else." He reached out and touched her swelling belly. "He is the first of a great house, Antonia."

"Oh, yes!" she agreed, catching his hand and kissing it.

Antonia's sons, he thought, as he tenderly caressed his adoring wife. They were young, and so fragile. The merest whisper of disease could take them. It really seemed a shame that the sons of Sextus Scipio should one day have anything of his. But of course, Antonia would not allow them to be disinherited. Though she was

not the best of mothers, she did dote on her children. Still, anything might happen, Quintus Drusus considered. *Anything.*

⊲⊱✕⊰⊳

Quintus Drusus's son was born on the Kalends of
March, exactly nine months to the day his mother had
married his father. The infant was a large, healthy child. Antonia's
joy at the birth of her child was short-lived, however, for the next
morning, the two little boys born of her marriage to Sextus Scipio
were discovered drowned in the atrium fish pond. The two slave
women assigned to watch over the children were found together in
most compromising circumstances; naked, entwined in a lascivious
embrace, and drunk. There was no defense for their crime. Both
were strangled and buried before the fateful day was over. Antonia
was hysterical with grief.

"I shall call him Posthumous in honor of his brothers," Antonia
declared dramatically, large tears running down her cheeks as she
gazed upon her day-old son. "How tragic that he shall never know
them."

"He shall be called Quintus Drusus, the younger," her husband
told her, slipping two heavy gold bracelets on her arm as he gave
her a quick kiss. "You must not distress yourself further, my dear.
Your milk will not come in if you do. I will not have my son suckling on the teats of some slave woman. They are not as healthy as
a child's own mater. My own mother, Livia, always believed that.
She nursed my brother, my sister, and myself most faithfully until
we were past four." He reached out, and slipping a hand beneath
one of her breasts, said with soft menace, "Do not cheat my son,
Antonia, of what is his right. The sons of Sextus Scipio were innocents, and as such are now with the gods. You can do nothing for
them, my dear. Let it go, and tend to the living child the gods
have so graciously given us." Leaning over, he kissed her lips
again.

The nursemaid took the infant from Antonia. She lay the child
at her master's feet. Quintus Drusus took up the swaddled bundle

in his arms, thereby acknowledging the boy as his own true off-spring. This formal symbolic recognition meant the newborn was admitted to his Roman family with all its rights and privileges. Nine days after his birth, Quintus Drusus, the younger, would be officially named amid much familial celebration.

"You will remember what I have said, my dear, won't you?" Quintus Drusus asked his wife as he handed his son to the waiting nursemaid and arose from her bedside. "Our child must be your first consideration."

Antonia nodded, her blue eyes wide with surprise. This was a side of her husband she had never seen, and she was suddenly afraid. Quintus had always been so indulgent of her. Now, it would seem, he was putting their son ahead of her.

He smiled down at her. "I am pleased with you, Antonia. It has been a terrible time for you, but you have been brave. You are a fit mother for my children."

He left her bedchamber and made his way to his library. The house was quiet now, without his stepsons running about. In a way, it was sad, but in a few years' time the villa would ring again with the laughter and shouts of children. *His children.* A single lamp burned upon the table as he entered his private sanctuary, shutting the door firmly behind him. Only the gravest emergency would cause anyone to disturb him once that door was closed. He had quickly trained the servants after his marriage to Antonia that this room was his sanctum sanctorum. No one came in but at his invitation.

"You did very well," he told the two men who now stepped from the shadows within the room.

"It was easy, master," the taller of the two answered him. "Those two nursemaids was easy pickin's. A little drugged wine, a little fucking, a little more wine, a little more—"

"Yes, yes!" Quintus Drusus said impatiently. "The picture you paint is quite clear. Tell me of the boys. They gave you no trouble? They did not cry out? I want no witnesses coming forward later on."

"We throttled them in their beds as they slept, master. Then we placed their bodies in the atrium pond. No one saw us, I guarantee you. It was the middle of the night, and all slept. We made that pretty tableau for everyone to find before we done the children. Quite a wicked pair, those girls looked," the tall man continued. He sniggered lewdly.

"You promised us our freedom," the other man said to Quintus Drusus. "When will you give us our freedom? We have done as you bid us."

"I told you that there were two tasks you must perform for me," Quintus Drusus answered him. "This was but the first."

"What is the second? *We want our freedom!*" the tall man declared.

"You are impatient, Cato," Quintus Drusus said, noting his look of distaste. It amused Quintus Drusus to give his slaves dignified, elegant-sounding identities. "In nine days' time," he continued, "my son will be formally named, and a ceremony of purification will be performed. It is a family event to be celebrated within the home. My father-in-law will come from Corinium; my cousin Gaius and his family from their nearby villa. It is my cousin and his family that I want you to study well.

"There is a Celtic festival in May. I remember it from last year. Gaius Drusus allows his slaves their freedom that night from sunset until the following dawn. I intend to pursue the same custom. On that night you will eliminate my cousin and his family. As an extra incentive, you may steal my cousin's gold from a certain hiding place I shall reveal to you when the time comes. In the ensuing uproar it will take several days for me to discover that those two new slaves from Gaul that I recently purchased are gone. Do you understand me?" He stared coldly at the pair, wondering if there was a way he could eliminate them as well and save himself the possibility of ever being discovered. No. He would have to rely on these two. If he was any judge of men, they would flee as fast as they could back across the sea to Gaul.

"Beltane," Cato said.

"*Beltane?*" Quintus Drusus looked puzzled.

"The Celtic festival you mentioned. It is celebrated the first day of May, master. There is no other spring festival of note."

"How appropriate," Quintus Drusus said with a brief smile. "I married my wife on the Kalends of June. Our son was born on the Kalends of March. Now on the Kalends of May I shall achieve the beginnings of my destiny. I do believe that the number one is a lucky one for me." He looked at the two Gauls. "I will dim the lamp a moment. Go out by the garden exit, and behave yourselves. *Both of you!* You must have easy access to the house when my cousin and his family are here. If you have been causing difficulties, the majordomo will send you to the fields. You are of no use to me in the fields."

In the morning, Quintus Drusus sent messengers to his father-in-law in Corinium, bidding him come, and to his cousin Gaius, inviting him and his family to the new Drusus's name day and purification. It was not until they arrived for the celebration that Gaius Drusus Corinium and his family learned of the deaths of Antonia's two older sons.

"Ohh, my dear," Kyna said, kissing the young woman on both cheeks, "I am so terribly sorry. Why did you not send for me? My mother and I would have come. Cailin too. It is not good for a woman to be by herself in a time of such great sorrow."

"There was no need," Antonia said softly. "My little ones are safe with the gods. Quintus has assured me of it. There is nothing I can do for them. I must think of the baby. Quintus will not have a slave woman nursing him. I cannot distress myself lest my milk cease. That would displease Quintus very much, and he is so good to me."

"She is mesmerized by him," Cailin said in disgust.

"She is in love with him," Kyna answered.

"I think it very convenient that Sextus Scipio's two sons are now gone," Cailin noted quietly.

Kyna was truly shocked. "*Cailin!* What are you saying? Surely you are not accusing Quintus Drusus of some unnatural act? He loved those two little boys and was a good stepfather to them both."

"I accuse no one of anything, Mother," Cailin said. "I have merely observed the convenient departure of Antonia's little boys.

You must admit that it can but suit Quintus that only his own child is left alive to inherit one day all he has gained."

"Why, when you speak of Quintus," Kyna asked her daughter, "are your thoughts always so dark, Cailin?"

The girl shook her head. "I do not know," she answered honestly. "My voice within warns me against him, calls to me of some nameless danger, yet I know not what. I thought when he married Antonia, these feelings would evaporate, but they have not. If anything, they have grown stronger each time I am in Quintus's presence."

"Are you jealous, perhaps, of Quintus's marriage?" Kyna probed. "Is it possible that you regret your decision not to wed him?"

"Are you mad, Mother?" The look of distaste on Cailin's beautiful face told Kyna that she was definitely on the wrong track.

"I only asked," Kyna said apologetically. "Sometimes we regret what we have refused, or thrown away."

They were called into the atrium, where the family altar was set up. Proudly, Quintus Drusus bestowed his own praenomen, or first name, upon his son. Gently he hung a beautiful carved gold bulla about the baby's neck. The locket, held together by a wide spring, contained a powerful charm within the two halves that would protect its wearer until he became a man. With the dignity befitting the patriarch of a great family, Quintus Drusus intoned prayers to the gods, and to Mars in particular, for this was the month of Mars. He prayed that Quintus Drusus, the younger, would live a long and happy life. Then he sacrificed a lamb, newborn on the same day as his son, and two snow-white doves to honor the gods so that his prayers would be favorably received.

Once the religious ceremony was over, the celebration and feasting began. Each member of the Gaius Drusus family had brought the baby a crepundia. Crepundia were tiny toys made of gold or silver in the shapes of animals, fish, miniature swords, flowers, or tools, which were strung together upon a chain and hung about the little one's neck to amuse him with their rattling and jingling. They were the traditional gifts brought to an infant's purification and name day.

Quintus Drusus was expansive in his good humor. Sharing wine with his cousins Titus and Flavius, he teased them, "I hear it said that there is a certain slave girl at your father's villa who ripens like a summer melon. Which one of you is responsible, eh?" He poked a playful finger in their direction and chuckled.

The twins flushed, and then laughed guiltily.

"We are not certain," Flavius admitted. "As has been our habit from childhood, we shared."

"Mother was quite angry with us. She says we are going to be matched and married before the summer is out lest we cause a scandal," Titus told his older cousin. "The girl has recently miscarried, at any rate, and so we shall never know who the father was, though perhaps we would not have known anyway."

"And Father says we are not to dip our buckets in any more wells, no matter how sweet the water," Flavius added.

"And have your brides been chosen, cousins?" Quintus asked.

"Not yet," Titus replied. "Father would go slightly farther afield than Corinium. He says it is time for fresh blood in the family. I think, perhaps, he is not pleased with the girls available to us here."

"The selection is not particularly great," Quintus observed. "I was fortunate in my darling Antonia. May the gods bring you both the same good fortune, my young cousins, and may I live to celebrate the name day of all of your children." He raised his goblet and drank.

They, in turn, saluted him.

"And what of Cailin?" Quintus asked. "Is she to be matched with a husband soon? She grows more beautiful every day." He looked across the room to where Cailin sat with his wife. "Had I not fallen in love with my Antonia on sight, I should have despaired at losing your lovely sister. Whoever she chooses will be a fortunate man."

"There seems to be no man who attracts our sister," Flavius said. "I wonder indeed if there is any man who will do so. She is sometimes strange in her ways, our sister. There is more Celt in her, we say, than Roman blood. What a pity if she were to die a virgin."

"More wine, master?" A tall slave stood by Quintus's elbow.
"Yes, Cato, thank you. And fill my cousins' goblets, too," he said
jovially.

⋘⋙

On Beltane night the bonfires blazed from every hill in
the province. The Celtic celebration in honor of the new
growing season was underway and shared by all. Class barriers
seemed to fade as men and women, freeborn and slave, danced together and shared potent cups of honeyed mead around the fires.

Gaius Drusus Corinium had just finished making love to his
wife in the privacy of their empty house when he thought he
heard a noise. Arising, he went out into the atrium to investigate.
He never saw the two intruders who came up behind him and
strangled him swiftly.

Kyna did not realize the thump she heard was that of her husband's body falling to the floor. She arose, and was but halfway
across the bedchamber when the room was invaded by two men.

"I told you she was a beauty," the taller said.

It was easy to divine their intent. Terrified, Kyna began to back
away. "I am the daughter of Berikos, chief of the Dobunni," she
managed to say, although her throat was tight with fear.

The taller man grabbed Kyna, his mouth pressing against the
mouth that had only just entertained her husband's sweet kisses.
Kyna fought her attacker like a lioness, clawing and spitting at
him. Laughing, the man pushed her upon her marriage bed, falling
atop her, his hands pushing up her sleep tunic. The other man was
quickly at her head, silencing her screams with his hand. Kyna
prayed to the gods for a quick death.

Brenna returned to the villa early. She had been chaperoning
Cailin at the celebration, but her granddaughter did not really
need her. There was no one who took Cailin's fancy, and besides,
the girl would not go off into the darkness with any man. She simply enjoyed the dancing and the singing.

Brenna stumbled over something in the dim atrium. Bending

down, she recognized with shock the face of her son-in-law. It was blue, and he was dead. She began to shake. With great effort, she pulled herself to her feet, and then, heart pounding, she ran to her daughter's bedchamber. Kyna lay naked, sprawled amid a tangle of bloody bedclothes. Brenna crumpled to the floor, not even realizing that she had been hit.

"The old woman was certainly easy," Cato remarked nonchalantly.

"But the younger one was more fun," his companion said. "What a good fight she gave us. The girl will be best of all, however. Let's dice for who takes her maidenhead and who gets the leavings before we kill her."

Titus and Flavius Drusus Corinium, coming home very drunk with honeyed mead, never saw their assassins. They were easily ambushed, quickly throttled, and then dragged along with their father's body into their parents' bedchamber, where Cailin would not stumble over them.

The two Gauls waited. The minutes slipped into an hour, and then another.

"Where the hell is that girl?" the shorter slave grumbled.

"We dare not wait any longer," Cato said. He pointed a finger through the window. "The sky is already lightening with the false dawn. We must fire the house so that it seems like just another Beltane fire, and be gone from here before the servants return. The girl isn't worth our getting caught. Do you think Quintus Drusus will save us if we do? A man who would murder his own stepsons so they could not inherit from him, and who would murder his cousin's family to gain lands, is not a man who would help us in our hour of need. Indeed I suspect he would kill us too if he could. The gold he promised us is in a hiding place beneath the statue of Juno in the alcove. Get it, and let us be gone. I do not trust that Roman scum to give us several days' lead. He'll be after us by tomorrow. We'll fool him, though. We'll not take passage for Gaul, but Ireland. They'll not suspect we've gone in that direction."

Brenna lay quietly, absorbing his words. She prayed they would not realize she was still alive. When they had gone, she would somehow escape to warn Cailin of the carnage. She stifled a groan, almost biting through her lip with the effort. Her head hurt fearfully. She suspected she had lost a great deal of blood, but if the gods would just grant her the power to remain alive long enough to avenge Kyna and the rest of her family, she would never again ask them for anything.

Brenna smelled the smoke of the burning bed and the gauze window hangings. Heard footsteps moving away from her. Saw the two pairs of boots as the murderers went out the door, leaving it ajar in their haste. She did not move. She needed to be certain that the two men had gone.

Soon the bedchamber began to fill with thick smoke. Gasping, her lungs burning with the acrid smell, Brenna realized that she could no longer lie where she was. Slowly, painfully, her head spinning dizzily, she crawled toward the open door and out into the atrium. There was no furniture to burn here as in the other rooms. Although the atrium was filling quickly with thick, black smoke, she knew her way to the door. Nausea almost overwhelmed her, and using a pillar for balance, she retched, racked by dry spasms, but she pulled herself to her feet. With an iron will Brenna stumbled across the atrium to the main entrance of the house. Pulling on the door handle, she staggered out into the cool, damp night air and collapsed several feet from the villa.

There was no one in sight. The assailants had gone. Brenna gulped in the clean air, noisily cleansing her lungs of the foul-smelling smoke. Above her a full moon beamed down placidly on the scene of the slaughter. *She had to find Cailin!*

Instead, Cailin found her. She came running down the lane, her long hair flying, but seeing her grandmother on the ground, the girl stopped and knelt down.

"Grandmother! The house is on fire! What has happened? Where are Mother and Father? My brothers?" She grasped the older woman by her arms, pulling her up. Brenna groaned. "Ohh! You are hurt, Grandmother! Why is there nobody to help? Why are the slaves not back from their celebrations?"

"Come away, my child! We must get away from the villa! We are in mortal danger! Help me! Hurry!" Brenna told her.

"The family?" Cailin repeated, already knowing in her heart the answer her grandmother would give.

"Dead. All of them. Come now, and help me. We are not safe here, Cailin. You must believe me, my precious one," Brenna said, sobbing.

"Why can't we wait for the slaves to return? We must inform the authorities," Cailin said desperately.

Brenna looked into her granddaughter's face. "I have no time to explain this to you now. You must trust me if you wish to live a long life. Come now, and help me. I am weak from loss of blood, and we have a ways to go before we are safe."

Cailin felt frightened. "Where are we going, Grandmother?"

"There is only one place we can go, my child. To the Dobunni. To your grandfather, Berikos. Only he can keep us safe from this evil." Grasping her granddaughter's arm, Brenna began to walk. " 'Tis but a few miles, although you did not know that, did you? Your whole life you have lived but a few miles from Berikos, and you did not know it." Then Brenna fell silent, realizing that she needed her strength if she was to get them to their destination alive. Berikos must know what had happened. Then, if the gods willed it, she would die. *But Berikos must know.*

"I do not know the way," Cailin whimpered. "Can you show me the way, Grandmother?"

The old woman nodded, but said nothing more.

They left the beaten path, and Brenna led her granddaughter up one hill and then down another. They made their way through a small, dense wood with only the light of the bright moon to show them the way. The night was silent, for the creatures belonging to it had long ceased their songs. Here and there a bird would trill nervously, certain that the bright white light signaled the dawn. Occasionally they would rest, but Brenna dared not stop for long. She did not fear pursuit, but rather she feared her own mortality. They crossed a large grassy meadow where deer were grazing in the early light, and then entered a second wood. Above them the sky was visibly lightening. They had been traveling for some time now, and Cailin had the feeling that they were moving up.

"How much farther is it, Grandmother?" Cailin asked after they had been walking for several hours, mostly uphill. She was weary from the unaccustomed exercise. She could only imagine how the older woman must feel. It had been a long time since Brenna had walked such a distance, and certainly never in such a precarious state of health.

"Not far, my child. Your grandfather's village is on the other side of this wood."

The forest began to thin out, and the sky was bright with color as they exited from the trees. Before them rose a small hill, and atop it was the Dobunni village. Suddenly a young man appeared before them. He had obviously been on watch, and was surprised to see someone out so early. Then his face lit with slow recognition.

"*Brenna!* Is it really you?"

"It is I, Corio," Brenna answered him, and her knees buckled beneath her.

"Help me, sir!" Cailin cried, attempting to keep her grandmother in an upright position, but it was futile.

Corio, after his initial amazement at seeing Brenna, jumped forward and caught the fainting woman up in his arms. "Follow me," he told Cailin, and without so much as a backward glance at her, he ran up the hill.

Cailin hurried behind him, her face creased with concern. Her curiosity was strong, however, and she noted that the hill was ringed with three stone walls. Behind the third wall, they entered into the village. Corio made directly for the largest house, and Cailin followed him through its entrance into a big hall. A woman, fully six feet tall and dressed in a deep blue tunic, came forward. She glanced briefly at Cailin, gave a start of recognition, then looked at the burden Corio carried.

"It is Brenna, Grandmother, and she is injured," Corio said.

"Put her there, boy, on the bench by the fire pit," the older woman commanded. "Then go and fetch my medicines." She looked at Cailin. "Are you squeamish, or can you help?"

"Tell me what you would have me do," Cailin answered.

"I am Ceara, Berikos's first wife," the tall woman said. "You are Kyna's daughter, are you not? You look like her, yet there is something a bit different about you."

"Yes, I am Kyna's daughter. My name is Cailin." The girl's eyes filled with tears. "Will Grandmother die?" she asked.

"I do not know yet," Ceara answered honestly. "What happened?"

Cailin shook her head. "I do not know. I came home from the Beltane festival. The house was ablaze, and Grandmother had collapsed outside. She says my family is dead, but I know nothing more. She was insistent we come here. She would not even allow me to inform the authorities, or wait for the slaves to return from their holiday."

"*Berikos!*" Brenna's voice rasped harshly. "*I must speak with Berikos!*" She struggled to rise from the bench where she lay.

"You must lie quietly, Brenna," Ceara told her. "I will send for Berikos, but if you persist in this behavior, you will not live to tell him whatever it is you must tell him. Rest now."

"Ceara! What is this I hear? Brenna has returned?" Another woman, not quite as tall as Ceara, but taller than Cailin, joined them. She had the prettiest, sweetest face that Cailin could ever remember having seen. There was something familiar about it, and yet Cailin could not place it. That face was now puckered with distress as she bent over the half-conscious woman. Her blue eyes filled with tears. "*Brenna!* It really is you! Ohh, I never thought to see you again!"

"*Maeve,*" Brenna said softly, but Cailin heard the affection in her grandmother's tone. "You are still a fool, I see."

Maeve bent down and kissed the injured woman's brow. "And you are still stubborn and filled with pride, my sister."

"*Sister?*" Cailin looked at Ceara.

"Maeve is your grandmother's younger sister. Did you not know that, child? No, I see you did not."

"Why does Grandmother call her a fool?" Cailin wondered, realizing that Maeve's familiar face was a slightly younger version of Brenna's.

"Your grandmother and Berikos were not a good match," Ceara said honestly. "They married in haste born of their overwhelming lust for each other. By the time they realized it, your grandmother was with child. Several years later your grandfather found himself truly in love with Maeve, and she with him. Brenna was appalled. She feared history would repeat itself, and she adored her sister, who is five years younger. She pleaded with Maeve not to wed Berikos, but Maeve refused to listen. Brenna called her a fool, and has referred to her as such ever since, despite the fact the marriage between Maeve and Berikos was a successful one." Ceara turned to the other woman. "Go and fetch Berikos, Maeve. He is at *her* house."

Corio returned with his grandmother's medicine basket, and Ceara began the task of examining Brenna's wound. She cut away some of Brenna's thick white hair, shaking her head at the size of the wound. This was far more serious than anything she had ever seen. Brenna's hair was severely matted with all the blood she had lost. The skull bone itself was open and had a large chip missing from it. Ceara wasn't even certain she could close the wound. Nature would have to do the job. As gently as she could, she cleaned the wound with wine, wincing when Brenna groaned. She sprinkled one of her healing powders generously over it, and then bandaged it with clean, dried moss. She had never felt so helpless in her entire life.

The girl had stood by her side, handing her what she needed, and never flinching once. Her presence seemed to soothe Brenna. Frankly, Ceara thought that only rest, time, and the will of the gods could make a difference now.

Corio had gone from the hall for a time and now returned, a small bowl in his hand. He gave it to his grandmother. "I thought that perhaps you would want this for Brenna," he said.

She smiled up at him approvingly. "Aye, 'tis just the thing. Here, Brenna, drink this. It will give you strength. Help her to sit up a bit, Cailin," Ceara ordered.

Cailin sat on the bench behind her grandmother and gently propped the older woman up. "What is she drinking?" she asked, noting that Brenna sipped the reddish liquid almost eagerly.

"It is cattle's blood," Ceara answered. "It is nourishing, and will help Brenna to rebuild her own blood." Ceara held back a smile at Cailin's look of distaste. At least the girl hadn't fainted.

"*Ceara!*" A deep voice thundered. "What is going on? Is what Maeve tells me true?"

Cailin looked up. A tall man with snow-white hair and matching twin mustaches had entered the hall. He was garbed in a dark green wool tunic embroidered with gold threads at the neck and sleeves. Around his neck was the most magnificent gold torque, worked with green enamel, that Cailin had ever seen. He strode directly up to the bench where Brenna lay and looked down.

"Hail, Berikos," Brenna said mockingly.

"So, you are back," Berikos said grimly. "To what do we owe this *honor*, Brenna? I thought never to see you again."

"Nor I you. You have grown old, Berikos," Brenna said. "I should not be here at all were it not for Cailin. I would have died in the forest safe in Nodens' care rather than come to you, were it not for our grandchild. I am here for her, Berikos, not for myself."

"We have no grandchild in common," he answered.

"*Berikos!*" Ceara's voice was sharp. "Do not persist in your stubborn folly over this matter. Kyna is dead."

A sharp look of sorrow swept over the old man's face and then was gone. "How?" he demanded, his voice impersonal, the pain forced back to where none could see it.

"Last night," Brenna began, "I went with Cailin to the Beltane fire, but I grew tired and returned home early. In the atrium of the villa I stumbled over the dead body of our son-in-law, Gaius Drusus. I ran to Kyna's bedchamber. She was dead upon her bed, ravaged and beaten to death. I never even felt the blow that felled me. When I regained my senses, I saw the bodies of Gaius and our two grandsons, Titus and Flavius, near me. The murderers were waiting for Cailin."

"*Quintus Drusus!*" Cailin cried, her face as white as milk.

"Aye, child, your voice within did not fail you." Brenna looked to Berikos and continued her horrific tale.

"What of your vaunted Roman magistrate at Corinium?" Berikos asked her scathingly when she had finished. "Is there no longer any Roman justice?"

"The chief magistrate in Corinium is Quintus Drusus's father-in-law," Brenna said. "What chance would Cailin have against him?"

"What is it you want of me, then, Brenna?"

"I want your protection, Berikos, though it galls me to ask it. I want your protection for Cailin, and for me. The slaves were still away from the villa when all of this happened. No one knows that we two alone have survived, nor must they ever know. Cailin is your granddaughter, and you cannot refuse me this request. I do not know if I will survive this attack. I am wounded, and my lungs yet ache with the smoke I inhaled. It took all my strength to bring Cailin here to you."

Berikos was grimly silent.

"You will both have the protection of the tribe," Ceara said finally. When her husband glared at her, she said, "Brenna is still your wife, Berikos; the mother of your only daughter. Cailin is your granddaughter. *Blood!* You cannot refuse them shelter or protection under our laws, or have you forgotten those laws in your ancient lust for Brigit?"

"I will accept your hospitality only as long as my grandmother lives," Cailin said angrily. "When she has passed through the door of Death into the next life, I will make my own way in the world. I do not know you, Berikos of the Dobunni, *and I do not need you.*"

A small winterly smile touched the corners of the old man's lips. With cold blue eyes he observed Cailin seriously for the first time since he had entered the hall. "Brave words, little mongrel bitch," he said, "but I wonder how well your soft Roman ways have prepared you for survival in this hard world."

"I am not afraid," Cailin told him defiantly, "and I am able to learn. I would also remind you that I am a Briton, Berikos. I was born here, as were my parents and my grandparents on both sides for generations before me. I have been raised to respect my elders, but do not try my patience, or you will find you cannot hide behind the wall of your many years."

Berikos raised his hand to her, but lowered it quickly, surprised by the venom he saw in her gaze. She was not as tall as a Dobunni, but neither was she tiny. She reminded him of Kyna in many ways, but her spirit was certainly that of her grandmother. That spirit was what had attracted him to Brenna in the first place. Unfortunately, he had not been able to live with it, and Brenna would not be tamed. He suspected this girl was very much the same. *Cailin. His granddaughter.* She would be a thorn in his side, he believed, but he had no choice but to grant her his protection and the shelter of his hall.

"You may stay," he said, and turning abruptly, walked away from them.

Brenna sagged against Cailin. "I am weary," she said.

"Corio," Ceara commanded, "take Brenna to the empty sleeping space by the south fire pit. It will be nice and warm there. Go with her, child. When you have settled her, come back. I will feed you. You must be hungry after your journey and the shock of all that has happened."

The young man gently lifted Brenna and moved her swiftly across the hall. Carefully, he lay her in the sleeping space. Cailin covered her grandmother with a lambskin, tucking it about her shoulders. She sighed deeply, a worried look on her face, but Brenna did not see. She was already asleep.

Cailin started at a touch on her arm. Turning, she looked into Corio's face for the first time. He was a pleasant-looking man with mild blue eyes.

"Come, and my grandmother will feed us. New bread is always best eaten warm. We are cousins, are we not? My father is Eppilus, Ceara's youngest son. I am only the first of your relations that you will meet. Your mother had ten brothers, all of whom are alive, and most have children, and in some cases grandchildren, of their own. You will not be lonely here."

Cailin looked to Brenna. She was pale, but her breathing was steady and even. The girl turned away and followed the young man back to where Ceara was busy preparing the morning meal. The big woman ladled cooked barley cereal into two fresh trenchers of bread, and handed them to the couple.

"There are spoons on the table, if you are dainty," Corio told her. "Come and sit down." He wolfed down a bite of his bread and cereal.

They sat, and Ceara plunked two goblets down before them. "Watered wine," she said, and then, there being no one else in the hall, she joined them. "You remind me of your mother, and yet you do not look quite as she looked at your age. Was she happy with your father?"

"Oh, yes!" Cailin said. "We were a happy family!" Abruptly, the enormity of the tragedy engulfed her. Only yesterday Kyna, her father, and her brothers were alive. There had been no warning at all of their demise—not that it would have been any easier to bear if there had been, but to have survived the murderous slaughter of her family only by chance was more than she could bear. Why should she live when they were all gone?

It was the very first Beltane festival that she had been allowed to stay at unchaperoned. Brenna had given Cailin her head that night, and once on her own, Cailin had begun to see things in a new light. All the young men had wanted to dance with her, and she danced about the leaping fires until almost dawn. She had not been ready to slip away into the darkness with any man yet, but drank her first cupful of honeyed mead and felt wonderful afterward. Cailin thought to return home with her brothers, but they had gone off much earlier, into the darkness with two maidens. She had not seen them again. Only when the false dawn began to lighten the skies, and the music finally stopped, did she wend her way back to the villa, to discover that death had been there before her.

Now, Cailin grew pale and shoved the trencher away from her. The very thought of food was nauseating.

Ceara divined the trouble immediately. "It is the will of the gods," she said quietly. "Sometimes they are kind, and sometimes they are cruel, and sometimes in being kind, unkind. You and Brenna are alive this day because your journey in this world is not yet done. Would you dare to question the wisdom of the gods, Cailin Drusus?"

"*Yes!*" Cailin cried. "Why should I live when my family does not? What could my brothers have possibly accomplished in this life that rendered their existence no longer necessary in this world? They were just seventeen!"

"I cannot answer you, child," Ceara said honestly. "All I can tell you is that everything happens when it is supposed to happen. What is death? It is but the doorway between this life and the next. We need not fear it. When your time comes, Cailin, those you love who have gone before you will be waiting on the Isles of the Blest for you. Until then it is your duty to the gods who created you to live out your destiny as they have planned you to live it out. You can, of course, whine, and despair about the unfairness of it all, but why would you so futilely waste the precious time allotted to you?"

"Am I not allowed to mourn then?" Cailin asked bitterly.

"Mourn the manner in which they met their ends," Ceara said, "but do not mourn them. They have gone on to a far better place. Now eat your breakfast, Cailin Drusus. You need your strength if you are to care for Brenna."

"Do not treat me as if I were a mindless child, lady," Cailin said.

"Then do not behave like a child," Ceara replied with a small smile, rising from her place at the board. "From the look of you, you are a girl full grown, and we are not idle people. You will be expected to earn your keep, which will leave you little time for feeling sorry for yourself." She turned from Cailin and began to serve breakfast to the others who were now entering the hall.

"Do not let my grandmother's bark fool you," Corio said with a grin as Cailin glared fiercely at Ceara's back. "She is noted for her soft heart. She only seeks to prevent you from hurting yourself."

"She has an odd way of showing it," Cailin muttered darkly.

"Would you like me to tell you about the family?" Corio asked in an attempt to distract her. When she nodded, he began, "Although our grandfather has sired ten sons, only three live in this village: my father Eppilus, and my uncles Lugotorix and Segovax, they are Bryna's sons. The others, and their families, are scattered about the other hill-fort villages belonging to the hill Dobunni. Our grandfather has five wives."

"I thought he had only four," Cailin interrupted.

"Four living, but he had a total of five. Bryna went to the Isles of the Blest some years back. Then Berikos married a woman named Brigit two years ago. She is not a Dobunni. She is a Catuvellauni. Our grandfather makes a fool of himself over her. She is not much older than you are, Cailin, but she is wicked beyond belief. My grandmother is chief of Berikos's women, but if Brigit decides to oppose Ceara's decisions, Berikos supports Brigit. It is very wrong of him, but it amuses him to encourage her in favor of his other women. Fortunately, Brigit is content to allow my grandmother and Maeve their responsibilities regarding the household. Such is not her forte. She prefers to spend her days in her own house, perfuming and preparing herself for my grandfather's pleasure. When she ventures out, she is accompanied by two serving girls who almost anticipate her every desire. They say she holds our grandfather by means of enchantment and secret potions."

Three tall men, one with dark hair, the other two with hair like Cailin's, came to sit down next to them.

"Mother says you are Kyna's daughter," the dark-haired man said. "Are you our sister's child, my pretty girl? I am Eppilus, the father of this handsome young scamp, and youngest son of Ceara and Berikos."

"Yes, I am the daughter of Kyna and Gaius Drusus. My name is Cailin," she replied quietly.

"I am Lugotorix," said one of the auburn-haired men, "and this is my twin brother, Segovax. We are the sons of Bryna and Berikos."

"My brothers, Titus and Flavius, were also twins," Cailin said, and then to her great mortification, tears began to slide down her face. Desperately she attempted to scrub them away.

The three older men looked away, giving the girl time to compose herself as Corio put a shy arm about his cousin's shoulder and gave it a squeeze. It was almost the undoing of Cailin, but she somehow managed to find humor in her situation. Poor, good Corio was making an attempt to soothe her, while in reality his kindness was close to sending her into a fit of hysterics. She needed to weep and to grieve for her family, but not now. *Not here.* It would have to be later, when she could find a private place where no one else would see her tears. Cailin drew a deep, calming breath.

"I am all right now," she said, removing Corio's protective arm.

Her three uncles met her steady gaze with admiration, and Eppilus said, "You still wear your bulla, I see."

"I am not married," Cailin told them.

"Inside your bulla there is a small bit of stag's horn, and a flat droplet of amber within which is a perfectly preserved tiny flower," Eppilus told her. "Am I not right, Cailin?"

"How did you know what my amulet contains?" she asked, surprised. "I thought that my mother and I were the only ones to know. Not even my grandmother knows what is within my bulla. It is blessed."

"Aye, but not by any of your phony Roman deities," he replied. "The stag's horn is consecrated to Cernunnos, our god of the Hunt. The amber is a bit of Danu, the Earth Mother, touched by Lugh, the Sun; the flower caught within it signifies fertility, or Macha, who is our goddess of both Life and Death." He smiled at her. "Your mother's brothers sent you this protection before you were even born. I believe it has kept you safe so that you might one day come to us."

"I never knew," Cailin said softly. "My mother said little about her life before she wed my father. I think the only way she could not hurt missing the ones she loved was to put them from her entirely."

Eppilus smiled. "How well you knew her, Cailin. Such wisdom in one so young is to be admired. I bid you welcome to your mother's family. I imagine that my father did not. He has never been able to forgive Kyna for marrying Gaius Drusus, and that prideful attitude has cost him so much. He loved your mother greatly, you know. She was his joy."

"Why does he hate Romans, or anything touched by their cul-

ture? Few real Romans have been in this land for years now. M
father's family has intermarried with Britons for so long that there
is little if anything Roman left in us. Only my original ancestor was
a pure Roman. His sons married Dobunni girls just as my father
did."

"Our father," said Lugotorix, "is a man very much enmeshed in
the past. Britain's past. The past glories of the Dobunni. A past
that began to fade and change with the arrival centuries ago of the
Romans. Our history is not a written one, Cailin Drusus. It is a
spoken history, and Berikos can recite that history like a bard. Ceara, who is closest to him in age, remembers Berikos as a young
boy. He was always consumed by our people and their past. He
knew that he would one day rule us, and he secretly longed to restore the Dobunni to their former glory. When the legions left, Ceara said he wept with joy, but in the years since, little has
happened to change Britain.

"Still, he saw the disintegration of the towns built by the Romans, and of the form of government that they left in place here.
Vortigern, who calls himself King of the Britons, has never really
consolidated the tribes. He is old now, and has no real power over
the Dobunni, or any of the other Celts. To Berikos, your mother's
marriage to your father was a great betrayal. He had planned to
match her with a warrior named Carvilius. Our father hoped that
Carvilius would help him regain all the Dobunni territory lost to
the Romans over the years, but it was not to be. Kyna loved Gaius
Drusus, and our father's dream was shattered."

"I know nothing at all about my mother's people. I will need to
learn more if I am to understand," Cailin said slowly. "My grandmother says we cannot go back to my home. She says my cousin,
Quintus Drusus, will kill me simply for my father's lands. I must
become a Dobunni, Uncles. Is such a thing possible, I wonder?"

"You are Kyna's daughter," Eppilus answered her. "You are already a Dobunni."

Chapter

3

The village in which Cailin now found herself was the main village of the hill Dobunni Celts. It was a hill fort, typical of Celtic villages in Britain. There were fifteen houses within the walls, her grandfather's being the largest. All the dwellings but Berikos's were built of wood, with walls of mud and wattle, and had thatched roofs. The chieftain's house was stone with a thatched roof. There were ten other villages belonging to the hill Dobunni, but each had only eight houses apiece.

While the houses were comfortable, they were a far cry from the villa in which Cailin had been raised. The villa's floors had been made of marble or mosaic. The floor in her grandfather's hall was stone, while in the other Dobunni houses they were hard-packed dirt. The walls in the villa had been plaster, painted and decorated. Cailin had to admit to herself that the mud and wattle walls, while certainly not beautiful, kept out the rain and the cold. That was, after all, the true purpose of a wall. In her father's villa she had her own small bedchamber. In her grandfather's house she shared a comfortable sleeping space with Brenna. It was built into the wall and, Cailin thought, quite cozy.

"You are not at all spoilt," Ceara noted as Cailin shelled peas for her one afternoon. "I would have thought that being raised as you were, with slaves around you, you would know little and complain much."

"I was taught," Cailin told her, "that in the early days of Rome, women—even of the highest social order—were industrious and knowledgeable in the domestic arts. They personally oversaw their households. Although my father's family has lived in Britain for hundreds of years, those values were retained. My mother taught me how to cook, weave, and sew, among other things. I will be a good wife one day, Ceara."

Ceara smiled. "Yes, I think you will. But who will be your husband, Cailin Drusus? I am surprised you are not already married."

"There is no one who pleased me, Ceara," Cailin said. "My father tried once to match me, but I would not have it. I will choose my own husband when the right time comes. For now, I need to be free to nurse my grandmother and earn my keep. There is much I do not know."

Ceara was silent. At the Lugh festival, after the harvest had been brought in, there would be a great gathering of all the hill Dobunni. Perhaps there would be a young man there who would please Cailin. She was fifteen, close to being past marriageable age. Ceara, however, knew all the young men in the various villages. She could not think of one who might be right.

Cailin would need a husband before the year was out. Brenna would not live much longer than that. Although she had not seemed injured by the fire at the villa, her lungs had probably been seared by the heat and the smoke of the blaze. She had never regained her strength. The least effort was far too strenuous for her. She spent most of her time sitting or sleeping. Walking, even a short distance, taxed her, so that Corio would now carry Brenna from one place to another so she might remain a participant in their family life. If Cailin did not see her grandmother fading away, Ceara and Maeve did.

Daily life in Berikos's village revolved around cultivation of the fields and care of the livestock. The land belonged to the tribe in common, but ownership of stock separated the social classes. Berikos had a large herd of short-horned cattle that were used for milk, meat, and sometimes were sold. He owned sheep that grew wool of an excellent quality. Each man in his family had at least two horses, but Berikos had a herd. He possessed hens, geese, and ducks, and he kept pigs. Celtic salt pork was famed throughout the western world, and the Dobunni exported it on a regular basis. Berikos also raised hunting dogs of which he was inordinately proud.

Cailin learned to work in Ceara's vegetable garden. This was a type of labor her family had left to their slaves, but although she was distressed by the condition of her hands after several days' labor, Cailin learned from her cousin Nuala, Corio's little sister, that a cream of rendered sheep fat and Mary's gold would cure rough hands, or any part of her skin needing attention.

Nuala, who was almost fourteen, took Cailin with her when she watched over the sheep. Cailin enjoyed those hours out upon the green hillsides. Nuala told her all she needed to know about her Dobunni family, and Cailin in turn shared her life before her family's murders with Nuala. She was the first real friend Cailin had ever had. She was far kinder than the Romano-Briton girls Cailin had grown up with, and a great deal more fun-loving. Taller than Cailin, she had wonderful long dark hair, and bright blue eyes.

Cailin rarely saw her grandfather, and counted it a blessing. He spent his nights with his young wife Brigit, in her house. Brigit, however, did not cook to suit the old man, so he took his meals in his own hall. Cailin avoided Berikos for Brenna's sake, but he had not forgotten her.

"Is she useless as all Roman women?" he asked Ceara one day.

"Kyna taught her to cook, weave, and sew," Ceara answered him. "She does them well. That joint you are gnawing on with such satisfaction was cooked by Cailin."

"Hmmmmm," the old man replied.

"And she tends my vegetable garden for me, Berikos. My bones are almost as old as yours are. I do not like getting up and down, weeding, hoeing, transplanting. Cailin does it all for me now. She learns quickly. Nuala has been taking her out to help tend the sheep. Cailin nurses Brenna, too. Kyna raised her well. She is a good girl, but we must find a husband for her. Brenna will not live much longer, and after her death, Cailin will feel that she has no one."

"She has us," Berikos said harshly.

"It will not be enough," Ceara told him.

"Well," the Dobunni chieftain said, "at least she is earning her keep, if you are to be believed, Ceara."

"I am not the wife who is prone to lying to you, Berikos," Ceara said sharply. "You must look to your Catuvellauni for lies."

"Why can you not get on with Brigit?" he grumbled at her.

"Because she has no respect for me, or for Maeve. She takes advantage of you, Berikos, and you let her. She calls to your dark side, and encourages it so that you do things you would have never done before you married her. She is wicked, and far too ambitious for a hill Dobunni chieftain's wife. But why do I waste words on you? You do not want to hear them. I have never lied to you, Berikos. Cailin is a good girl," Ceara finished quietly.

In mid-June the spelt, a species of early wheat, was harvested. In late July the einkorn, a single-grained variety of wheat, was harvested along with barley, rye, and millet. The grain to be kept for seed or barter was put in stone subterranean silos, closed with clay seals. The grain for everyday use was stored in the barns. The hay was cut and set out to dry upon wooden racks.

Nuala and Cailin collected leaves of woad, carefully filling their rush baskets with the greenery; when processed, it made a marvelous blue dye for which the Celts were famous. They also dug madder root, which yielded an excellent red dye. When the two were mixed together, a royal-purple resulted, which was very much in demand. The colors would eventually be used on garments made from the flax and hemp that were also being harvested.

August first was the feast of the great Celtic sun god Lugh. It was marked all over Britain by a general military truce between the tribes. The main harvest done, there would be a great gathering of all the hill Dobunni, with games, races, music, and poetry recitals. Cailin was familiar with the festival. In Corinium there had been a fair at Lugh's feast.

She wondered if she would ever see the town again. Shortly after her family's deaths, her uncles Eppilus and Lugotorax had made a trip to Corinium to learn what was being said about the deaths of Gaius Drusus and his family. Stopping at the main tavern, they mentioned to the tavern keeper the burned-out villa they had seen some miles from town.

"It appears to have been a recent fire," Eppilus said casually.

"Was anyone hurt?" Lugotorax asked.

The tavern keeper, a gossipy soul with little business this sunny day, took a deep breath and replied, " 'Twas a great tragedy. The villa belonged to Gaius Drusus Corinium. It had been in his family since the time of the Emperor Claudius, hundreds of years ago. Nice people. A very respectable family indeed. There were three children, I'm told. Two boys and a girl. And the wife's mother, too. All dead now. The villa caught fire Beltane last, and the whole family perished."

"Is the land for sale, then?" Eppilus inquired politely.

"No," said the tavern keeper. "What was bad luck for Gaius Drusus Corinium was good luck for his cousin, Quintus Drusus. That young man came from Rome just a couple of years ago. Married the daughter of the chief magistrate here in Corinium, a rich woman in her own right. Now he's inherited the lands belonging to Gaius Drusus Corinium. Well, you know what they say, my friends. The rich get richer, eh?"

As they journeyed back to their village, Eppilus said, "I'd like to lie in wait one dark night for this Quintus Drusus, and slit his greedy throat for him. Murdering the family was bad enough, but you know what Brenna told us they did to our sister Kyna before she died."

"Killing Quintus Drusus won't bring our sister and her family back among the living," Lugotorax answered his brother. "We have to think of Cailin now. Ceara says Brenna will not live much longer. We must find a good husband for our niece."

"Perhaps at Lugh," Eppilus replied thoughtfully, "when all the hill Dobunni are gathered. Are there any among our brothers' sons whom you think would suit the girl? Whoever he is, he must be a man of property. Whatever Father may feel, Cailin is our blood."

A troupe of strange, dark people in colorful garb, traveling in three closed wagons, arrived at Berikos's village the evening before Lugh. Because of the season, they were warmly welcomed and invited to remain for the festivities.

"Gypsies," Nuala said wisely. "They are very good with horses, and some even have a gift for prophecy, 'tis said."

Indeed, the next morning as the celebrations began, one wrinkled old woman among the Gypsies set herself up beneath a striped awning and offered to tell fortunes for barter.

"Ohh!" Nuala said excitedly, "let us have our fortunes told, Cailin! I want to know if I shall have a handsome young husband with an unquenchable thirst for my flesh." At Cailin's shocked look, Nuala giggled mischievously. "Celts speak frankly," she told her cousin.

"I have nothing to offer the old woman," Cailin said. "If it were not for your grandmother, I should have nothing but the tunic I came in when I arrived here. Why, the only jewelry I possess are the garnets in my ears and the gold and enamel brooch I was wearing on Beltane. You go, Nuala, and get your fortune told. I will listen."

"Give her a pot of that salve I taught you to make," Nuala said. "It will be more than enough, I promise. We'll go in together, but I'll go first, and give her this bronze and enamel pin. It's really generous, but I don't like it any longer."

The two cousins approached the awning. The old woman beneath it was certainly an ancient-looking creature. Her black eyes surveyed them as they came. She resembled a turtle sunning itself upon a rock in the early spring, Cailin thought.

"Come! Come, my pretties," she greeted them, cackling. "Do you want old Granny to tell you the future?" She smiled a toothless grin at them.

Nuala held out the pin, and the old woman took it, looking it over carefully, nodding with pleasure.

"No one does finer enamel work than you Celts," she said admiringly. "Give me your hand, girl. I will see what life has in store for you, eh?" Chortling, she took Nuala's hand and looked deeply into the palm. "Ahhhh!" she said, and then she looked again. "Yes! Yes!"

"What is it?" Nuala cried. "What do you see, old woman?"

"A strong, handsome man, my girl, and not just one. You will be wife to two men. You will have many children, and grandchildren. Aye! You will live a long life, my girl. It will not always be an easy life, but you will not be unhappy." The Gypsy dropped Nuala's hand.

"Two husbands?" Nuala looked nonplussed, and then she giggled. "Well, if one is not enough, I shall be happy to have another. And *many* children, you say? You are certain?"

The old woman nodded vigorously.

"Well," Nuala said, "it's a good fate, and I will be happy with it. What better for a girl than marriage and children?" She pulled Cailin forward. "Now, tell my cousin her future! It must be at least as good as mine is. Give her the salve, Cailin!" Nuala finished impatiently.

Cailin handed the small stone pot of salve to the Gypsy, who took the girl's palm and peered into it.

"You have but recently cheated death," the fortune-teller said. "You will cheat it more than once, girl, before your time here is done." She looked into Cailin's face, and Cailin shivered. The Gypsy looked down into her hand again. "I see a man; no, more than one." She shook her head. "Golden towers. Aiiii, there is too much confusion here! I cannot see what I need to see." She loosed Cailin's hand. "I cannot divine further for you, my child. I am sorry. Take back your salve."

"No," Cailin replied. "Keep it if you can but tell me one thing, old woman. Will I lose a loved one to death soon?"

The Gypsy took Cailin's hand again and said, "You have lost several loved ones recently, my child, and yes, the last tie binding you to your old life will soon be severed by death. I am sorry for you."

"Do not be," Cailin told her. "You have but confirmed what my own voice within tells me. May your gods protect you." She turned away, Nuala in her wake.

The younger girl's face was worried. "It is Brenna, isn't it?" Nuala asked.

Cailin nodded. "I try to put a good face on it for her sake," she said. "Everyone pretends in my presence that they do not notice, but we all know, even Grandmother. She has been with me my entire life. She saved me from death and brought me to safety. I want so much for her to grow well and live many more years, but she will not, Nuala. She is dying a little bit each day, and for all my love, there is nothing I can do to help her."

Nuala put a comforting arm about her cousin's shoulder and squeezed her. "Death is but the doorway between this life and the next, Cailin. You know that, so why do you already grieve before Brenna has even taken the first step through that doorway?"

"I grieve because I cannot take that step yet, Nuala. I will remain alone on this side of the door while my family lives on the other side of that door. I miss my parents, and my brothers!"

There was simply nothing Nuala could say that would comfort Cailin, and so she remained silent. She had all her family yet about her. She could only barely imagine what it must be like to be without one's family, and that small imagining came close to making her weep. Attempting to change the subject, she suggested, "Let us go and watch the footraces. My brother Corio is very swift. All the young men from the other villages will unwisely try to beat him."

"And they will not?" Cailin asked with a small smile. Nuala's love for her brother bordered on worship.

"No one can beat Corio," Nuala insisted proudly.

"*I can!*" came a young voice, and the cousins turned to see a handsome young man with dark hair pulled back by a leather thong.

"Bodvoc the Boastful," Nuala mocked him. "You could not best my brother at Lugh last. Why would you think you can best him now?"

"Because I am faster this year than last," Bodvoc said, "and when I win the race, Nuala, you will reward me with a kiss."

"I most certainly will not!" Nuala said indignantly, blushing, but Cailin noticed her protest was not really as vigorous as she wanted it to seem.

Bodvoc grinned engagingly. "Yes, you will," he said, and then went off to join the other young men preparing to race.

"Who is he?" Cailin asked.

"Bodvoc. His father is Carvilius, headman of one of our grandfather's villages. Your mother was to have married Carvilius, but when she chose your father instead, he married a Catuvellauni woman. Bodvoc is the last of their children."

"Bodvoc likes you, Nuala," Cailin teased her younger cousin.

Nuala giggled. "Well," she allowed, "he is handsome."

"And has, I suspect," Cailin told her, "an unquenchable thirst for your flesh. Could it be he is the first of your husbands?"

"Ohh, don't tell anyone the Gypsy said I will have two husbands," Nuala begged Cailin. "No man will want to take a chance on me if he thinks by doing so it will shorten his life. Then I will die an old maid!"

"I won't tell," Cailin promised Nuala, "but let us go watch the race, and see if you will indeed owe Bodvoc a kiss."

No one believed that Corio could be beaten, but to everyone's surprise, Bodvoc finished a full length ahead of the champion this time. Dressed only in a pair of leather briefs, his muscular chest wet with his exertion, he strode over to a very surprised Nuala.

"You owe me a kiss, Nuala of the blue, blue eyes," he said softly. And a slow smile lit his handsome features.

"Why would I kiss a man who's bested my favorite brother?" she asked him a trifle breathlessly, feeling just a little bit weak in the region of her knees. He was so ... *so gorgeous!*

Bodvoc did not argue with her. Instead he reached out, and pulling Nuala against his body, he bent to kiss her. Nuala sighed deeply and sagged against him for a long moment as her lips softened beneath his. She almost fell when he gently released her from his embrace and set her back. Her pale skin flushed a deeper hue as about her the racers, including her own brother, chuckled with amusement.

"Nuala?" Cailin spoke low.

The sound of her cousin's voice galvanized Nuala into action. Rearing back, she hit Bodvoc with all her might. "I did not say you might kiss me, you sweaty oaf!" she shouted, and ran from him, her dark hair flying.

"She loves me!" Bodvoc exulted, and turned to Corio. "Tell your father that I want Nuala for my wife," he said, then ran off after the fleeing girl.

The crowd was dispersing. Cailin looked at Corio. "Will she have him?"

"Nuala has liked Bodvoc for several years, and she's fourteen now. More than old enough to be a wife. It's a good match. He's eighteen, and strong. They'll make beautiful babies, Cailin. Now we must find a husband for you, too, cousin. I don't suppose you would consider me for a mate, would you?" For a small moment an almost hopeful look entered his eyes, and Cailin realized to her surprise that her cousin Corio harbored feelings for her that, if encouraged, could grow into love.

"Oh, Corio," she said, and touched his arm. "I love you, but my love is like that of a sister for a brother. I do not think it will ever be anything more." She hugged him. "I think at this time in my life I need a friend more than a husband. Be my friend."

"The most beautiful girl I've ever seen, and she wants to be my friend," said Corio mournfully. "I have surely displeased the gods that they would visit such a burden upon me."

"You are a rogue, dearest cousin," Cailin laughed, "and I do not feel one bit sorry for you. Your path is strewn with broken hearts."

That evening Cailin got a little more insight into her Dobunni heritage when her grandfather stood before a huge audience in his hall and recited the history of their Celtic tribe. Next to him a young harper stood playing, his music alternately sweet and wild, depending upon the portion of the tale being recited at the time. Ceara and Maeve bustled about the hall, seeing to the comfort of their guests; but at the high board, Berikos's youngest wife, Brigit, sat proudly on display.

In the three months she had lived among the Dobunni, Cailin had seen Brigit rarely, and she had never spoken with her. Brigit was beautiful, in a cold way, with her skin as flawless as marble, her icy silver eyes, her black, black hair. She held herself aloof, believing that her aged husband's protection was all she needed.

"And when he dies, does she wonder what will become of her?" Ceara demanded bitterly one day.

"She will find another foolish old man," Maeve said matter-of-factly. "No young man would have her, as she obviously lacks a heart. But an old man can be gulled into thinking he will be the envy of all for possessing a fair young wife."

⋙✦⋘

In the days that followed the celebration of Lugh, the final harvest was completed. The apples and pears were gathered from the orchards. The fields were plowed once again, and the winter wheat planted. Cailin dug carrots, turnips, and onions for cold storage.

"Leave the cabbage," Ceara said, "until there is danger of a hard frost. It's better in the garden. But pick all the lentils that are left, child. I want to dry them out and store them myself."

"Look after Cailin when I am gone," Brenna said to Ceara one afternoon. "Everything she has ever known is gone from her. She is brave, but I have heard her weeping at night in our sleeping space when she thinks I am asleep and cannot hear. Her pain is very great."

"Why not Maeve?" Ceara asked. "She is your sister."

"Maeve is ever a fool over Berikos," Brenna said, "and besides, Cailin has taken to you, Ceara. She will give Maeve honor, but it is you she trusts and is learning to love. Promise me you will look after her, dear old friend. My time is growing shorter with every passing hour, but I cannot go easily unless I know Cailin has a friend and a protector in you."

"When you have passed through the door," Ceara promised her, "I will watch over Cailin as I would one of my own granddaughters. I swear by Lugh, Danu, and Macha. You may rest easy in my word."

"I know I can," Brenna said, her relief obvious.

Brenna died on the eve of Samain, six months after incurring her injuries. She went quickly to sleep, but did not awaken the following morning. Cailin, in the company of Ceara and Maeve, washed the body and dressed it for burial. As refugees, Cailin and her grandmother had possessed little, but decorated pots, bronze vessels for food and drink, small bits of jewelry, furs, cloth, and other things considered necessary to a woman began to appear by the body in order that she be buried properly, as befitted a Dobunni chieftain's wife.

Brenna was interred several hours before sunset, when the Samain feasting would begin. The harper played a liltingly sad tune as the mourners followed the body. Berikos accompanied his estranged wife to her final resting place along with the rest of the family. Even Brigit was among the official mourners. As always, she sought to divert the focus of Berikos's attention to herself.

"Could she not have waited until the new year was begun before dying?" she whined at her husband.

"It seems appropriate to me that Brenna chose this last day of the year to end her existence here and walk through the door," Berikos answered his wife sharply.

"There will be a pall over the feasting tonight," Brigit said.

Ceara saw it coming, but she was powerless to stop it.

Cailin turned and placed herself directly in front of Brigit, making it impossible for her to move forward. "How dare you speak with such disrespect at my grandmother's funeral?" she demanded. "Is this how the Catuvellauni raise their daughters to behave? My grandmother was a woman of virtue and kindness. She was held in esteem by all who knew her. All you care about is yourself and your selfish needs!"

"Who is this ... *this girl?*" Brigit said angrily to her husband.

"My granddaughter, Cailin," he said. "Brenna's grandchild."

"Ohh, the mongrel bitch," Brigit sneered, and there were gasps.

"I am no mongrel," Cailin said proudly. "I am a Briton. Do not think your blood so pure, Brigit of the Catuvellauni. The legions, I am told, plowed many a furrow amongst the women of your tribe. Your Roman nose gives you away. I am surprised my grandfather did not notice it, but he is so overcome with his lust for you that he sees nothing except a pair of full breasts and firm buttocks."

"Are you going to let her speak to me that way, Berikos?" Brigit demanded, her cheeks red with her outrage.

"She is right, Brigit. You are disrespectful of the dead, and I am overcome with my lust for you," Berikos replied with some humor.

"She should be beaten!" Brigit insisted.

"Are you brave enough to try, Catuvellauni woman?" Cailin retorted. "No, you are not! You hide behind my grandfather's authority, and snivel at him when you do not get your own way. We all know you for what you are—the plaything of a foolish old man whose lust has made him a laughingstock. What will you do when Berikos walks through the door himself, Brigit of the Catuvellauni? Will you seek out another old man to entice with your youth and your pretty face? You will not be young forever!"

Berikos's face now darkened with anger. *"Be silent, Cailin!"* he ordered her. "I thought that we had come to bury Brenna this day, but I hear her voice coming from your mouth, excoriating me as she was ever wont to do. You speak of respect, but where is your respect for Brenna that you would disrupt her burial in such a manner? Now, be quiet, girl! I do not want to hear another word from your mouth this day."

Cailin glared at him defiantly, but she said nothing more. Brigit, however, burst into tears and ran from them, her two serving women chasing in her wake.

Berikos groaned. "The gods only know what *that* will cost me," he grumbled to Ceara and Maeve. "Perhaps I should beat the girl."

"Cailin's anger is but a reflection of her pain, Berikos," Ceara said wisely. "Remember that only six moon spans ago her entire family was cruelly wiped out by treachery. Only Brenna survived, and Cailin lived for Brenna. She has nursed her devotedly."

"My sister was all Cailin believed she had left," Maeve chimed in. "Now Brenna is gone, too. Cailin is overwhelmed with her loneliness. Kyna was a good wife and mother. Her family was a close one."

"Aye," Ceara said. "Think, Berikos. How would you feel if everyone you loved and held dear was no longer here, and you were the only one left? Cailin will never be able to replace those she has lost, but we must help her to make peace with herself and begin a new life."

"The girl has to learn to hold her tongue," Berikos replied, his ego still stinging at his granddaughter's harsh words. "You had best teach her some Dobunni manners. The next time I will beat her," he threatened. He looked over to where the grieving girl now stood, some distance from them, by Brenna's grave. Then Berikos walked away from his two wives, heading to his hall, where the Samain feasting would soon start.

Ceara shook her head in despair. "They are so alike," she said. "Cailin may be outspoken like Brenna, but she is every bit as stubborn as Berikos. They will clash again you may be certain."

"And Brigit will be seeking some sort of revenge," Maeve fretted. "She is not used to being insulted in public, nor is she used to having Berikos not come to her defense at the merest slight."

That evening, Ceara kept Cailin busy helping with the Samain feast. Brigit, in the place of honor by her husband's side, had dressed herself with special care. Her scarlet tunic dress was embroidered with gold at the neck and sleeves. About her slender neck was a delicate gold torque, filigreed and inlaid with red enamel. Pearls hung from her ears, and she wore her long black hair unbound, held only with a gold-and-pearl band about her high forehead.

She watched her enemy and contemplated her vengeance. Nothing she had thought of so far was quite right. The time was obviously not right now, but when it came, she would certainly know it. In the meantime she would bind Berikos even closer to her so he would acquiesce to whatever she desired when the moment for her revenge was at hand.

Berikos, in an effort to mend fences with his young wife, told her, "I will share a secret with you, Brigit." He leaned close to her, and his head spun with the intoxicating fragrance she wore.

"Tell me," she said, her red lips pouting seductively, "and then I shall tell you a secret in return, my dear lord."

"I have sent to the Saxons for a warrior to come and teach our men what they have forgotten about fighting. If all goes as I hope it will, we may begin taking back the Dobunni lands stolen by the Romans next summer. With the legions long gone and certain not to return, all that are left of the Romans are farmers and fat merchants. We will destroy them. They think the Celtic tribes have grown into lap dogs, but we will show them otherwise, Brigit. We will regain what is ours with sword and fire! Our success will encourage the others to take their lands back as well. Britain will be ours once more. It will be like the old days, my beauty. Now, what have you to tell me?"

"Do you remember the Gypsies that came on Lugh? Well, one of my serving women learned a secret from them that will give you pleasure such as you have never dreamed of, my lord." Her voice was breathy, and his heart beat faster with his excitement. "It has taken me all this time to learn the technique to perfection, but I have finally mastered it. Tonight, I shall show you. Do not drink to excess, Berikos, or my efforts will be wasted upon you." She licked her lips suggestively.

He shoved his goblet aside. "Let us go now," he said.

"But if you leave," she protested faintly, "the feasting must be done. It is early yet, Berikos. Let us wait a bit longer, I beg you."

"The Samain fires are long burned out," he replied. "My fire for you, however, blazes hot, Brigit, my wife."

"Bank your fire for a little time, my lord." She smiled winningly. "Will it all not be the better for the waiting?" She kissed him hard on his lips.

"As my granddaughter so forcefully reminded me this afternoon," Berikos said grimly, "I am no longer a young man." He stood up, pulling Brigit with him. "Come! The night grows older as quickly as do I."

They left the hall, and Ceara smiled bitterly. "Brigit reminds us once again that it is she who guides the old stallion leading this herd."

"I wonder what she did to get him to go so early?" Maeve said.

"Some suggestion of lustful games, you may be sure," Ceara said. "He always had a large appetite for women's flesh. His appetite is obviously still large, but can it overcome his age?"

"You sound jealous," Maeve said, astounded.

"Aren't you?" Ceara replied. "I may be considered an old woman by virtue of my years, but why should my desires not rise as hot as Berikos's desires? I would not mind if he visited my bed now and then. He was always a good lover."

"Aye," Maeve agreed, "he was. Now that we are older, no one admires us, or asks Berikos's permission to share our beds. It is lonely."

"Remember when we were younger," Ceara said, "Berikos was so proud of how other men desired his wives when they came to visit. It always gave him great pleasure to extend his hospitality to our beds. And he had his share of the visiting women as well. Do you remember the time when those three chiefs of neighboring tribes arrived to discuss an alliance, and they admired us?"

Maeve laughed at the memory. "Aye! They had come alone so others would not know of their coming. Berikos was forced to parcel us out, and then he was left without a bedmate that night. Brenna was almost ready to have Kyna, and so she could not be with him. The only other women available were all related to him. Ohh, it seems so long ago!"

"It was," Ceara said. "The old ways are dying, and men are not so ready to share their women now as they were then. It is too bad, isn't it? The right precautions kept one safe from unwanted pregnancy, but a child from an honorable man was considered a blessing. I must admit to enjoying the variety offered on those rare occasions."

The days were growing shorter with the approach of winter. The sun did not rise until late, and set by what would have been mid-afternoon in the summer. Ceara and Maeve decided to visit their sons and grandchildren in two of the other villages before the snows set in. As they would be going to the village where Bodvoc lived with his family, Nuala decided to accompany her grandmother.

"You just want to go so you can share a bed space with him," Cailin teased her cousin. "You are sure to have a big belly by the time you two are wed on Beltane next." Beltane was a traditional time for weddings among the Celtic tribes.

"If I have a big belly when we are finally married, no one would be more pleased than Bodvoc and his family. It would show them I am a fertile field, and that Bodvoc's seed is strong. There is no shame in it among our peoples, Cailin. Is it not the same for the Britons, then? Your blood is so intermingled that I thought you would follow many of the same customs as do the Dobunni."

"We follow many customs belonging to the Celtic peoples, Nuala," Cailin said, "but among the Romans, a maiden goes to her marriage bed a virgin. That custom seems to have continued among the Britons."

"What a pity," Nuala remarked. "How can you please your husband if you know nothing of what is involved in lovemaking?" Then her blue eyes grew wide with sudden awareness. *"You have never been with a man, Cailin, have you?"* she said in shocked tones. "Not even Corio? Ohh, when I return from visiting Bodvoc, I shall have to remedy this gap in your education, dear cousin. It is all very well to be able to read, but a woman must know far more than that to please a man in bed."

"I don't think I want a man in my bed just yet," Cailin ventured.

"You are going to be sixteen in the spring, cousin," Nuala said. "I will teach you everything you need to know, and then we will find a nice man for you to practice on. Bodvoc would be perfect!"

"But you are to marry Bodvoc!" Cailin squeaked nervously.

"I'm not jealous. After all, you don't love him. He's a marvelous lover, Cailin. Just perfect for a first experience! I'm certain he would be happy to oblige us in this matter."

"I do not know if I can do such a thing, Nuala. I have not grown up as freely as you have. These are not my ways," Cailin said.

"We do not hold that lovemaking between two consenting parties is wrong, Cailin," Nuala explained. "There is nothing evil about giving and receiving pleasure. Your mother was certainly no virgin when she wed your father." She patted her obviously distressed relative. "We will speak on this when I return from my visit to Carvilius's village."

Cailin's mother had never told her these things. Brenna had never told her these things. While many girls her age and younger had spoken of the mysterious ways of love, Cailin had never been particularly curious about it. There had been no man who attracted her enough to rouse her interest. While she had grown in height and breadth, and her chest had sprouted round little breasts two years ago, she had never considered life as a grown woman one day. Now it appeared that she must.

Ceara and Maeve were hardly subtle in their quest for a husband for her. Their reasoning was sound. She needed a protector. Berikos barely tolerated her, and given the chance, would have been rid of her by now. She no longer had any family. Oh, Ceara and Maeve looked after her, but what would happen to her when they were not here?

"Stay away from your grandfather while we are gone," Ceara warned Cailin in the morning of her departure. "Brigit has yet to attempt any revenge against you, but she will try, particularly if there is no one here to defend you. Are you sure you do not want to come with us, my child? You would be most welcome."

Cailin shook her head. "You are good to ask me, but I need to be alone with myself, and my thoughts. There has been no time for that since I came here. I will keep from Berikos's sight, I promise you, Ceara. I do not want him to disown me as he did my mother. At least she had my father to go to, but I have no one."

"Be certain the slaves have his meals prepared on time, and that they are hot. You will have no trouble with him then. His stomach, and his manroot, are the center of his life these days. You take care of the stomach, and Brigit will see to the other," Ceara told her wryly.

Cailin laughed. "If Berikos heard you, he would say it sounded like Brenna talking, I am certain. Do not fear, I will oversee the slaves properly."

For two days all went well, and then in mid-morning of the third day, Brigit came into the hall, looking agitated. "Where is Ceara?" she demanded of Cailin, who was alone at her loom, weaving.

"Gone two days ago to visit her sons," Cailin answered politely. "Did you not know it, lady?"

"Know? How could I know? Who tells me anything?" Brigit complained. "Then Maeve! Find Maeve!" she demanded excitedly.

"Maeve has gone visiting as well," Cailin replied.

"The gods! What am I to do?" Brigit cried.

Cailin swallowed hard. Brigit seemed genuinely disturbed, and although they were scarcely friends, Cailin heard herself ask, "Can I help you in some way, lady?"

Brigit's blue eyes narrowed and she observed Cailin thoughtfully. "Can you cook?" she finally said. "Can you prepare a small feast for tonight? Berikos has an important guest arriving. We must extend him our best hospitality." She flushed, and then admitted, "I cannot cook, at least not well enough to prepare the kind of meal that must be served."

"I am a good cook, and with the slaves to do my bidding, I can prepare a meal worthy of an important guest, lady," Cailin told her.

"Then do it!" Brigit commanded her ungraciously. "And it had better be good, mongrel, or this time I will see your grandfather has you beaten for your insolence. There is no one here to defend you now." She turned and hurried from the hall, her yellow skirts thrashing.

"I should have gone with Ceara and Maeve," Cailin muttered. "Then she would have been in the soup, and what would Berikos have thought of his beautiful young wife then, the ungrateful bitch! Well, I shall do it because Ceara would want me to, and she is good to me."

Cailin hurried off to the cook house, which was located just behind the hall. There she instructed the servants in the preparation of a thick pottage with lentils and lamb, while upon the open spit a side of beef was to be slowly roasted. There would be cabbage, and turnip, and onions braised in the coals of the fire. Fresh loaves were baked that afternoon, which would be served with butter and cheese. Cailin polished a dozen apples to a bright shine and piled them artistically in a burnished brass bowl. Taking them into the hall to place them upon the high board she complimented the young slave girl who had just finished polishing the board with beeswax. The huge table was Ceara's pride and joy. She reveled in the fact that in other halls the high boards were worn and pockmarked by knives and goblets. In *her* hall, the high board glowed and shone like new.

The slave girl brought heavy brass candle holders. "The mistress always uses these for important guests," she told Cailin.

Cailin thanked her and set them on the table, taking the large fat candles from the serving wench and placing them carefully on the iron spikes that held them. She stood back and smiled to herself. The high board looked as if Ceara had set it herself. Berikos would have no cause for complaint.

It was then that Cailin realized that someone was staring at her. She turned and, looking down the hall, saw a great, tall man standing there. His look, even from a distance, was bold.

"Who is that?" she asked the slave.

"It is your grandfather's guest," the girl whispered. *"The Saxon."*

Cailin turned and stepped down from the dais. She walked with measured steps toward the man. "May I be of service to you, sir?" she asked politely, not even stopping to think he might not speak Latin.

"I would ask permission to sit by your fire, lady," the answer came. "The day is chill, and I have had a long journey."

"Indeed, come by the fire," Cailin replied. "I will fetch you a goblet of wine, unless, of course, you would prefer ale."

"Wine, thank you, lady. May I ask whom I have the honor of addressing? I would give no offense in this hall."

"I am Cailin Drusus, a granddaughter of Berikos, the chieftain of the hill Dobunni. I apologize for your poor welcome, but the lady Ceara, who is mistress here, is away visiting her grandchildren before the winter snows come. We did not know you were expected, or she would have never gone. Has your horse been stabled properly, sir?" Cailin poured some wine into a silver goblet decorated with dark green agates, and handed it to the huge Saxon. She had never seen such a big man before. He was even larger than the Celtic men she knew. His garb was most colorful: red braccos cross-gartered in deep blue and gold, and a deep blue tunic from which his chest threatened to burst forth with every breath.

"Thank you, lady; my horse has been taken care of by your grandfather's servants." He drained the goblet and handed it back to her with a dazzling smile. His teeth were large, white, and amazingly even.

"More?" she inquired politely. He had shoulder-length yellow hair. She had never seen hair naturally that color before.

"Nay, it is enough for now. I thank you." Dazzling blue eyes, the blue of a summer's sky, looked into hers.

Cailin blushed. This man was having the oddest effect on her.

"My name is Wulf Ironfist," he told her.

"It is a ferocious-sounding name, sir," she answered.

He grinned boyishly. "I gained it as a mere stripling because I could crack nuts with one blow of my fist," he told her, chuckling. "Later, however, my name took on a different meaning when I joined Caesar's legions in the Rhineland, where I was born."

"That is why you speak our tongue!" Cailin burst out, and then she blushed again. "I am too forward," she said ruefully.

"Nay," he said. "You are blunt, honest. There is no crime in that, Cailin Drusus. I like it."

Her cheeks warmed at the sound of her name on his lips, but her curiosity was greater than her shyness. "How came you to Britain?" she asked.

"I was told there is opportunity in Britain. *Land!* There is little unclaimed land left in my homeland. I spent ten years with the legions, and now I would settle down to farm my own land and raise my children."

"You are wed, then?"

"Nay. First the land, and then a wife, or two," he told her in practical tones.

Cailin smiled shyly at Wulf Ironfist. She thought the Saxon quite the handsomest man she had ever seen. Then, remembering her duties, she said, "You must excuse me, sir. With the lady Ceara gone, the kitchens are in my charge. My grandfather is very fussy about his meals, and he likes them piping hot. Stay by the fire and make yourself comfortable. I will send for Berikos to let him know that you have arrived."

"My thanks for your kindness and hospitality, lady."

Cailin hurried from the hall, and directed the first male servant she saw to go and fetch his master. Then she returned to the kitchens to oversee the final preparations for dinner, requesting that pitchers of wine, ale, and honeyed mead be made ready for the evening's meal. She tasted the pottage, and directed the cook to add a bit more garlic. The beef sizzled and spat over the fire. It smelled wonderful.

"I sent a man down to the stream to look in the fish trap, little mistress," the cook told her. "He found two fine fat perch. I've stuffed them with scallions and parsley, and baked them in the coals. Better to have too much than too little. I'm told the Saxon is a giant of a man, and he's had a long ride. He'll have a good appetite for his supper, I'm thinking."

"Will there be enough, Orna?" Cailin fretted. "Berikos will be angry if he thinks we've slighted his guest. I've never had to prepare for a person of importance before. I don't want to shame Ceara, or the Dobunni."

"There, there, little mistress," the ruddy-cheeked cook soothed the girl. "You've done well. A nice thick pottage, beef, fish, vegetables, bread, cheese, and apples. 'Tis a very good meal."

"Have we a ham?" Cailin wondered aloud, and when the plump Orna nodded vigorously, Cailin said, "Then let us serve it as well, and boil up a dozen or more eggs. And pears! I'll put pears with the apples. Oh, please be sure there is plenty of bread, Orna."

"I will see to it," Orna said. "Now go and put on your prettiest gown, little mistress. You are far more beautiful than the Catuvellauni woman. You must sit at the high board with your grandfather in the lady Ceara's place tonight. Hurry along now!"

4

C *ailin left the cook house* and walked back to the
hall. She hadn't thought about joining her grandfather and
his guest. She had taken to eating in the cook house since Ceara
and Maeve had left. Brigit would not like it at all if she showed up
this evening, but then Brigit could go to Hades, Cailin decided.
Orna was right. She must take Ceara's place. Cailin hurried to her
sleeping space to change clothes. To her surprise, there was a small
basin filled with warmed water awaiting her. She smiled. The servants were certainly united in their dislike of Brigit, and obviously
determined that she should outshine Berikos's young wife.

Cailin drew off her tunic dress and set it aside. Opening her
small chest, she drew out her best gown. It was a beautiful light
wool garment that had been dyed with a mixture of woad and
madder. The rich purple color was stunning. There were gold and
silver threads embroidered at the simple round neckline and on
the cuffs of the sleeves. Ceara had given it to her at Lugh, and
Cailin had never worn it. She bathed carefully, using a small sliver

ented with woodbine. When she had stored the tunic
a all day in the chest, she slipped the purple garment over
en camisa. Corio had made her a pearwood comb. Cailin
ed as she drew it through the tangle of her thick russet curls.
imple fillet of freshwater pearls and chips of purple quartz dec-
rated her head; Maeve's Lugh gift to her.

Hearing her grandfather's voice, Cailin hurried from her sleeping
space and signaled the waiting servants to begin serving the meal.
She took her place at the high board, nodding politely to Berikos,
who bobbed his head slightly in her direction. When Brigit opened
her mouth to voice what Cailin was certain would be a complaint
about her presence, Berikos glowered fiercely at his wife, and
Brigit's mouth snapped shut before she uttered a single word. Cailin bit her lip to keep back her laughter. She knew it was not that
Berikos had grown any softer toward her, but that the old man was
wise enough to realize that Brigit could not direct the servants to
his satisfaction. Cailin, he knew from Ceara, could.

Brigit sat between her husband and their guest. She gushed and
flirted with Wulf Ironfist in what she believed was a successful effort to win him over to Berikos's plans for the region. The young
Saxon was polite, and more than slightly amazed by his host's wife.
He had heard the Celts were a hospitable people, but a man's wife
was a man's wife. Every now and then his gaze would stray to Cailin, silent on the other side of Berikos. Her only words were
directed to the servants, and she managed them well, he saw. She
would make some man a good wife one day, if she was not already
wed, and he somehow did not think she was. There was an innocence about her that indicated she was yet a maid.

Brigit noticed that the handsome Saxon's attention was drawn to
her husband's granddaughter. A wicked plan began to form in her
mind. She had so patiently bided her time these last weeks, waiting for the right moment to have the perfect revenge upon Cailin
Drusus. Now she believed she had found that moment. Cailin had
embarrassed her publicly before the whole village, and what was
worse, Berikos had refused to discipline the wench. How those two
old crows, Ceara and Maeve, had gloated over it, protecting Cailin

from her wrath, but now they were out of the way. Unobtrusively Brigit filled and refilled her husband's goblet, first with a rich red wine, and then with honeyed mead. Berikos had a strong head for liquor, but in recent years his tolerance had been lower than in his youth.

The steaming hot pottage was put upon the table along with the beef, ham, and fish. Platters of vegetables, cheese, and bread followed. In a burst of generosity, Berikos nodded his approval to his grandchild. The assembled ate and drank, the Saxon matching the old man goblet for goblet until finally the food was cleared away and the discussion of business began in earnest.

"If I train your young men and lead them, Berikos, what will you give me in return for my services?" Wulf Ironfist asked. "After ten years with the legions, I can teach your Celts to fight like Romans. The Romans have the best army in the world. My knowledge is valuable. I must have equal value in return."

"What do you want?" growled the old man.

"Land," was the simple reply. "I have had my fill of war, but I will do this for you if you give me land for my own."

"No," said Berikos. "*No land!* I would drive all Romans and other foreigners from Britain, and have it belong to our people again as it once did. Why else would I begin such an endeavor in my old age?"

"The only foreigners here in Britain now are we Saxons," came Wulf Ironfist's amused reply. "The true Romans departed years ago, and those you call Romans are in reality Britons, Berikos. Their blood has been intermingled with that of you Celts for so many generations that they are no longer alien. If you would make yourself king of this region, I will help you in exchange for land, and I will pledge you my fealty; but the idea that you can drive everyone from Britain but those of pure Celtic blood is a foolish and impossible task."

"But if I am successful," Berikos insisted, "more tribes—the Catuvellauni, the Iceni, the Silures, and others—will join me." In his enthusiasm he knocked his goblet over, but Brigit quickly righted it and refilled it. Berikos drank it down.

"No, they will not. They, too, are used to peace now," the Saxon said. "They want nothing more than to pursue their daily lives. You are living in another century, Berikos. Times have changed; are changing even as we sit talking this night. Now we Saxons are coming into Britain. In another fifty years our descendants will be native-born as well. One day there will come another people after us, and they will also overwhelm and intermingle with Britain's inhabitants until they, too, become native-born. This is the way of the world: One tribe overcoming another, mingling with its blood, to become a different people. You must accept it, for you cannot change it, Berikos, any more than you can change the phases of the moon, or the seasons. I will train your Celts in the military arts so that you may become the strongest warlord in this area, if you will, in exchange, give me my own lands to farm. Perhaps I will even find a wife or two among your women. It is a fair offer, Berikos."

Berikos said nothing at first in reply to the young Saxon. He sat silently pondering, not really willing to give up his dream. Until now no one but Ceara had dared to tell him that his proposed plans for the region were impossible. Once he would not have needed to send for a Saxon warrior to teach his men to fight, for the Celts had been famed for their battle prowess. But in his time he had seen the men of his tribe grown soft with good living. They were content to farm the land and keep their cattle and sheep. This was what Rome had done to them. It had taken the heart from them.

In Eire, he heard, the Celts were still real men. They lived to do battle with an enemy. Perhaps he should have sent to the Irish for a battle-hardened warrior to reeducate the Dobunni in the ways of war. He reached for his goblet again and swallowed down the honeyed mead Brigit had poured for him. It was potent, burning as it reached his belly. He was feeling tired, and confused by the younger man's words. His Catuvellauni in-laws were nearer to the Saxon shore of southeast Britain. He had arranged for them to find him a respected military man from among the Saxons, and Wulf Ironfist had come highly recommended. Still, Berikos could not be content with what the Saxon had told him.

Brigit leaned over and whispered softly in her husband's ear, "We can win the Saxon over to our side if we are patient, my lord," she murmured. "Let us offer him Celtic hospitality as of old. We will send a beautiful woman to his sleeping space to warm his bed, to give him a night's sport. Not a *real* Dobunni woman, but your granddaughter, Cailin Drusus. We must not allow one of *our* women to mingle her juices with the Saxon's. Cailin is not really one of *us*, is she, Berikos?"

He shook his head, and murmured low to her, "But what sport can the little mongrel bitch give him, Brigit? She is an untutored virgin."

"All the better reason to give her to the Saxon. First-night rights are considered a special privilege among all tribes. You honor the Saxon by giving him those rights with one he will consider to be of your own blood."

Berikos looked craftily at the young girl next to him. She certainly was beautiful, he thought grudgingly. Her coloring was unique and had a certain provocativeness to it. It was past time she lost her virginity. They would have to find her a husband soon, and she would need to know how to please a man. No man wanted a bride who was frightened, or clumsy in bed. He turned back to Wulf Ironfist. "We have spoken enough on this matter tonight, my young friend. I do not know if I agree with you, but you have given me pause for thought. I am not so old that I cannot change if I must. Let us speak on this again on the morrow. It is our custom to honor a guest by giving him one of our women to warm his bed. I will give you my granddaughter, Cailin. She will share her sleeping space with you this night, *will you not, girl?*"

If he had struck her, Cailin could not have been more surprised. Then she saw Brigit smiling broadly at her, and Cailin knew instantly who had put the old man up to this mischief. Her instinct was to refuse and flee the hall. What Berikos was asking of her was unthinkable. But then as reason quickly overcame her overwrought emotions, Cailin realized that to refuse would not only enrage Berikos, but embarrass him, and the Dobunni as well. She had never felt more alone in her entire life. The smirking Brigit had certainly enacted a fine revenge. She knew that the Romano-

Britons kept their daughters virgins until marriage, unlike the Celts. Yet whatever husband they found for her would be a Celt. He would not consider her lost virginity a deficit. She had no other choice.

"*Well, girl?*" the old man snarled threateningly.

"As you will, Berikos," she answered him, looking directly into the old man's eyes until he turned away. She had never been more frightened in all her life, but she would not give Brigit the satisfaction of knowing it.

"Good, good," he muttered, then turned to his wife. "It is time for us to retire, Brigit. Bid our guest good night. I will join you shortly at your house."

Brigit arose from the table all smiles. "Good night, Wulf Ironfist. May your pleasures be great, and many," she tittered. "I will await your coming with eagerness, my lord," she told Berikos, and then with another bright smile, Brigit hurried from the hall.

"Go to your bed space now, Cailin," her grandfather ordered her. "Wulf Ironfist and I will have a final cup of mead together while you await his coming."

Cailin stood up and moved slowly from the high board. She said no word of farewell to Berikos, and certainly none was necessary for the handsome Saxon who sat with him. Berikos would surely direct the young man to her sleeping space when the time came. She frankly wasn't certain what kind of protocol was involved in such an arrangement. It was better she remain silent.

Reaching her sleeping space, Cailin opened her little storage chest, removed her gown, and stored it neatly away with her little jeweled fillet. Should she remove her camisa? She honestly did not know. She had never in her whole life seen her parents abed together. She knew absolutely nothing of what would transpire between herself and Wulf Ironfist. No mother in her culture would discuss such serious matters with her daughter until she was ready to marry. As Cailin had never settled upon a husband, there had been no talk about the intimacies shared by a man and a woman. Her twin brothers had been as protective of her as were their parents.

It would be best, Cailin finally decided, to err on the side of caution, lest she be considered wanton. She slowly slipped off the soft felt slippers she wore in the house, and putting them in the chest, too, she closed it. Then she climbed into the sleeping space, which was set into the stone walls of the building.

The mattress was newly made, filled with a mixture of sweet hay, lavender, heather, and rose petals. The inner covering of the mattress was a close-woven linen, but the outer cover was a finer, soft linen fabric of a natural hue. There was a beautiful coverlet of red fox, which kept her warm in the coldest, dampest weather. In a small niche above her head a little stone oil lamp burned, illuminating the sleeping space. Cailin considered dimming it, but decided to leave it burning for the present. It cast a comforting golden light over everything, and she needed all the courage she could muster to face whatever lay ahead.

Wulf Ironfist was shown to the sleeping space by a servant. Sitting upon the small chest, he pulled his boots off and set them neatly aside. Then he stood and removed his tunic and braccos. The servant girl, who had hidden in the shadows that she might see him nude, almost swooned at the sight. Never in all her life had she seen such a man! He had broad, broad shoulders and a wide back. When he turned to stretch, the serving wench was treated to the sight of well-muscled arms and a smooth bronzed chest. His legs were like tree trunks, massive and well-shaped, covered with a golden down. Her wide eyes slid down the tantalizing torso following his treasure trail, and her mouth formed a small O of worshipful admiration. Silently the girl backed away, envying the fortunate young mistress who would certainly be wellpleasured by the Saxon's passion this night.

Wulf Ironfist undid the thong holding his hair back, and the blond mass fell forward, touching his shoulders. The glow of the light in the bed space was welcoming. Reaching out, he pulled the fur coverlet aside and climbed in. For a brief moment he thought he was alone, for Cailin was pressed against the far wall of the enclosure, her back to him, and at first he did not see her. Although he had earlier thought her demeanor a pleasingly modest one, he had expected a warmer welcome to her bed. Was she teasing him? Or was she merely shy? Rolling onto his side to face her, he reached out and pushed the delightful tangle of her curls aside to bare her neck. Then, leaning forward, he kissed the slender column warmly.

"Your skin is like silk," he told her admiringly, and he stroked the back of her neck gently.

Cailin, who had shivered just slightly at the touch of his lips on her flesh, now shuddered hard at his touch.

Wulf Ironfist was not an insensitive man. He could see that the girl was holding herself stiffly. Then he realized that she was also still wearing her camisa. An uncomfortable thought crept into his head, but he pushed it away for the moment. He needed to know more. "You have not removed your camisa," he said quietly. "Let me help you now."

"I did not know if I should," came the muffled reply, and she seemed to move even farther away from him, although he knew it impossible given the dimensions of the bed space.

"I have been told that Celtic girls celebrate the Mother goddess," he replied, reaching down to slide the camisa up and off her cringing figure. Rolling over, he tossed the garment upon the chest and turned back to the girl. The line of her back was beautiful, and her skin was exquisitely fair. He touched her shoulder with gentle fingers, and she started violently. "Do you not wish to share your sleeping space with me, Cailin Drusus?" he asked quietly. "I have been told this is a common custom among your people. What is the matter?"

"For an unmarried maiden to share a sleeping space with a man is not how I was raised, Wulf Ironfist, but I am bound to obey the wishes of my grandfather. Just a few months ago I foolishly told Berikos that when my grandmother stepped through the door from this life to the next, I would leave the Dobunni; that I could take care of myself. But the truth of the matter is that I cannot fend for myself no matter how much I would wish to do so. Therefore I must obey when Berikos commands. He is not particularly fond of me as it is." Her young voice trembled slightly at the last.

"You are not a Dobunni?" What mischief was this? Wulf wondered.

"My mother, the child of his third wife, was Berikos's only daughter," Cailin said. "Her name was Kyna. My grandfather loved her dearly, I am told, but he disowned her when she married my father, whose family descends from a Roman tribune. I liked what you said to my grandfather this evening about us all being Britons. Unfortunately, Berikos doesn't see it that way."

Cailin went on to tell Wulf Ironfist how she had come to Berikos's village, and of her grandmother's death just a few weeks prior. "I am not unhappy here among my mother's people. They are kind and good to me. But my grandfather will not forgive me the slight amount of Roman blood that flows in my veins," she finished.

"The lady Brigit does not like you," Wulf noted astutely.

"No, she does not. It was she who suggested this arrangement, but then it is customary for the Dobunni to offer an important visitor a bedmate for the night. Brigit thinks to kill two birds with one stone. She can revenge herself on me, and she hopes to influence you to aid my grandfather, which will gain her greater favor with him."

"What do you think of his plans for Britain?" Wulf Ironfist asked Cailin. He had liked this beautiful, and obviously intelligent girl from the first moment he had seen her this afternoon with her bowl of brightly polished apples. He did not want to hurt her.

"I think you are right, sir, and that Berikos deludes himself," Cailin said honestly. "Will you help him?"

"Turn around, Cailin Drusus, and look at me. It is difficult speaking to your back," he replied, and there was just a hint of laughter in his deep voice as he cajoled her gently.

"I cannot," Cailin admitted. "You are naked, are you not? I have never seen a man naked . . . completely naked," she amended, remembering the wrestlers who had entertained at her brothers' Liberalia feast.

"I will keep my half of the furs wrapped tightly about my body," he promised her. "Only my arms, shoulders, and head will be visible to you. And you must be as tightly wrapped for your own comfort. I would not embarrass you, Cailin Drusus, but I would like to see your lovely face when we speak. It is very dim in this sleeping space. I feel as if I am speaking to some disembodied creature," he teased.

She thought a long moment, and then said, "Very well, but do not look too closely at me. I cannot help being shy, sir. This is all quite new to me, though not quite as frightening as I earlier thought." Cailin rolled over carefully, clutching the furs to her chest. He smiled encouragingly down at her, and she blushed to the roots of her auburn hair. "Will you help Berikos?" she repeated, struggling not to burst into tears, for her fear had suddenly returned at the sight of him, and her heart was pounding.

For a quick moment he caught a glimpse of her eyes. They were like wet violets. Then her lashes swiftly lowered, brushing her pale cheeks like dark, dancing butterflies. "Berikos, it would seem, is not willing to meet my price," Wulf Ironfist answered her.

"Land," Cailin said, and suddenly she had a marvelous idea. "I will meet your price, sir," she told him, "and in exchange I will ask but two things of you. You will find, I believe, that mine is the better bargain."

"You will give me land for training and leading the Dobunni?" he said, quite confused by her offer.

Cailin laughed. "No. You are correct about the Dobunni's chances of restoring the Celtic tribes to their former prominent position; there is no chance. But I would be revenged upon the man who engineered the murders of my family, and would have killed me but for happenstance. The lands of the Drusus Corinium family are mine by right as the sole, surviving member of that family. Alone I can do nothing to claim my rights. My cousin, Quintus Drusus, would find some way to kill me to hold on to what he has stolen. But you could kill Quintus Drusus for me, Wulf Ironfist. And if you wed with me beforehand, then my lands would become yours, would they not? It is a far better opportunity than my grandfather can give you," Cailin concluded, surprised at her own daring in even suggesting such a thing. Perhaps she was learning how to survive without the Dobunni after all.

"Are your lands fertile? Is there sufficient water?" he asked, amazed that he was even considering her proposition, but then why shouldn't he? He wanted lands of his own, and he would need a wife. The girl's idea was a perfect solution to both their problems.

"Our lands are fertile," she assured him, "and there is plenty of water. There are good fields for grain, and other fields for grazing cattle and sheep. There are orchards, too. My family's villa is gone, but we can build another dwelling, sir. The slaves belonging to my father will also be mine. Berikos will have to give us a generous bridal gift as well. Ceara and Maeve will see that it is a good portion."

Wulf Ironfist needed no time to consider. Her offer was an excellent one, and only a fool would refuse it. "I will do it," he told her. "We will wed, and then I will regain your lands for you, Cailin Drusus. I will even aid that old reprobate, your grandfather, somewhat. We will be forced to winter here. During the next few months I will train any young Dobunni who wishes to learn the arts of war. The final test of their skills will be when we retake your lands from your wicked cousin. Then Berikos may have them. If you are right about these people, they will not follow him any farther than the boundaries of their own fields." He looked hard at her. "You are clever, lambkin." Reaching out, he tipped her face up and touched his lips briefly to hers. "We will not tell your grandfather of our plans, though. I will tell him only that I want you for my wife."

"He will not refuse you that," she said, feeling a flush suffuse her whole body at the touch of his mouth on hers. "Indeed, both he and Brigit will think it fitting that the mongrel bitch, as they like to call me, has mated with a foreigner, as they call you Saxons."

"We have not mated yet," he said softly, his gaze direct.

"We have not wed yet," she countered quickly, her heart skipping a beat.

"We cannot insult your grandfather, lambkin, nor will he believe me overcome by my hot passion for you if we do not do what is expected of us tonight." He tangled his big hand in her hair, cupping her head. "I like the color of your hair, and the charming confusion of your curls, Cailin. Saxon girls have straight, blond hair. They wear it in two plaits, and it is often cropped to their skulls when they wed, to show their subservience to their husbands. I could not do that to your sweet curls, so it is fortunate you are a Briton and not a Saxon," he finished with a smile at her. Gently, but firmly, he pulled her head back, exposing the line of her throat. Then pushing her onto her back, he pressed slow, hot kisses on her milky flesh.

Cailin clutched her furs desperately to her breasts. She didn't know what to do. She didn't know if she should do anything. Suddenly his blue eyes were staring deeply into hers. She found she could not look away. She was growing warm again, she thought irrationally, longing to toss off the coverlet, but not daring to do so.

Wulf Ironfist was absolutely certain of the answer he would receive to the question he now asked her. "Are you a virgin, lambkin?" Of course she was a virgin. Her face mirrored her confusion, as she alternated between fear of the unknown and curiosity.

"Yes," she said low. "I'm sorry I won't be able to give you pleasure. I just don't know what to do."

"I like it that you are a virgin," he told her tenderly, "and I will teach you everything you should know to please us both." He pressed a handful of curls to his lips for a moment.

"I don't even know how to kiss," she said dejectedly.

"It is an easily learned art," he assured her seriously, but his blue eyes were dancing with amusement. "In many it is instinctive. When I kiss you, just kiss back. Let your heart guide you. I will instruct you in certain refinements later on." Lowering his head, he kissed her gently, and after a moment of hesitation Cailin kissed him back. "That is very good," he praised her. "Let us try again."

This time his kiss was firmer, and she felt her lips give way slightly beneath his. She gasped faintly as the very tip of his tongue brushed sensuously and lightly over her mouth. The sensation caused her head to whirl dizzily. Cailin put her arms about him to steady herself, for she felt as if she were falling.

He released her lips and buried his head in her hair. "You taste delicious, lambkin, and you smell delicious. I never met a girl who smelled as good as you do. Why is that?" He now looked down into her eyes, and Cailin colored once more. "Will you always blush when I look at you?" he asked her softly. "You are so fair!"

"Your praise is extravagant, I think, sir," she answered him, and then realizing that her arms were about him, she unwrapped herself from him, but he protested her actions.

"I like that you held on to me, lambkin. I think for all your maidenly fears, you know me to be a man who can be trusted. I am not a man who scatters compliments like raindrops. When I offer you praises, it is because you deserve them, Cailin Drusus. *You are beautiful.* I have never known such a beautiful woman. I will be proud to have you for my wife, and I will be jealous of any man who looks at you, lambkin. We are going to make fine, strong children together."

"*How?*" she boldly asked him, surprising them both.

He grinned boyishly. "So you are curious, are you? Then we must continue with our lessons." Reaching out, he began to draw back the fox coverlet.

Cailin cried out softly, attempting to stop him, but he would not be stayed. The look of awe upon his handsome face, however, when he gazed upon her nudity for the first time, gave Cailin a tiny glimpse of the power a woman holds over a man. He did not touch her at first. Rather, his eyes drank in her smooth, fair flesh; her small round breasts; the graceful curve of her waist; her slender, but well-fleshed thighs; the tightly bunched curls upon her Venus mont.

He smiled, almost to himself, and touched her there with a single finger. "These curls match those upon your head," he said.

She watched him wide-eyed, silent.

Then he said, "Remove my half of the coverlet, lambkin."

She pulled the furs back, and caught her breath at the sight. He had called her beautiful, and yet it was he who was beautiful. He had the body of a god, surely. Everything was in proportion; perfect, perfect proportion. There was nothing that surprised her but for the appendage between his legs. She stared at it curiously, touching it gingerly with a finger even as he had touched her. "What is it?" she asked him. "What use does it serve for you? I do not have one."

Wulf Ironfist swallowed hard. Her curiosity was almost detached. "Nay, you do not have one, but your brothers did. Did you never see theirs?"

"What is it?" she repeated.

"It is called a manroot."

"And my brothers had them, too? No, I never saw them. My parents believed in modesty. They said a great many of Rome's problems today stemmed from a lack of morals. They did not believe we should be ashamed of our bodies, but they also did not believe that we should flaunt them lewdly. What does your manroot do?"

"It is the means through which my seed will flow into your womb, lambkin. Encouraged, my manroot will grow large, and hard. I will sheath it within you, releasing my seed. The act will give us both pleasure."

"Where will you sheath it? Show me," she demanded.

He bent and kissed her once more, and as he did so, he took a single finger and, pushing gently between her nether lips, touched the entry to her woman's passage. *"There,"* he told her, lifting his mouth from hers.

"Ohhh!" she answered. That single light touch had not simply startled her. It was as if something had burst in her midsection. Tiny tremors of sensation pulsed throughout her entire being.

"We have a ways to go before that," he told her, removing the invasive digit. "I will answer all your questions later, lambkin, but perhaps it would be better if we did not talk so much right now."

"Why do you call me 'lambkin'?" she persisted nervously.

"Because you are an innocent little lamb, with your big purple eyes and your naughty russet curls; and I am the wolf who is going to eat you up," he responded. Then his mouth pressed down hard on hers. He wanted to be gentle. He wanted to be patient. But her nearness was driving him wild with longing. He needed to get on with it, and if the truth be known, the longer he waited, the harder it was going to be on Cailin. Her lips softened beneath his, and he pushed his tongue into her mouth. She tried to draw back, but he held her firmly.

At first she tried to elude the tongue seeking hers, but he would not let her. She could taste the honeyed mead on his breath, and it excited her. Tentatively her tongue sought his out; joining it in an exquisite dance that gratified both their senses. Her arms tightened about him once again, drawing him half over her, her young breasts pushing up to meet his smooth chest.

Pulling away, he took her heart-shaped face in his hands and covered her face with kisses. His lips trailed once again down her straining throat, moving into the valley between her breasts. When she cried out softly, he soothed her. "No, lambkin, do not be afraid."

Her breasts felt as if they were swelling beneath his kisses. When he cupped one in his hand and tenderly fondled it, her cry was one of relief. She had wanted him to touch her there. She wanted him to keep touching her there. Her heart was beating so violently that she thought it would come through her chest, but his touch was far more compelling now than her fears.

Wulf bent and kissed the young breasts in his charge. His tongue began to tentatively lick at her nipples, first one, and then the other, teasing the soft flesh into tight, hard spear points of tingling sensation. Cailin's breath sounded ragged in his ears as he finally closed his mouth over her left nipple and began to suckle strongly. *"Pleasure,"* he heard her half sob as he moved to her other nipple, offering it the same erotic homage he had offered its sister.

Cailin watched him through half-closed eyes as he worshiped her body. She felt weak with unfamiliar longing, but in her heart she felt stronger than ever before. She realized suddenly that he had swung himself over her, as bending forward he caressed and kissed her torso. Thrusting from his body was ... was ... *his manroot!* But it was suddenly enormous. It could not possibly fit within her young body. He would tear her apart! "You are too big!" she cried, her voice genuinely frightened, her palms against his chest, pressing away. "Please don't! I do not want to do this thing now!" She arched, struggling against him.

He groaned. It was a desperate sound. "Let me fit just the tip of it in your passage, lambkin, and you will see it will be all right."

"Just the tip?" she quavered.

He nodded. Gently he guided himself with a hand. She was wonderfully moist with her excitement, and he easily fitted himself into her waiting passage. The heat of her flesh welcomed him as she closed tightly about the tip of his manroot. Wulf wondered how long he was going to be able to maintain his control. She was simply delicious. What madness had made him propose such foolishness? He wanted to bury himself as deeply within her as he could. He took a deep breath. "There," he crooned to her. "That is not so terrible, is it, my lambkin?"

The invasion was a tender one. She felt it most distinctly. The tip of him was stretching her, but it did not really hurt her.

He kissed her lips softly and murmured against them, "If you will let me come just a bit farther, I will give you sweet pleasure." When she did not answer him, he began to press his advantage forward, moving with delicate, quick strokes within her, while continuing to kiss her mouth, her face, her neck.

Cailin closed her eyes and allowed him his will. Although the feeling was new, it was not altogether unpleasant. In fact she was beginning to grow quite warm, and when she felt her body start to move in rhythm with his, she was surprised, but she could not refrain from the motion. Indeed, as she moved with him she began to find herself overcome with a sensation of overpowering sweetness. It was as if a hundred butterflies were caught within her body. Cailin suddenly took Wulf Ironfist's face between her hands and kissed him passionately for the first time.

He had watched the changing expressions on her face. It was like watching a clear sky turn stormy. "Can you feel the pleasure beginning, my lambkin?" he whispered to her. "Is it good? Let me complete what we have started. I long to possess you completely!"

"*Yes!*" It was clearly said.

She felt his muscled thighs pinion her firmly. He began to piston her with quicker strokes of his manhood. Faster, and faster, and faster, and then a sharp burning pain overwhelmed her as her maidenhead shattered before the onslaught of his weapon. The pain swept up her torso, filling her achingly as he sheathed himself completely within her with a triumphant cry. Cailin gasped as the fire filled her belly. Her nails clawed at his straining back. She would have screamed in her terrified agony had he not covered her mouth with his own at the precise moment he deflowered her.

He had hurt her! He hadn't even warned her of this torture! Of course he hadn't. He knew full well she would have not allowed him the liberty of her body had she known of this horrendous pain. She hated him! She would never forgive him. She . . . she . . . she was suddenly aware of a new and absolutely delicious sensation sweeping over her. The pain had vanished as rapidly as it had come. Nothing remained but warm, sweet pleasure. Wulf was moving again upon her, and the honeyed fire pouring through her veins was akin to nothing she had ever experienced before.

"Ohhhh!" she half sobbed as he released her lips. "Oh!" There was a hot tightness building inside her. "What is happening to me?" she moaned desperately as she felt her body beginning to spiral out of control. She was soaring! It was wonderful! She didn't want it to stop! Up. Up. Up. She could go on forever like this. Then the sensation climaxed, bursting like a thousand shooting stars inside both her body and her brain. *"Ohhhh!"* she cried, overwhelmed by the pleasure, and disappointed as she felt the deliciousness melting away as quickly as it had come upon her.

"No!" Cailin said, and then she opened her eyes and looked into his. *"More!"* she demanded.

Wulf Ironfist burst out laughing, but there was no mockery in the sound. It was the laughter of a happy and relieved man. He smoothed her hair from her face and rolled off of her, kissing the tip of her nose as he did so. Then propping himself up against the wall of the bed space, he looked down into her face and said, "I hope you gained as much pleasure from our passion as I did, lambkin." Then he drew her into the safety of his strong arms.

Cailin nodded, turning her head to look up at him. Her euphoria was abating slightly, but she was not unhappy. "After the pain it was wonderful," she told him shyly.

"There is only pain the first time," he promised. "We shall make fine children. The gods have been kind to us, Cailin Drusus. We are well-mated and well-matched, I think."

"Your seed is fierce," she said, blushing with the remembrance of how she felt it flooding her with sharp bursts. "Perhaps even now we have begun our first son, Wulf Ironfist," she finished as they slipped beneath the coverlet again.

He lay his great blond head upon her breasts, and was pleased when she cradled him as protectively as he had her. He had come to the Dobunni seeking land. The gods, in their wisdom, had given him Cailin, and a brand new future.

"If we were in your world," he said, "and I had asked your father for you, and he had consented, how would our marriage be celebrated?"

"The ceremony would begin at my father's villa," Cailin told him. "The house would be decorated with flowers, if there were any, and boughs of greenery, finely spun colored wool, and tapestries. The omens would be taken in the hour of the false dawn, and being auspicious, the guests would begin arriving even before the sunrise. They would come from all the neighboring villas, and from the town of Corinium, too.

"The bride and the groom would come to the atrium, and the ceremony would begin. We would be brought together by a happily married matron who would be our pronuba. She would join our hands before ten formal witnesses, although actually all our guests would be present."

"Why ten?" he asked her.

"Ten for the ten original patrician families of Rome," she answered him, and then continued, "I would then say the ancient words of my consent to our marriage. 'When—and where—you are Gaius, I then—and there—am Gaia.' We would then move to the left of the family altar and face it, sitting on stools covered with the skin of sheep sacrificed for the occasion. My father would then offer a cake of spelt to Jupiter. We would eat the cake, while my father prayed aloud to Juno, who is Goddess of Marriage. He would pray to Nodens, and to other gods of the land, both Roman and Celtic. Afterward we would be considered truly wed. There are other forms of the marriage ceremony, but this was the one always used by my family.

"My parents would then host a great feast which would last the entire day. At the end of it pieces of our wedding cake would be distributed to our guests for luck. Then I would be formally escorted to my husband's home. You would seize me from the shelter of my mother's arms, and I would take my place in the procession. We would be led by torch bearers, and musicians, and anyone along the way might join in the parade. Indeed, this procession was considered the final stamp of validity to a marriage in the old days.

"It is customary for a bride to be attended by three young boys whose parents are both living. Two would walk next to me and hold my hands, while the third would go before me carrying a branch of hawthorn. Behind me would be carried a spindle and distaff. I would have three coins of silver; one I would offer to the gods of the Crossroads, the second I would give to you, representing my dowry, and the third I would offer to your household gods."

"And would I do nothing except stride proudly along?" he said.

"Oh, no," Cailin told him. "You would scatter sesame cakes, nuts, and other sweetmeats among the bystanders. When we reached your house, I would decorate the door posts with colored wool, and anoint the door with precious oils. Then you would lift me up and carry me across the threshold. It is considered bad luck if a bride's foot should slip while entering her new home."

"I would not let you slip," he promised, and lifting his head up, he kissed her lips. "Is that all?"

"No," Cailin said with a little laugh. "There is more. As you carried me into the house, I would repeat the same words I had said to you at our marriage ceremony. Then the door would be closed to the crowds outside."

"And we would be alone at last!" Wulf Ironfist said.

"No," Cailin answered, giggling. "We would have certain invited guests with us. You would put me upon my feet and offer me fire and water as a token of the life we would share, and as symbols of my duty in our home. There would be wood and kindling already set in the hearth, which I would light with the marriage torch. Then I would toss the torch among our guests. It is considered very lucky to gain possession of a marriage torch."

"Then our guests would go home, and we would *finally* be alone," he said. "Am I right, Cailin Drusus?"

She chuckled. "No."

"*No?*" he said in exaggerated tones of outrage.

"I would have to recite a prayer first," she said.

"A long prayer?" He pretended to look aggrieved.

"Not too long," she replied, "and afterward the pronuba would lead me to our marriage couch, which would be placed in the center of the atrium on the first night of our marriage. It would always remain in its original position as a symbol of our union."

" 'Tis a long day for a bride and groom," he said.

"How do the Saxons celebrate their marriages?" she asked him.

"A man buys his wife," Wulf Ironfist replied. "Of course he usually makes certain first that the maid is of a similar frame of mind. Then he approaches her family—through an intermediary, of course—to see what and how much they will take for the girl. Then the offer is formally made. Perhaps it is accepted, or perhaps a little more dickering goes on. Once the bride price is agreed upon and exchanged, a feast is held, and afterward the happy couple go home—without their guests, I might add," he concluded.

Then he took her chin between his thumb and forefinger. "Say your words to me, Cailin Drusus." His voice was soft, his tone caressing, his manhood beginning to stir once again. "Say your words to me, lambkin. I will be a good husband to you, I swear by all the gods, both yours and mine."

"When—and where—you are Gaius, I then—and there—am Gaia," Cailin told him. How odd, she thought. I waited all my life for the right man to say those words to, but never did I think to say them, stark naked, in a bed space in a Dobunni village to a

Saxon. Still, Cailin decided she was fortunate. She sensed that Wulf Ironfist was an honorable and a good man. She needed his protection, for without her family she had no one. Ceara and Maeve did the best they could for her, but they had gone away, and she had found herself at the mercy of Berikos and his vicious Catuvellauni wife. It would not happen again. Then she heard the Saxon's voice, strong and sure, and she looked into his blue eyes.

"I, Wulf Ironfist, son of Orm, take you, Cailin Drusus, for my wife. I will provide for you, and protect you. This I swear by the great god Woden, and by the god Thor, my patron."

"I will be a good wife to you," Cailin promised him.

"I know," he told her. Then he chuckled. "I wonder what your grandfather, and that witch Brigit, will think of this turn of events?"

"He will ask payment of you for me, I am certain. Give him nothing!" Cailin said. "He deserves nothing."

"That for which we pay nothing is worth nothing, lambkin," Wulf told her. "I value you above all women. I will give him a fair price of which you need not be ashamed."

"You are too good," she said. "How can I repay you for your kindness to me? You might have had a night's sport, and then sent me away. If you had, however, I know I ought not have been shamed, for it is the Dobunni way, but I would have been shamed in my heart nevertheless."

A slow, mischievous grin lit his strong, handsome features. "I know just how you may begin your repayment, lambkin," he said, and he brought her hand to his manroot, which was again in a state of eager readiness. "I intend to exact full payment, lambkin, not just this night, but in the nights to come."

Her young face took on a seductive look he had not seen before. "It is fair, my husband," she agreed. "You will hear no complaint from me in this matter. My family always taught me to repay my debts." Then she pulled his face back to hers, her lips ready and eager for his kisses.

Chapter

5

Berikos *looked at his guest.* "You slept well?" he asked. "You have reconsidered our conversation of yesterday?"

"Your granddaughter is a charming companion," Wulf Ironfist replied, and gulped down a draught of brown ale. "I am honored to have had her first-night rights, Berikos. You have made it plain how much you desire my aid, but I, in turn, still believe your idea is doomed to failure. You cannot turn back time. No one ever has, my friend."

"I will meet your price," Berikos said desperately.

"*Land?*" The Saxon raised an eyebrow questioningly.

Berikos nodded bleakly.

"You would make a bad neighbor, feeling as you do," Wulf told the old man. "I would never really be able to trust you ... unless...."

"*Unless what?*" Berikos pounced upon the small thread of hope.

"Assign me a portion of land for security now. When I have

trained your men, I will exchange it with another Celt living on the Saxon shore," Wulf Ironfist said. "I will have my land, and the land you give me will belong to another of your race. Perhaps not of your own tribe, but you Celts can work that out amongst you."

Berikos nodded. "Aye, we can, *and* when the day comes when we drive your people back to the Rhineland, you cannot complain to me, can you? I will have kept my part of our bargain. Good! I agree!"

"Not quite so quickly, my friend," Wulf Ironfist said. "I want one other thing of you. I think you are most apt to keep your bargain with me if we are related by blood. Your granddaughter pleases me. I need a wife. Her mixed blood disturbs you, but it does not disturb me. I will pay you a fair bride price for her if you will give me your consent."

"Under our laws, she must give her consent, too, Wulf Ironfist. If she does, I will be glad to accept a bride price for her," Berikos answered, "although I should not. You will be doing me a favor by taking Cailin off my hands. My wife Ceara has been nagging me to find her a husband. What will you give me for her?"

The Saxon tossed his companion a coin. It flashed and glittered as it flew through the air. Berikos's fist closed about it. His eyes widened. He bit the coin as hard as he could, his look one of surprise.

"*Gold?* This is a gold coin, Wulf Ironfist. One girl is hardly worth an entire gold coin," Berikos said slowly. He wanted the Saxon's gold, but his conscience would never leave him in peace if he weren't honest. "Besides, the wench has not yet given her consent to the match."

"She has given her consent," the younger man told him. "It is a fair price, for it will ensure that you will not take my life when my use to you is over and done with, Berikos of the Dobunni."

The old man chuckled. "You do not trust anyone, Wulf Ironfist, do you? Well, you are wise not to, for no one can be completely trusted in this world. Very well, I accept your terms, and the girl is now your wife. You may think it a poor bargain when she shows you the rough side of her tongue, but I will not take her back." He spit in his right hand and held it out to the Saxon, who, spitting in his own right hand, clasped Berikos's outstretched palm in a firm grip.

"Agreed, Berikos, but I will not regret the bargain, I assure you. Cailin will make me a good wife. Her mother taught her well the duties a woman has to her husband and house."

"Aye," the old man responded softly, "Kyna was a good girl."

"Good morning, and was your night filled with many pleasures?" Brigit tittered, entering the hall. Her sky-blue tunic dress with its silver embroidery floated about her gracefully as she came, smiling falsely.

"Indeed, lady, my night was a very good one," Wulf Ironfist answered.

"Wulf has agreed to aid us," Berikos said, pleased. He explained to his young wife the land transaction involved. "And," he concluded, "I have given him Cailin as a wife."

"*You have done what?*" Brigit's eyes widened with shock. This was not at all the way she planned it. She had intended only for the Saxon to roughly violate Cailin and break her spirit. She wanted the girl shamed, and hurt.

"Wulf asked me for Cailin's hand," Berikos repeated. "Her tainted blood does not bother him. My granddaughter has agreed." He held up the coin, saying, "Wulf has given me *this* for the wench's bride price. It is gold. Your father was content to accept a silver piece and a breeding pair of hunting dogs for you, Brigit."

Brigit's eyes glittered at the sight of the gold, and Wulf thought that Berikos would not have his granddaughter's bride price for very long if Brigit had her way. The woman's mouth was sullen, however, and she finally said, "Is there no food in this hall that we might break our fast? Cailin is derelict in her duties, or has her marriage gone to her head? A good wife should have the morning meal ready at a respectable hour. I hope Ceara returns soon."

"Perhaps if you did not sleep half the morning away, Brigit," Cailin said as she entered the hall, "you would find the meal ready. Berikos and my husband ate hours ago. If you go to the cook house, however, they may give you something if you tell them I said to do so." She smiled brightly at the woman. "I must be about my duties. A runner arrived this morning from Carvilius's hill fort. Ceara and Maeve are expected before sunset. We will eat as soon as they arrive. Do try to be on time, lady." She turned to her grandfather. "Is the bargain made between my husband and you, Berikos?"

"It is," he said, the corners of his mouth twitching just slightly. The girl was tough, and refused to be beaten. He'd give her that. "Speak more gently to my lady wife in future, mongrel," he warned her. "She is deserving of respect."

"Only if she earns it, Berikos," Cailin shot back, and turning on her heel, left them.

"*There!*" Berikos crowed. "You have seen the rough edge of her tongue now, Wulf Ironfist, but it is too late! She is your wife."

"The barb was not directed at me, Berikos. I like a woman who speaks her mind. I will only beat her if she defies me," he answered.

Ceara, Maeve, and Nuala arrived even as the mid-afternoon winter sunset was turning the sky glorious shades of red, orange, gold, and dark purple. One cold bright star hung over Berikos's hill fort, as if guiding them to the warm safety within. Nuala was excited to be home, and hugged her cousin tightly while her elders removed the cloaks.

Before they might hear it elsewhere, Berikos told his two older wives of Cailin's marriage. Both were clearly horrified, and equally furious at Brigit's part in the matter.

"She did it to be cruel," Maeve cried in a rare show of anger before her husband. "You were filled with wine and mead, I've not a doubt, and went along with the bitch's mischief! Oh, shame, Berikos!"

"You do not have to accept him as a husband, my child," Ceara said, her calm tones belying her outrage. "There is no shame among our peoples if a woman samples pleasure with several men. If she learns to give equal pleasure, it but enhances her reputation as a possible wife. You can withdraw your consent, Cailin, if you wish. Berikos can return the Saxon's gold piece. It can be done honorably."

"I do not wish to withdraw my consent, Ceara," Cailin said calmly. "Wulf Ironfist is a good man. I am content to be his wife. There is no other to whom I am attracted. Have you not been nagging me about marrying, lady?" she teased.

"But when he has finished his work here," Ceara wailed, "he will take you away to the Saxon shore, and we will never see you again!"

"Good riddance, I say!" Brigit sneered.

Ceara rounded on her. "Shut your mouth, bitch! I should have killed you when I first laid eyes upon you. You are nothing but trouble!" Then she turned on her husband. "I have honored you my entire life, Berikos," she began. "I have defended your decisions even when I knew them to be wrong. I stood silently by when you disowned your only daughter, and never said a word in Kyna's defense when I should have. I gritted my teeth when you would not allow us to share the joy of the births of Brenna's grandchildren, and I stood by silently again when Brenna left us to be with Kyna and her family.

"You are a foolish old man, Berikos! You wish to restore the Dobunni to greatness. What greatness? We never had any greatness! We are a simple clan. If you try to drive the Britons from their lands, they will fight back to defend these lands they have farmed for the last few hundred years. You will not succeed in this mad scheme even if I cannot prevent you from pursuing it; but I will not let Brenna's only surviving grandchild leave us! You will give this Saxon the lands you promised him, and they will remain here. Unless, of course," she concluded, "you wish to spend your days alone without Maeve and me."

Berikos was flabbergasted. In all the years they had been married, Ceara had never spoken so harshly to him, privately or in public. He had also never seen her so angry. "What do you mean *without* Maeve and you?" was all he could think of to say. He did not even rail at her for her overly frank speech.

"We will leave you, Berikos," Ceara said grimly. "We will go to other villages and live with our sons. But you need not fear. I am certain Brigit will keep your house, and nurse you tenderly when you grow sickly, and see that your food is cooked to your liking. Does she even know how you like your meals prepared? Probably not, but I am sure that you will tell her."

"There is no need for that," Berikos grumbled nervously.

Ceara cocked a bushy eyebrow quizzically. "Indeed?" she said.

"We will make some accommodation, lady, I swear it," Berikos promised the angry woman. "There is no need for rashness."

"We will see, old man," Ceara answered him in dark tones.

Cailin looked up at her husband, her eyes twinkling with their conspiracy. They had agreed within the cozy closeness of their bed space early that morning that no mention would be made of her lands until they were ready to make their move. They would not press Berikos to keep his bargain. When the time came, they would retake the property belonging to the Drusus Corinium family.

The word was passed among the Dobunni villages that any wishing to relearn the ancient arts of war were to come to Berikos's village, where they would be housed, fed, and taught in exchange for their service. Several wooden barracks were built within the walls of the hill fort for the prospective warriors. One hundred fifty young men, ranging in age from thirteen to eighteen, came. Berikos was disappointed with the small number. He had honestly believed there would be more.

"What did you expect?" Ceara said to him. "There are only a thousand of us. Many of the young men are already married, and do not choose to leave their families. Why should they?"

"What of honor?" Berikos said, outraged by her words.

Maeve chuckled. "Honor has little hope of keeping a man warm on a cold winter's night. And what woman wants to spend her winter alone, or with only her children, or great with child, and no man to comfort her?"

"*This* is what the Romans have done to us!" Berikos said grimly.

"The Romans did nothing to us we did not allow to be done," Ceara told him matter-of-factly. "Besides, what sensible people do not prefer peace to war?"

"Our people," Berikos said. "Our people who came out of the

darkness, and across the plains and the oceans to Britain, Eire, Cymry, Gaul, and Armorica. *Our Celtic race!*"

"When will you accept the fact that that time is past, Berikos?" Ceara said quietly to her husband. She put a comforting hand upon his arm, but he shook it off.

"*No!* It cannot be. It will come again!" he insisted.

"Then train your warriors, you stubborn old man," she said irritably. "When the spring comes, we will see what happens."

The winter came with its cold winds, icy rains, and snow. Wulf Ironfist worked with his recruits, taking them on daylong marches in all kinds of weather with fifty-pound packs of equipment upon their backs. When they complained at first, he said coldly, "Rome's legions carry more. Perhaps that is why you are no longer masters of your own land. You prefer drinking and telling outrageous tales to military training." The young Dobunni gritted their teeth and complained no more. The clang of swords rang in the clear air of the hill fort, along with the *thunk* of the javelin meeting its target as the warriors-to-be honed their battle and survival skills.

Yet as harsh a taskmaster as Wulf Ironfist was in training his men, he was a completely different man with his wife. Ceara and Maeve both agreed that the Saxon, though he would be a fierce opponent upon the battlefield, was a gentle soul with Cailin and with the children of the hill fort who followed him admiringly, begging for his favor. More often than not he would take two of the littlest ones up in his arms and walk through the village carrying them as he went about his business. There was not a child who did not adore him, nor a young girl who did not try to attract his attention. After all, there was nothing limiting Wulf Ironfist to only one wife. The maidens, however, were doomed to disappointment, for the Saxon had no time for anyone or anything but Cailin and his duty.

Cailin was content with her life. She had an attractive husband who was kind and regularly made passionate love to her. It seemed to be enough, particularly as she quickly found herself with child. She realized that her parents had had a different sort of relationship than she had with Wulf Ironfist, but she did not understand what that relationship had been.

Cailin's swelling belly pleased her husband. Here was proof of his virility for the Dobunni. Berikos was not pleased. Now he would never get rid of the Saxon. If Ceara and Maeve were determined that he and Cailin stay before this, they would be implacable now. Berikos sighed to himself. What difference would one damned Saxon make anyway? And there was always the chance Wulf would be killed in battle.

Cailin enjoyed the long, dark winter nights spent in Wulf's arms. Once she divulged her condition to him, he was more careful of her, but no less vigorous a lover. He liked cuddling her spoon-fashion, his big roughened hands cupping her round, little breasts, which were swelling now with her condition. Her nipples, always sensitive, became even more so with each passing day.

"What a little wanton you have become," he said to her one night as he sheathed his great weapon gently in her passage from behind so that his weight would not harm the child. He fondled her bosom, wickedly teasing the hard buds of her nipples. He then slipped his hands down, grasping her about the hips, drawing her firmly against his belly. He sunk his teeth into the flesh of her neck, nuzzled at the marks, and then placed a kiss on the flesh.

Cailin squirmed against him. "Are wives not allowed to be wanton, my husband? Ohhhhh," she squealed softly as he probed her more deeply, and her hips began to rotate just slightly against him.

Wulf groaned. He had never known any woman to have the effect on him that Cailin did. She roused him quicker, and brought him on quicker. He wasn't certain that he liked it, but he certainly did not dislike it. Unable to help himself, he began to pump her, her little staccato cries of pleasure only increasing his own.

Cailin thought dizzily that she should be used to him by now, but each time he took her, the excitement built and built until she could scarcely bear it, it was so achingly sweet. He seemed to grow and swell within her until finally they would both burst with pleasure, and yet the afterglow was delicious as well. Even now when the child moved within her she enjoyed his attentions. "Ahhhhhhh!" she sighed at last.

"Soon we must cease this," he told her reluctantly.

"Why?" she asked him.

"I fear I might hurt the child," he replied.

"Will you take another woman?" she asked, and he heard the edge of jealousy in her voice, which pleased him inordinately.

He was silent a long moment. "Would you mind if I did?" he asked, affecting a nonchalant air.

Now it was Cailin's turn to be silent for a time. *Would she mind?* And if she did, why would she mind? "Yes," she finally answered him. "I would mind it if you took another woman to your bed. But do not ask me why, because I do not understand it. I just would!"

"Then I will not," he told her. "If I cannot keep my desires in check like a man, then I am no better than a green boy. Besides, I have seen the difficulties your grandfather has with more than one wife. I think I should just as soon avoid such difficulties, although I do not promise I will always feel so, lambkin."

Cailin found herself smiling at his words. There would be no other wives if she could help it. One wife was more than enough for any man, even a magnificent, marvelous man like Wulf Ironfist. She would always be more than enough woman for him. Then a thought struck her. Why did it matter to her? Was it possible she cared for him? Was his thoughtfulness a sign he might care for her? Cailin slid into a contented slumber, her last waking memory that of her husband's deep sleepy breath humming against her ear. It was a comfortable feeling.

Several days later, on a bright April morning, Wulf Ironfist put his plan to regain his wife's property into effect. Assembling the young warriors he had spent the winter months training, he asked them, "How would you like to demonstrate your skills to me by helping me take a villa owned by a Roman called Quintus Drusus?"

The young men looked distinctly uncomfortable. Then Corio, Cailin's cousin, said, "Most of the lads want to return to their villages, Wulf. The planting is already under way, and their families need them. You never really expected that they would form an army for Berikos and carry out his foolish plans, did you?"

Wulf Ironfist laughed. "No, Corio, I did not. However, Quintus Drusus is the fellow who murdered Cailin's family, and was responsible for Brenna's death. I promised Cailin when I wed her that I would regain her family's lands for her, and for our children."

Corio's blue eyes widened, and then he grinned. "So that is why you have never pressed grandfather about the lands he promised you! You knew all along that you would have Cailin's property."

"I will only have it if you and the lads will help me to retake it, and mete out justice to this Quintus Drusus," Wulf Ironfist said honestly. "I cannot do it without your help, Corio."

Corio turned to the other young men. " 'Twill only take a few days of our time," he told them. "We will right a wrong, and Cailin can go home again to raise her children, to give honor to her dead family, to live in peace as we would live." He looked to his companions, and when each head among them nodded in assent, he turned back to Wulf Ironfist, saying, "We'll do it!"

"Get a good night's rest, then, my lads," the Saxon told them. "We leave in the morning." Then he dismissed them, but Corio touched his arm, obviously wishing to speak further with him as the others hurried off in all different directions. "What is it, Corio?"

"I must tell you something, Wulf," the younger man said. "It's about my grandfather, but you must keep what I reveal secret for now."

"I agree," Wulf said.

Corio did not dissemble, but came right to the point. "The men have had a clandestine meeting. As you know, Berikos lives in the past—a past he was not even a part of, which makes it even odder. As he grows older, this determination of his to drive all the *Romans* from Britain grows and eats at him. Brigit encourages him in it. We have no wish to join him in his folly, but while he is our chief we must give him obedience. However, we have the option of replacing him with another. My father, Eppilus, has been chosen to lead the hill Dobunni. Berikos can retire with honor and spend his days amusing himself in whatever manner he chooses."

"When will this happen?" Wulf Ironfist asked.

"Just before Beltane," Corio answered him. "We will retake Cailin's lands, and then we will return to help the others depose my grandfather."

"I think it a wise decision that has been made," Wulf said. "Some men in power grow old, and their wisdom but increases along with their age. Their judgment remains sound, and good. Others, however, lose their sense of proportion with the passing years. Berikos is one of these, I fear. Your people will never truly have peace as long as he is your ruler. I understand your desire for peace. I have seen enough war to last me a lifetime. I will not fight again except in defense of my lands and my family. There is no other reason for it."

"I have lived my entire life here among these hills," Corio replied. "The farthest I have ever been away is to the town of Corinium. It is a wondrous place, with its paved streets, its shops and pottery works, the theaters and the arena. Still, I could not have lived there, Wulf. It is too noisy, too busy, too dirty; and there are, I am told, places even larger than Corinium, even here in this land. They say there is a huge town in the southeast called Londinium. Two roads from Corinium lead to it if one rides far enough, but I never have had the desire to follow either of those roads.

"I have heard your stories of the battles you fought in Gaul and in the Rhineland. They did not fill me with excitement like they did some of the lads. They frightened me, and Celts are not supposed to fear anything. Like you, I can see no reason for fighting except to keep one's lands and one's family from harm. The majority of us feel this way, and so Berikos must go. He will not be happy, but he will have no choice but to accept the will of the Dobunni."

"Brigit certainly will not be happy," Wulf noted. "You had best beware her. She is a wicked woman, and will not hesitate to do a bad turn to those she thinks have betrayed her, or Berikos."

"You do not have to tell me about Brigit," Corio said quietly. "When she first came to our hill fort as my grandfather's bride, she tried to seduce me. She has never forgiven me for repulsing her. I am not the only man she has approached, either. It would be one thing if Berikos offered her, but he has not. He is very proud of her, and jealous of any man who looks her way. You are right when you say she will not be happy. To be a chieftain's wife gives her a certain rank, but to be simply the wife of an old man does not." Corio smiled. "I think I shall enjoy her discomfort, and I shall not be the only person who revels in her downfall. Few like her."

"She thought to do Cailin a bad turn when she encouraged Berikos to put her in my bed the night I first came here," Wulf said. "She knew that the Dobunni ways were not Cailin's customs, and hoped to shame and degrade her by using me as her weapon."

"I know," Corio said softly. "Had it not turned out as it did, I would have strangled Brigit with my own two hands."

Wulf Ironfist looked intently at the younger man. For a brief moment he saw something in Corio's face that he had never seen there, but it was quickly gone. "You care for Cailin," he said.

"I offered to make her my wife shortly after she came here, but she did not love me, at least as a man. She said she felt for me as she had her brothers." He grinned wryly. "Now what man in love with a girl wants to hear that he reminds her of her kin? You do not remind her of her brothers, I will wager. Do you love her? I know you are good to her, but one day that will not be enough for Cailin. She is more Celt than Roman. She needs to be loved, not simply made love to."

The big Saxon thought carefully. He had not considered loving Cailin. The kind of love that Corio was speaking of was a luxury between men and women. A man sought a wife who would be a good breeder, a good helper, and perhaps if he were fortunate, a good friend. *Love.* He turned the word over in his brain as if he could examine it. Did he love her? He knew he wanted to be with her whenever he was not about his duties. Not just to make love to her, but to be with her; to see her smile aimed in his direction; to smell her fresh fragrance; to talk with and nestle with her on a chilly night. He thought of the mixed feelings he had had of late when other men looked admiringly at his pregnant wife. He was proud, yet he was a little jealous, too. He considered what life would be without her, and found he could not even imagine such a thing now. The realization stunned him, and he heard himself say to Corio, "Yes, I do love her," and the mad thing was that as the words rang in the springtime air, he knew in his deepest heart of hearts that it was true!

"Good," Corio said with a smile. "I am glad you love her, because Cailin loves you."

Corio's declaration surprised Wulf Ironfist. "She does?" he said. "She has never told me so, even in the heat of passion. How is it you know she loves me? Has she said it to you?"

He shook his head. "No, Wulf, but I see it in her face each time you pass by; in her eyes as they follow you about the hall; in the way she smiles so proudly when you are praised in her presence. These are all signs of her feelings for you, but because she was so sheltered by her family, she is not aware yet of what these feelings within her mean. She will be one day, but in the meantime you must not hide your feelings from her."

"I told her I would not take another woman, even when she and I could not love for the sake of the coming child. It seemed to please her very much," Wulf Ironfist told Corio.

Corio laughed. "You see!" he said triumphantly. "She is jealous, and that, my friend, is the sure sign of a woman in love."

The two men walked, still conversing, into the hall. Cailin was seated by her loom weaving cloth. She looked up, and a welcoming smile turned her mouth up prettily. "Wulf! Corio." She arose. "Are you hungry, or thirsty? May I get you something?"

"We leave tomorrow for your villa," Wulf began.

"I am coming with you," Cailin said.

"You cannot," he told her. "This is man's work."

"Neither my father's lands nor my cousin's are defended. There was never any need for that kind of defense. You will meet with no resistance, I promise you. Quintus Drusus will protest, but even his father-in-law, the chief magistrate of Corinium, will not deny me what is rightfully mine."

"You will not be safe," Wulf Ironfist said, "unless I kill this Quintus Drusus. Remember, he had no mercy upon your family."

"I will never forget his treachery as long as I live," Cailin replied. "Of course you must kill him, but not in such a way that the magistrate can charge you with his murder. My son must have his father."

"And my son's mother must remain here where she will be safe," Wulf countered with what he thought was sound logic.

"If I do not go with you, then how will they know I am alive? I want Quintus to see me, and know that I have come not just to reclaim what is rightfully mine, but to expose his wickedness to the world."

"You cannot ride a horse, Cailin," Corio said.

"There is little to riding pillion behind my husband," Cailin replied. "My belly is not that big yet. The child is not due until after the harvest. I must be there. It is my right to see justice served!"

"Very well," her husband answered, "but we leave before dawn, Cailin. If we meet with any resistance, you must get down and hide. Will you promise me that, lambkin?"

"Yes," she said, and then she smiled almost cruelly. "It will be very frightening to see a large party of armed warriors coming from the forest and across the fields. It has been over a hundred years since such a thing has occurred, and certainly not in the memory of anyone living hereabouts now. You will strike terror into all who see you." She looked at the two men. "Does Berikos know of your plans?"

They shook their heads.

"We will only tell him we are taking the men on a practice march," Wulf said. "He doesn't have to know any more than that."

"No," Cailin agreed. "He does not. He grows stranger as each day passes, and spends all his time with Brigit. We only see him for meals in the early morning and at night. Frankly, I prefer it."

Her two companions said nothing. Berikos's overthrow was not Cailin's business. It would happen soon enough.

It was dank and chilly as they arose in the dark of the night to dress for their departure. Wulf handed his wife a pair of braccos.

"Corio gave them to me to give you," he said. "They are lined in rabbit fur, and big enough for your belly."

Cailin was delighted to have the garment. She made a belt from a length of ribbon to hold up the braccos, and then slipped her camisa and tunic dress on over them. Her boots were fur-lined as well, and absorbed the chill from her feet even as she slid into them. She ran the pearwood comb through her hair and, taking up her cloak, silently followed her husband outside, where Corio and the others were already waiting upon their own animals.

Wulf Ironfist mounted his horse, then reached down and pulled Cailin up behind him. She put her arms about his waist, and they were off. There was a waning moon that gave them scant light, and the forest was particularly dark, but with each foot forward that they traveled, the sky above them faded from pitch-black to gray-black, and finally to an overcast gray as they crossed the great meadow Cailin remembered from her journey to the Dobunni hill fort almost a year ago. Birds chirped cheerily as they passed through the second wood and then over the hills that led to the home Cailin had once known.

On the crest of the final hill they stopped, and looking down Cailin could see the ruins of her family's home. They looked undisturbed; the rubble uncleared, although the surrounding fields were plowed and the trees in the orchards appeared to be well-pruned. "Take me to the villa," she said softly. "It is early yet, and there is no one about to give the alarm."

Wulf Ironfist led his warriors down the hill. They stopped before the ruined building, and Cailin clambered down from the horse's back. For a long moment she stood just staring, and then she entered. Carefully she picked her way through the atrium, stepping over the fallen timbers that lay strewn across what had once been a magnificent stone floor inlaid with mosaic designs. Wulf, Corio, and several of the other men followed her.

Reaching her parents' bedchamber, Cailin moved into the space. Nothing was recognizable—nothing except the bleached bones, and the four skulls that lay at various angles upon the floor. "It is my family," Cailin said, tears springing to her eyes. "He did not even have the decency to bury them with honor." As the tears slipped down her face, she continued, "See, there. That is my mother, Kyna, upon the bed, all burnt but for a few large bones, and her skull which lies in what was once a place of loving refuge for her. And there, in a row, lie my father and brothers. My father's skull would be the largest, I imagine." She knelt and touched one of the smaller skulls. "This is Titus. I can tell, for one of his front teeth his chipped. I hit him with a ball when I was little, and did the damage. I did not mean to, but after that I could always tell my brothers apart. And this is Flavius. They were so handsome and so full of life the last time I saw them."

She suddenly felt very old, but nonetheless pulled herself to her feet. "Let us go now. When we have secured my lands, we will return to bury my family with the dignity that they deserve." She turned and walked back through the ruins, out into the morning.

Corio shook his head. "She is Celt," he said admiringly.

"You breed strong women," Wulf Ironfist replied. The men rejoined Cailin. "Where does Quintus Drusus have his lair?" the Saxon asked his wife.

"I will lead you," Cailin answered him in a strong, cold voice.

The slaves in the fields belonging to Quintus Drusus saw the armed and mounted party of Dobunni coming. They quailed at the terrible sight and froze where they stood. The Dobunni paid them no heed. There was, Wulf assured them, no true sport in killing unarmed slaves. When they reached the magnificent, spacious villa belonging to Cailin's cousin, they brought their horses to a stop. The slaves raking the gravel driveway had melted away before them. As prearranged, fifty of the men remained mounted before the villa's entrance. Cailin, Wulf, Corio, and the hundred other men entered the house unannounced.

"Wh-Wh-What is this? You cannot enter here!" the majordomo cried, running forward as if he might stop them.

"We have already entered," Wulf Ironfist said in a severe voice. "Fetch your master immediately, or would you prefer to be skewered upon my sword, you fat insect?"

"This is the house of the magistrate's daughter," the majordomo squeaked, desperately striving to do his duty.

"If the magistrate is in residence, then fetch him also," Wulf ordered the man, and he prodded his plump midsection with the tip of his sword. "I am growing impatient," he growled.

Giving a small cry of horror as the sword point cut through the fabric of his tunic, the majordomo turned and fled; the laughter of the Dobunni causing his ears to redden as he went.

"From Antioch to Britain they are all alike, these upper servants," Wulf noted. "Pompous, and filled with their own importance."

As they stood in silence waiting, the Dobunni snuck looks about the atrium, for most of them had never been in so fine a house. Then suddenly Quintus Drusus entered the room. From her place behind her husband Cailin peeked at her cousin. He had put on weight since she had last seen him, and was almost fat. He was still handsome, however, but his eyes were now openly hard, and his mouth a trifle sullen.

"How dare you enter my home unannounced and uninvited, you savages," he blustered at them, but Quintus Drusus knew as he spoke the words he could not have stopped these men. "What do you want? State your business with me, if indeed you have any business with me, and then get out!"

Wulf Ironfist took the measure of the man before him and could see that he was soft. This was no warrior; just a carrion creature who allowed others to do the killing for him, and then moved in to take the largest portion of the spoils. The Saxon moved just slightly to one side, allowing Cailin to step forward.

"Hail, Quintus Drusus," she said, enjoying immensely his look of amazement which was quickly followed by one of fury.

"You are dead," he said.

"Nay, I am very much alive, *cousin.* I have returned to claim what is rightfully mine, *and* to see that justice is done," she told him. "I will show you no more mercy than you showed my family!"

"What is this? What is this?" Anthony Porcius entered the atrium, followed by his daughter.

It was Antonia who saw Cailin first, and she gasped with surprise. "Cailin Drusus! How can this be? You surely died in that tragic fire almost a year ago! But I can see you did not. Where have you been? And why are you wearing those dreadful clothes?"

Cailin nodded to Antonia, but her words were for Anthony Porcius. "Chief magistrate of Corinium, I claim justice from you."

"You will have it, Cailin Drusus," the magistrate answered solemnly, "but tell me, child, how is it you survived that terrible fire, and why is it you have not revealed yourself until now?"

"For reasons I will never understand," Cailin told him, "the gods spared me death in the conflagration that destroyed my home. I had stayed late at the Beltane celebrations. When I arrived back at the villa, it was in flames, and my grandmother Brenna was collapsed outside. She insisted we flee, saying the danger to our lives was great. We walked the rest of the night, until at dawn we reached the hill fort of my grandfather, Berikos, chieftain of the hill Dobunni. It was there that she told us what had happened."

"What had happened?" Quintus Drusus demanded edgily.

"You piece of Roman filth!" Cailin cried angrily. "You are an embarrassment to the name of Drusus. *You* murdered my family, and *you* dare to play the innocent? I pray the gods strike you down before me, Quintus Drusus!"

Cailin looked again to the magistrate. "My cousin arranged for two Gauls he owned to gain their freedom by doing his heinous bidding. They gained entry to the villa, killed my parents and my brothers, and felled Brenna with a single blow. Unbeknownst to them, it did not kill her. She lay waiting until she could make her escape. She overheard these Gauls bragging about how well they had carried out their master's bidding—first by murdering his two little stepsons and making it appear as if the nursemaids had been negligent. The murder of my family was to complete their service to Quintus Drusus. They even knew where my father kept his gold, and they looted it before fleeing.

"I, too, was to be killed, but it grew late. The Gauls feared exposure and execution if they did not soon flee, so they fired my home and departed. My grandmother escaped, crawling through the flames and smoke. We fled to my grandfather, fearing that if my cousin learned of our survival, he would seek to finish the task he had started. Brenna never recovered; she died at Samain. Now I have returned, Anthony Porcius. I claim what is rightfully mine as the sole surviving member of the Drusus Corinium family. I am a married woman now, and my child will be born after the harvest. I want my lands back. I want this murderer punished," Cailin concluded.

It was a great deal to absorb. Anthony Porcius had never liked Quintus Drusus, but he had swallowed his own feelings for he had not liked Sextus Scipio, either. He had assumed that as a doting father it was his nature to dislike Antonia's husbands. He realized now that perhaps he had been right all along, and his daughter was incapable of choosing a good man. Now Cailin was accusing her cousin of not only the murder of her family, but of his two little grandsons as well. It was horrifying, but in his heart of hearts he believed it to be true. Quintus was a cold, hard man. Still, Anthony Porcius was a chief magistrate. Everything he did must be done exactly according to the letter of the law.

He drew a deep breath. "I can, of course, return the land to you, Cailin Drusus. It is indeed yours by right of inheritance, and you have a husband to work and protect it. As for your accusations against Quintus Drusus, what proof can you give me other than this story your grandmother told?"

Cailin looked bleakly at him and said, "Once my mother told me that before she married my father, while she was living with my grandparents in Corinium, you fell in love with her. She, however, loved my father, but when she turned you away, it was with gentleness, for she respected you. If there is any pity in your heart, Anthony Porcius, help me avenge her death. Do you know what my cousin's Gauls did to her? They raped and beat her until they killed her. My grandmother said her last glimpse of her daughter was her bloodied and battered face and body. She was once a very beautiful woman. This murderer that your daughter has wed has not even had the kindness to bury her bones or those of the rest of my family. They lie where they were killed, while Quintus Drusus tills *our* fields with *our* slaves. *Is this the Roman justice of our ancestors?*"

The magistrate looked as if he would cry. She was telling the truth; in his very heart and soul the part of him that was Celtic knew it; but he could not help her. "The law, Cailin Drusus, requires proof. You have no proof but the words of a dying old woman. It is not enough. I would help you if I could, but I cannot. *There is no proof.*"

Cailin burst into tears. "Have I survived everything, and come to you for justice, only to be denied? Must I live the rest of my days knowing that Quintus Drusus continues on in comfort when my family is dead and gone?" She wiped her tears away with the heel of her palm, and then her moment of weakness passed. She looked at her cousin. "You know what you did, Quintus Drusus. Do not rest easy feeling that you have escaped punishment. If you are wise, you will never close your eyes in sleep again. I will see you punished if it is the last thing I ever do, you murderer!"

"You have gone mad, or else your natural grief has addled your wits, Cailin, my dear," Quintus said in a bored and superior tone. He hated losing his cousin's lands after all his hard work, but he would correct that. He just needed time, and since his father-in-law maintained that a lack of hard evidence made it impossible to prosecute him, he would have that time.

"Well," Antonia said, "now that is settled, may I offer you wine?" She smiled brightly, as if she had heard nothing of what had transpired.

"Nothing is settled until your husband pays for his crimes," Cailin said coldly. "By the gods, Antonia, do you not realize what Quintus has done? Not just to me, but to you as well!"

"Quintus is a good husband to me, Cailin," Antonia said primly.

"Quintus is a heartless bastard!" Cailin snapped. "Before he murdered my family, he had his Gauls murder the sons you birthed by Sextus Scipio. They were innocent children!"

"My sons drowned in the atrium pond because their licentious nursemaids were negligent," Antonia replied, but her voice quavered with the secret doubts she had always harbored about the incident.

"Your husband's Gauls throttled your children in their beds, and then placed their lifeless bodies in the atrium pool," Cailin told the woman bluntly, cruelly.

"It isn't true!" Antonia began to sob.

"It is true!" Cailin said harshly. "Does it hurt you to know what Quintus did? Perhaps then you will understand some of what I feel, Antonia."

"Quintus! Tell me it isn't so," Antonia wept. *"Tell me!"*

"Yes, cousin," Cailin mocked him. "Tell her the truth, if indeed you even know how to tell it. Have you ever told the truth in your whole life? Tell your wife, the mother of your only son, that you did not arrange to have her sons from her first marriage disposed of; and then tell her that you did not have those same Gauls murder my family in order that you would inherit my father's lands. *Tell her, Quintus!* Tell her the truth, if you dare—but you do not, do you? *You are a coward!*"

Quintus Drusus's face was contorted with terrifying fury. "And you are a bitch, Cailin Drusus!" he hissed at her. "Who among the gods hates me so that he protected you from death that night when I had arranged for everything to be ended so neatly?"

Cailin threw herself at her cousin and raked her nails down his handsome face. *"I will kill you myself!"* she screamed at him, teeth bared.

Quintus Drusus raised his hands to strike out at her, but suddenly his arms were grasped and pinioned hard behind him. Panic rose in his chest as he saw the huge Saxon warrior push Cailin firmly behind him. Quintus Drusus knew from the look upon the man's face that he was going to die. "Noooooo!" he howled, struggling desperately to free himself from the iron grip holding him.

Wulf Ironfist slid his sword from its sheath. It was a two-edged blade, thirty-three inches in length, made of finely forged steel, with an almost round point. Grasping the weapon firmly by its pommel, the Saxon thrust it straight into Quintus Drusus's heart, twisting the blade just slightly in order to sever the arteries. His blue eyes never left those of his panicked victim. His look was pitiless. The undisguised terror he saw in return was small payment for all the misery and heartache Quintus Drusus had caused those about him, especially Cailin. When life had fled the Roman's eyes, Wulf pulled his blade from the dead man's chest and wiped it clean on Quintus's toga. Corio then allowed the body to fall to the floor.

The Saxon looked challengingly at the magistrate, but Anthony Porcius said smoothly, "He condemned himself with his own words." He put a comforting arm about his daughter. "Wait here," he told them, and then he led Antonia from the atrium.

"A realistic man," Corio noted dryly.

"He was always practical," Cailin told him. "My father said for all his girth, Anthony Porcius had to be lighter than thistledown, for he could blow in any direction with any wind, just like a duck feather." She looked down at the lifeless body of her cousin. "I am glad he is dead. I'm just sorry he did not suffer like my mother did."

"Your mother is with the gods," Corio told her. "This Roman is not, I am certain." He looked to Wulf. "I think the men can wait outside now. There is no danger here."

"Dismiss them," Wulf Ironfist said, and then he told his wife, "Come and sit down, lambkin. It has been a long morning for a woman in your condition. Are you tired? Would you like something to drink?"

"I am all right, Wulf," she told him. "Do I look like some delicate creature who must be pampered?" But she sat nonetheless on a small marble bench by the atrium pool. It was empty of water now.

Anthony Porcius came back into the atrium. "I have given my daughter into the keeping of her women," he said. "She is, unfortunately, with child again." He sat down next to Cailin. "My dear, what can I say that would possibly ease your suffering?" He shook his head wearily. "You never liked him, I know. I did not, either, but I thought I was a foolish old man jealous of his only child's husband. Well, he is dead now, and will not harm you or Antonia again. What is past is past. When I return to Corinium, I will see your survival is made known, and I will have your lands legally restored. Your family's slaves, and other goods of course, will be returned. Where will you live? The villa is in ruins."

"The Dobunni warriors with us will help to raise a hall for us.

We will bury my family with honor, then clear away the rubble and begin. There is nothing salvageable. We will have to start from the beginning, just like my ancestor, the first Drusus Corinium, did," Cailin said.

"The big Saxon is your husband?" Anthony Porcius asked curiously.

"Yes. We were wed five months ago," she told him, and then seeing the worry in his face, she continued, "It was my choice, Anthony Porcius. Celts do not force their children into marriage."

"I know," he rejoined. "For all my Roman name, Cailin Drusus, I am every bit as much a Celt as you."

"I am a Briton," she told him. "I am a Briton, and Britain is my land. I will not take sides against one part or the other of myself. I am proud of my ancestry, of its history. I honor the old customs when I can honor them, but I am a Briton, not a Roman, not a Celt. My husband, Wulf Ironfist, is a Saxon, but our children will be as I am. They will be Britons. I will teach them my history, and Wulf will teach them his, but they will be Britons. We must all be Britons now if we are to survive this dark destiny before us, Anthony Porcius. Everything as we knew it has changed, or is changing. It is a hard world in which we live."

"Yes, my child, it is," he agreed. He arose and drew her up with him. "Go now, Cailin Drusus. Go with your strong, young husband, and make this new beginning. In time the horror of today will fade. My grandchildren will play with your children, and there will be peace between us then, as there has always been between our families." He kissed her brow tenderly and then put her hand into Wulf's. "May the gods be with you both," he told them.

Together they walked from the atrium of the villa, Corio in their wake.

"A new beginning," said Wulf Ironfist. "I like the sound of it."

"Yes," Cailin agreed, and she smiled up at both men. "A new beginning for us all. For Britain, *and for the Britons.*"

Chapter

6

True to his word, Anthony Porcius returned to Corinium and removed Cailin's name from the list of the dead, restoring her property to her legally. He then closed up his own house in the town and made his way back to his daughter's home. Instinct told him that she would need a man's presence in her household. She had no other family besides him. He knew her grief would be deep, for she had truly loved Quintus Drusus and had refused to acknowledge his faults.

To his great surprise, Anthony Porcius did not find his daughter prostrate with grief. He instead found her embittered and angry. Worse, she had become overdoting of her little son, Quintus, the younger. Antonia had loved all of her children, but had never bothered a great deal with them, preferring to leave them to the servants; a practice her father abhorred but could do nothing about. Now, suddenly, she could barely stand to have her son out of her sight.

"You must not allow him his way in everything, my daughter,"

Anthony Porcius chided her the afternoon of his return. Little Quintus had just thrown a tantrum and, having calmed her son, Antonia then rewarded him with a new toy.

"He is alone in the world, but for us, Father," she answered angrily. "Thanks to Cailin Drusus, my little Quintus and the son I carry in my womb are fatherless. I must be both father and mother to my babies now. *All because of Cailin Drusus!*"

"Antonia, my dearest," her father reasoned, "you must face the truth. You cannot live with a heart that is filled to overflowing with bitter vetch. Cailin Drusus is not responsible for your husband's death. Did you comprehend nothing that was said the day he died? Quintus Drusus had Cailin's family murdered, and then burned their villa to cover his crime in order that he might have their lands for himself. He admitted it. Why will you not understand?"

"I will not believe it!" Antonia said stubbornly.

"Why would Cailin make up such a story, Antonia?" her father persisted. "What purpose would she have in doing so? If it were not true, then why did she and Brenna flee to Berikos? If the fire had been an accident, why not simply say she escaped it?"

"Perhaps because she killed her family, Father. Did you ever consider that possibility? No, of course not!" Antonia cried.

"Antonia!" He was horrified by her words, for they were totally irrational. "What reason would Cailin have for doing such a thing?"

The grieving widow looked bleakly at him in silence.

"Antonia," her father continued, "how can you mourn a man who saw to the murder of your own two sons?"

"*It isn't true!*" Antonia shrieked. "*It cannot be true!*"

"It horrifies me as well as it does you, but there is a certain logic to it. Antonia, was Quintus Drusus such a gentle and perfect man that there was never a time when you were afraid of him?"

"There was one time," Antonia said low, "Just after Lucius and Paulus were found dead, when our son was but a day old. I was filled with grief, but Quintus grew hard with me for he feared my bereavement might impede the flow of my milk. He became very angry with me, Father. He said his son must be nursed by his mother, not some distressed slave woman. I was afraid of him in that moment, but it passed."

So that was why Antonia suckled her youngest son, Anthony Porcius thought. She had never nursed the elder boys.

"He could not have killed my sons," Antonia protested further. "He loved them! Besides, the two nursemaids were found in the most lewd and compromising of positions, reeking of wine."

"Had these women ever been found drunk, or judged guilty of lascivious behavior before, my daughter? I remember them both. They were faithful women, and loved my grandsons. You chose each of them carefully yourself after Lucius and Paulus were born, Antonia. They nursed those boys devotedly. Yet before they might even defend themselves, they were adjudged guilty and strangled. Who did this?"

"It was Quintus," Antonia said.

"Quintus," her father replied softly. "Ah, yes, Quintus. I find that interesting, my dear. The household slaves are your province, Antonia. Should he not have waited for your decision in the matter? Perhaps he did not because he knew if he had, those poor women would have implicated his murderous Gauls, and they in turn, to save their own skins, would have implicated Quintus Drusus. My reasoning is sound, I believe."

Antonia stubbornly shook her head. "It is Cailin's fault!"

"How is it Cailin's fault, Antonia? *How?*" he demanded.

"Oh, Father, do you not see? If Cailin Drusus had not come back, none of this could have happened! Quintus would be alive this very minute, and my sons would have their father. But she returned with her accusations, and then her husband killed mine!"

"What of your two elder sons? And what of the Drusus family?" the magistrate said. "All brutally slain; the villa burned; the Drusus family's bones left to bleach in the wind and rain? Have you no pity for anyone but yourself, Antonia? The gods! I am ashamed of you! I did not raise you to be so selfish!" Anthony Porcius turned away from his daughter, angry and disappointed.

"Am I selfish to have loved my husband, Father? If that is so, then I do not care what you think of me! Quintus Drusus was the man I loved, and Cailin took him from me. I care for nothing else. If I am wrong, then what matter? I am condemned to live the rest of my days without my love. My children are sentenced to grow up without their father, and for these and other crimes, I hold Cailin Drusus responsible. *I hate her!* I only hope she someday knows the pain and suffering she has inflicted upon me. *I hate her! I will never forgive her!* It is not fair, Father, that she now have the handsomest man in the province for a husband instead of me. She has taken Quintus Drusus from me, and she has that magnificent Saxon to comfort her. I have no one to comfort me!"

His daughter's unbalanced thinking disturbed Anthony Porcius greatly. He could understand her anger somewhat, but this sudden irrational envy of Cailin's husband made him very uncomfortable. Perhaps, he considered, with time Antonia would learn to accept the reality of what had happened. She would come to terms with herself, and everything would be all right. Quintus Drusus was newly dead. Anthony Porcius knew his daughter. She would grieve dramatically for a time, and then another handsome man would catch her eye, and Quintus Drusus would be forgotten. It had always been that way with Antonia when she lost a man. Another soon took his place.

After spending several days with his daughter, the magistrate took his horse and rode across the fields to the Drusus Corinium estate. The rubble of the burned villa had been cleared away, and a timber and stone hall was being raised over the marble floor that ran from the entry through the atrium and into the dining room of the old building. The wings of the villa where the sleeping chambers, baths, and kitchen had been located were not to be restored. It would be a far simpler and more practical lifestyle that Cailin would have to accustom herself to, Anthony Porcius realized, and he sighed.

All over Britain others were being forced to do the same thing in order to survive. The age of gracious living as embodied by the elegance and the lavish lifestyles of their Roman ancestors had drawn to a close. In order to continue on, people would have to learn to make do. Although, he realized, some would make do better than others. He smiled to himself. It was not really so bad. Cailin and Wulf had good lands, each other, and the hope of many children. In the end, when all else was stripped away, that was what was important.

The young couple greeted him politely. They showed him the new graves of Cailin's family. A marble cutter had been sent for from Corinium, and would make a memorial to the family using marble from the villa's wings. The new hall would not be a great one to begin with, but eventually, Wulf told their guest, they would build a larger and far grander hall. Even so, there would be a room called a solar located above part of the main hall that would offer them some privacy. The fire pits would be lined in brick; the roof expertly thatched with neatly woven, tight smoke holes.

"I have been able to salvage some items from the old kitchen," Cailin told the magistrate proudly. "The pots and the Samianware did not burn. With cleaning I believe they will be usable again."

"But what will you do for other household items and furnishings?" he asked her. "Perhaps Antonia has some things she does not need, and would send them over to you," he said doubtfully.

"I want nothing from your daughter," Cailin said proudly. "The Dobunni will give us what we need. Berikos owes me my dower rights, and Ceara will see he gives them to me."

"And I am capable of carpentry, for all my military calling," Wulf joined in. "Then, too, there will be some among our slaves who are capable of like tasks. It will simply take time, and time is the one commodity with which we are most generously blessed, Anthony Porcius."

"You will not be able to do much more with the hall until the harvest is in," the older man replied. "The coming summer months you must spend attending to your fields, which are already planted and greening. Your harvest will be your most important asset. You will need a barn or two."

"I agree," Wulf said, "but there will be those who cannot work in the fields, and there will be rainy days when the fields cannot be worked. We will manage to finish what must be finished before winter."

They returned to Berikos's hill fort for Beltane and the wedding of Nuala and Bodvoc. Eppilus was already chieftain of the hill Dobunni. It had not, however, been necessary to depose Berikos. He had been spared that indignity. Several days after Cailin, Wulf, and his men had departed to revenge her family, her grandfather had suffered a series of seizures that left the old man paralyzed from the waist down. His speech was also affected. Only Ceara and Maeve could really understand what he was trying to communicate.

Consequently, the Dobunni men had not had to remove him from his high office. A physically impaired man could not rule his fellow men. As far as everyone was concerned, the gods had taken care of the matter, and Berikos had been retired, albeit forcibly, with honor. The old man, however, was still filled with venom, most of which was now directed at Brigit.

"She has left him," Ceara told Cailin in a rather satisfied tone. "No sooner had his condition been ascertained, and the fact that he would not recover fully made known, than she was gone." Ceara smiled grimly. "She took her serving women, her jewelry, and everything else of value he had lavished upon her. We awoke one morning, and she had vanished, along with a foolish half-grown boy who shall remain nameless. The lad came back, his tail between his legs, several days later. Brigit had returned to her Catuvellauni kin, and immediately took herself a new husband. We did not tell Berikos that. There is no need to add to his pain."

"I can almost feel sorry for him," Cailin said, "but then I remember that he disowned my mother, and that he was so unkind to my grandmother when we came to him for aid. I cannot forget that he forced me to Wulf's bed when he knew I was a virgin and unused to such behavior."

"But you are happy with Wulf, are you not?" Ceara asked her.

"Yes, but what if Wulf had not been the kind of man he is?"

Ceara nodded. "Yes, you have a just grievance, but try to forgive him, Cailin. He is a foolish, stubborn old man. He cannot change, but you, my child, can. He did love your mother, and I suspect he loves you as well, for you are Kyna's daughter, though he is too proud to say it."

"He sees too much of Brenna in me," Cailin said softly, "and he will never forgive me for it. He does not see my mother when he looks at me. He hears Brenna speaking out of my mouth." She smiled. "I will try, though, for your sake, Ceara. You have been good to me."

Nuala and Bodvoc were wed during the festive celebration of Beltane. The bride's belly had already grown quite round, and while Bodvoc was congratulated, Nuala was roundly teased, but she did not mind.

"Perhaps we shall leave here, and settle near you and Wulf," Nuala said to her cousin.

"Leave the Dobunni?" Cailin was surprised by Nuala's words. Celtic life was a communal life of kin and good friends. She was startled to think that Nuala and Bodvoc would give all that up.

"Why not?" Nuala replied. "Times are changing for us all. Life is too constricted here for Bodvoc and for me. There is no opportunity to do anything except what has always been done. We love our families, but we think perhaps we should like to be a little bit away from them. You and Wulf have no one but each other. If we came and lived by you, you would have us, and we would be near enough to the Dobunni villages to have the rest of our family available when we wanted to visit, or if they needed us, or we them. There is more than enough land for us, isn't there?"

Cailin nodded. "When Anthony Porcius returned my father's lands to me, he included the river villa that had been given to Quintus Drusus when he came from Rome. You and Bodvoc could have that land. Wulf and I will give it to you as a wedding present! You will have to build your own hall, but the lands are fertile, well-watered, and there is a fine orchard, Nuala. It would be good to have you near."

"Our children will grow up together," Nuala said with a smile.

Cailin found her husband and told him what she had done.

"Good!" he said with a smile. "Bodvoc will be a good man to have as a neighbor. We'll help him to build his home so that by the time their child comes, they will have a place of their own."

With the sunset, the Beltane fires sprang to life, and the feasting, drinking, and dancing continued. During the day, Cailin had been absorbed with her relatives and the wedding, but now a deep sadness came upon her. Just a year ago her family had been murdered. She wandered among the revelers, and then suddenly found herself by Berikos. Well, she thought, now is as good a time as any to try to make peace with this old reprobate. He was seated on a bench with a back. She sat down upon the ground by his side.

"Once," she began, "my mother told me of how, when she was a little girl, no one could leap higher across the Beltane fires than you could, Berikos. I think it was the only time I ever heard her speak of you. I believe she missed you, especially at this time of year. I am not like her, am I? Well, I cannot be anyone but who I am."

Surprised, she felt the old man's hand fall heavily upon her head, and turning, she looked up at him. A single tear was sliding down his worn face. For a brief moment Cailin felt her anger rising. The old man had no right to do this to her after all his unkindness and cruelty—not just to her, but to Brenna and to Kyna. Then something inside her popped and she felt her anger draining away. She smiled wryly at him.

"We're alike, Berikos, aren't we? It isn't just Brenna that makes me who I am. It is you as well. We are quick with our tongues, and have a surfeit of pride to boot." She patted her rounded belly. "The gods only know what this great-grandchild of yours will be like."

He half wheezed, half cackled at her remark. "Guud!" he said.

"Good?" she answered him, and he nodded vigorously, a chuckling noise coming from his throat. "You think so, do you? Well, we shall see after Lugh's feast if you are right," Cailin replied with a small smile.

Before Cailin and Wulf departed the next morning, Ceara came to her and said, "You have made Berikos very happy, my child. Your mother would be proud of you and of what you have done. I think it has helped him to make peace with himself, and with Kyna."

Cailin nodded. "Why not?" she said. "Last night the doors between the worlds were open. Perhaps not as widely as at Samain, but open nonetheless. I felt my mother would want me to be generous toward Berikos. It is strange, is it not, Ceara? Just a few weeks ago Berikos was strong and vital, the lord of his world. Now he is naught but a weak and sad old man. How quickly the gods render their judgment when they decide that the time has come for it."

"Life is fragile, my child, and appallingly swift, as you will soon find. One day you are filled with the juices of fiery youth and nothing is impossible! Then just as suddenly, you are a dried-up old husk with the same desires, but no will left to accomplish the impossible." She laughed. "You have a little time yet, I think. Go with your man now. Send for me when the child is due. Maeve and I will come to help you."

Cailin took the time to stop by the bench where her grandfather sat in the sunshine of the May morning. She bent to kiss his white head, and taking his hand in hers, gave it a squeeze. "Farewell, *Grandfather*," she said quietly. "I will bring you the child after it is birthed."

She and Wulf returned to their own home, and Cailin, finding more strength in herself than she would have thought, helped to seal the walls of the new barn with mud daub and wattle while Wulf worked in their fields with the servants. It was a good summer, neither too dry, nor too wet. In the orchards the fruit grew round and hung heavy upon the boughs of the trees. The grain ripened slowly while the hay was cut, dried, and finally stored in the barns for the coming winter.

The cattle grew fat, their herds having increased quite sizably that spring with the birth of many calves. In the meadows the sheep had multiplied, too, and shearing time was drawing near. Cailin, sitting outside the hall one warm day, looked across the shimmering fields contentedly. For a moment it appeared as if nothing had changed, and yet everything had changed. It was a different time, and she was beginning to sense it most strongly.

One evening she and Wulf lay upon their backs on the hillside looking up at the stars. "Why do you never mention your family?" she asked him. "I am to bear your child, yet I know nothing of you."

"You are my family," he said, taking her hand in his.

"No!" she persisted. "What of your parents? Did you have brothers and sisters? What has happened to them? Are they in Britain?"

"My father died before I was born," he told her. "My mother died when I was just past two. I remember neither of them. They were young, and I was their only child."

"But who raised you?" she said. She was sorry he had no close relatives, but on the other hand it meant that he was all hers.

"Kin raised me, in my village along a river in Germania. I was passed from one relation to another like a lovable but unwanted animal. They were not unkind, mind you, but life was hard. No one really needed another mouth to feed. I left them when I was thirteen, and joined the legions. I have never been back. This is my land now, my home. You and our child are my family, Cailin. Until I found you, I was alone."

"Until you found me," she told him, "I was alone, too. The gods have been kind to us, Wulf."

"Aye," he agreed, and looking up, they saw a falling star blazing its way across the heavens.

⋘⋟⋞⋙

A *slave came* from Anthony Porcius one day with a message. Antonia had gone into labor, and the magistrate was at a loss. He wrote that Antonia's women seemed helpless; although they should not be, Cailin thought. He begged that Cailin come to the villa to aid them. Wulf Ironfist was not happy about it, but Cailin did not think in light of the magistrate's kindness to them that she could refuse.

"We will pad the cart out, and I will travel in complete comfort," she told her husband. "Our child is not due for another few weeks. Even if we go slowly, I can be there by day's end."

Anthony Porcius was grateful when Cailin arrived. Antonia was still in labor and was having great difficulty. "She sent all the women who had always been with her away after Quintus's death, and replaced them with a group of fluttery girls. I do not understand why," he told Cailin, answering her unspoken question.

"It probably had something to do with making a new start," Cailin suggested. "Perhaps the other women, who were with her when she was married to Sextus Scipio and to my cousin, made her sad. They were only reminders of all she had lost, of better times now gone."

"Perhaps you are right, Cailin Drusus," he answered.

"You have asked me to come, and I came," Cailin replied, "but how will Antonia feel about my presence? I will help her, of course, but I am no expert. Why did she have no midwife among her staff?"

He shrugged helplessly. "I do not know."

"I have never birthed a child before, Anthony Porcius, but I know what must be done. Antonia will be able to help me, for this is her fourth child. Take me to her."

When they reached Antonia's quarters, they found her alone, her maidens having fled. Glimpsing her father's companion, Antonia's blue eyes flashed angrily for a moment, but hiding her ire, she said, "Why have you come, Cailin Drusus?"

"Your father called me to help you, though the truth is you know more about birthing a child than I do. Still, I will do what I can, Antonia. Your young women seem very helpless."

Antonia whimpered as a contraction tore through her, but she nodded. "You were good to come," she answered grudgingly.

The child, who came shortly afterward, was born dead, the cord wrapped about its little neck. It was a boy, and quite blue in color. Cailin wept openly with sadness at Antonia's misfortune. Though she had detested her cousin Quintus, she knew that Antonia had loved him greatly. Loving Wulf as she did, Cailin could but imagine Antonia's deep sadness at losing the posthumous son of Quintus Drusus.

Antonia, however, was dry-eyed. "It is better," she said fatalistically. "My poor little Marius is now with the gods, with his father." She sighed dramatically.

Quintus is hardly with the gods, Cailin thought sourly, as Anthony Porcius attempted to comfort his daughter. "I will stay the night and return home on the morrow," Cailin told them, wincing just slightly as she felt a mild cramp in her belly. She started nervously.

"What is it?" Antonia, sharp-eyed, demanded.

"Just a twinge," Cailin told her with more self-assurance than she was actually feeling. She hated being here, and the morning could not come quickly enough for her.

"Do not leave me so quickly, Cailin Drusus," Antonia pleaded. "Stay with me a few days, at least until my initial sorrow is past. You are no use to that handsome husband of yours in your present condition. Bide with me a little bit. I will wager you would enjoy soaking in my baths. You have no such amenities in your hall, I believe."

Cailin considered Antonia's tempting offer. She really wanted to go home; frankly, Antonia made her uncomfortable now. If she had any real sorrow over the loss of her poor little son, there was none that Cailin could see. What kind of a woman was she? Still, her pleading tone seemed genuine, and the offer of the baths was an enticing one. Cailin did not mind the more primitive life she was living, except for one thing. She really did miss the baths, with their hypocaust heating system, that had been in her family's old villa. It had been well over a year since she had had the luxury of a long, hot soak. It would be nice to remain for a short while to indulge this familiar luxury.

"Well," she said, "I'll stay, Antonia, but only for two or three days." Then she wrapped the tiny corpse in a swaddling cloth and removed it for proper burial, sending Antonia's silly maidens back in to attend to their mistress's needs.

Their mistress hardly noticed them. She was too busy plotting. She had seen the spasm that had crossed Cailin's face. Was it possible the girl was going into an early labor? Or perhaps she had miscalculated the time of her child's arrival. Antonia Porcius knew she would never again have such an opportunity for revenge, and she wanted that revenge badly. If Cailin would deliver her child here, alone, and without her Saxon husband, then both Wulf Ironfist's wife and child would be at her mercy. Oh, Quintus, she thought. Help me to avenge your unjust death at the hands of that barbarian. Let me make him suffer as I have suffered! Why should he be happy when I am not?

"You are very good to stay with Antonia," Anthony Porcius said to Cailin that evening as they shared a meal. "This tragedy could not have come at a worse time for me. I have found a buyer for my house in Corinium. I mean to remain here with Antonia, as she is widowed. There are few young men about now, and she may not have the opportunity to marry again. My grandson will need a man's influence. If Antonia does remarry one day, no good son-in-law would refuse me my place in this house. And though she will not admit it, I think my daughter needs me."

"You need to travel to Corinium shortly?" Cailin guessed.

"Yes, I do, my dear. I have let my home run down a bit in the years since Antonia first married Sextus Scipio. I was alone, and it really didn't matter to me then. Now, however, I must make several repairs before the new owners will agree to my price. They wish to take possession as soon as possible. I am lucky to have found buyers at all in these hard times. I plan to oversee the work personally, so I will have to be away for several weeks. I know you cannot stay with Antonia all that time, but if you will visit with her for just the next few days, it will help her to overcome her sorrow." He smiled fondly, seeing his daughter as no one else certainly did. "She indulges little Quintus far too much," he confided, "and without me, there is no discipline at all."

"Two days, three at the most," Cailin told him, "but no more. My child must be born in his father's hall. My grandfather's wives, Ceara and Maeve, are coming to midwife me. I can stay but a short time, and then I must go home, Anthony Porcius. You do understand?"

He nodded. "I will ask no more of you than two days, Cailin Drusus, and I thank you for your kindness to my child. She has not always been kind to you, I know, but surely you are her dearest friend."

Anthony Porcius departed the following morning for Corinium. Watching him go, Antonia felt relief. It would have been far too difficult to execute her plans if her father had remained. Oh, yes, the gods were certainly on her side in this matter, and her pleasure increased threefold knowing that they approved her revenge. In a way, she was to be their instrument of retribution against Cailin Drusus and her husband.

Cailin found herself quickly bored. Even when her parents were alive and she had lived a life similar to Antonia's, she had never been as idle as this woman seemed to be. Antonia had seemingly recovered from the ordeal of childbed instantly. She spent her time fussing over Quintus, the younger, and beautifying herself. The tinkling, vapid girls who surrounded her did naught but giggle.

Cailin knew from her conversations with Anthony Porcius that his daughter had been devastated and embittered by her husband's death; yet here was Antonia, freshly widowed, her newborn dead, behaving as if nothing at all was amiss in her little world; and acting gracious to the wife of her husband's executioner. Cailin found herself growing more and more uncomfortable. Why in the name of all the gods had she agreed to keep this woman company, even for just a couple of days? Worse, she could not seem to escape Antonia, who seemed to be everywhere she went, and always chattering, chattering, chattering about nothing. The longer Cailin remained with Antonia, the more her voice within nagged at her; particularly when her hostess brightly informed her, "I sent a messenger to Wulf Ironfist this morning telling him to fetch you in three days."

"How kind of you to think of it," Cailin replied, wondering why she had not thought of it herself. Being here must be addling her wits. Well, at least this day was almost done.

The evening meal was a particular trial. Antonia had always loved good food and good wine, which certainly accounted for her plumpness. She pressed dish after dish upon her guest, piling her own plate high with fish in a creamy sauce, game, eggs, cheese, and bread. She fussed at Cailin for not eating enough. "You will offend my cook," she said.

"I am not particularly hungry," Cailin replied, nibbling at some fruit and a bit of bread and cheese. Her stomach was in knots.

"Are you all right?" Antonia inquired solicitously.

"Just a bit of a queasy belly," Cailin admitted reluctantly.

The little fool was in labor! She was in labor, and she did not know it, Antonia thought triumphantly. Of course she wouldn't know it. She had never borne a child before. But Antonia was certain of it. "Wine is good for an upset in your condition," she counseled, and she poured Cailin a large gobletful. "This is my favorite Cyprian vintage, and you will feel much better after you have drunk it. Take a bit of bread to cleanse your palate," she instructed, and while Cailin was thus diverted, Antonia flipped the catch on a large cat's-eye beryl ring she wore and slipped a pinch of power from the secret compartment into the wine, where it dissolved instantly. She held out the goblet to the girl. "Drink it up now, Cailin, and you will soon feel better."

Cailin sipped slowly at the wine while she watched the half-full dishes of food being returned to the kitchens. No one, she thought, could eat all that food. Such a waste when so many are going hungry. Then she gasped as a hard pain tore through her.

"You are in labor," Antonia said calmly. Of course she was in labor. If her earlier pains had been but false labor, the drugged wine had ensured the onset of the child's birth.

"Send for my husband," Cailin said, trying to keep the fear from her voice. "I want Wulf here for his child's birth!" Oh, the gods! Why had she promised to remain here for even a day?

"Of course you want Wulf here by your side," Antonia cooed. "I remember when I bore my darling son how very much it meant to me to have my Quintus with me. I will send a slave for Wulf. Do not fear, dear Cailin. I will take good care of you." She helped Cailin into her bedchamber.

Leaving her maidens with Cailin, Antonia sent for a young male slave she had intended to make her lover. It was unfortunate, she thought, but she would have to kill him for his part in this matter, and she would not even get to enjoy him for a night. "Go to Simon, the slave merchant in Corinium. He sends consignments to Londinium monthly and will be dispatching a caravan shortly. Say I have a female slave I wish to rid myself of and he must send someone tomorrow to fetch her. She is a troublesome creature, and a liar. She must be kept drugged until she reaches Gaul. I want her sent as far from Britain as possible. Do you understand, my handsome Atticus?" Antonia smiled up into the young man's face while caressing his buttocks suggestively.

"Yes, mistress," he answered her, returning the smile. He was new in the household, but he had heard she was a lusty woman. She would certainly have no complaints over his performance when she was healed from her childbirth and ready to take a lover.

"Tell Piso to give you the fastest horse in the stable," Antonia instructed him. "I want you back by dawn. If you are not, I shall whip you." Her hand moved about to fondle his hardening manhood. "You are well-made," she noted. "Did I buy you, Atticus? I do not remember."

"Your father bought me, mistress," he replied with more aplomb than he was feeling. He was as hard as iron within her hot hand.

"We shall have to find a suitable position for you shortly," Antonia remarked, thinking that perhaps she would not kill him immediately. After all, he would not understand what she had done. "Now, go!" She turned away from the slave and hurried back to her patient.

⋘⋙

All through the night, Cailin struggled to birth her baby. Her body was wet with perspiration. She strained under Antonia's direction to bring forth the child. *"Where is Wulf?"* Cailin repeated over and over again to the older woman. "Why does he not come?"

"It is dark," Antonia told her. "There is no moon. My messenger must go slowly over the fields to reach your hall. It is not as if he could simply gallop easily down the Fosse Way from my home to yours, Cailin. He must pick his way carefully. He will get there, but then he and your husband must come back just as slowly. Here." She put her arm about Cailin's shoulders. "Drink some of my Cyprian wine. You will feel better for it. I always do."

"I don't want it," Cailin cried, pushing Antonia's hand away.

"Do not be such a silly goose," Antonia told her. "I have put some herbs in it that will ease your pain. I take them myself when I am in the throes of having a child. I see no reason to suffer."

Cailin reached out, and taking the goblet from Antonia, drank it slowly down. She immediately felt better, but her head was also spinning. Another pain tore through her, and she cried out. Antonia knelt and examined her progress. She began to smile and hum to herself.

"Can you see the baby's head?" Cailin asked her. "Ohh, I wish Ceara and Maeve were here with me. I need them!"

"They could do nothing for you that I cannot," Antonia replied sharply, then her tone softened a bit. "I can see the baby's head. Be brave, Cailin Drusus, just a few more minutes and your child will be born."

"The gods!" Cailin groaned. "Where is Wulf? Antonia, I am very dizzy. What exactly did you put in that wine?" Another pain came.

Antonia ignored Cailin's questions. *"Push!"* she commanded the straining girl. "Push hard. *Harder.*"

The infant's head and shoulders appeared between its mother's legs. Antonia smiled, well-pleased. Cailin did not realize it, but she was having an easy labor. The baby would be born in just another moment.

Cailin was having difficulty keeping her eyes open. Her head was whirling violently and she felt as if she were beginning to fall. Another terrible pain washed over her. She heard, if somewhat distantly, Antonia's voice demanding she push again. Cailin struggled to obey. She couldn't allow herself to become unconscious. Making a supreme effort, she pushed with all her might. She was rewarded by the sudden cry of a newborn baby, and her heart accelerated with excitement and joy. Then, as suddenly, the darkness rushed up to claim her. She fought valiantly against it, but it was no use. The last thing she remembered was Antonia saying, "She is so sweet. I have always wanted a little girl," and then Cailin remembered no more.

⟨⊱⊰⟩

W hen *Wulf Ironfist arrived* to reclaim his wife two days later, Antonia came slowly into the atrium to greet him. She was crying, the tears sliding down her fair skin. "What is it?" he asked, a sinking feeling overcoming him even as he put forth the question.

Antonia sobbed and threw herself into his startled embrace. *"Cailin!"* she wept piteously. "Cailin is dead, and the child—your son—with her! I could not save them. I tried! *I swear I tried!*"

"How?" he said, stunned. "How could this happen, Antonia? She was healthy and well when I saw her last."

Antonia stepped from the shelter of his arms and, looking up at him with her wide blue eyes, said, "Your son was large. He was not properly positioned. A child is born head first, but this boy came feet first. He tore poor Cailin almost in two. Her suffering was a terrible thing to behold. She bled to death. The child, so long in birthing, did not survive her by more than an hour. I never imagined such a thing could happen. I am sorry, Wulf Ironfist."

"Where is her body?" he demanded. His voice was hard and cold. *Cailin!* His beloved lambkin dead? It could not be! It could not be! He would not believe it! "I want to see my wife's body," he repeated. The pain in his chest was fierce. Could a heart break in two, he wondered, for he believed that it was happening to him now.

"She was so torn apart," Antonia explained, "that we could not prepare her properly for burial. I had her cremated, the way our Celtic ancestors used to cremate their dead. I put the baby in her arms so that they would reach the gods together."

He nodded, numb with grief. "I want her ashes," he said stonily. "Surely you have her ashes. I will take her home and bury her on her land with the rest of her family. Cailin would want that."

"Of course," Antonia agreed softly, and turning about, she picked up a prettily decorated polished bronze urn from the atrium bench. "Cailin's ashes, and those of your son, are within this vessel, Wulf Ironfist." She handed it to him with a sympathetic smile. "I understand your grief, having just recently lost both a mate and a child myself," she said.

He took the urn from her, almost reluctantly, as if he could still not believe what she had told him. Then he turned wordlessly away from her and started for the door.

Antonia silently exulted in his pain. Then a wicked thought came to her, and she acted impulsively upon it.

"Wulf." Her voice was suddenly seductive.

He turned back to her, and was shocked to see that she had removed her robe and was stark naked. She was all pink and white, and plump. There was not a mark upon her to spoil the perfection of her smooth skin. He found her appallingly repulsive. For a moment he was rooted to the spot where he stood, staring at her repugnant nudity.

"I am lonely, Wulf Ironfist," Antonia said softly. *"So lonely."*

"Lady, put your robe back on," he said.

"You killed my husband, Wulf Ironfist. Now I am lonely. Do you not think you should compensate me for the loss of Quintus Drusus?" Antonia purred to her horrified audience. She slipped her hands beneath her large breasts, with their deep rose nipples, and lifted them as if she were offering them to him. "Are you not tempted to sample these fine fruits, Wulf Ironfist? Is that weapon beneath your braccos not already hard with your longing for me?"

"Clothe yourself, lady," he said coldly. "You disgust me."

She launched herself at him, her naked body pressing against him. He was overpowered by the scent of musk. "You are the handsomest man in the province, Wulf Ironfist," she said, panting with desire. "I always have the handsomest man in the province for my mate." Her arms slipped tightly about his neck. "Kiss me, you Saxon brute, and then you must take me. *Here!* Where we stand on the floor of the atrium. Stuff me with your manhood and make me scream with pleasure. I am so hot for you!"

Wulf took her arms from him and thrust her away. He felt near to vomiting. "Lady, your grief has made you mad. First your husband and child, and then my wife and son. I am sorry for you, but

I must master my own grief. It is already tearing me apart. *I loved my wife.* I do not know how I will go on without her. What is left for me? Nothing! *Nothing!*" He turned and stumbled from the atrium.

"*Go!*" Antonia shrieked after him. "Go, Wulf Ironfist! If you are in pain, I am glad! Now you will know how I felt when you butchered my Quintus! May the sorrow eat your heart out! I will be glad of it!" Bending down, she picked up her robe and slipped it back on. "I wish I could have told you the truth, Wulf Ironfist," she said softly to herself, "but I could not. Then my father would find out, and I cannot have that." She laughed. "Still, I have had my revenge upon you, and Cailin Drusus. If no one knows but me, what difference will it make?"

When Anthony Porcius returned from Corinium several weeks later, his daughter was prepared and waiting. They sat together in the mid-autumn air of her garden while Antonia nursed the infant at her breast.

"I was shocked, Father," she said. "He didn't want her. He was ready to expose her on the hillside, had I not begged him for the child. All that mattered to him was that Cailin had not given him the son he wanted. These Saxons are cruel people, Father. Fortunately, little Quintus was ready to be weaned, and my milk is rich, so I decided to take the baby and raise her with my son. It almost makes up for having lost my own baby. Poor Cailin!"

"Where is Wulf Ironfist now?" the magistrate asked.

"He has disappeared." Antonia replied. "No one knows where he has gone. He made no provision for his slaves. He simply left. The land, of course, now belongs to my little Aurora. I call her that because she was born with the dawn, even as her mother died. I sent my majordomo to drive off those Dobunni who had begun to build a hall at the river villa. They said that Cailin had given them the land for a wedding gift, but I told them it was mine by right of inheritance, and that Cailin was dead in childbirth and not here to enforce their supposed rights. They did not give me much difficulty, and are now gone."

Anthony Porcius nodded. It was all so much to take in, he

thought, but one good thing had come of it. Antonia seemed to be her old self again. Taking in the orphaned daughter of Cailin Drusus had obviously been good for her.

"You will stay here with us, Father, won't you?" Antonia said. "I do need you so very much. I shall not marry again, but will devote my life to my two children. It is, I feel, what the gods desire of me."

"Perhaps you are right," he said, reaching out and taking her hand in his. "We will be a happy family, Antonia. I know it in my heart!"

BYZANTIUM

A.D. 454-456

Chapter 7

I *do not believe it!*" Phocas Maxima said, surprised. "This cannot be the same girl you purchased in the market this morning, Jovian. That creature was a filthy, sore-ridden horror. This girl is lovely. Her skin is like cream. There isn't a mark on her, and that hair! The rich auburn color, those marvelous little curls!"

They are one and the same, brother dear," Jovian Maxima said in smug tones. "You are a true businessman; you have absolutely no imagination, Phocas. The moment I laid eyes upon the girl, I knew she was a treasure. All it took was hot water and soap to clean her up. Not only that, her Latin is flawless, but for a slight provincial accent which can be corrected—although some may find it most charming." He looked to the slave girl who accompanied his new purchase. "Isis, remove her tunica, please."

Phocas Maxima stared hard at the girl when she finally stood nude before him. "She's a bit slender for my taste," he noted, "but we can fatten her up. I don't imagine she's been getting a great deal to eat recently. Her feet looked dreadfully roughened."

"She's done a lot of walking, I would imagine," Jovian replied.

"We can eventually correct it," his brother said. "Her breasts are very nice; small, but well-formed. Well, I must admit it, you did get us quite a good bargain in this girl. Does she understand what is expected of her, or are we going to have to train her? She is pagan, I hope."

It was as if she did not exist except as an object, Cailin thought as she listened to the two brothers chattering back and forth about her and her eventual fate. Not that it really mattered. Nothing mattered anymore. It was all so confusing. She didn't even understand why she was still alive when all she wanted was to be dead; but something inside her would not allow her to die. It made her angry, but there was naught she seemed to be able to do about it.

She thought back over the many days that had passed since she had lain in labor at Antonia's villa. The last thing she remembered was the cry of a baby as she sank into unconsciousness. When she came vaguely to her senses, she was in a dirty room in a strange house. The woman who brought her food told her she was in Londinium, which amazed Cailin. She had heard of Londinium, but had never thought to see it in her lifetime. As it turned out, she did not see it, for when she asked what she was doing in this place, she was told that the lady Antonia had sold her to Simon, the slave merchant, and that shortly she would be transported to Gaul and beyond.

"But I am no slave!" Cailin protested.

"That is what the lady Antonia said you would say," the woman replied sourly. "She says you're real troublesome and have ideas above your station, girl. Why, you even seduced her late husband, and bore his bastard. Well, she'll have no more of you, wench."

"Where is my baby?" Cailin demanded.

"The brat died, I'm told," was the cold reply.

Cailin began to weep hysterically. "I do not believe you!" she protested. Before she knew it, a bitter liquid was being forced down her throat and she was sliding into darkness again.

For days afterward she drifted between reality and nightmare. When she finally was allowed to come to herself again, she was in

Gaul, traveling south with a shipment of other slaves down the backbone of the land, toward the Mediterranean Sea. Not long after, one particular beautiful young woman attempted to escape, for unlike many of the slaves traveling with them, she wore no collar, nor was she chained. She was quickly recaptured, being unfamiliar with the land.

The slave master debated on her punishment. To beat her would mark her fair skin, and that same fair skin was an asset that could bring him a pretty penny for the girl. He elected to make his point by raping her, which he did before the entire party of travelers. "Run again, bitch," he threatened as he jammed himself into her, "and I'll give you to my men! Perhaps you'd like that, wench, eh?"

The look of terror on all the women's faces told the slave master that he would have no more difficulty with any of them. Indeed, after that Cailin went out of her way to make herself invisible. She allowed her hair to go unwashed and uncombed. Her tunica, which was the only garment she possessed, grew more worn with each passing day. She did not dare wash it for fear that it would disintegrate and leave her naked, like some of the other women. She did not expect she would be supplied with other clothing if she lost what she possessed.

When they reached the coast, the slaves were separated, some being put aboard ship for a town called Carthage, while Cailin and the rest were being sent to a place called Constantinople. It was, she later learned by listening to others, the great capital city of the Eastern Empire. The male slaves in her group were chained to the oars of the galley. They would be sold when and if they reached their destination, but in the meantime they would provide the manpower to get there. The women were penned below in barely habitable quarters; a square space with no sleeping accommodations but the floor; a wooden bucket for their needs; little light, and less air.

Each night, the first mate would arrive grinning, and select several of the women, whom he would take away. They returned with the morning, usually laughing, with extra food or water for themselves, which they usually chose not to share. Their own survival was paramount. Cailin instinctively hid herself in the darkest corner when the first mate came. She did not need to be told what the women were doing, or why they were given gifts. She grew thinner with the meager rations supplied her, but somehow remained alive to reach Constantinople.

The morning of their arrival, the slave master came to carefully look over the women. He selected several who appeared more attractive than the others. They were immediately removed. Some of those not chosen tried to plead with the slave master to take them, and they wept when he roughly shoved them away.

"Where have the others gone?" Cailin asked of an older woman.

The woman looked at her and replied, "They are considered the best of us. They will be taken to a private slave market where they will be bathed, perfumed, and clothed in fine raiment before being auctioned off. They will get wealthy masters, and live comfortably if they please those masters."

"What will happen to us?" Cailin inquired curiously.

"It's the public market for us," the woman said fatalistically. "We'll be bought as house or field slaves, or for some waterfront brothel."

"What is a brothel?"

The look of astonishment on the woman's face was almost comical, but before she might answer Cailin, the slave master's minions came below and began herding the women up onto the deck. They blinked uncomfortably in the sunshine, their eyes unused to bright light after their many days at sea spent in the semidark of the hold. Gradually, as they adjusted to the daylight, they were led off the vessel and through the city streets to the public slave market.

Cailin was astounded by the four and five-story buildings along their route. She had never seen buildings so big. And the noise! There seemed to be no quiet in this place. She couldn't imagine how people managed to live amid the cacophony and such dirt. The streets were strewn with garbage, and both human and animal waste was littered all about. Her bare feet cringed with every step.

At last they reached the open slave market, where little time was wasted. One after another, the slaves who had traveled with her were put up upon the block to be quickly sold off. Again Cailin hid herself among the others, until finally there was no longer any place to hide. She was roughly pulled by the arm onto the little platform.

"Here's a fine, strong young girl, good for house or field," the slave dealer said. Turning to Cailin, he ordered, "Open your mouth, wench." He peered in, and then announced to his audience, "She has all her teeth. What am I bid?"

The spectators looked up at the creature offered. She was tall and pitifully thin. Her hair, of an undistinguishable color, was filthy and matted. There was nothing at all about her that could be considered attractive. Despite the slave merchant's spiel, she did not look particularly strong or healthy. They shuffled their feet, and several began to slowly drift away.

"Offer me something," the slave merchant pleaded with his audience. "She speaks good Latin. Cleaned up, she would make a good nursemaid, or tavern servant. *Smile, girl!*" he hissed angrily at Cailin.

She ignored him. If no one bought her, perhaps they would kill her, and then she would be out of her misery. Then suddenly into her view came the most astounding creature Cailin had ever seen. He was plump, with rosy cheeks and merry dark brown eyes that surveyed her quite carefully. He was dressed in a plum-and-gold-striped silk dalmatica. His round head was covered in a profusion of tight black curls. The creature pursed his pink lips thoughtfully, and then said in a clear, sweet voice, "I will give you two folles for her."

"*Two folles?*" The slave merchant pretended outrage, although he was relieved to be offered anything for the wretched creature. He was just about to accept the gentleman's offer when the elegant spoke again.

"Oh, very well, I shall give you four folles. I'll not have you whining afterward that I cheated you. You slave merchants are all alike when a man snatches a bargain from under your very noses.

You cannot see the value in what you have—but if someone else does, you howl and cry to the gods—er, God," the gentleman amended.

"Jovian," the plainly dressed gentleman who accompanied the elegant said irritably, "the girl isn't worth five nummi, let alone four folles."

"She is worth a dozen solidi, brother, even if you cannot see it right now. Trust me. You know I have an eye for such things," the curly-haired man murmured, extracting the coins from his purse and handing them to the slave merchant. "Here, fellow, is your coin. Will you accept it?" He pierced the merchant with a direct look.

The man snatched the money from the elegant's fingers and shoved Cailin toward him. "Go with your master now, girl," he growled.

Jovian's nose wrinkled with distaste as Cailin approached him. "The gods, girl! When was the last time you bathed?"

"What is today's date?" she asked bluntly. "One loses track of time in the hold of a slave galley, sir."

"It is the ides of April," he answered her, curious. She was not at all a subservient creature. Indeed, she gave every indication of being strong-willed. It was all to the good, he thought, pleased.

"Then it has been almost eight months since I last bathed," she told him. "Will I be able to bathe wherever it is you are now taking me, sir? I would be grateful to know that I could bathe properly again."

"*Eight months!*" both men chorused in unison, looking horrified by Cailin's revelation. Then the more somber of the two said darkly, "You have made a dreadful error, I fear, Jovian."

The plump gentleman chuckled. "Nay, Phocas, I have made no error. Wait and see! Wait and see!" He turned to Cailin. "Follow us, girl, but be mindful not to become lost in the crowds. With us, you will suffer no ill treatment, but if you try to flee, you could find yourself in far greater difficulties. This is a cruel place."

Cailin needed no warning. Nothing could be worse than the last few months she had spent in captivity. She had come close to losing track of her own identity. Whoever these two men were, they were certainly not threatening, and at this point she would have followed anyone who promised her a bath. She wondered, in fact, whether she would ever be able to really get clean again. Before her captivity she would not have believed that anyone could become so filthy as she now was. Mindful of his warning, she hurried along after the elegant and his companion.

They walked swiftly through the noisy city, and everywhere she turned there was something to catch Cailin's eye. She wished she were not as she now was, that she might ask questions of the two men. It was all very overwhelming, and not just a little frightening. She was not at all used to the idea that she was a slave. As she followed the two men off the wide avenue and into a narrow, quiet street, she saw them turn through the wide gates of a large house. Well, at least they were wealthy and could afford to replace her worn tunic, which was practically falling off her as she walked.

A majordomo hurried forward to greet the two gentlemen, his eyes widening with shock at the sight of the girl following them. "My lord?" he questioned faintly. "Is this *person* with you?"

"Jovian has bought her in the public market, Paulus," the sterner man replied. "You will have to ask him what he wants done with her."

The majordomo looked to Jovian, and the plump man laughed at the servant's distress. "I shall take her to the baths myself, Paulus," he said. "Make certain the bath attendants are on duty. They certainly have their work cut out for them, don't they, but wait until we have finished. This filthy piglet I have purchased will turn into a peacock, I promise you. *And I only paid four folles for her!*" He turned to Cailin. "Come, girl. That bath you so desire is but steps away."

"My name is Cailin," she replied, following him.

"Is it? And what kind of a name is 'Cailin'?" They exited the large atrium and moved through a scented corridor lined with many doors. "And," he continued, "where is Cailin from?"

"My name is Celtic, sir. I am a Briton," she told him as they entered the reception room for the baths. Two attractive women came forward, bowing to Jovian and looking slightly dismayed by the sight of the girl accompanying him.

"You have a great deal of work to do with this one, my dears," Jovian told the bath attendants. "She tells me she has not bathed in eight months." He chuckled. "I shall join you while you attend to the girl. Her name, she says, is Cailin. I like it. We shall let her keep it."

"I will answer to no other name," Cailin said firmly.

"You were obviously not born a slave," Jovian noted.

"Of course not," Cailin replied indignantly. "I am a member of the Drusus family of Corinium. My father, Gaius Drusus Corinium, was a decurion of the town. I am a married woman of property and good reputation."

"Who is now a slave in Constantinople," Jovian answered dryly. "Tell me how you came to be here," he said as they entered the dressing room.

Cailin told him what she could remember and what she had managed to piece together during her months of travel, while the bath attendants undressed them and brought them into the tepidarium, a warm anteroom where they would wait until they began to perspire. The fact that she was now naked, as was Jovian, did not trouble Cailin. She felt no danger from this man. Indeed, she felt he might become her friend. Seeing their perspiration begin, the bath attendants scraped away the dirt and sweat with silver strigils as they talked.

"You were obviously betrayed by this Antonia Porcius," Jovian noted wisely. "A woman who believes herself wronged is a very dangerous enemy to have, my dear. Selling you into slavery was her revenge upon you, and upon your poor husband. No doubt she told him you were dead. If not, he would have forced her to reveal your whereabouts and come after you, I expect. The news of your death, however, would cause him the same deep pain that his execution of her husband caused her. She has been quite clever, this Antonia. It is a plot worthy of a Byzantine. You survive to suffer in slavery, not knowing what happened to your child, while your husband suffers anguish over your alleged death."

Cailin was silent. How succinctly Jovian had put it, and he was probably correct. What was worse, there was absolutely nothing she could do about it. She was helpless, and so far from her beloved Britain that she would never be able to get back. Until this moment she had not even considered it, but now she had no choice but to face reality. She was alive, and obviously likely to remain so. She had her future to consider.

"Why did you purchase me?" she asked Jovian as they moved on into the caldarium to be bathed.

"I could see that beneath the dirt you were beautiful, and beautiful women are my business," he told her, then turning, said to the bath attendants, "Wash her hair first, my dears. I want to see its true color. It is so mud-caked I cannot tell."

"My hair is auburn," Cailin told him. "I take my coloring from my mother, a Dobunni Celt." Then she could say no more, as the two girls bathing her began to scrub her head and scalp with great vigor. "Ouch!" Cailin complained as their fingers forced themselves through the almost impossible tangles her hair had knotted itself into over the last months. Finally her hair was rinsed with warmed water that smelled of a pungent substance. "What is in the rinse water?"

"Lemon," Jovian said. "The gods! Your hair is wonderful!"

"What is *lemon?*" Cailin demanded.

"I'll show you later," he said. "Come now, and let the girls bathe you, my beauty. No." He motioned to the bath attendants. "I shall care for myself. Devote your time to Cailin."

They washed her with a soft soap that seemed to melt the remaining dirt from her skin. Cailin could scarcely contain her delight at being clean again. They continued on into the frigidarium for a quick, cold plunge bath, and then into the unctorium, where they stretched out side by side on two benches to be massaged with sweet oils.

"How are beautiful women your business, sir?" Cailin asked.

The two bath attendants giggled.

"This is Villa Maxima, Cailin," Jovian explained. "It is the most elegant brothel in all of Constantinople. We serve both ladies and gentlemen seeking entertainment of a more exotic, exciting kind."

"What is a brothel?" she asked him, annoyed to hear the two girls' renewed amusement. They sounded so smug.

Jovian raised his head up in surprise and looked at Cailin, who lay comfortably next to him, enjoying her massage. "You do not know what a brothel is?" he said, amazed.

"I should not have asked you if I knew, sir," Cailin replied.

"You say you come from Corinium," he began, but she interrupted.

"My branch of the Drusus Corinium family came to Corinium in the time of the emperor Claudius," Cailin told him, "but I was raised away from the town. I only visited it three times in my whole life, the last time being when I was six years of age. I am the only daughter of a good patrician family. I do not know what a brothel is. Should I?"

"Oh, dear," Jovian said, almost to himself. "Finish your massage, Cailin, and then I will explain to you what you need to know." Then he glared in an unusual show of irritation at the giggling bath attendants, who immediately fell silent. It was rare for Master Jovian to grow angry, but when he did, it was highly unpleasant.

When the bath attendants had finished their work, they escorted their charges into a warm dressing room, where Jovian donned a fresh dalmatica, this one of sky-blue silk. A fresh white silk tunica, belted with a gold cord, was supplied for Cailin.

"Come, my dear," he said, taking her hand in his. "We will have honey cakes and wine in my private garden, and I will tell you everything you need to know."

The garden was exquisite; small and surrounded by a wall covered in ivy. A little marble fountain was in its center, shaped like a shell, from which water dripped into a rounded basin. There were half a dozen damask rose bushes already coming into bloom, perfuming the air with their luxurious sweetness.

"Come, and sit by me," Jovian said, settling himself upon a marble bench. "Ahh, the wine has been iced. Excellent!" he said with a smile at the slave serving them. "Now, Cailin, to answer your question. A brothel is a place where women sell their bodies for the amusement of men. You do understand what I mean by that, don't you?"

She nodded, her eyes wide, and he noted their marvelous violet color. "I have never heard of such a thing," she answered him. "I know that men lie with women other than their wives, but I never knew women got paid for such things."

"Oh, there is nothing unusual in it," he replied. "It is done all the time, and has been done since the beginning of time. There are, however, varying degrees of such an arrangement. Some women sell themselves in the streets. They are called whores, or prostitutes. They couple with their customers up against walls and in alleys. They cannot be discerning about the men with whom they involve themselves, either. Consequently they end up diseased, and often dead at an early age, which is probably a blessing. It is not easy being a woman of the streets. They can fall prey to a single man who steers other men their way, but takes most of their pitiful earnings for himself. It is a hard life.

"Women in brothels are usually better off, although there are different sorts of brothels. Those serving the lower classes tend to treat their women little better than those poor souls plying their trade in the streets of the city. These brothels exist because there is always an unending supply of poor girls willing to take their chances making their fortunes within their walls, but alas, few, if any, do escape to live to a grand old age in comfort."

"Why do they do it, then?" Cailin asked him.

"Because they have no other choice," he told her frankly. "Villa Maxima, however, is not like most other brothels. We cherish our women, and pamper them in luxury. They are not common whores, but courtesans, highly trained, and skilled in giving the men who come to patronize them the utmost in pleasure. We also have handsome young male courtesans who are much in demand among certain wealthy women of the city and the court. There are men among our clients who enjoy—indeed they prefer—the company of other men; and women who would rather have a woman for a lover. We cater to every taste."

"It is all very strange to me," Cailin told him.

He nodded. "Yes, I imagine it would be, considering your former life in Britain. I know it will be difficult for you, but you will adjust to this new life if your mind is open. Are you perchance a Christian?"

Cailin shook her head. "No. Are you?"

He chuckled. "It is now the official religion of the empire," he said. "Like a good citizen, I obey the emperor in all things."

Cailin laughed for the first time in many months. "What a prevaricator you are, sir. I fear I do not believe you."

Jovian shrugged. "I do what I must to avoid difficulty," he said. "This new church fights among itself as to what is correct and proper doctrine, and what is not. When they have settled it among themselves, perhaps I shall find my faith. Until then . . ."

"You will give lip service to it," she told him. "I know very little about the Christians, sir. I think, however, that I prefer my own gods: Danu, the mother, and Lugh, our father. They are represented by the earth and the sun. Then there is Macha, Epona, Sulis, Cernunnos, Dagda, Taranis, and my favorite, Nodens, the Goddess of the Forest. My mother particularly loved Nodens. The Christians, I am told, have but one god. It seems a poor religion to me that only has one god."

"You should learn about it, as you are to live in Constantinople," Jovian told her. "I will have a priest tutor you in the intricacies of the religion. We have several rather important clerics as clients."

"Am I to be a courtesan, then, sir?" Cailin asked him.

"Not immediately, my dear. You lack training, for one thing, and for another, I must be certain you are disease-free. The women who live in this house are healthy. I do not allow them to consort with men who are not. Some brothel owners are penurious when it comes to the health of their women. My brother and I are not. For a single solidus a good Greek physician can be purchased in the market. We own one who lives here and oversees to the health of all the residents of Villa Maxima."

"Then once he has decided that I am healthy," Cailin said, "you will have me trained to be a courtesan."

"Eventually," he answered. "Does it disturb you to know that you will be expected to entertain a variety of lovers, my dear?"

Cailin considered his words. In another time and another place, the mere thought of such a thing would have horrified her beyond anything, but this was not Britain. She was so far from home she could not even ascertain the distance. Her husband probably did believe her dead. Mayhap he had already taken another wife. *Wulf.* For a moment she saw his strong, handsome face before her, and tears sprang to her eyes. She quickly blinked them away. It would not be easy at first to take another man between her thighs, but she supposed in time she would grow used to it. "What future have I beyond my youth?" she asked Jovian.

For a moment surprise suffused his features, and then he said in admiring tones, "How wise you are, my dear, to consider the future. So many of them do not. They think they will be young and desirable forever. Of course, that is not the case. Well, I will tell you what that future can hold for you if you will trust me. Learn your lessons well, Cailin, and you will, I promise, attract the best lovers Constantinople has to offer to your bed.

"Learn more than just the sensuous arts, my dear. Many do not realize that to be truly fascinating a woman must be a clever and a knowledgeable conversationalist as well as a desirable female. Lovers will shower such a woman with expensive gifts, gold, jewelry, and other valuables. Eventually you will be able to purchase your freedom.

"At the beginning of each year we put a value upon each woman in our house. If during that year she decides she wishes to buy her freedom, there is no argument over price, for it is already set. Today I purchased you for four folles, but your value is already more now that your beauty is visible to all. You are worth at least ten solidi."

"How many folles is that, sir?" Cailin queried him.

"There are one hundred and eighty copper folles to each gold solidus. Eighteen hundred copper folles equals ten gold solidi, my dear," he said with a grin. "I am almost tempted to take you back now to that foolish slave merchant who allowed you to go so cheaply for want of a little water. No, I cannot. He will howl, and cry he's been cheated, despite the fact that I warned him. They are all alike, those people." He stood up. "Come, we will go and show my brother Phocas that I have not lost my ability to see a perfect gem beneath the mud in the road. Isis," he called to an attending slave. "You will accompany us." Then he turned back to Cailin. "You will address gentlemen who enter this house as 'my lord.' My brother, and myself, as well. 'Sir' is such a provincial mode of address, dear girl."

"Yes, my lord," Cailin answered him, following Jovian through the house to where Phocas sat awaiting them. When she was disrobed the elder of the Maxima brothers expressed his surprise at and his approval of her newly restored appearance. She stood silent as they spoke, until finally her garment was restored to her.

"Isis," her new master instructed the slave girl, "take Cailin to the quarters I have ordered prepared for her." When the two women had departed, Jovian turned to his brother, an excited look upon his face. "I have the most marvelous plans for that girl," he said. "She is going to make us a fortune, Phocas, and our old age will be secure!"

"No single courtesan, however well-trained," his elder brother answered, "can make us that much gold."

"This one will, and she will not have to personally entertain any of our clients. At least not for some time, brother dear," Jovian finished. Rubbing his hands together gleefully, he sat down next to Phocas.

They were a study in contrasts, these two brothers. Although they were of almost equal height, Phocas being slightly taller, no one who did not know them would have realized they were siblings, born of the same parents. Their father had been a courtier, their mother his mistress. Villa Maxima had been her home. Phocas favored the paternal side of his family. He was slender, with a long aristocratic face made up of a slim nose, narrow lips, and deep-set dark brown eyes. His hair was dark and straight, cut medium-short, and brushed away from the crown of his head. His clothing was expensive and simple. Phocas Maxima was the sort of man who could easily disappear amid a crowd. It was said by the women he owned that he was a lover of epic proportions who could make the most hardened courtesan weep with joy. His business acumen was admired citywide, and his generous works of charity kept him in favor with the church.

His younger brother, Jovian, was his opposite. Elegant, classically educated, a slave to fashion, he was considered one of the greatest wits of his time. He adored beautiful things: clothing, women, works of art, and particularly beautiful young men, of whom he kept several to see to his every need. His dark curls in careful and deliberate disarray, he was easily recognizable at the races, the games, the circus. The success of Villa Maxima was largely due to him, for although Phocas could keep the books and see to the budget needed to run the brothel, it was Jovian's wonderful imagination that set Villa Maxima above all the other expensive brothels in the city. Their late mother, a famous courtesan of her day, would have been enormously proud of them.

"What have you in mind?" Phocas asked him, his curiosity provoked by his brother's particularly excitable state regarding the girl, Cailin.

"Are we not famous the length and breadth of the empire for our entertainments?" Jovian said.

"Absolutely!" Phocas agreed.

"Our living tableaux have no equal. Am I correct?"

"You are correct, brother dear," Phocas answered.

"What if we took a living tableau a giant step further?" Jovian suggested. "What if, instead of a tableau, we staged a playlet of delicious depravity so decadent that all of Constantinople would want to view it—*and would pay handsomely for the privilege.* No one, brother dear, would be allowed to view this playlet at first but our regular clients. They, of course, would talk about it, intriguing their friends, and their friends' friends.

"Only those personally recommended by our clients would be permitted to enter here to view our little entertainment. Soon we would have so many requests for entry that we could charge whatever the traffic would bear, and thus make our fortunes. No one has ever before done anything such as I propose to you. Others will, naturally, copy us, but they will not be able to maintain the level of genius and imagination as we can. Cailin will be the centerpiece of the performance."

Phocas could fully appreciate his brother's plan. It was absolutely brilliant. "What will you call your playlet, and how will it be performed, Jovian?" he asked his sibling, fascinated.

" 'The Virgin and the Barbarians!' Is that not marvelous?" Jovian chortled, most pleased with himself and his cleverness. "The scene will open with our own little Cailin seated before a loom, modest and innocent in white, her hair unbound, weaving a tapestry. Suddenly the door to her chamber bursts open! Three magnificent naked barbarians enter, swords in hand, their intent quite plain. The frightened maiden leaps up, but alack! They are upon her, rending her garments asunder as she shrieks her protest! They violate her, and the curtain descends to the cheers of our audience."

"Boring," Phocas said dryly.

"*Boring?*" Jovian looked offended. "I cannot believe you would say such a thing to me. There is nothing boring about the scene I have described to you."

"Violation of a virgin is an ordinary topic of living tableau," Phocas answered, disappointed. "If that is all there is to it, Jovian, then it is boring."

"The gods!" Jovian exclaimed. "It is all so clear to me that I have not explained it in detail to you. Our virgin is violated by three barbarians, Phocas. *Three!*"

"Indeed were it one or three, it is boring," his brother repeated.

"*All three of them at one time?*" Jovian slyly elucidated.

Phocas's brown eyes grew wide. "*Impossible!*" he said breathlessly.

"Not at all," his brother answered, "but it must be choreographed most carefully, as one would choreograph a temple dance. It is not, however, impossible, dear brother. Oh, no! Not at all; and nothing like it has ever been presented here in Byzantium. Does not the church itself constantly decry the wickedness of man's nature? There will be riots before our gates in an effort to see the performance. This girl will make us our fortunes. We shall retire to that island in the Black Sea that we bought several years ago and have not seen since."

"But will the girl cooperate?" Phocas asked. "You are, after all, expecting a great deal of an unsophisticated little provincial."

"She will cooperate, brother dear. She is very intelligent for a woman, and because she is a pagan, she has no foolish qualms. Since she is not a virgin, she has no respectability to lose in this. Do you know what she asked me? What her future held after her youth and beauty had fled. Of course I told her she might eventually purchase her freedom if she were clever, and I believe she certainly is. With the proper training, Cailin will be the greatest courtesan this city has ever known."

"Have you decided upon the men involved?" Phocas said, now all business. "And how often shall we schedule this spectacle?"

"Only twice weekly," his brother replied. "The girl's physical well-being must be protected, and the unique nature of the performance involved considered. Better our clientele be left begging for more than our little playlet become too ordinary too quickly. As for the men, I saw just the trio I will need at Isaac Stauracius's private slave market two days ago."

"What if they are already sold?"

"They will not be," Jovian said. "I thought I might want them then, although I wasn't certain. I gave Isaac five gold solidi to hold them for me. I was to tell him by tomorrow, but I shall go today. They are quite magnificent, Phocas dear. Brothers, all identical in features and form down to the last detail. Big, blond Northmen. They have but one tiny flaw. It is not visible to the eye, but Isaac wanted me to know. They are dumb. The fool who captured them had their tongues torn out. A pity, really. They seem intelligent, and hear quite well."

"Go and fetch them, then," Phocas replied. "Do not let Isaac cheat you, Jovian. After all, he does not know how we are going to utilize these young men. Their physical defect should certainly lower the price he will ask appreciably. But wait! What of their

male organs? They are large? No matter how beautiful these creatures, they must have big manhoods. How can you be certain of
that without Isaac suspecting something of the use to which we
will put this trio?"

Jovian looked drolly at his elder sibling. "Phocas, my dear
brother, you wound me deeply. When did I ever purchase any
male slave for this house that I did not inspect their attributes
most thoroughly first? At rest the manhoods of these three hang
limply at least six inches. Aroused they will lengthen to eight, if I
am not mistaken, and I rarely am."

"Your pardon, brother," Phocas said with a brief smile.

With an answering smile and a bow, Jovian departed his brother's presence. Calling to his favorite body slave, and current lover,
to come and join him, he walked swiftly through the gates of Villa
Maxima and out into the street.

Chapter

8

Cailin had always believed that the home in which she had grown up was luxurious, but life at Villa Maxima was a revelation to her. No windows despoiled the outside walls of the building facing the street. One entered through bronze gates that led by way of a narrow passage into a large, sunny, open courtyard. The flooring in the courtyard was designed of square blocks of black and white marble. Great pots were set about the perimeter of the space. They were planted with small trees and pink damask rosebushes. There were always attractive slaves on duty within the courtyard to welcome visitors and to direct them up the two wide white marble steps onto the colonnaded portico, and through it into the atrium of the villa.

The atrium was magnificent. It had a high, curved, vaulted ceiling divided into sunken panels that were carved and decorated in red and blue, and gilded with gold. The walls were decorated with panels of white marble, and the baseboards were overlaid in silver. The entry to the atrium had two squared columns and four rounded pillars in red and white marble, all topped with gilded cornices. Above the entry were three long, narrow, latticed windows.

The doors leading from the atrium were of solid bronze, and the door posts sheathed in green marble, carved and decorated with gold and ivory. The floor was of marble tiles of various, contrasting shades of green and white arranged in geometrical patterns. In the recessed wall niches set about the room were marvelous marble sculptures of naked men and women, singly, or in pairs, or groups, all in erotic poses calculated to titillate the viewer. There were marble tubs filled with brightly colored flowers, and several marble benches where clients sat waiting admittance as their identities and credit were checked.

What little of the rest of the villa that Cailin saw in her first weeks in Constantinople was equally magnificent. The walls were all paneled, and centered upon them, painted pictures in frames. The subject of most of these paintings was erotic in nature. The ceilings were all paneled, and decorated with raised stucco work which was gilded or set with ivory. Doors were paneled and carved with colorful mosaic thresholds. The floors were either of marble of various hues, or mosaic pictures made of pieces so tiny that they appeared to be painted. The floor of the main chamber where the entertainments took place had the story of Leda and Jupiter illustrated in exquisitely colored pieces of mosaic that gave a jeweled effect.

The furniture found at Villa Maxima was typical of a wealthy household. Couches were everywhere, and they were ornately ornamental in design. Wonderfully grained woods were used for the legs and the arms, which were often carved. Tortoiseshell, ivory, ebony, jewels, and precious metals were used to decorate them. The couch coverings were of the finest fabrics available, embroidered in both gold and silver threads as well as sewn with jewels.

The tables were equally beautiful, the best being made from African cedar. Some had bases of marble, others of gold or silver, and yet others of gilded woods. There were chests for storage, some simple and others of elegant design. The candelabra were of bronze, silver, and gold, as were the lamps, both on the tables and hanging. There was nothing that could be considered lacking in grace or beauty about the villa and its furnishings.

Cailin had been assigned a charming little room with a mosaic floor whose center decoration was of Jupiter seducing Europa. About the walls, frescoes showed young lovers being encouraged and bedeviled by a host of amusing, little winged cupids. There was a single bed, a lovely little decorated wooden chest, and a small round table to furnish the space, which had but one window looking out over the hills of the city to the sea beyond. The room was sunny most of the day, and the light gave it a cheerful outlook that made Cailin feel comfortable for the first time in almost a year. It was not a bad place to begin her new life.

For almost two weeks that life was uncomplicated and pampered. She was fed more food than she had ever before eaten. She was bathed and massaged three times daily. Her feet and her hands were attended to, the nails pared, her skin creamed to soften it. She was made to rest continuously, until she thought she would die of boredom, for Cailin was not used to being idle. She saw no one but Jovian and the few servants who attended to her. In the evenings she could hear laughter, music, and merriment from elsewhere in Villa Maxima, but her chamber was very isolated from the rest of the house.

One day Jovian came and took her in a highly decorated—and to Cailin's taste—flamboyant litter to tour the city. He was a font of fascinating facts and general information. A town had been founded a thousand years before by the Greeks on this very site, Cailin learned. Located at the junction of the east-west trade routes, the town had always flourished, even if it was not particularly distinguished. Then, just over a hundred years ago, the emperor Constantine the Great had decided to leave Rome, and chose for his new capital the town of Byzantium. Constantine, the first emperor to embrace Christianity, consecrated the city on the fourth day of November in the year A.D. 328. The city, renamed Constantinople in his honor, was formally dedicated on May 11, 330, with much pomp and ceremony. Already building and renovation was then in progress.

Constantine and his successors were always building, and little remained now of the original Greek town. Constantinople currently had a university of higher learning; its own circus; eight public and one hundred fifty-three private baths; fifty-two porticos; five granaries; four large public halls for the government, the senate, and the courts of justice; eight aqueducts that conveyed the city's water; fourteen churches, including the magnificent St. Sophia; and fourteen palaces for the nobility. There were close to five thousand wealthy and upper-middle-class homes, not to mention several thousand houses and apartments sheltering the plebian classes, the shopkeepers, the artisans, the humble.

The city had been built on trade, and trade prospered there. Since it was set where the land routes from Asia and Europe met, Constantinople's markets were filled with goods of all kinds. There was porcelain from Cathay, ivory from Africa, amber from the Baltic, precious stones of every kind found on the earth; silks, damask, aloes, balsam, cinnamon and ginger, sugar, musk, salt, oil, grains, wax, furs, wood, wines, and of course, slaves.

That afternoon, they traveled the length of the city to the Golden Gate, and then back along the Mese past the forums of Constantine and of Theodosius. They skirted the Hippodrome and moved on past the Great Palace. As they were carried by the great church of St. Erine, Jovian said, "I have not yet chosen a priest for you, Cailin. I must remember to do so."

"Do not bother," she told him. "I do not think I could be a Christian. It seems a difficult faith, I fear."

"Why do you say that?" he asked her, curious.

"I have been speaking to your servants, and they tell me that to be a Christian you must forgive your enemies. I do not think I can forgive mine, Jovian. My enemy has cost me my family, my husband, and my child. I do not even know if that child was a son or a daughter. I have been taken from the land I love best, enslaved and generally terrorized. We Britons are a hardy race, which is probably why I have survived all of this, but I am angry, and I am embittered. Given the opportunity to take my revenge upon Antonia Porcius, I would gladly do so! I cannot forgive her for what she has done to me, or taken from me."

"Your fate is now here," Jovian told her quietly, and reaching out, he took her hand in his, squeezing it to comfort her.

Cailin's violet eyes surveyed him calmly. "I have learned to put my trust in no one, my lord. It is wiser, and I shall not be disappointed."

How cold she is, he thought, wondering if her husband had ever been able to ignite passion in her. Yet she was exactly what he needed for his new entertainment; a perfect marble Venus. Beautiful. Untouchable. Icy. And heartless. She would be a sensation, and her performance would bring all of Constantinople to its knees in their admiration. "Tomorrow," he said, "you will begin your training. You will be taught to do certain things that may at first frighten you or seem repugnant to you, but you can believe me, Cailin, when I tell you that I will not allow you to be injured in any way. In this one instance you may put your trust in me. I have too great an investment in you to allow you to come to harm, my dear. Oh, yes. You may trust Jovian Maxima, but no other."

"You have an investment of four folles, my lord." She laughed. " 'Tis hardly a great amount, as you yourself explained to me."

"Ahh, but remember that having cleaned you up, I told you that your worth had increased to ten solidi. Once you are trained, your worth will be a hundred times that, Cailin."

She was fascinated by what he was saying. She had absolutely no idea what her *training* was going to involve. She had no idea exactly what went on at Villa Maxima during those long evenings when the enticing noises from the main part of the villa teased at her sleepy ears. All she knew about brothels was that bodies were sold for a night's pleasure. There was obviously a good deal more, if her instincts proved correct.

The next morning she was brought by the slave girl Isis to an interior room where Jovian awaited her with several others. All of them but Jovian, resplendent in a red and silver dalmatica, were naked. There was a beautiful dark-haired woman of Cailin's height, and three tall young men with long golden locks. For a moment it was as if a hand had clutched at her heart, Cailin thought upon seeing them. Although there was nothing in the trio other than their size and coloring to remind her of Wulf, it was more than enough. For a moment she was angry at Jovian, but then she realized he could not know, so she steeled herself for whatever was to come because it meant the first step along her road to freedom.

Yesterday, discussing her anger with Jovian, Cailin had suddenly known that what she desperately wanted was to return to Britain, no matter how far away it was or how difficult the journey. The realization of such a dream was impossible without gold and power behind her. She knew not if Wulf was dead or alive. Even if he lived, he might not want her back. But her father's lands were hers, *and* there was that faceless, sexless child, too, who belonged to her. She wanted them back, and she wanted her revenge on Antonia Porcius. Only by becoming famous here in Constantinople did she have the slightest chance of returning to Britain and foiling Antonia's evil scheme. In her innocence, Cailin vowed she would do whatever she had to do to attain her goal.

"This is Casia," Jovian said, introducing the dark-haired woman. "She has been with us for two years and is most popular with the gentlemen. I have asked her to join us because she will demonstrate what I have in mind for you. Remove Cailin's tunica for her, Isis, and then you may leave us."

Cailin swallowed her apprehension at being nude before strangers. No one else was embarrassed. It was obviously a normal procedure in circumstances such as these. The obvious admiration for her in the blue eyes of the male trio was flattering. "Who are they?" she asked Jovian.

"Your fellow players," he said smoothly, and then asked her, "How did you and your husband make love, my dear? The positions you assumed, I mean," he further explained. Then he continued, answering his own question, "You lay upon your back, I surmise, and he rode you?"

Cailin nodded, swallowing silently. She was suddenly cold.

Casia put her arm about her. "Do not be frightened," she said in kindly tones. "No one is going to hurt you, Cailin. You are really very fortunate to have been chosen by Jovian for this entertainment."

"Surely you are not fearful?" Jovian fussed at her. "I told you that in this one matter you could trust me. It is simply the unknown that distresses you. Very well then, let us demystify your fears. Your fellow players cannot speak, although they hear. I have decided to call them Apollo, Castor, and Pollux. The physician tells me you are healthy in all respects, and more than ready to receive a man's homage. These three are to be your lovers."

"They are slaves as I am," Cailin said. "Where is the profit in that my lord? How can I earn my freedom lying with slaves?"

Jovian chuckled. She might be afraid, but she had not lost sight of all he had told her. "Your lovemaking shall be an entertainment for our clients, Cailin. Twice weekly you four shall perform a playlet of my devising." He then went on to explain what would be required of her: "I realize that you have never had a man enter through your temple of Sodom. That is why Casia is here today. It is a particular specialty of hers. If you see her carrying out this manner of lovemaking, you shall see there is nothing to be apprehensive about. Casia, take your position. Pollux and Castor, attend her. Now watch carefully, Cailin. You will be required to do what Casia does."

Casia fell to her knees. Castor, standing before her, rubbed his male organ against her lips. Opening her mouth, she absorbed him before Cailin's shocked eyes. She suckled strongly upon his manhood.

"She is arousing him by means of the sucking action, and by teasing his flesh with her tongue," Jovian explained matter-of-factly. "See, he is already engorged with his lust. He's an eager young fellow."

Casia could no longer contain the Northman within her mouth. She positioned herself on her hands and knees. Castor moved behind her and knelt. Using his hand to guide himself, he pushed between the tight half-moons of her bottom. Casia groaned softly, and as she did, Pollux tipped her head up with one hand while offering the girl his manhood to entertain within her mouth. Grasping her hips in his big hands, Castor very slowly inserted himself within the kneeling Casia. Then he began to pump her with equally slow, long, majestic strokes of his manhood.

"I cannot possibly do that," Cailin protested.

"Of course you can, and you will not only do that, but more, my dear," Jovian assured her. "You will note how careful he is with her. As filled with lust as he is, he is tender. He must be lest he damage her. He would forfeit his life if he did, and he knows it." Jovian suddenly put an arm about Cailin, and drawing her next to him, he put a hand between her nether lips, to her shocked surprise. "Ahh, good, you are already moist with beginning desire, despite those maidenly protests you are going to make to me. Apollo, come here and sooth our little novice. Lay her on her back and give her a good fucking."

Strangely, it was the gentle pity in Apollo's eyes that hardened Cailin's heart that day. She realized then that if she were not the mistress of this situation, the three brothers would bully her in their performance ever after. She lay down upon a mat placed on the marble floor and, spreading her legs wide, observed to Jovian, "He is as ready to couple as I am, my lord. His manhood is certainly a fine one, though I have seen bigger. Come, Apollo, and do our master's bidding."

She felt absolutely nothing as he reamed her vigorously. She was as cold as ice. Finally Casia, her own performance concluded, knelt by Cailin's head and softly instructed her, "You must always let a man believe you are feeling passion such as you have never felt before, even when you are not. Thrash your head back and forth. Good! Now moan, and claw at his back." She smiled up at Jovian as Cailin complied. "She is an apt pupil, my lord."

I am dead, Cailin thought, and this is Hades. But it was not. For several weeks she was instructed in the erotic arts, and to her own surprise, she seemed to excel in them. Finally came the day when Cailin and the trio of young Northmen brought Jovian's playlet fully to life before his delighted eyes. Two days later they performed a dress rehearsal before all the residents of Villa Maxima. Afterward both Cailin and Jovian were congratulated; Jovian for his creative abilities, and Cailin for her acrobatically inclined performance.

"Next week," Jovian said enthusiastically. "We begin our performances next week. There is just enough time to let our special clients know that something extraordinary will be happening. Oh, my brother! We are going to be rich!"

The Virgin and the Barbarians was an immediate success. Never had anything like it been seen in the history of Constantinople. It was all going exactly as Jovian had predicted it would. Phocas, in a rare show of excitement, could scarcely contain his glee over the thousands of gold solidi piling up in their strongbox. Twice weekly the playlet was performed before several hundred guests, each paying five gold solidi apiece to view the performance.

One night Jovian sought out his elder brother and told him excitedly, "The empress's brother has come, *and* General Aspar with him! I have seated them in the first row for the best viewing. The gods! I knew I was right! I am going to start designing another playlet, Phocas."

I *wonder if* this is as fascinating as the rumors insist," Prince Basilicus murmured to his companion. The prince was an elegant man with fair skin, black hair, and deep brown eyes. Cultured and educated, it was unusual to find him in such an atmosphere, particularly given his public piety and his circle of religious friends. "I am going to be sorry that I allowed you to drag me here tonight, Aspar."

The general chuckled. "You are too serious, Basilicus."

"And I should be more like you? A lover of plays and public spectacles, Aspar? If you weren't the finest general the empire has ever seen, you would not be tolerated by the court."

"If I were not the finest general the empire has ever seen," Aspar said quietly, "your sister, Verina, would not be empress."

The prince laughed. "It is true," he admitted. "You made Leo emperor even as you chose Marcian before him. You would be emperor yourself were it not for my friends in the church. They fear you, Aspar."

"They are fools, then," was the reply. "Thank God for my lack of orthodoxy, Basilicus. I should rather be an emperor-maker than an emperor. That is why your friends really fear me. They do not understand why I choose to be as I choose to be. Besides, times have changed. Byzantium needs a great general more than she needs a great emperor right now; and the days are long past when a single man could be both."

"Your modesty touches me," the prince said ironically. "My God! Is that Senator Romanus's wife with that muscle-bound boy? *It is!*"

Aspar chuckled. "We probably know half the people in this room, Basilicus. Look, over there. There is Bishop Andronicus, and just look whom he is with. It is Casia, one of the finest courtesans Villa Maxima has to offer. I have enjoyed several evenings in her company. She is a charming and a most talented girl. Would you like to meet her one day? I do not think I dare intrude upon the bishop tonight, however."

The room was totally filled now. Naked young boys and girls began to move about, snuffing out the lamps until the room was in total darkness. Aspar smiled to himself, hearing the low moans and heavy breathing about him. Already some in the audience were taking advantage of the darkness to make love. Then the heavy curtain shielding the stage was drawn aside, revealing a second diaphanous curtain. The stage was very well lit, with lamps set along its rim and several others that hung down from the stage beams.

The sheer draperies were slowly drawn back to completely reveal a beautiful young woman seated at a loom. Her face was serene, but it was her charming, long auburn curls that Aspar found delightful. The girl was dressed in a modest white tunica; her slender feet were bare. She worked knowledgeably at the loom. Her very demeanor was of purity and innocence.

Soft music played in the background from unseen musicians setting the peaceful scene. The general gazed about him. Among the audience, lovers were beginning to become quite entwined. Senator Romanus's wife was seated facing the stage, upon her lover's lap. Her gown was pulled well up, as was the tunic of the young man upon whom she sat. Their activity was obvious. Aspar smiled, amused, and turned back to the stage. The girl looked up from her weaving, and Aspar saw that her eyes held no expression at all. For a moment he wondered if she were blind, but he could see she was not. The vacant look touched him in a strange fashion. He realized he felt sorry for the beautiful young woman.

Then suddenly the door to the little theatrical chamber burst asunder. The audience gasped as three naked, oiled warriors strode onto the stage. They were all identical in features. Each wore a helmet with a horsetail, and carried a sword and a decorated shield; but it was their large male organs that intrigued both the men and the women in the audience.

"God in his heaven!" murmured Basilicus. "Where did those three come from? Surely they aren't going to ... ah, yes, they are!" He leaned forward, fascinated, as the three barbarians began their violation of the hapless virgin.

Cailin's gauzy little garment was torn violently from her voluptuous body. Raising her right arm, she pressed the back of her hand against her forehead while her left arm was positioned down and slightly back. This clever little piece of staging allowed her audience a perfect view of her beautiful naked body. For the briefest of moments the three barbarians stood silent, as if they too were admiring their victim. Then suddenly one of them grabbed the girl and kissed her fiercely, his big hands roaming over her lush form, fondling it vigorously. A second barbarian tore the maiden from his companion and began to plunder her lips, only to have the third man in their trio demand his share of the sweetness as well. For a few minutes the barbarians kissed and caressed Cailin beneath the collective hot gaze of their audience.

"*Oh, the gods!*" a faceless female voice half moaned in the darkness as the three golden barbarians suddenly turned to face the audience, revealing their engorged manhoods in all their epic proportions.

There were more lustful sighs and groans as the playlet continued onward to its conclusion. Clutching the girl to prevent her escape, the three barbarians diced to see who would take the virginity contained in her temple of Venus. Unknown to the audience, this was the one part of the act that was left to chance each time the quartet performed. Jovian believed if his male actors played exactly the same role in each performance, they would become stale in their parts, and hence boring.

Apollo won the first toss, and grinned delightedly. He had been relegated to the role his brother Castor would play tonight for the last three performances. He groaned with genuine pleasure as Cailin was forced down upon his manhood. Pollux knelt down behind the girl, grasping her hips tightly while she balanced herself upon her hands, and slowly inserted himself in her temple of Sodom. The audience chuckled as Castor, apparently left out of the fun, looked downcast. Then a wicked smile crossed his face. Walking over to the entwined group, he stood over Apollo, and reaching down, lifted Cailin's head up. He rubbed himself against her lips until, with what appeared a demure reluctance, she opened her mouth and took his manhood in, at first shyly, and then with a noisy suckling. Carefully, the other two men began to move on the girl as well. Her ravishers howled with their pleasure.

It was clever, the general thought. The girl looked as innocent as a young lambkin. The blankness in her eyes, however, told him that she was doing what she had to do to survive. She was certainly not enjoying the three men now pushing themselves into the three orifices of her lovely body. About him Aspar saw men and women in the audience slack-jawed and wide-eyed with lustful enjoyment. Several couples, physically involved themselves, were moaning their own pleasure as the players upon the stage were bringing this little piece of depravity to its natural conclusion. As the quartet collapsed in a heap of entwined limbs, the curtains were drawn back across the stage.

Jovian appeared, to the cheers and shouts of the audience. "You have enjoyed our little entertainment?" he asked coyly, a winsome twinkle in his eyes.

They shouted their approval at him, and he beamed, pleased.

"Are there any ladies here tonight who would like to enjoy the special attentions of one of our handsome young barbarians?" Jovian inquired slyly. He was immediately bombarded with eager requests. The three brothers were quickly auctioned off, appearing from behind the curtain to join their happy partners for the night. To Basilicus's astonishment, Senator Romanus's lusty wife gained possession of one of the players, and disappeared with both him and her young lover.

"What about the girl?" came a shout from the audience.

"Oh, no!" Jovian answered with a little laugh. "Our *virgin* is not for anyone else's amusement—for the time being. Perhaps one day, gentlemen, but not right now. My brother and I are pleased that you have all enjoyed yourselves at our playlet. There will be another performance in three nights. Do tell your friends." Then he disappeared behind the curtain like a small fox popping back into its den.

Aspar stood up. "I have some business to conduct," he said to his companion. "Will you remain, Basilicus?"

"I think so," the prince said. "After all, I am here."

Smiling to himself, Flavius Aspar left the small theater. He had sought light amusement at Villa Maxima for a number of years, and he knew precisely where he was going. He found the two Maxima brothers in a small interior room, gleefully counting their proceeds from tonight's performance.

"My lord, it is good to see you!" Jovian hurried forward while Phocas looked up just long enough to nod at the general. "Did you enjoy our little entertainment? I saw Prince Basilicus with you."

"Nothing escapes your sharp eyes, does it, Jovian?" the general said with a laugh. "The performance was unique. A bit hard on the girl, I would say. Is that why you limit her appearances to twice weekly?"

"Of course, my lord. Cailin is very valuable to us. We would not want to harm her in any way," Jovian said.

"I want to buy her," Aspar said quietly.

Jovian felt his heart jump in his chest. His eyes met those of his brother nervously. This was certainly not something that they had even considered. "My lord," he said slowly, "she is not for sale. Not now, perhaps later." He felt a tiny bead of perspiration begin to slide down his backbone. This was the most powerful man in the Byzantine empire. More powerful than the emperor himself.

"One thousand gold solidi," Aspar said, and he smiled to show he was unoffended by Jovian's refusal.

"Three thousand," Phocas answered. There was no sentiment in Phocas Maxima. Jovian might protest, but another girl could be trained to take Cailin's place. Besides, the playlet was no longer fresh.

"Fifteen hundred," the general countered quickly.

"Two thousand," Phocas replied.

"Fifteen hundred," the general replied firmly, indicating the bidding was done. "Have the girl delivered to my private seaside villa. It is just five miles past the Golden Gate. When you arrive tomorrow, the majordomo there will have your gold for you. I trust that will be satisfactory, gentlemen." He did not for a single moment believe he would be denied.

"We would prefer, my lord, if the gold were delivered here to us. I do not think either of us relishes returning from beyond the city walls laden with such a treasure," Phocas explained. "When the purse is brought to us, we will gladly send the girl to you." He bowed politely.

"Very well," Flavius Aspar answered, and then seeing Jovian's downcast features, he said, "Do not be sad, my old friend. *The Virgin and the Barbarians* was becoming quite commonplace. Shortly no one will believe that your little protégé—what did you call her?—is a virgin. Create a new playlet for your audience, Jovian. You will lose nothing by it. Those who have not seen this playlet will be twice as eager to see the next one, and those who have seen it will be equally eager to see what is next."

"*Cailin*. Her name is Cailin. She is a Briton," Jovian said. "You will be kind to her, my lord? She is a good girl fallen on hard times. If you ask her, she will tell you her tale. It is most fascinating."

"I did not purchase her to hurt her, Jovian," the general told him. Then he said, "Gentlemen, no word of this transaction is to be gossiped about, even to my friend Basilicus. I do not want any-one to know of my purchase."

"We understand perfectly, my lord," Jovian said smoothly, now beginning to recover his aplomb. Knowing Cailin's history, he had always secretly felt a bit guilty about making her the centerpiece of his entertainment. He realized that as General Aspar's mistress she would be far safer, and possibly even happier. "We will see less of you now, I expect," he finished.

"Perhaps," Aspar answered. Then nodding to the two men, he departed the chamber, closing the door behind him as he went.

"The gods!" Phocas exclaimed. "We have had the girl in our possession less than three months, brother dear. Her performances made us fifteen thousand solidi, and her sale has brought us an-other fifteen hundred solidi. An excellent return on a slave who only cost us four folles to begin with, even considering the cost of her keep, which was really quite negligible. I salute you, Jovian Maxima! You were correct!"

Jovian smiled broadly. A compliment from Phocas was as rare as finding a perfect pearl in an oyster. "Thank you, brother," he said.

"You will tell the girl?"

"I will speak to her in the morning. On the nights she gives her performance, she bathes, and goes to her bed immediately follow-ing it. She will be sleeping now, and she always sleeps like the dead afterward."

Sleep. It was her only escape. Cailin had believed she was strong. She had almost convinced herself that she could do what they asked of her. But she did not think she could bear much more. It was not that anyone was unkind to her. Indeed, everyone went out of their way to make certain she was comfortable. She was pam-pered and fussed over by everyone at Villa Maxima. Jovian was al-most devoted to her. Apollo, Castor, and Pollux adored her openly. They had even gone as far as to show her a lion designed in a mo-saic, point to it, tap their chests, and then point to her. They were telling her, in the only way they could, that she had the courage of a lion. It was flattering, but it was not enough. She had recently overheard Jovian speaking about a new entertainment he was conceiving for her. It surely couldn't be any worse than what was happening to her now.

To her surprise, Jovian joined her the following morning for the first meal of the day. "I could not sleep," he told her, "and so I went early to the marketplace. See the fine melon I have brought you. We will enjoy it together while I tell you that you have had the most incredible piece of luck, Cailin."

"Fortuna is not a goddess who has been kind to me of late," Cailin told him, handing the melon to Isis to split.

"She smiled quite broadly on you last night, my dear," Jovian said archly. "Flavius Aspar, Byzantium's most powerful man, was in the audience."

"I thought the emperor was your most powerful man," Cailin replied.

"Flavius Aspar is the empire's most famed general. He has personally chosen the last two emperors. Both the late emperor, Marcian, and this emperor, Leo, owe their positions to Aspar."

"And what has your general to do with me, my lord?" Cailin took a slice of melon offered her by Isis. It was wonderfully sweet, and the juice ran down her chin. She flicked out her tongue to catch it.

"I have sold you to him," Jovian said, biting into his own piece of the ripe fruit. "He paid fifteen hundred gold solidi for you, my dear. Did I not tell you that your value would increase?"

"You also told me that I should be able to purchase my freedom eventually," Cailin said bitterly. "Did I not say I should trust no one? But you swore to me that you could be trusted, my lord!"

"Dear girl," Jovian protested, "we did not solicit your sale. He came to us after last night's performance and said he wished to purchase you. He is truly the most powerful man in the empire, Cailin. There was no way my brother and I could refuse him and continue to prosper. To deny Aspar what he wanted would have been tantamount to suicide." He patted her arm. "Do not be afraid, my dear. He will be kind to you. I do not think the general has ever kept a mistress. When he wished to have a woman other than his wife, he would come here, or to some other respectable house such as ours. You should feel honored."

Cailin glared at him. "How will I ever get back to Britain to take my revenge on Antonia Porcius now?" she demanded furiously.

"A clever woman—and I do believe you are clever, Cailin—would see the great opportunity offered her. Aspar will lavish gifts upon you if you please him. He may even free you one day," Jovian said.

"I have none of the skills of a courtesan," Cailin told him. "Those lessons were to come later. All I am capable of doing is . . ." She flushed angrily. "Well, you know what I can do, my lord Jovian, for you conceived the Hades I have been living in for the past weeks! Will not your powerful general believe he has been cheated when he finds out that the woman he bought last night is not at all skilled in the arts of erotica?"

"I do not think it is a trained courtesan he wants, Cailin," Jovian told her. "He is a strange man, Aspar. For all his military skills he is a very kind person in a very cruel world. Make no mistake about him, however. He is a man used to being obeyed. He can be hard."

At that moment Phocas came bustling into Cailin's small chamber. "The messenger has arrived with the gold," he said, attempting to restrain his glee. "I have counted it, and it is all there to the last solidus, brother dear. Have you told Cailin? Is she ready to leave us now?"

"I must wash my hands and face first," Cailin answered for Jovian, "and then I am ready to leave, my lord Phocas."

There was nothing else left to say. Isis brought a basin of water, and Cailin removed all traces of the melon from herself. Then bidding Isis farewell, she was escorted by the two brothers to the courtyard, where a litter was waiting. She wore a simple white chiton belted with a gold rope. The sleeves of the garment flowed gracefully to her mid-arms. Her feet were bare, for she had needed no sandals within Villa Maxima, and none had been given her.

Casia came out into the courtyard and said, "You cannot allow her to leave without these." With a small smile she fastened amethyst, pearl, and gold dangles in Cailin's ears. "Every woman deserves some jewelry. The gods go with you, my little friend. I do not think you realize how fortunate you truly are."

"Thank you, Casia," Cailin exclaimed. "I have never had lovelier earrings than these; and thank you for the rest."

"Be yourself, and you will succeed admirably with him," Casia promised.

"I will call on you soon," Jovian told Cailin brightly, and helped her into the litter. "Take Casia's advice. *She knows.*"

Cailin felt a momentary panic as the litter was lifted and the bearers moved off through the gates of Villa Maxima. Once again she was facing the unknown. It seemed so odd after the quiet life she had lived in Britain that within the space of two years her fate had taken such twists and turns. Cailin leaned back and closed her eyes as they hurried through the city. At the Golden Gate the litter stopped in the line of traffic waiting to be passed through. She heard a rough voice say, "And what have we here?"

"This woman belongs to General Aspar, and is going to Villa Mare," came the curt reply.

"I'll just have a look," the voice answered, and the litter's diaphanous draperies were yanked aside.

Cailin stared coldly at the soldier peering in.

The draperies fell back. "*She* belongs to old Aspar?" the guard at the gate said, whistling admiringly. "What a beauty! Pass on!"

The litter was picked up again, and moved forward. Cailin peeped between the draperies after a while. The road stretched across a flat, fertile plain with wheat fields, orchards, and olive groves along both sides. Beyond lay the sea. She could not see it, but she could smell it, the sharp, pungent tang of the salt air tickling her nose. She was beginning to feel better. The sea was a means of escape, and now that she was free of Villa Maxima, she would never again have to degrade herself as she had the last five weeks.

They moved along at a smooth pace, and then she felt the bearers slowing, turning. Peeking out again, she saw they had passed through an iron gate and were going down a tree-lined lane. She was in the country again, she thought, relieved to be free of the noise and stink of Constantinople. The bearers stopped and the litter was set down again. The curtains were drawn aside and a hand extended to her. Cailin stepped out to discover the hand belonged to an elderly white-haired man of small stature.

"Good day, lady. I am Zeno, the majordomo at Villa Mare. The general has bid me welcome you. This is your home, and we are all at your command." He bowed politely, his worn face breaking into a friendly smile.

"Where is your master, Zeno?" she asked him.

"I have not seen the general in several months, lady. He sent a messenger early this morning with his orders for you," Zeno replied.

"Is he expected soon?" Cailin asked. This was odd.

"He has not informed me so, lady," Zeno told her. "Come in now and take some refreshment. The day is growing warm, and the sun is very hot for late June. The city, I can but imagine, was a tinderbox."

Cailin followed after him. "I do not like the city," she said. "The noise and the dirt are appalling."

"Indeed," he agreed. "I have served the general for many years, but when he offered to make me his majordomo at Villa Mare, I kissed his feet in gratitude. The older I get, the less tolerance I seem to have, lady. You are not a citizen of Byzantium?"

"I am a Briton," Cailin told him, and accepted a goblet of chilled wine from a smiling servant.

"It is a very savage and barbaric land, I am told," Zeno said with utmost seriousness. "It is said the people are blue in color, but you are not blue, lady. Am I mistaken, then?"

Cailin couldn't refrain from one little giggle, but she quickly soothed the majordomo's feelings by telling him, "In ancient times the warriors among my people painted themselves blue when they went into battle, Zeno, but we are not blue-skinned by nature."

"I can see that, lady, but why did they paint themselves blue?"

"Our warriors believed that although the enemy might kill them and strip them of their possessions, as long as they were painted blue, their honor and their dignity could not be taken from them," Cailin explained to him. "Britain is not a savage land. We have been part of the empire for over four hundred years, Zeno. My own family descended from a Roman tribune who came there with Emperor Claudius."

"I can see I have a great deal to learn about the Britons, lady. I hope you will share your knowledge with me. I greatly value knowledge," Zeno said.

During the next few days Cailin explored her new surroundings. Villa Mare was very much like her home in Britain had been; a simple but very comfortable country villa. The atrium had a dear little square fish pond, and she enjoyed sitting there in the heat of the day when the outdoors was not particularly comfortable. Her bedchamber was large and airy. There were no more than half a dozen servants, all older. It was obvious to Cailin that General Aspar sent those slaves he wished to semiretire to the Villa Mare, where they would have a simpler and easier time of it. It seemed a kind act, and she grew more curious about the man who had rescued her from Villa Maxima; but he was not, it seemed, expected by his household at any time soon. It was as if he were deliberately leaving her in peace to recover from the ordeal she had suffered these last months. If this was indeed fact, Cailin appreciated it.

Zeno was fascinated by her stories of Britain. He had never, it seemed, been anywhere in his entire life but Constantinople and the surrounding countryside. Cailin was surprised to find he was a very cultured man despite his status. He could both read and write Latin and Greek as well as keep accounts. He had, he explained, been raised with the son of a noble of the court of Theodosius II, and had come into General Aspar's household when his master had died deeply in debt; then he, along with the other slaves of the household, were sold.

"You were not born a slave, my lady Cailin," Zeno said.

"No," she told him. "I was betrayed by a woman I believed a friend. A year ago at this time I was in Britain, a wife, an expectant mother. If I had been told that this would be my fate, I should have never believed it, Zeno." She smiled softly, almost to herself. "I will go home one day, and I will revenge myself on that woman. I swear it!"

It was obvious to him that she was of the upper class, but because Zeno had been born a slave, the son and grandson of slaves, he did not inquire further. It would have been a presumption on his part, and he could not, despite his curiosity, change the habits of a lifetime. It did not matter that she was also a slave. She was a slave who had been born a patrician. She was his better, no matter her youth.

"Tell me of your master?" Cailin asked him.

"You do not know him?" Zeno said. This was interesting.

"I do not even know what he looks like," Cailin admitted candidly. "The master of the house in which I served came to me one morning and told me that I had been seen and admired by General Aspar, who had bought me from him. I was then sent here. I find it all quite strange."

Zeno smiled. "No," he said, "it is the kind of thing he would do, my lady. We who have been with him for so long know his kind heart, although it is not his public reputation. He would be, should be, emperor of Byzantium, my lady, but instead he has placed Leo on the throne."

"Why?" she asked, curious. She motioned Zeno to sit with her by the atrium pond, encouraging him to continue.

"He descends from the Alans, my lady. They were once a pastoral, nomadic clan living beyond the Black Sea. The Alans were driven from their homeland by the Huns, a fierce, warlike tribe who until recently were ruled by an animal called Attila. Although the general is a Christian, he is an Arian Christian. Whereas the Orthodox Christians believe that their Holy Trinity, consisting of God the Father, the Son, and the Holy Spirit are one in three, and three in one, the Arians believe that the Son is a different being from the God Father, and subordinate to him.

"They argue back and forth over doctrine. Although some of our emperors are intrigued by the Arians, the Orthodox church holds sway in Byzantium. They will not allow an openly Arian Christian to be crowned emperor. The bishops respect General Aspar, and they know there is no finer military man alive; but they would not allow him to be emperor. I honestly do not think he wants to be emperor, my lady. The emperor is never a free man. Much of the general's heritage remains in him, I believe. He would rather be a free man than a king."

"Does he have a wife, Zeno? Or children?" Cailin wondered.

"For many years the general was wed to a good woman of Byzantium, the lady Anna. In the first year of their marriage they had a son, Ardiburius, and then later a daughter, Sophia. Nine years ago the lady Anna, after many years of barrenness, bore our master a second son, Patricius. The birth weakened her. She remained an invalid until her death three years ago. Villa Mare was bought for her pleasure because it was thought the sea air would be salubrious for her.

"We thought the general would remain a bachelor, but last year he married again. It is a political alliance, however. The lady Flacilla is a widow with two married daughters. She does not even live in our master's house in the city, but remains in the home she has had for many years. She is a woman of the court with powerful connections, but I fear she is a poor companion for the general. He is lonely."

"The trouble with old and valued servants," came a deep voice, "is that they know far too much about one, and are given to idle chatter."

Zeno leapt up and, kneeling before the man who had entered the atrium, kissed the hem of his cloak. "Forgive an old fool, my lord," he said, and then, "Why did you not send word you were coming?"

"Because this house is always in perfect order to receive me, Zeno," Aspar said, helping the old man to his feet. "Now, go and bring me some chilled wine, the Cyprian wine, for I have had a long, hot ride." Having dismissed the servant, he turned to Cailin. "You are well-rested?" he asked politely.

"Thank you, my lord." She tried not to stare.

"Zeno has made you comfortable?" he said. God, she is beautiful, he thought. He had bought her on a whim, out of pity, but now he realized perhaps he had not been foolish after all. It had been a long time since any woman had made his heart race and his loins stir with desire.

"I have been treated with nothing but kindness, my lord," Cailin told him softly. He is a very attractive man, she considered, realizing the place she would occupy in this house from his look. "Here, let me take your cloak," she said, unfastening the diamond button of the garment and laying it aside. He stood just two or three inches taller than she was. He was not nearly as tall as Wulf or the trio of Northmen had been, but his body had a solid, almost square look to it. He was obviously a general who kept himself in as good condition as his own men were required to keep themselves.

"What is the fragrance you are wearing?" he asked her. It was intoxicating him with its elusiveness.

"I wear no fragrance, my lord, but I do bathe daily," Cailin told him nervously, stepping away from him. "It is probably the scent of the soap that lingers on my skin."

"We will bathe together after I have had my wine. The ride was hot, and the city even hotter. Do you like it here by the sea?"

"I was raised in the country, my lord, and lived there until I came to Constantinople. I prefer it to the city." She answered him calmly, but her heart was thundering in her ears. *We will bathe together.* If there had been any doubt in her mind as to what position she was to hold in his life before, there was certainly none any longer.

Zeno returned with the wine, and Aspar sat down on the marble bench by the fish pond, sipping the cool beverage slowly and with obvious appreciation. Cailin stood silently by his side watching him. His hair was deep brown, sprinkled with bits of silver. It was cut short and brushed away from the crown of his head. It was a practical style for a military man. The hand holding the goblet was large and square, the fingers long and powerful-looking. There was a big gold ring upon his middle finger. The ruby in it was cut to resemble a double-headed eagle, the symbol of Byzantium.

He felt her stare and looked up suddenly. Cailin blushed, caught at her scrutiny. He smiled. It was a quick, mischievous smile like that of a small boy. His teeth were white and even, and the eyes that twinkled at her a silvery gray. The lines about his eyes that crinkled with amusement told her that he smiled easily. "I think my nose too big. What do you think, Cailin?" He smiled again, and her knees went just a trifle weak. He wasn't quite handsome, but there was something about him.

"I think your nose very nice, my lord," she replied.

"The nostrils flare a bit too much," he told her. "Now my mouth is very well-proportioned, neither too big nor too little. Our friend, Jovian, has a cupid's bow of a mouth, quite unsuitable for a man, don't you think? It was probably charming when he was a child."

"Jovian is still a bit of a child," Cailin observed.

Aspar chuckled. "So there is a keen eye, and, I suspect, an intellect to go with that beautiful face and form."

"I was not aware that my face was particularly visible when you saw me last, my lord, and my form was quite contorted, or so it felt," Cailin said humorously. Then she grew serious. "Why did you buy me, my lord? Is it your habit to purchase inmates of brothels?"

"I thought you the bravest woman I had ever seen," Aspar told her. "You were struggling to survive at Villa Maxima. I saw it in the blank stare you favored the audience with, and the stoic way in which you accepted the degradation visited upon you in that obscene playlet of Jovian's.

"The empire that rules the world, or at least most of it, is governed by those same deviates who found your shame entertaining. I am a member of that ruling class, but I find those people more frightening than any danger I have ever faced in battle. When I impulsively purchased you from Jovian—who by the way would not have dared to refuse my request—I was doing so because I felt your bravery should be rewarded by freeing you from the hell you so gallantly endured. Now, however, I think perhaps there was another reason as well. You stir my blood, it seems."

His frankness amazed her. Cailin struggled for composure. "There must be many beautiful women in Byzantium, my lord," she said. "It is, I have been told, a city of uniquely beautiful women. Surely there are others more worthy of your attention than myself, a humble slave from Britain."

His laughter startled her. "By God, I would not have thought coyness a part of your nature, Cailin. It does not become you, I fear," Aspar told her.

"I have never been coy in my entire life!" she sputtered indignantly.

"Then do not start now," he chided her. "You are a beautiful woman. I desire you. Since I bought you, there is, it would seem, little you can do except bear with the horrendous fate I have in store for you." He put down his goblet and arose to stand facing her.

"Yes, you own me," Cailin said, and to her dismay, tears sprang into her eyes which she seemed powerless to control. "I am bound to obey you, my lord, but you will never have all of me, for there is a part of myself that only I can give, no man can take!"

He caught her chin between his thumb and forefinger, stunned by her honest declaration and moved by her passionate defiance. Tears slipped slowly down her smooth cheeks like tiny crystal beads. "My God," he exclaimed, "did you know that your eyes glisten like amethysts when you weep like that, Cailin? You break my heart. Cease, I beg you, my beauty! I surrender humbly before your feet."

"I hate being a slave!" she told him desperately. "And why is it that you can penetrate the defenses I have so carefully built up around myself these last months when no one else could?"

"I am a better tactician than any of the others," he told her teasingly. "Besides, Cailin, although you tempt my baser nature, I find you fascinating on several other levels as well." He brushed away her tears carefully with a single finger. "I have finished my wine now. We will become better acquainted in the bath. I promise I will try not to make you cry again if you will not be coy. Do we have a bargain, my beauty? I think I am being most generous."

She could not be angry with him. He was really very kind, but she was a little fearful of him nonetheless. "I agree," she said finally.

"Come then," he said, taking her hand and leading her from the atrium.

Chapter

9

The bath at Villa Mare was unique in that it was not
an interior room. It faced the sea, and had an open portico
that could be closed off by means of shutters in cold or inclement
weather. The view from the room was both beautiful and soothing.
The walls were decorated in mosaic. One pictured Neptune, the
sea god, standing tall amid the waves, a trident in one hand and a
conch shell in the other, upon which he was blowing. Behind him
silver-blue dolphins leapt. A second wall offered a scene of Neptune's many daughters cavorting among the waves with a troupe of
sea horses; while the third wall showed the mighty king of the sea
seducing a beautiful maiden in an underwater cave. The mosaic
floor of the bath pictured fish and sea life of every kind known to
the artist. It was both colorful and amusing.

There was a tiled dressing room off the bath, but the main room
served all the steps necessary to bathing, unlike the elegant bath
complex at Villa Maxima with its many different rooms. The bathing pool was set in sea-blue tiles, and the water gently warm. A

corner fountain with a marble basin ran with cool water. There were shell-shaped depressions with drains for rinsing and benches for massage.

Aspar dismissed the old slave who served as bath attendant. "The lady Cailin wishes to serve me," he told the woman, and she grinned a toothless grin that bespoke pure conspiracy, cackling as she departed.

"Discretion is wasted here," Cailin told him, pinning up her long hair.

"Remove your chiton," he said. "I want to see you as God made you, Cailin. Bent over as you were the last time I viewed your charms, I could see little of much note, so covered were you by those Northmen."

"You may be sorry you did not buy one of them," she teased him mischievously, and slipped the simple garment over her head, tossing it carelessly upon a bench. Then she stood silent and still, amazed that she was not mortified; but then her stay at Villa Maxima had, she suspected, rid her of all false modesty.

"Turn slowly," he commanded her quietly, his admiration obvious. Then he removed his own garments, unfastening the cross-gartering on his braccos and slipping them off, to be followed by his drawers, tunic, and fine linen chemise.

As Cailin turned back to face him, she found Aspar quite as naked as she herself was. Startled by his action, she blushed. He stood quietly, allowing her the same advantage as he had had, and then he turned, too. Her first impression had been a good one. His body was firm, well-muscled, and kissed by the sun. He was not fat, nor was he large-boned. There was a solid stockiness to him that she found comforting. His arms and legs were hairless, as was his chest. He had longer legs than she would have expected, and a well-sculpted, hard torso. His buttocks were tight.

His male organs seemed smaller than she was used to, but she suspected he was of quite average size. Her "barbarians" and Wulf had been the exceptions to the rule, Casia had assured her when they had once spoken on it. Her curiosity had led her to question the lovely courtesan who had tutored her so well in the arts of

Eros. Casia had been a font of useful and rather fascinating information for Cailin, who was so lacking in practical experience regarding men and lovemaking.

His voice brought her back to the present. "Do you find me as beautiful as I find you, Cailin?" he asked her.

"Yes," she said quietly. He was an attractive man, and she saw no reason not to tell him so.

"Take up the strigil, now, and scrape me," he ordered her. "I am filthy from my ride. The roads are particularly dusty at this time of year."

Cailin picked up the silver bathing tool and began to remove the sweat and grime that his ride in the heat of the day had deposited on his skin. She had watched the bath attendants at Villa Maxima at their trade, for Casia had warned her that men frequently enjoyed being served this way by their lovers. Slowly, carefully, she worked, moving from his shoulders and chest, down his arms and back and legs.

"You have a skill for this work," he said softly as she knelt before him, carefully running the bath instrument over his thighs.

"I am a novice at such a task," she said, "but I am glad I please you, my lord." She rinsed him with a basin of warm water taken from the bathing pool, and he took the strigil from her hands. "I will scrape you now," he said softly, plying the tool. Cailin stood very still as he moved the strigil gently over her delicate skin. She found this love-play rather charming. His restraint in claiming his rights was very reassuring. She sighed as he rinsed her, and turning to face him, she said, "Now, my lord, I will wash you before we enter the bathing pool."

He stood in one of the hollowed mosaic shells in the floor. Cailin placed an alabaster jar of soft soap on the floor nearby and took up a sea sponge. Scooping some soap from the jar, she spread it over his shoulders, and then worked up a lather using the sponge. Slowly, carefully, she washed him, working in an efficient manner, turning him about as she knelt, adding more soap, scrubbing with the sponge. She blushed self-consciously as she bathed his manhood, but to his credit he said nothing, remaining quiet as she worked. Cailin stood, swirling the soapy sponge over his belly and up his broad chest. Finished, she rinsed him again with warm water, relieved the ordeal was over. She had never bathed a man before. Wulf had always washed himself, usually in the fast-running stream near the hall, even in winter.

"Now you may enter the bathing pool," she told him.

"Nay," he answered her, and took the sponge from her hand. "You must be washed first, my beauty." Bending, he rinsed the sponge in the bronze basin, and tipping the dirty water out, refilled it with fresh.

"I can bathe myself," she said shyly.

"I'm certain you can," he said, laughter evident in his tone, "but would you deny me the pleasure serving you will give me?" Not waiting for her answer, he dipped his three fingers into the alabaster pot and began to slowly spread soap over her shoulders and back. The slow, circular motion of the sea sponge on her skin was almost mesmerizing in its sensuous movement. She thought she felt his lips touch the back of her neck, and then the soapy sponge swirled over it, leaving her confused. Kneeling, he washed her buttocks, kissing them first, and then moved on to her legs. *"Turn,"* he said, and she obeyed, although her body was already beginning to feel heavy with desire. How lovely all of this was. Bathing with a man was most pleasurable.

He lifted her left foot and washed it, then the right. The sponge swept slowly up her legs, which were tightly closed. Gently he pushed them slightly apart, the sponge sliding over her sensitive skin. Cailin turned her head and looked away. She was unused to seeing her Venus mont so pink and smooth, devoid of its little curls, but only men, peasants, and savages, Jovian had assured her, kept such body hair. A woman must be silken all over. Her stomach knotted itself as his hand rubbed soap over the quivering flesh. Cailin closed her eyes as the sponge rubbed round and round and round.

His hand gently drew her forward, and Cailin gasped, startled as his mouth closed over the nipple of her right breast. His teeth lightly scored the flesh; his tongue teased insistently at her; and then he suckled hard on the tight little nub even as his left hand caressed then crushed her other breast until her knees began to buckle. Standing quickly, he pulled her hard against him, his mouth finding hers with a burning kiss that left her breathless. Then his gray eyes held her in thrall as he rinsed her slowly, being certain that every bit of soap was washed away. Finally placing the basin down, he took her by the hand and led her down the steps into the bathing pool.

The warm water lapped softly at their bodies. Cailin felt weak in the sudden heat. Seeing how pale she was, he drew her against him again. When he felt her trembling, Aspar said softly, even as he began to place little kisses all over her face, "I do not want you to be fearful of me, Cailin, but you must know I want to make love to you. Do you know how sweet lovemaking can be between a man and a woman, my beauty? Not that ugly animal coupling you were forced to endure at Villa Maxima, but true passion between lovers. Tell me, were you a virgin when you first came to Constantinople, or did some other lover initiate you into the wondrous sweetness two people can create?" Tenderly he nibbled on her earlobe, and then he looked directly into her violet eyes.

"I . . . I had a husband," Cailin told him.

"What happened to him, my beauty?" Aspar gently encouraged her.

"I do not know, my lord. I was betrayed into slavery," she told him, and then went on to explain briefly. "Jovian says that Wulf was probably told I was dead," she finished. Several tears slid down her cheeks. "I think he is correct. I just wish I knew what happened to our child. I am so afraid that Antonia may have sold it, too, if indeed it lived, but our child would be strong. I know it is alive!"

"You cannot change the past," he counseled her wisely. "I understand that better than most, Cailin. If you will trust me, I will give you a happy present, and your future will be everything you could ever want."

"It would seem, my lord, that I have no choice," she replied. *Trust,* she thought, wryly. Why were men always asking you to trust them?

"Oh, my beauty," he said with a smile, "we always have a choice. It is just sometimes our choices are not particularly pleasant. Your choices, however, are. You may love me now, or you may love me later."

Cailin giggled. "Your choices, my lord, bear a great similarity to one and another." She already liked this man. He was kind, and he had humor. These were not bad traits in one so powerful.

He smiled back at her. She excited him very much; rousing him in a way no woman really ever had, even his beloved Anna. It had been a long time since he had really desired a woman, although he had visited Villa Maxima quite regularly. He firmly believed that a man should not allow his juices to be pent up for too long. To do so foggled the brain and made a man irritable. He knew, however, looking at this beautiful girl before him, that he would never visit Villa Maxima again.

"I like it when you laugh, my beauty," he said softly.

"I like it when you smile at me, my lord," she responded, and then she kissed him on the lips, quickly, without passion, but sweetly.

In answer he cupped her head in one hand and began to kiss her face and throat with warm lips that sent tingles of pleasure throughout her entire being. She moaned low in the back of her throat, arching her body as his other hand began to knead at a breast and he pushed her back against the side of the pool. He ran his tongue over her lips, nibbled at her eyelids, tongued the column of her straining neck. His hand dug into the tightly bunched curls pinned atop her head, and then he groaned as if pained when her body pushed against his lower torso. Her arms slipped about his neck. Cailin, returning his kisses with fervor, realized she had no need to employ Casia's tricks with Aspar. She felt his hungry arousal against her thigh, pushing, pressing with urgency.

"I want to wait," he half sobbed, "but I cannot, Cailin!"

"Do not, my lord," she encouraged him, tightening her hold about his neck as he slid his hands beneath her buttocks and sheathed himself within her passage, sighing with deep relief. He pumped her with long slow strokes of his weapon, and she felt him, hard but loving, within her body. She murmured low as he moved inside her over and over again until he could bear no more and his lover's tribute exploded in hot bursts of passion that left him weak and Cailin shocked that she had felt nothing but his physical presence. She shuddered, horrified.

Aspar opened his eyes. "What is the matter?" he asked her. "You had no pleasure of it, did you, Cailin? Yet I think I do not displease you, my beauty, do I?" He was free of her body now, and they stood together facing each other, her back still against the bathing pool.

"Is there only pleasure with a husband?" she asked him, honestly confused, and needing desperately to know. "I felt no pleasure when I was forced to couple with Jovian's trio of Northmen, but I thought it was because I did not love them, because what they were doing to me was wrong. You are not my husband, but you are kind to me. I want to serve you like a wife. Should there not be pleasure then, my lord? You do not repel me! *You do not!*" Her voice cracked, and she began to weep wildly. "What has happened to me, my lord, that I can feel no pleasure with you?"

He took her in his arms and soothed her as best as he could. He was not a doctor, but he knew that the mind was probably the most powerful weapon that God had ever created. He had seen strange things happen to soldiers in the field, particularly after a cruel battle: Men, normally hardened and fierce, who would break down weeping. Men who could never look at weapons again without breaking into a fit of trembling sweats. Perhaps the brutal savagery Cailin had endured had hurt her in a similar way. He remembered the blank look in her eyes the night he had attended the entertainment at Villa Maxima. She had, in a sense, removed herself from what was going on upon the stage because it was the only way she could survive it.

"What has happened to you since you left Britain has hurt you in some unseen manner," he told her comfortingly. "If you will trust me, I will help you to heal yourself, my beauty. I very much want you to have the same pleasure of me as I have had of you. Unlike most men of my age, I have a rather unusually large capacity for lovemaking, Cailin. We will continue on until you, too, are pleasured, no matter how long it takes." He took her hand. "Come now before we are so weakened that we are washed away in this bath."

He led her from the bathing pool, and they dried each other off. Then, taking her hand again, he brought her to their bedchamber. Cailin was surprised to see that her pretty, narrow little couch had been removed from the dais and pushed against a wall. In its place upon the raised platform was a large striped mattress and several large, colorful pillows. Aspar began kissing her again, and shortly they fell to the bed, their limbs intertwined. The sensation of his body against hers was totally different here than in the bathing pool. He seemed harder.

"Lie still," he commanded her, and pushing two of the pillows beneath her hips to raise her up, he told her, "I want you to spread your legs wide for me, my beauty," and when she obeyed him, he leaned forward, gently spread her nether lips with his thumbs and began to touch her lightly and softly with his tongue.

Cailin gasped with shock and surprise. Her first thought was to push him away. This was an invasion of such a deeply intimate nature such as she had never experienced. Yet there was a tenderness to it, and a sweetness that hypnotized her so thoroughly that she found she was unable to deny him his way with her. His tongue gently caressed her flesh, then began to tease at the tiny core of her very being. Cailin felt heat suffusing her entire body, yet she shivered. The little nub began to sharply tingle, the sensation growing in intensity until she thought she could simply bear no more, but for the life of her she could find no voice to beg him to stop.

She let the deliciousness take her, and she heard herself, as if from a distance, moaning with her own pleasure. Her limbs were heavy with a longing she had never experienced but did not find unpleasant in the least. The feeling was building even more with each passing moment, until finally an intense sweetness swept over her like a wave from the sea, and receded as quickly, leaving her weak, but most strangely satisfied. "Ahhhhh," she exhaled breathily. Then quite unexpectedly, she began to cry softly.

Aspar pulled himself up and gathered the girl in his arms. He said nothing. He simply stroked those riotous little auburn curls, marveling at their softness as his fingers became tangled amid the silk of her lovely hair. She pressed herself against him as if seeking his protection, and he was overwhelmed by his own desire to keep her safe from all the cruelty of the world. No matter what had happened to her, Cailin was in her heart an innocent. He was not going to let her be hurt again.

Finally her sobs subsided and she said, "You received no pleasure, my lord, yet I did. How can this be? I did not know a woman could be pleasured in such a way." She looked up at him, and he thought that her beautiful eyes resembled violets, wet with a spring rain.

"There is pleasure in just giving pleasure, Cailin; not perhaps as intense for me as when I am encased within you, but pleasure nonetheless. There are many ways of giving and receiving pleasure. We will explore them all. I will never intentionally do you harm, my little love," he told her, stroking her cheek with a gentle finger.

"They say you are the most powerful man in the empire, my lord. Even more powerful than the emperor himself," she said.

"Never say that aloud to anyone else, Cailin," he warned her. "The powerful are jealous of their power, and would not share it. My survival depends upon remaining a good servant of the empire. It is really the empire I honor. God, and the empire. No man. But that, my little love, must remain our secret, eh?" He smiled at her.

"You are like the Romans of old, I think, my lord. You honor the new Rome, Byzantium, as they once honored the old Rome," Cailin said.

"And what do you know of Rome?" he asked her, amused.

"I sat with my brothers and their tutor for many years," Cailin said. "I learned the history of Rome and of my native Britain."

"Can you read and write?" he questioned her, fascinated.

"In Latin," she responded. "The history of my mother's people, the Dobunni Celts, is an oral history, but I know it, my lord."

"Jovian told me little of your background, Cailin. Your Latin is that of a cultured woman, if a bit provincial. Who were your people?"

"I descend from a tribune of the Drusus family who came to Britain with the emperor Claudius," Cailin said, and then, as they lay together, she told him her family's history.

"And your husband? Who was he? Also of a Romano-Briton family?"

"My husband was a Saxon," Cailin said. "I married him after my family was murdered at the instigation of my cousin Quintus, who wanted my father's lands. My cousin was unaware I had escaped the slaughter until I came with my husband, Wulf Ironfist, to reclaim what was rightfully mine. Wulf killed Quintus when he attempted to attack me. It was his wife, Antonia, who betrayed me, but you already know that part of my story, my lord."

"It is amazing that you have survived it all," Aspar said thoughtfully.

"Now you know everything about me. Zeno has told me that your first wife was a good and an honorable woman. What he did not say about the wife you now have is more of interest," Cailin said. "If you would tell me, my lord, I should like to know."

"Flacilla is a member of the Strabo family," Aspar began. "They are very powerful at court. Our marriage was one of convenience. She does not live with me, and frankly I do not even like her."

"Then why did you marry her?" Cailin asked curiously. "You did not need to marry again at this time, my lord. You have one grown son, Zeno says, and a second son as well as a daughter."

"Did Zeno mention my grandchildren?" Aspar demanded with a certain humor in his voice. "My daughter Sophia has three children, and my eldest son has four. Since Patricius, my youngest, shows no signs of wanting to be a monk, I can assume he, too, will give me more grandchildren one day when he is grown and wed."

"*You have grandchildren?*" Cailin was astounded. He did not look *that* old, and his behavior was certainly not that of an old man. "How old are you, my lord Aspar? I was nineteen in the month of April."

He groaned. "Dear God! I am certainly old enough to be your father, my little love. I am fifty-four this May past."

"You are nothing like my father," she murmured, and then she boldly pulled his head to her and kissed him softly, sweetly.

His head swam pleasantly with her daring. "No," he said, his gray eyes smiling into her violet ones, "I am not your father, am I, my little love?" He kissed her back; a long, slow, deep kiss.

Cailin's senses reeled. Finally, when she recovered herself, she said, "Tell me more about your wife, my lord Aspar."

"I like the sound of my name upon your lips," he said.

"The lady Flacilla Strabo, my lord Aspar," she insisted.

"I married her for several reasons. The late emperor, Marcian, whom I placed upon the throne of Byzantium and married to the princess Pulcheria, was dying, and there were no heirs.

"Marcian came from my own household. He had served me loyally for twenty years. When I realized his end was near, I chose Leo, another of my household, to be the next emperor. I needed certain support from the court, however. The patriarch of Constantinople, the city's religious leader, is a relation of the Strabo family, and family ties are strong here. Without him I could not have hoped to place Leo on the throne. To ensure his support, and that of the Strabo family, I married the widowed Flacilla. She was pregnant with a lover's child at the time, and was causing her family untold embarrassment."

"What happened to the child?" Cailin wondered aloud.

"She miscarried it in her fifth month," he said, "but it was too late. She was my wife. In return for my aid, the patriarch and the Strabo family supported my choice of Leo. Of course, other patrician families followed suit. This allowed us a peaceful transition from one emperor to another. Civil war is unpleasant at the least, Cailin. And Flacilla is to all outward appearances a good wife. She has taken my little son, Patricius, in her charge, and is a very good mother to him. He is being raised in the Orthodox faith. I hope to match him with the princess Ariadne one day, and make him Leo's heir, for the emperor has no sons."

"What do you want of me, my lord, I mean other than the obvious?" Cailin asked him, and then she blushed at her own audacity. Still, her life since leaving Britain had been so unsettled. She needed to know if she was to have a permanent home.

He thought for several long minutes. "I loved my first wife," he began. "When Anna died, I thought that I should never again care for a woman. I certainly do not like Flacilla, but I serve a purpose for her. Her social stature is practically as high as the empress Verina, for I am the General of the Eastern Armies, and the First Patrician of the Empire. Flacilla, in turn, mothers my orphaned son, but that is all she does for me.

"I am powerful, Cailin, but I am alone, and the honest truth is, I am a lonely man. When I saw you that night at Villa Maxima, you touched me as no woman has ever really touched me. I need your love, I need your gentleness, and I need your companionship in my life. Do you think that you can give it to me, my beauty?"

"My grandfather said I had a sharp tongue, and I do," Cailin told him slowly. "I am practical to a fault. If there is any gentleness left in me, my lord Aspar, you are possibly the only one to see it. Now what I must say to you will sound hard, but I have learned in the last year to be hard in order to survive. You are not a young man, yet I am your slave. If you should die, what will happen to me? Do you think that your heirs will treat the slave mistress of their father with kindness? I think not.

"I believe that I shall be disposed of with all the other possessions that you own that will be considered unnecessary. Can I love you? Yes, I can. I believe you to be kind and good, but if you truly care for me, my lord, then make provisions to keep me safe when you are not here to do so yourself. Until that time I will serve you with all my heart and soul."

He nodded quietly. She was right. He would have to make arrangements to protect her when he no longer could. "I will go to the city tomorrow and arrange for everything," he promised her. "You will be free upon my death, and have an inheritance to keep you. If you bear my children, I will provide for them, and recognize them as well."

"It is more than fair," Cailin said, relief sweeping over her.

When she awoke in the morning, Aspar was gone from their bed.

"He has gone to the city," Zeno said, smiling. "He says to tell you that he will return in several days' time, my lady. He has also told me that you are to be considered mistress here, and we will obey you."

"My lord Aspar is a generous man," Cailin said quietly. "I must rely upon you, Zeno, to help me do what is proper and correct."

"My lady's wisdom is only excelled by her great beauty," the elderly majordomo replied, pleased by her tactful response and the certainty that everything would remain the same.

Aspar returned a few days later from Constantinople. Within a short time it was obvious to his servants that he intended to make Villa Mare his primary residence. He left only to attend to court business and oversee his duties as general of the Eastern Armies. He was rarely away overnight. He and Cailin had settled down to a very quiet domestic existence.

Cailin was surprised to learn that Aspar owned all the farmland about the villa for several miles. There were vineyards, olive groves, and wheat fields, all contributing to the general's wealth. He thought nothing of helping out in the fields, or working to harvest the grapes. She rather suspected he enjoyed it.

I n the city, Aspar's absence from his elegant palace was not noticed at first, but the empress Verina, a clever woman, kept her ear to the ground in all quarters. She and her husband had not the advantage of inheritance to keep their thrones safe. Aspar was important to them. Although an excellent public servant, Leo was not a master of intrigue at this early point in his reign; but his wife, raised in Byzantium, knew that the more one knew, the safer one was. A servant's idle gossip caught her ear at first, and then she heard it again, this time from a minor official. The empress invited her brother Basilicus to come and visit her.

They sat on a terrace overlooking the Propontis, called by some the Marmara, one afternoon in late autumn, sipping the first of the new wine. Verina was a beautiful woman with ivory skin and long, black hair which she wore in an elaborate coiffure of braids that were fastened with jeweled pins. Her red and gold stola was of rich materials, and the low neckline showed her fine bosom to its best advantage. Her slippers were bejeweled, and she wore several ropes of pearls so translucent they seemed to shimmer against her skin and gown. She smiled at her brother.

"What is this I hear about Aspar?" she purred.

"What is it you have heard about Aspar, my pet?" he countered.

"It is said that he has closed up his palace and now lives in the countryside outside the city," the empress said. "Is it true?"

"I would not know, sister dear," Basilicus replied. "I have not seen Aspar socially for months now. I see him only when we have mutual court business to attend to, which is infrequently. Why would you care where Aspar lives, Verina? Although he is responsible for Leo's ascent, you have never cared particularly for him. I know for a fact that his presence irritates you for it only serves to remind you that he is responsible for your good fortune."

"It is said there is a woman living with him, Basilicus," the empress said, ignoring her brother's astute observation. "You know that Aspar's wife, Flacilla, is my friend. I would be very distressed to have Flacilla embarrassed by her husband's peccadillos."

"Nonsense, sister, you are simply consumed by curiosity," Basilicus replied. "If indeed Aspar is living with some mistress, nothing, I suspect, would please you more than to drop a hint in Flacilla's shell-like ear, thereby enraging her. You know that Aspar agreed to marry her only if she would remain discreet in her little adventures and not embarrass her family again. Aspar is not a man to install a mistress in his house, but if indeed he has, then by living in the country he is making an attempt to be circumspect in his affair. Besides, there is nothing wrong with a man taking a mistress, Verina. It is my opinion that our good general deserves a modicum of pleasure in his life. He will never obtain it from your dear friend Flacilla, who takes lovers like some women gather flowers in a field, and with less discretion, I might add."

"Flacilla is young yet. She is many years her husband's junior," the empress said. "Aspar could not keep up with her, I assure you."

"She could not keep up with him," Basilicus said with a laugh.

"Aspar is known to be a prodigious lover, my dear sister. An eighteen-year-old could not keep up with him, I am told by most reliable sources. Besides, Flacilla has two grown daughters. She is hardly in the first bloom of youth herself."

"She had her children when she was fifteen and sixteen," Verina said in defense of the lady. "They were fifteen and sixteen when she married them off last year. That only makes her thirty-two. Aspar is at least twenty years her senior. If he has taken a mistress, it will make my poor Flacilla the laughingstock of all of Constantinople. You must find out!"

"*Me?*" Basilicus looked horrified. "How could I find out?"

"You must go to visit Aspar in the country, Basilicus. Perhaps these rumors are nothing more than that, rumors, but if they are true, then I must inform Flacilla before she is shamed before the court."

"*Go to the country?* Verina, I detest the country! I haven't left the city in several years. There is nothing to do in the country. Besides, Flacilla should be delighted if Aspar has taken a mistress. It will keep him occupied, amused, and uninterested in her affairs. She almost caused a dreadful scandal again last week when the young gladiator she had been amusing herself with decided he was in love with her after she attempted to discard him."

"I didn't hear *that*," the empress said, annoyed and curious as to why her network of spies had not reported this rather interesting tidbit to her. "What happened, Basilicus? I can see you know every delicious detail. Tell me at once, or I shall have you blinded!"

He chuckled and, pouring himself another goblet of wine, began, "Well, my dear sister, your friend Flacilla had taken a young gladiator to her bed whom she had first seen at the spring games. A Thracian named Nichophorus; rather beefy I thought, but those muscular thighs of his were irresistible, I suspect. As is usual with Flacilla after a few months' time, familiarity began to breed contempt. She grew tired of her muscular Adonis and, besides, her eye had lit upon Michael Valens, the young actor. Our Flacilla was struck anew by Cupid's dart."

"What happened to the gladiator?" Verina demanded.

"He caught them at the very same trysting place Flacilla had once shared with him," Basilicus replied. "She is not a woman of great imagination, is she, sister? You would have thought she would have chosen another site to carry on her little passion, but no, 'twas the very same spot. Nichophorus, informed by some mischief maker, found them there. He howled and raged, beating upon the door of the chamber in which your friend and her lover were cowering. Finally he broke the door down.

"Michael Valens, no hero, fearful that his beautiful face would be destroyed, escaped through a window naked as the day his mother had birthed him, I'm told, leaving a semi-garbed Flacilla to contend with the outraged gladiator. He railed loudly against her, cursing her and naming her a whore to all who would listen. The innkeeper finally called out the guard, who chased after Nichophorus as he ran screaming after Flacilla's litter, which was making its way down the streets of the city at an unusually great rate of speed." Basilicus laughed. "The captain of the guard and his men were, of course, bought off by the patriarch. The scandal was hushed up. Nichophorus was sent to Cyprus. It is a very good thing Aspar was not in the city when it happened. He warned Flacilla when they married that if she caused any public scandal, he would send her to St. Barbara's Convent for the rest of her life."

The empress nodded. "Yes, he did, and the patriarch agreed to support him in such an instance. The Strabo family is not just a little annoyed by Flacilla's indiscreet behavior, and their patience is worn thin by her. Hmmmmm, I wonder to what use I may put all this information, but of course the puzzle is incomplete until I know exactly what is going on at Aspar's villa." Her amber eyes glittered wickedly. "You will leave in the morning, brother."

He groaned as he arose, kissing her hand. "The empress's wish is my command, but Verina, I will expect the favor of my choice for this little task I undertake on your behalf. Remember that!"

"Within reason, Basilicus," she purred, smiling broadly after him. He was such a good brother, the empress thought fondly as she watched him leave. Whatever was happening at the general's villa, Basilicus would obtain the entire story, analyze it, and return to her with it. If she could not decide how to use his information, he would be able to advise her. They were very close, and always had been.

Basilicus left the city early the following day. He traveled in a large, comfortable litter, preferring not to ride in the warm sun. To his surprise, he napped most of the way, awakening as they entered through the gates of the villa. Zeno, the majordomo, greeted him politely, recognizing the prince from his own days at the general's house in Constantinople.

"Where is your master?" Basilicus asked.

"He is walking by the sea, my lord," Zeno replied.

Basilicus was about to tell Zeno to send a servant for Aspar, but instead decided that he might learn something of value if he took his friend unawares. "Thank you, Zeno," he said. "If you will but direct me." He followed the majordomo through the atrium of the villa and across the interior garden, out into a large open garden that looked over the Propontis, and beyond into Asia.

"There is the path, my lord," Zeno told him, pointing.

Basilicus hurried along the gravel walkway. It was a marvelous day with a flat, bright blue, cloudless sky above. The autumn sun was warm, and about him the damask rosebushes sported a mixture of late blooms and large, fat, round red-orange rosehips. Then he saw them—Aspar and a woman, laughing together upon the beach. The woman wore a white chiton and was barefoot, as was her companion, who was garbed in a short red tunic. The sea was almost flat, a mixture of azure, aquamarine, and teal-green stretching like an iridescent fabric across to the hills on the other shore. Above them the gulls mewled and cried, swooping to the water and then pulling up sharply to soar in the windless sky.

Basilicus watched them for a long moment, enchanted by the picture they made, and then he called out, raising his hand and waving at the couple. "Aspar, my friend!" He stepped from the pathway to the sandy beach and began walking toward them.

"Jesu!" Aspar swore softly beneath his breath. "It is Basilicus."

"The empress's brother?" Cailin replied. "Did you invite him?"

"Of course not. He has obviously heard something, my little

love. He is a clever, and a sly fox. He has come with a purpose, you may be certain. I can only wonder at what it is."

"He is very handsome," she observed.

Aspar felt a twinge of jealousy at her words. He had no cause, he knew, to doubt her. She was simply making an observation, and yet he felt resentful. He did not want to share Cailin with anyone, he thought, as Basilicus finally reached them. "Is there some emergency that you invade my privacy?" he said ungraciously to his friend.

Basilicus was somewhat taken aback by the unfriendly tone of the general's voice. Dear lord! Caught between his sister's unbridled curiosity and the annoyance of the most powerful man in the empire. No one would envy him his position at this moment. "There is no emergency," he said. "I simply felt like a day in the country, Aspar. I did not believe my arrival would cause you to behave like a bear with a sore paw," Basilicus replied, put off but determined to remain.

"Your guest will be thirsty and hungry, my lord," Cailin said quietly. "I will go and make certain that Zeno has refreshments prepared." She nodded politely at the prince, and left the two men on the bench.

"What a glorious creature!" Basilicus said. "Who is she, and where, you fortunate man, did you find her?"

"Why are you here?" his companion demanded bluntly. "You detest the country, Basilicus. There is another reason, I know."

"Verina sent me," Basilicus admitted. Honesty always worked with Aspar, the prince knew. Besides, Aspar was not a man to trifle with, particularly when he was in a difficult mood such as now.

"Good lord! What does your sister want of me that she would send you to the country after me, Basilicus? Tell me! We will not return to the house until you do." Then Aspar chuckled, obviously finding humor in the situation. "Your poor body will soon go into shock, my friend. I do not believe it has been in the warmth of the sun in years."

"Verina heard that you had closed up your house in the city and moved out to your villa. She has also heard that you have taken a mistress. You know her curiosity is greater than most women's," Basilicus said to Aspar. "And, of course, she is Flacilla's friend."

"And she hopes to get me in her debt," Aspar observed wisely.

"How well you seem to know my sister," Basilicus said mockingly.

"I also know of the recent scandal involving my wife that the patriarch hushed up," Aspar replied. "I may be living in the country, Basilicus, but my channels of information have simply stretched a bit farther. There is little happening in the city that I do not know about. Because I am happy, and because my wife's relations have quieted the gossip surrounding her and her recent lovers, I am content to let the matter rest, lest my own arrangement be brought to light. You know as well as I do, Basilicus, that Flacilla is perfectly capable of creating a scandal around this villa and its inhabitants simply to deflect attention from her own outrageous behavior. Because she is not a happy woman, the idea that I should be happy would be galling to her. That is why I live here now rather than in the city. My conduct is subject to less scrutiny at Villa Mare, or so I believed until today."

"You do not seem to be living a very profligate life, Aspar," Basilicus observed as they now walked from the beach up the garden path to the villa. "Indeed, if I had not known you, I would have assumed you were simply a well-to-do gentleman and his wife. Now tell me, before I die of curiosity, who the girl is and where you found her."

"You do not recognize her, Basilicus?"

The prince shook his dark head. "No, I do not."

"Think back, my friend, to a night several months ago when you and I together visited the Villa Maxima to take in a notorious and particularly salacious entertainment that had the city agog," Aspar said.

Basilicus thought a moment, and then his dark eyes grew wide. "No!" he said. "It cannot be! Is it? You bought *that* girl? I do not believe it! That exquisite creature with you on the beach is patrician-born without a doubt. She cannot be the same girl!"

"She is," Aspar said, and then offered his friend a brief history of Cailin and how she had come to Villa Maxima.

"So you rescued her from a life of shame," Basilicus noted.

"What a soft heart you have, Aspar. It would be better that others, including my sister and your wife, not know it, I suspect."

"I am only softhearted where Cailin is concerned," the general told his friend. "She makes me happy, and is more a wife to me than Flacilla has ever been. Anna would have liked her, too."

"You are in love," Basilicus accused, almost enviously.

Aspar said nothing, but neither did he deny the charge.

"What will you do, my old friend?" Basilicus asked. "You will not be content to live in the shadows with your Cailin for very long, I know."

"Perhaps I will seek a divorce from Flacilla," Aspar said. "The patriarch cannot deny me, particularly given this recent scandal she has caused. It is past time she was shut up in a convent. She is a constant embarrassment to her family. Eventually she will do something so mad that they will not be able to cover up her behavior."

They walked across the portico facing the sea, and into the interior garden of the villa, where chilled wine and honey cakes awaited them. Cailin was nowhere to be seen, and they were served by a silent slave who, at a sign from his master, withdrew to allow them privacy.

"Even if you were allowed to divorce Flacilla Strabo," Basilicus observed, "you would never be allowed to marry a woman who had begun her life in Constantinople as performer in the city's most notorious brothel. Surely you realize that, Aspar. You must realize it!"

"Cailin is a patrician, born into one of Rome's oldest and most distinguished families," Aspar argued. "Her tenure at Villa Maxima was not of her own making. She was not used as a common whore, and she only performed in that obscene playlet less than a dozen times. My God, Basilicus, there were women in the audience the night I first saw her who were coupling with slave boys, and all were of good family."

The prince sighed. "I cannot argue with your logic, but neither can you argue with the plain facts. Yes, there were women of distinguished families seeking illicit entertainment, *but* they were not performing for the delectation of several hundred people twice weekly. Even my sister could be moved by Cailin's story, but she would still not approve a marriage between you. Besides, the girl is a pagan."

"She could be baptized, Basilicus, by the patriarch himself, ensuring that I would have an Orthodox wife, and children," Aspar said.

"You are living in a fool's paradise, my old friend," the prince told him. "You are too important to Byzantium to be allowed this romantic folly, and you will not be, I assure you. Keep the girl as your mistress, and continue to be discreet. It is all you will be allowed, but at least you will be together, Aspar. I will not tell my sister of your other desires. They would frighten her, for they are so unlike you."

"I am the most powerful man in Byzantium, the king-maker, they say, and yet I cannot have my own happiness," Aspar said bitterly. He swallowed several gulps of wine. "I must remain married to a highborn bitch who whores among the lower classes, but I must not marry my highborn mistress because for a short time she was forced into carnal slavery."

"Have you freed her?" Basilicus asked.

"Of course," Aspar answered. "I told Cailin she would be freed legally upon my death, but actually she is free now. I feared she might leave me if she knew the truth, although she is really quite helpless. She wants to return to her native Britain to avenge herself upon the woman who sent her into slavery, but how could she do it without help? And who would help her? Only those seeking to take advantage of her."

"And besides," Basilicus said gently, "you love her. Do not regret what you cannot have, Aspar. Take what you can have. You have Cailin, and she is yours for as long as you desire her. No one will deny you your mistress, even if Flacilla protests to the heavens over it. The court knows your wife for what she really is, and no one would seek to see you unhappy. Do you understand what I am saying to you, Aspar?"

The general nodded bleakly. "I understand. What will you tell your sister, Basilicus? It must be enough to keep her content."

He laughed. "Yes, Verina is more curious than a cat. Well, I shall tell her that you have taken a charming, beautiful mistress to your bed, and are living quite contentedly with her at Villa Mare in order to avoid any scandal, or public argument with Flacilla. She will think you justified despite her *friendship* with your wife, and that will be the end of it, I suspect. Verina thinks I do not lie to her, although I find I must sometimes in order to protect her, or to protect myself." The prince chuckled. "Besides, I shall not be lying. I shall simply not be telling her the entire truth. But then she really does not need to know the whole story, does she?" He grinned at Aspar.

"I do not know why Leo does not use you in the diplomatic service," Aspar said, his gray eyes twinkling.

"My brother-in-law does not trust me," Basilicus replied. "He also does not like me, I fear. His high office has turned him from a dull little man into a dull little man who grows more righteous and more pious as each day passes. The priests adore him, Aspar. You had best watch that quarter lest they convince Leo of his own infallibility, and that generals are unnecessary to God's grand design for Byzantium."

"You may not like Leo, or he you," Aspar said, "but he is the perfect man to be emperor, and he possesses more common sense than you would suspect. For now he lacks ego, although eventually, as with all men in power, the ego will rear its ugly head to cause him difficulties. He loves Byzantium, Basilicus, and is a good administrator. I chose the right man, and the priests know I did. Although they forced me into that little bargain to gain their most vocal support, they are content with Leo, and so are the people. Marcian gave us prosperity, and more peace than we had had in many years. Leo is his most worthy heir."

"I would think you would not care much for peace," the prince said.

Aspar laughed. "Twenty, thirty years ago I could not get enough of war, but now I have had my fill. I am in the twilight of my life. I wish nothing more than to live in peace here with Cailin."

"May God grant you that wish, Aspar, my friend. It seems a very little wish to me," Basilicus told the general. "Now, am I to be introduced to that exquisite girl, or must I return to my sister's with the news I neither saw nor spoke with this divine creature who has made you depart your palace in Constantinople?"

Chapter

10

I *s she beautiful?*" the empress demanded of her brother.
"Outrageously so," Basilicus replied, smiling. He had left
Villa Mare in early afternoon of the same day he had arrived, hur-
rying back to the city to report to his eagerly waiting sister.

"Fair of skin?" Verina asked.

"Her skin is as white and as smooth as a marble statue, my
dear."

"What color are her eyes?"

"It depends upon the light," Basilicus told his sister. "Sometimes they are like twin amethysts, and at other times they appear
like early spring violets," he reported poetically.

"And her hair?" Verina was growing more intrigued as her
brother spoke. Basilicus was not a man to lavish praise easily.

"Her hair is auburn, a mass of little ringlets that fall to just below her hips. She wears it loose, and it is most charming."

"Do not tell me," the empress said. "Her curls are natural, I am
certain. How fortunate she is, but who is she, Basilicus?"

"A young patrician widow of Roman ancestry from Britain," he answered serenely. "She is most charming, Verina, and she loves Aspar. If you saw them together, you would assume them to be a happily married couple."

"How did this woman arrive in Byzantium, my brother? A widow, you say? Was her husband a Byzantine? Does she have children? Come now, Basilicus, you are not telling me everything you know." The empress looked sharply at her brother.

"Her husband was a Saxon, I am told. Their child was lost to them. I have absolutely no idea how she came to Byzantium. Really, Verina, it was embarrassing enough cross-examining Aspar for you simply to satisfy your childish curiosity. I have done my best and will do no more!" he huffed.

"How old is Aspar's little mistress, and what is her name?" the empress pressed him. "Certainly you know that much."

"The girl is nineteen, and her name is Cailin," Basilicus answered.

"*Nineteen?*" Verina winced. "Poor Flacilla!"

"Flacilla deserves whatever she gets," snapped Basilicus, eager to escape his sister's questioning before he told her something he should not tell her. For some reason, Verina was making him very anxious. She knew something, but he did not know what she knew. He shifted nervously.

Verina saw her brother's discomfort. "I had a visitor this morning, brother dear," she said sweetly. *Too sweetly.* "I probably should not confide this to you. Men are so foolish about these things, but since you are obviously holding something back from me, I must tell you so that you will speak freely to me. You know that Leo rarely visits my bed any longer. He listens to his clerics who declare women unclean, a necessary evil for reproduction who should otherwise be avoided. I do not know how he thinks we will get a son unless we couple. It is all very well for the priests to tell him to pray for an heir, but there is more to getting a child than just prayer!" The empress flushed irritably, but then she continued smoothly.

"I dare not take a lover yet to satisfy my own needs. The church considers a woman's natural urges evil. I have no real privacy, and I am constantly watched, as you know. I have thought about it for some time, and it finally came to me! If I am to entice my husband back to my bed, I must take drastic action! I realize I am not supposed to know of things like this, but we have, I am told, several very fine brothels in Constantinople. I decided to engage a courtesan to teach me the erotic arts so that I might lure Leo into doing his duty by us both."

"You did what?" Basilicus gasped, totally stunned by his sister's revelation. A good Byzantine wife was not supposed to be aware of such things. He did not know whether to be shocked or amused by what she had done.

"I hired a courtesan to help me become more sensual," Verina repeated. "Flacilla helped me. She sometimes visits a place called Villa Maxima. It has wonderful entertainments, and marvelous young men for hire as lovers, she tells me. Do you know it, Basilicus?" And while he gaped at her in wonder, she answered her own question, "Of course you know Villa Maxima, brother dear. You are one of its distinguished patrons on occasion.

"One of those occasions was several months ago when you visited the place in the company of our good general. There was a particularly notorious and most lewd entertainment being performed twice weekly that had the entire city talking of its perversity. Flacilla says it was wonderful! I wish that I had been able to see it, but how could I go to such a place, even in disguise? Someone would be certain to recognize me."

He nodded. "It would be unwise, indeed, Verina," he told her.

She smiled at him, and then took up the thread of her story. "The courtesan sent to me is a lovely creature named Casia. It is she who told me that Aspar had purchased from the owners of the brothel the female member of that depraved entertainment. *A young patrician widow of Roman ancestry from Britain?* Really, Basilicus!"

"She is precisely as I have described her to you, Verina. I did not think it necessary to reveal her unhappy months in slavery, a condition that came about through nothing of her making. Aspar freed her immediately after he purchased her. He recognized her patrician blood and felt sorry for her. Now he is in love with Cailin!"

"I cannot believe that you would lie to me, brother," the empress pouted.

"I did not lie to you, Verina," the prince said irritably.

"You did not tell me all that you had learned. I cannot forgive you for it."

"I did not tell you because I did not want to embarrass Cailin, Verina. Aspar would not have told me but that I recognized her. It is an episode that both of them would like to put behind them," Basilicus said. "All they desire is to live quietly together at Villa Mare." Then he grew serious. "Leo will never be so safe that you do not need Aspar, sister mine. Offend Aspar, and God knows what might happen to you, and your family. The empire is relatively stable right now, but one never knows when something may set the masses to rebellion and discontent.

"I will tell Aspar that you know his secret, and how you learned it. You will keep that secret, and by doing so our general will be deeply in your debt, Verina. That is far more valuable to you than any momentary satisfaction you might gain by revealing all this to Flacilla Strabo."

The empress considered her brother's words, and then she nodded. "Yes, you are correct, Basilicus. Aspar's goodwill is far more important to us than that of his whorish wife. She has a new lover now, you know, and this time she has chosen a man from among our own class."

"Did she tell you that?" Basilicus asked. "Who is it, Verina?"

"Justin Gabras! Scion of the great patrician family in Trebizond," the empress responded. "He is twenty-five, and said to be very handsome."

"What is he doing in Constantinople, and how has Flacilla intrigued him into a carnal liaison?" Basiclius wondered aloud, but seeing the sparkle in his sister's eye, he knew she would tell him everything.

"It is whispered," Verina began, "that Justin Gabras has a very quick temper. He has killed several people whom he believed offended him. His last victim, however, was a cousin of the bishop of Trebizond. It was necessary, I am told, to remove the murderer as quickly as possible from the scene. They say that the Gabras family was forced to pay the bishop's family a huge bounty for their relative's life. Justin Gabras was expelled from Trebizond for a period of five years.

"Already his reputation in Constantinople grows for its wickedness. He has bought an enormous mansion overlooking the Golden Horn, and an estate in the country. They say his parties and his entertainments rival those at the city's best brothels, Basilicus. Are you surprised that Flacilla should find him?"

"I am surprised that the church does not interfere," the prince said.

"His generosity to the patriarch's favorite causes has earned him a blind eye in that quarter," the empress told her brother knowledgeably.

"If this Justin Gabras is all you say he is, I think perhaps Flacilla has gotten in over her head this time," Basilicus noted.

"If she has, it might solve many problems," the empress observed wisely. "The Strabo family would no longer have to worry about Flacilla's behavior, nor would Aspar have to be burdened with her."

"And then he could marry his beloved Cailin," Basilicus said casually, looking to see what his sister would say.

"Marry the girl he found in a brothel? No, brother dear, it simply could not be allowed. He need not marry again at all, but it would never do for the First Patrician of the empire, Byzantium's greatest general, to marry a girl who worked in a brothel, no matter how blue her blood is. The empire would be a laughing stock, and we cannot have that," Verina said.

Of course, Basilicus thought sadly, they would never allow Aspar to marry Cailin. Had he not told his friend so? Still, when he had heard of Flacilla's latest lover, and his rather unsavory reputation, he had thought that just perhaps the empire would reward its favorite son with permission to marry the woman he loved, who would tend him with devotion and love in his old age. Basilicus thought of himself as a sophisticate, but sometimes even he longed for a simpler life.

⟨⟩

Autumn slipped into winter. The winds blew from the north, and at Villa Mare the shutters upon the portico were drawn tight, while the braziers filled with charcoal warmed the rooms on cold days. Cailin and Aspar lived quietly. They seemed to have a need only for each other. There were no further visitors to the villa after Basilicus's surprise arrival that autumn day. They preferred it that way.

Aspar spent several days each week in the city attending to his duties. He saw his eldest son, Ardiburius, quite often, and one day in the senate Ardiburius boldly asked his father, "Why did you close our palace?"

"Because I prefer living in the country," Aspar replied.

"They say you have a young mistress with you," Ardiburius said.

A small smile touched Aspar's lips, but was quickly gone. "*They* are correct," he told his son. "Unlike your stepmother, I prefer to conduct my affair in a discreet manner. Cailin is a gentle girl, and prefers the country to the city. It pleases me to please her."

Ardiburius swallowed hard. "Do you care for her, Father?"

Aspar stared at his son, wondering just where this was leading. Finally he said, "Yes, I do, and your mother would have liked her, too."

"You do not love the lady Flacilla?"

"No, Ardiburius, I do not. I would have thought that obvious to you from the beginning. The marriage was political. I needed the patriarch's approval of Leo, and I gained it by taking Flacilla off her family's hands," Aspar said. "What is it you want to tell me, my son? You have never been a man for this many words. You are a soldier, as I am. Speak!"

"You must remove Patricius from the lady Flacilla's care, Father. He should not remain in her house any longer," Ardiburius said.

"*Why?*" The word was sharp.

"She has a very evil lover, Father. A man of wealth and great family. He has, I have it on the most reliable authority, debauched children as young as eight. Patricius is almost ten, and grows more beautiful every day. He is a charming child, as you know, and always eager to please. Your wife's lover has not yet violated him, but he has of late shown an interest in Patricius that is not healthy. My source is totally reliable, Father. My little brother must be protected."

"You and Zoe must take him, then," Aspar said. "Sophia is not used to little boys, and he lacks respect for her. Patricius adores you, Ardiburius, and your wife knows well how to deal with rambunctious little boys. I will tell Flacilla that Patricius needs the company of other children, and as there are none in her house, I have decided to give him to you and Zoe. It will not seem like a criticism if I handle it that way. Hopefully her *new* interest will keep her amused, so she will not take offense. You know I cannot bring Patricius to Villa Mare. Cailin, of course, would adore it. She is meant to be a mother, but it would cause the very reaction I seek to avoid—a scandal. You understand, my son?"

"Yes, Father," Ardiburius said. "Will you take Patricius today? It should be done as quickly as possible. I have already discussed the possibility of his coming to us with my family. Your grandson, David, is delighted to have his uncle join us. Being the eldest with two sisters after him, and his brother just a baby, it is hard for him."

"You spoil him," Aspar growled, "but he seems a good lad despite it. He is six now, is he not? He and Patricius will get on quite well." He sighed gustily. "As much as I detest having to meet with Flacilla, I shall go now and fetch Patricius from her. Go home, Ardiburius, and tell Zoe that he will be coming to you by nightfall."

The general left the senate and, mounting his horse, rode unescorted through the streets of the city to his wife's home. He needed no guard to keep him safe, and many recognized him, calling out to him, wishing him well. The gatekeeper at Flacilla's mansion greeted him pleasantly, and the majordomo, after hurrying

forward to welcome him, sent a slave to his mistress to announce
her husband's arrival.

Flacilla Strabo was a beautiful woman. Small and delicate, she
possessed gorgeous blond hair and sea-green eyes. She had been
entertaining her lover when news of her husband's sudden and totally unexpected visit was brought to her. "Damn him!" she said
irritably. "How like Aspar to come without any forewarning. My
God! What if he has heard about us? He threatened to put me in
St. Barbara's if I caused any new scandal, and my family will support him if he does!"

Justin Gabras smiled lazily at her from the couch where he was
reclining. A single black curl fell directly in the center of his forehead. He was tall and lean, and had dark eyes that seemed fathom-
less. "I would very much regret losing you, Flacilla," he drawled.

"You must leave now!" she said fearfully as the silent slave
stood waiting for her instructions to take back to the majordomo.

Reaching out, Justin Gabras yanked Flacilla down into his lap,
pulled the neckline of her chiton as low as he could, and lifting a
plump breast out, began to fondle it vigorously. "Have your husband come in, Flacilla. I am very much looking forward to meeting
him. His fame as the empire's general precedes him. I do not believe I have ever really met a truly brave man, but Aspar is said to
be one."

She struggled to escape him. "Are you mad?" she gasped as he
lowered his head and he began to suckle strongly on her nipple. In
answer, Justin Gabras bit sharply down on Flacilla's tingling breast,
causing her to cry out. His eyes met hers, and Flacilla said weakly
to the slave, "Have my husband join us here on the terrace,
Marco." Then she gasped again as her lover slipped a hand beneath her gown, slid it quickly up her leg and began to tease at her
little jewel. She moaned desperately, knowing that he would not
cease until she gave him complete satisfaction, and that it would
not matter in the least to him if Aspar walked in and found them
in such a compromising attitude. Justin Gabras was the most per-
verse man she had ever known, and even though she was some-

times frightened of him, she could not resist him. "Ahhhhhh!" she moaned as he forced her to completion.

He laughed, releasing her, and watched as Flacilla quickly straightened her garments and attempted to regain her composure. "He was probably on the stairs even as I made you obey me," he mocked her. "Did you think of him coming toward us as I played with you, my pet?"

"You are a wicked man," she said, now angry that he had frightened her so greatly. "You love danger, but you involved me in it then."

"And you loved it, Flacilla," he mocked her. "You are the perfect woman for me. You have breeding, and you are a very skilled whore. As your husband is leaving us today, I will have another little surprise in store for you, my pet. Does it excite you to think on it?"

Before she could answer, however, Aspar came out onto the terrace. Flacilla arose and came forward to greet him. "My lord, why did you not tell me you were coming? Patricius will be so delighted to see you. He has been doing very well at his studies lately, his tutors say."

"I apologize for interrupting you, and your guest, Flacilla," Aspar said with a hint of censure in his voice.

She heard it, and quickly replied, "This is Justin Gabras, a gentleman from Trebizond, my lord. He is now making his home in the city. The patriarch has asked him to help me in a project to aid the poor. We were just discussing it when you arrived. Will you join us?"

A small amused smile touched Aspar's lips, but it was quickly gone. "I have come for Patricius," he said. "I have decided to send him to live with Ardiburius and Zoe. You have been a good mother to him, Flacilla, but he is at an age now where he needs the company of other children. My grandson David is just slightly younger than Patricius, and will benefit as well from their shared companionship. Since both my elder son and daughter-in-law follow the Orthodox faith, Patricius will, of course, continue in that instruction. Will you send for him?"

Flacilla was astounded, and frankly curious as to his apparently sudden decision, but she nodded. Calling a servant, she gave instructions that the boy be brought to them. "May I see Patricius on occasion, my lord?" she asked her husband. "I have grown fond of the child."

"Of course," he said, smiling. "You are always welcome at my elder son's home to visit Patricius. He is fond of you also, I know."

Justin Gabras was fascinated. He had never seen two more poorly matched people. He would be sorry to see the boy go, too. Only recently he had begun to consider what an appetizing little tidbit the child would be. As Patricius was sweet-natured, and eager to please, seducing him would have been a simple matter. And afterward he would have taught him how to please his lusty stepmother as well. Bad luck, he thought, an opportunity lost, but another will appear.

The general and his wife had grown silent, for they had little if nothing to say to each other. Aspar looked like a dull fellow, Justin Gabras thought. Brilliant in the field, but boring in the bedchamber. Flacilla politely offered wine, and then mercifully the boy came.

"Father!" Aspar's youngest child ran into the room, his face joyful at the sight of the general. "What a grand surprise, Father!"

Aspar caught the boy in an embrace, and then stepping back, said, "You have grown again, lad! And the lady Flacilla says your tutors give good reports of your studies. You make me proud, and I have come with a surprise for you. You are to go and live with your brother and his wife. Your cousin David is most eager for your arrival."

"Ohh, Father! That is splendid news!" Patricius cried. "When am I to go?" Then his face fell, and turning toward Flacilla, he said almost apologetically, "I will miss you, lady. You have been good to me."

Flacilla smiled, but there was no warmth in it. "I think your father has made an excellent decision, Patricius. You should be with other children, and my household is long past children."

"If we left now, my lad, would that suit you?" Aspar asked his son. The boy nodded vigorously, and Aspar said to his wife, "Have old Marie pack my son's things up. You may send her and his tutors to Ardiburius's home tomorrow. Now, we will take our leave of you, my lady, and you may return to your business with this gentleman." He bowed politely to Flacilla first, and then to Justin Gabras. Taking Patricius's hand in his, they departed the terrace.

When they were safely out of hearing, Patricius said to his father, "I am glad to be going to my brother's house, Father. The lady Flacilla entertains too many gentlemen, and this latest fellow frightens me. He was always watching me."

"He did not touch you, or hurt you, my son, did he?"

"Oh no, Father!" the boy assured his parent. "I never let him come *that* close to me. Marie says he is a very bad man."

"You listen to your old nurse, Patricius. She loves you well," Aspar told his child. "Your mother picked her especially to care for you."

Upon the terrace, Flacilla watched through the latticed screen that topped one of the low walls as her husband and his child rode off down the wide street. Justin Gabras stood behind her, his hands upon her hips, plunging himself in and out of her woman's passage as she leaned upon the parapet. "It was so sudden," she said irritably. "How typical of Aspar to make this surprise visit with its surprise ending."

Her lover ground himself slowly into her, and bending over, whispered in her ear, "He thinks you no longer fit to watch over the child, my pet. Oh, he masked his intent with sweet words, but it was obvious to me what he was really thinking, Flacilla. What will the gossips make of it, I wonder, for it will certainly provide grist for their mills."

She felt her crisis approaching, and moaned hungrily, thrusting her hips back to meet him. "I will ... go ... to the empress!" she gasped.

Justin Gabras pushed Flacilla farther over so that she was almost bent double, enjoying her surprised scream as he moved from her temple of Venus and jammed himself into the entry of her temple of Sodom. His hands held her firmly, stilling her feeble struggles as he leaned forward and bit her neck. "You will be the laughingstock of Constantinople, my pet. Everyone knows you for a whore, but now they will know you for a bad mother as well. Do you not ever wonder why your daughters do not visit you, Flacilla? Their husbands' families will not let them associate with you, I am told." His lust exploded into her aching body, and finally, with a satisfied groan, he withdrew from her.

Flacilla burst into tears. "Why do you tell me these lies?" she demanded of him.

"Because you have a delightful talent for perversion to match mine, my pet. You have barely scratched the surface of your own wickedness yet, but under my tutelage you will become a mistress of evil. Do not weep. You are too old to do so publicly; and your face is getting puffy. 'Tis most unattractive. I do not lie to you, Flacilla, when I say you are the perfect woman for me. I want to marry you. You have powerful family connections, and if I must remain here in Constantinople, then I want a wife such as you, my dear. A young girl would bore me. She would whine and complain about my tastes. You, however, will not, will you?"

"You would let me take lovers?" she asked him nervously.

"Of course," he said, laughing, "for I will take lovers, too." He took her hand and they lay together upon the couch. "Think of it, Flacilla! Think of what we could share together, and with no recriminations on either side. We could even share lovers. You know I enjoy both women and men as you do. Shall we go to Villa Maxima tonight and choose a lover to share? What about one of those wonderful dumb Northmen Jovian so favors? Or perhaps Casia is more to your taste? What say you?"

"Let me think," she said. "Ohh, I wish that girl that Jovian featured in the first of his playlets was still here. She was so beautiful, but she disappeared very quickly. You did not see the performance, of course, not having yet come to Constantinople, but the girl took all three of those Northmen into her body at one time! Jovian never allowed anyone else to have her, and then suddenly she was gone. He would never explain what had happened to her. I think she may have killed herself. She did not look like a whore."

"Let us have all three of the Northmen, then, Flacilla. You shall play the girl's part for me, and we shall have Casia as well," he said, kissing her quickly. "It will be a celebration of our engagement."

Flacilla sat up. "My family would never allow me to divorce Aspar and marry you," she said. "They value Aspar's influence too much. Though they forced him to wed me in order to gain their support for Leo, they have gotten much through his influence, Justin. They will not easily give all that up."

"Do not ask your family, Flacilla. Ask your husband for a divorce. I suspect he wants to ask you for one, and removing his child from your care is his first step along the road to ridding himself of you. Once again Aspar will embarrass you and hold you up to ridicule. Strike first, my pet! I doubt he cares as long as he is rid of you."

"What if he refuses me?" she said. "You never know with Aspar."

"Then you can go to your family," Justin replied. "Your husband is not a god, Flacilla. There must be some weakness of his you can play upon. Have you learned nothing in the time you were married to him?"

"Actually," she admitted, "I know little of him. We have never lived together, nor slept together. He is an enigma to me."

"Then you must spy upon him to learn what we need to know, my pet, for I will have you, or no one will!" He kissed her hard.

After a night of particularly wild debauchery, Flacilla awoke clear-headed and determined. "Send a messenger to my husband's palace," she told her majordomo, "and say that I wish to visit him this morning. I shall arrive before the noon hour."

"The general is not at his palace, my lady," the majordomo said. "He closed his palace up some months ago, and lives at Villa Mare now. Shall I send a messenger to the country to inform him you are coming, my lady? The villa is just five miles beyond the gates."

"No," Flacilla said. "Do not bother. I will simply go. By the time a messenger went and returned, I could be there myself. Have my litter made ready." She dismissed the majordomo and called her maids.

Wanting to make a good impression, Flacilla chose her garments carefully. Her stola was blue-green in color, and matched her eyes. It was shot through with gold threads, and the fabric was very rich. The sleeves were long and tight, and the garment was belted at the waist with a wide gold belt that was most flattering. Her gold slippers were beautifully bejeweled, and her hair was a mass of golden braids, fastened high and decorated with jewels. A matching cloak lined in fur completed her outfit. Flacilla stared hard at herself in the polished silver mirror. Then she smiled, well-pleased. Aspar would be impressed.

Her bearers hurried along the Mese and through the Golden Gate. The day was pleasant, and she could see through the bit of drapery she left open the cattle grazing in the fallow fields. Here and there peasants were pruning trees in the orchards that occasionally lined the road. It was a soothing and most pastoral scene, Flacilla thought, if not just perhaps a bit boring. Why was Aspar living in the country? The litter turned into the gates of the Villa Mare, and entering the courtyard, came to a stop. The vehicle was set down and the curtains drawn back. A hand was extended to help her out.

"Who are you?" Flacilla demanded of the elderly servant.

"I am Zeno, General Aspar's majordomo," was the polite reply.

"I am the lady Flacilla, the general's wife. Please tell him that I have arrived," she said grandly, "and you may show me into the atrium now, Zeno, and bring me some wine."

Zeno was horrified, but his face did not show his consternation. "If my lady will follow me," he said calmly.

It was a charming little villa, Flacilla thought. She had never been here before. A bit too rustic for her taste, but peaceful. She could not, however, understand why Aspar would prefer it to his palace in the city. Making herself comfortable upon a marble bench, she sat down to wait for her wine and for her husband to make an appearance.

Aspar arrived before her refreshment. His greeting was less than cordial. "What are you doing here, Flacilla? What could have possibly brought you into the country on a winter's morning at so early an hour?" He looked distinctly uncomfortable, and she wondered why. Then it dawned upon Flacilla that her husband, the morally upright Aspar, had taken a mistress. He was living with her and wanted no one to know of it. Why, the old fox! Flacilla almost laughed aloud. "I have come on a matter of some importance," she began, swallowing to conceal her amusement.

"Yes?" he said, shifting on his feet.

"I want a divorce, Aspar!" Flacilla burst out. This was no time to be coy. She didn't give a damn if he had one or a hundred mistresses tucked away here in the country. She had been twice wed to please her family. Now she wanted to marry for her own sake.

"You want a divorce?" His look was almost incredulously comical.

"Ohh, Aspar," she said with utmost candor, her words tumbling out quickly, "our marriage was one of politics. You got what you wanted—the support of the patriarch and the Strabo family in Leo's behalf. I got what I thought I could live with, being the wife of the most powerful man in Byzantium. But ours has been no true marriage. We detested each other on sight! We have never spent a single night, including our wedding night, in the same bed, or under the same roof. You do not really want me. You have even taken Patricius from my care.

"Well, I am no longer a girl, and for the first time in my life I am in love. I want to marry Justin Gabras, and he wants to marry me. Let me have a divorce, and in exchange I will be your eyes and ears in Verina's court. Verina is very ambitious for both herself and Leo. She would dispose of you if she thought she could, and one day she may think to do so. If I am there for you, you will have no unpleasant surprises to contend with from that quarter. It is a fair offer!"

He was astounded. If they both wanted the divorce, then the patriarch could hardly contest them, and the Strabos could not be offended. "Yes," he said slowly. "It is a fair offer, Flacilla. Why did you not speak to me about this yesterday when I came for Patricius?"

"Justin asked me the same thing," Flacilla lied, "but as I told him, I was so distraught by Patricius's departure that I was not thinking clearly; and then you were gone with the child. I promised him, however, that I would come to you this very day and settle the matter."

"I have brought wine, my lord." Zeno had reappeared. He set the goblets and the carafe on a small inlaid table.

"You need not bother to pour," Aspar said. "I will. Return to your *duties*," he finished meaningfully, hoping Zeno understood.

"*At once*, my lord," was the emphasized reply, but at that moment disaster descended as Cailin entered the atrium.

"I have been told we have guests, my lord," she said.

Flacilla Strabo's mouth dropped open. She stared hard at the girl, and then managed to gasp, "*You! It is you!*"

Cailin looked confused. "Lady, do I know you?" she replied.

"*You are the girl from Villa Maxima!* Do not bother to deny it! I recognize you!" Flacilla shrieked, and then she began to laugh. "Ohh, Aspar," she chortled, "you were faithful to Anna, and then waited years past the time when most men take a mistress. Now, in the twilight of your years, you choose one, and she is the most notorious girl in all of Byzantium! You will give me my divorce, and we will call the matter even. If you do not, I shall tell the world of your whore, and then you will be the laughingstock of the empire. Your usefulness will be over, and where will your power be? You will be helpless! I can scarcely believe my good fortune! *The girl from Villa Maxima!*"

"Who is this coarse creature, my lord?" Cailin said icily.

"*Coarse? Me?*" Flacilla glared angrily at the girl. God! She was so young!

"May I present my wife, Flacilla Strabo," Aspar said formally. What an incredible piece of bad luck that Cailin should come into the atrium before Zeno could find her and warn her off. Well, it could not be helped. He would have to make the best of it. He looked at Flacilla. "I was not aware that you patronized Villa Maxima."

"Occasionally," Flacilla answered carefully. "Jovian's little playlet was the rage of the city early last summer. She does not look like a whore, Aspar."

"I am not," Cailin replied sharply. "My blood is nobler than yours, lady. I am a Drusus of the great Roman family."

"Rome is finished. It has been for eons, and since Attila pillaged it several years ago, there is little of any consequence left, including its families. This is the center of the world now," Flacilla sneered.

"Do not boast so proudly, lady," Cailin returned. "This center of the world you so loftily hail is as rotten as an egg that has lain in the sun all day. In Britain we do not debase our women before an audience of lewd and cheering lechers! You should be ashamed to admit to what you saw, but why should it surprise me? Even your priests came to see Jovian's entertainments. The outward beauty of your city cannot make up for the darkness in your hearts and souls. I pity you."

"Will you allow this slave to speak to me so?" Flacilla demanded. She glared angrily at Aspar. "I am still your wife, and will have respect!"

"Cailin is not a slave," Aspar said quietly. "I freed her months ago. She is your equal, Flacilla, and may speak to you as she chooses." He took Cailin's hand in his and then continued, "I will give you your divorce, Flacilla. I will go with you myself to the patriarch, and we will tell him of our wishes. I have no quarrel with you, and never have had. If you have found happiness, as I have found it, then I wish you well, and will do whatever I can to ensure your good fortune."

Flacilla's anger was almost immediately tempered. "That is most generous of you, my lord," she said slowly.

"There is one condition," he told her. "You will not gossip about Cailin's past, Flacilla. You must swear to me that you will be silent, or I will not acquiesce in this matter. A divorce is more to your advantage, my dear *wife*, than it is to mine. And you will still be my eyes and ears at Verina's court. Those are my terms. Will you swear?"

"Why is this more to my advantage than to yours, Aspar?" Flacilla said.

"You wish to marry Justin Gabras, do you not? You cannot marry him without a divorce. I, on the other hand, will never be permitted to marry Cailin because of her unusual beginnings in Constantinople. The fact that I keep her with me as my mistress is not a crime, nor is it considered unique for a man of my position. Whether you are my wife or not, Flacilla, Cailin will remain my mistress; but to marry your lover, my dear, you must be free of me. So it is more to your advantage that I agree to divorce you than it is to mine. Would you not say I am correct?" He smiled at her in a friendly manner, cocking his head to one side questioningly. "Well, Flacilla, what say you, my dear?"

She nodded. "As always, Aspar, you are correct. I must tell you that I have ever found this trait of yours most irritating, however. Very well, I swear on the body of our crucified Lord that I will not gossip or speak ill of your little barbarian pagan lover. I rarely give my word, as you know. You also know you may trust that word."

"I do, Flacilla," he said. "Now when would you like to meet with your cousin, the patriarch? I am at your disposal in this matter."

"Let us do it today!" she said eagerly. "Let us simply call upon him, without warning. If we take him unawares, he is more likely to cooperate than if he sits down with his council of bishops and they natter on about the matter. I know just the argument to sway him, Aspar."

"Go on ahead of me," he told her. "I will ride, and catch up with you before you even reach the city gates. Allow me to escort you to your litter, Flacilla. Cailin, remain here."

"I am content to do so," she said, and he heard ice in her tone.

Aspar walked with his wife to where her litter awaited her.

"What a pity you cannot marry her," Flacilla said wickedly. "She loves you like Anna did, and is obviously meant to be a good wife; but she has spirit, like I do. The perfect mate, Aspar, and you cannot have her. It hardly seems fair after all your service to the empire," Flacilla mocked him. "Tsk! Tsk!"

He smiled, unaffected by her cruel barbs, more concerned with Cailin, whom he knew was going to be furious with him for not telling her that she was already a free woman. "It will be as God wills it, my dear," he replied smoothly, spoiling Flacilla's obvious glee as he helped her into her luxurious litter. "I will be with you as quickly as I can." Closing the curtains of the vehicle smartly, he told the bearers, "Take the lady Flacilla to the palace of the patriarch at once." Then Aspar turned about and went back into the atrium of his villa.

Cailin was pacing around the fish pond. She whirled at the sound of his step and shouted at him, "How could you keep such a thing from me, my lord? Or was it a lie told simply to annoy that dreadful creature?"

"It is true," he said. "You have been a free woman again since that day I promised it to you. I could not tell you the whole truth, Cailin. I am not a young man, but God help me, I love you! I feared if I told you that you were free, you would leave me; that you would attempt some foolish flight back to Britain, and end up in a worse situation than the one from which I rescued you."

For a moment pity welled in her eyes, but it was quickly gone. "Oh, Aspar," she said to him. "Do you not know that I love you also? Until you found me, and yes, even for a time afterward, I dreamed of returning to Britain to avenge myself upon Antonia Porcius. But what good would it do me? Would vengeance return me to my family? My husband? My child? I do not think so. Antonia's revenge certainly did not return Quintus to her. Wulf Ironfist will have found himself another wife by now. Perhaps they even have a child. He husbands the lands that were once my family's. My return would bring but unhappiness to all involved. It is a new age for Britain, and it would seem that I am not meant to be a part of it. This is where my fate has brought me, and here I will remain, by your side and in your heart as long as you will have me, Aspar." She surprised herself with her own words, but even as she had spoken them, she realized it was time to put her dreams aside and face reality. It was unlikely that she would ever see Britain again.

"They will not let us marry, Cailin," he said sadly.

"Who? Your Christian priests? I am not a Christian, Aspar. I am, what was it your wife called me? A pagan. Do you remember the old words of the Roman marriage? Perhaps you do not, but divorce Flacilla, and I will teach them to you that we may say them to each other. Then whatever others may say, we will be bound together for all eternity, my dearest lord," Cailin promised him. Slipping her arms about him, she pressed herself hard against him and kissed him with all the passion her young soul could muster. Then looking up at him, she said, "And you will *never*, ever again keep things from me, or tell me half-truths, my darling lord, or I shall be very, very angry. You have not yet seen my wild temper in full force, and you do not wish to, I promise you!"

She astounded him, and the happiness filling him would only allow him to say, "You love me? *You love me!*" He caught her up in his arms and swung her about happily. "Cailin loves me!"

"Put me down!" she said, laughing. "You will have the servants thinking that you have lost your wits entirely, my lord."

"Just my heart, my love, and that you will keep safe for me, I know it!" He placed her gently upon her feet.

"Go to Constantinople now, my lord, and convince those you must to rid you of that harpy you wed for expediency's sake," Cailin told him. "I will eagerly await your return."

"I will legalize any children you bear me," he promised her.

"I know you will do the just thing," she replied. "Now go!"

He did not even have to give orders. Zeno appeared to inform his master that his horse was saddled and awaiting him in the courtyard. Aspar laughed aloud. It was a conspiracy, he thought to himself. His servants adored Cailin and would do whatever they must to ensure both her happiness and his. He rode off down the road to the city, eventually catching up with Flacilla's litter. Together they traveled the rest of the distance to the patriarch's palace, where they were admitted immediately and announced to Constantinople's religious leader.

The patriarch looked warily at the couple before him. "And to what do I owe the pleasure of seeing you both?" he murmured nervously.

"We want a divorce," Flacilla said bluntly. "Both Aspar and I are agreed upon it. You cannot refuse us. We have no marriage, and never have, my lord. We have not even cohabited once, and I have constantly betrayed my husband with men of low degree," she finished.

"*Constantly?*" Aspar said, one dark eyebrow arching quizzically.

"You rarely knew," Flacilla said smugly, and then she laughed almost ruefully. "They do not all end as scandalously as did the little episode of the gladiator and the actor, my lord."

The patriarch paled. "You knew of that unfortunate incident?" he asked Aspar.

"I knew," the general replied. "My sources are even better than yours are, my lord patriarch. I chose to overlook it."

"Because of your little mistress?" the patriarch countered, his black robes swirling about as he paced the room edgily. "You will never be permitted to marry her. Your prestige is too valuable to Byzantium, Flavius Aspar. Your behavior is tolerated because you have been discreet, but only for that reason. Go home, both of you."

"I have twice married for the good of my family," Flacilla said, taking up the argument. "I was content to remain a widow when my husband Constans died, but the Strabos would make me this man's wife. Well, I have served my purpose for them, and for you. Now I want to be happy with a man of my own choosing."

Her blue eyes glared fiercely at the patriarch. "Cousin, I wish to marry Justin Gabras, and he wishes to marry me. He is the first lover with whom I have been involved who is my equal. The Gabras family is, as you well know, the first family of Trebizond. The emperor is in your pocket now, and Aspar is the most loyal citizen in this land. You need fear neither of them. I would be far more useful as Justin Gabras's wife, as this should give you an important toehold in Trebizond. Refuse us, and we will cause such a scandal that neither you nor this emperor will survive it! I mean it, cousin, and you know that I am capable of such destruction," Flacilla finished threateningly.

"You are content to allow this marriage?" the patriarch said feebly to Aspar, but even as he spoke he knew that Aspar undoubtedly considered this situation a pure stroke of luck.

"I have no quarrel with Flacilla," Aspar replied smoothly. "If this marriage can make her happy, why should we refuse her, my lord? To what purpose? She is correct about the Gabras family, and they would, I suspect, even be grateful to Flacilla. Her lover has never before married, and a marriage may settle his rather erratic personality. That would certainly reflect well on the Strabos, and upon you. And if marriage does not settle him, we are, none of us, any the worse off." He shrugged. "As for my situation, I will continue to remain discreet. Little can be said about an unmarried man who keeps a mistress and is faithful to her, my lord. It is small reward I ask for all my services to the empire."

"She must be baptized," the patriarch said. "We can tolerate a Christian mistress, Flavius Aspar, but never a pagan. I will choose a priest myself for her instruction, and when he tells me she is ready to receive the sacrament, I will baptize her myself into the true Orthodox faith of Byzantium. Will you accept my decision in this matter?"

"I will," Aspar said, wondering just how he was going to explain it to Cailin. She would find it very irrational, but in the end he knew she would do it to please him, and because it was the only way that their relationship would be tolerated by the powers that be.

The patriarch turned to Flacilla. "You will have your divorce, cousin, and before your Strabo family relations even know it. I do not intend to argue with them over this matter. Choose a wedding date, and I will personally marry you to Justin Gabras. It is to be done, however, privately and with a little decorum, Flacilla. I will not allow either of you to make a circus of this matter. And afterward you will hostess a family party to properly celebrate this new union. There will be no orgy. Do you understand? Will Justin Gabras understand?"

"It will be as you desire, my lord patriarch," Flacilla said meekly.

The cleric laughed humorlessly. "If it is," he said, "then it will be the first time you ever really obeyed me, *cousin.*"

Chapter

11

S*pring always came sooner* to Byzantium than it did to
Britain, Cailin noted, not displeased by the early display of
flowering trees in Aspar's orchards. The general was a good master,
as each peasant she met was quick to assure her. While many on
neighboring estates were worn down by the incredible taxation
placed on the farmers by the imperial government, Aspar paid the
taxes imposed on his people so that they would not have to leave
their own small bits of land. Taxes unfortunately could not be paid
in kind. They had to be paid in gold, yet the price of all produce
and farm animals was strictly regulated by the government, making
it nearly impossible for freedmen to meet their obligations. The
government kept these prices artificially low to satisfy the populace. Many small farmers attached to other estates had practically
sold themselves into serfdom to their overlords so that they and
their families might just survive.

"If you had no farmers," Cailin said to her lover, "where would
we get our foodstuffs? Does the government not consider that?
Why are the merchants taxed so little, and the farmers so much?"

"For the same reason ships docking in the Golden Horn are only charged two solidi on their arrival, but fifteen solidi on their departure. The government wants luxury goods and staples brought into the city, but not traded away out of it. That is why the merchants are charged such low taxes. Someone has to make up the deficit. Since the farmers have no choice but to farm the land, and are so scattered throughout the country they cannot unite and complain, the heaviest burden of taxation falls upon them," Aspar told her. "Governments have always acted thusly, for there is always someone willing to farm the land."

"That is totally illogical," Cailin responded. "It is the luxury goods that should be taxed, and not the poor souls who supply the necessities of everyday life! Who makes such foolish laws?"

"The senate," he said, smiling at her outrage. "You see, my love, the bulk of the luxury goods are sold to the ruling class, and the very rich have a strong aversion to heavy taxation. The government keeps the majority of the populace content by regulating the price of everything that is sold. The poor farmers, a minority, can cry out all they want. Their voices will not be heard in either the senate or in the palace. Only when the majority of the people threaten rebellion do those in power listen, and then not particularly closely, but just enough to save their own skins," Aspar finished cynically.

"If they tax the farmers out of existence," Cailin persisted, "who will grow the food? Has the government considered that?"

"The powerful will grow the food, using slave labor," he said.

"That is why you pay your tenants' taxes, isn't it?"

"Free men are happier men," Aspar said, "and happier men produce far more than those who are not happy, or free."

"There is so much beauty here," Cailin said slowly, "and yet so much wickedness and decay. I miss my homeland. Life in Britain was simpler, and the boundaries of our survival were more clearly defined, even if we had not the luxuries of Byzantium, my dear lord."

"Your thoughts are complex even for a wise man," he replied, taking her hand and kissing the inside of her wrist. "Your heart is great, Cailin Drusus, but you must accept the fact you are only a woman. There is little you can do to right the world's ills, my love."

"Yet Father Michael tells me that I am my brother's keeper," she answered him cleverly, and he smiled at her tenacity. "This Christianity of yours is interesting, Aspar, but its adherents do not always do what they preach a good Christian should do, my lord. I like your Jesus, but I think he would not like some of the ways in which his teachings are interpreted by those who claim to speak in his name. I have been taught that one of the commandments handed down says that we shall not kill our fellow man, and yet we do, Aspar. We kill for foolish reasons, which is worse. A man does not worship as we think he should worship, and so we kill him. A man is of a different race or tribe than we are, so we kill him! This is not, I think, what Jesus meant. Here in Byzantium there is so much evil amid so much piety. Yet that evil is ignored by even those in the highest places who proudly worship in the Hagia Sophia, and then run off to commit adultery, or cheat their business associates. It is all very confusing."

"Do you tell Father Michael of your thoughts and concerns?" he asked her, not knowing if he should be truly amused or fearful for her.

"No," she said. "He is too intense in his religious fervor, and very bound up with the correctness of his worship. He says that I am far from ready for baptism, which is, I think, a good thing, Aspar. A good Christian woman, it is said, must either be a wife or go to live in a convent. I am told I cannot be your wife, and I certainly have no desire to live a cloistered existence. Therefore, once I accept the rite of baptism, I must either leave you or be forever damned. It is not a particularly broad choice, my lord, that is offered me." Cailin's violet eyes twinkled with amusement. Then she slipped her arms about his neck and kissed him slowly. "I am going to avoid baptism as long as I can, my lord."

"Good!" he answered her. "It will give me time to overcome this ridiculous notion that we cannot be married. Flacilla whored all over Byzantium, and was allowed to wed Justin Gabras, but you, my love, who in your innocence was cruelly abused, are denied the right to marry. It is not a situation that is to be tolerated, and I will not tolerate it!"

"We are together, and that is enough for me, Aspar," Cailin told him. "I want nothing more than to be by your side for eternity."

"How would you like to go to the games with me in May?" he asked her. "Special games are held each May eleventh to commemorate the founding of the city of Constantinople. My box is right next to the imperial box. Have you ever seen chariot races, Cailin? The Hippodrome has the finest course in all Byzantium."

"If you are seen in public with me, will that not cause a scandal?" she asked him. "I do not think it wise, my lord."

"There is nothing unusual about a man bringing his mistress to the games, particularly a bachelor such as myself," Aspar answered. "Casia, the girl you knew at Villa Maxima, is now Basilicus's lover. He has given her her own home in the city, and visits her regularly. We will ask her to join us, as well as some of the city's more famous artisans and actors. I am known to keep such company, to the despair of the court, but frankly, those who create are far more interesting to me than those who govern and intrigue." He chuckled. "We will fill the box with interesting people, and few will know just who is who."

"Perhaps it would be nice to see other people," Cailin observed. "When you are away on your official duties, I grow lonely sometimes."

Her admission startled him, for she had never complained about her solitude before. Aspar had never considered that she might be weary of being companionless.

Several days later Zeno was sent to the city, and when he returned, he brought with him a young girl with large, frightened blue eyes, and flaxen braids.

"The master thought you would like a young maidservant to keep you company," Zeno said, smiling. "We are all so old here, but you, lady, are like springtime, and need a fair flower to serve and amuse you. She speaks no language I can understand, lady, but she seems pleasant and biddable."

Cailin smiled at the girl and then asked, "From where does she come, Zeno? If I knew, perhaps I might find a language in which we could communicate. If I cannot speak with her, then all my lord's good intentions are for naught."

"The slave merchant said she comes from Britain!" Zeno said triumphantly. "Surely you can communicate with her, my lady."

"Yet she speaks no Latin," Cailin mused to herself. She turned to the young girl. "What is your name?" she asked in her own native Celtic tongue. If the girl didn't speak Latin, she must speak Celtic.

"Nellwyn, lady," the girl said slowly.

"Are you Celt?" Cailin said.

The girl shook her head. "Saxon, lady, but I understand the tongue you speak. I come from the Saxon shore, and there are many Celts there."

"How came you to Byzantium?" Cailin continued.

"*Byzantium?*" Nellwyn looked confused. "What is Byzantium, lady?"

"This place, this land. It is called Byzantium. The city in which you were in is its capital, Constantinople by name," Cailin explained.

"Northmen raided our village," Nellwyn told her. "My parents and my brothers were slaughtered. My sisters and I and the other women who could not escape were carried off. They took us to Gaul first, and then we traveled by sea again to come here. Many died on the way. The sea was horrible!"

"Yes, I know," Cailin said. "I came to Byzantium almost two years ago from Britain in a similar fashion. My home was near Corinium."

The girl's eyes grew wide. "Are you a slave, too?"

"No longer," Cailin replied.

"Is this your house, lady?" Nellwyn recognized quality when she saw it, and this beautiful woman was obviously nobility.

"No," Cailin told her. "It is the house of Flavius Aspar, Byzantium's most famous warrior, and a great nobleman." There was no need to explain anything else. Nellwyn would soon figure it out, if indeed she had not already. "My lord has brought you to be a companion to me, Nellwyn. You are safe now, and need fear no longer. Do you understand?"

"Yes, lady," Nellwyn replied, kneeling before Cailin. "I will serve you loyally, I swear by Woden!"

"I am pleased to hear it," Cailin said. "Now get up girl, and go with Zeno, who is master of the servants in this house. He will show you where you are to sleep, Nellwyn. You will have to learn the language spoken in this land, or it will be difficult for you, I fear. The tongue is called Latin. Many spoke it in Britain."

"I have heard the words of that tongue," Nellwyn answered. "I have a good ear, my father always said, and learned Celtic quickly. I am sure I will learn Latin as well, lady, and make you proud of me."

"Good! Now, whatever Zeno tells you to do, you must obey him," Cailin explained to the girl. Then she turned to her major-domo. "She has some words of Latin, and claims she can learn quickly, Zeno. See she is given a bath. She smells like a stable. Then give her fresh clothing and a sleeping space. She may come to me in the morning, and I will assign her duties and begin to teach her myself."

The elderly servant bowed and, signaling to the girl, led her off. Very shortly he returned, however, and said bluntly, "She will not let us bathe her, my lady. She screams like a rabbit in a trap."

"I will come," Cailin said, and followed him to the servants' quarters, where Nellwyn, naked now, stood sobbing piteously. "Come, girl, you must wash," Cailin scolded her. "In this land we bathe with regularity. Your pretty hair will be crawling with lice, I've not a doubt, and must be cleaned, too. Follow Tamar to the bath now!"

"They would drown me, lady!" Nellwyn wept. "I know how to wash, but properly in a basin, not with all that water!"

Cailin swallowed her laughter. "In Byzantium we wash with lots of water," she explained. "Now you must trust me, Nellwyn, and obey me when I command you, for I am your new mistress. Go with Tamar."

Reluctantly the girl obeyed, casting a teary glance over her shoulder as she followed the older woman into the servant's bath.

"It is a pretty toy you have given me, my lord," Cailin told Aspar that evening as they ate. "She speaks no Latin, and I must teach her; is afraid to bathe, but she appears sweet-tempered and eager to learn."

"You said you were lonely. She is young as you are young, my beauty. She will keep you amused when I am away," he responded, smiling.

"She is thirteen, and believed she was about to be drowned in the servant's bathing pool." Cailin giggled. "Where did you find her?"

"I asked a slave merchant I know to find me a young female Briton," he said.

"She is a Saxon from the Saxon shore of Britain," Cailin told him.

"Then she is not one of your people," he remarked, irritated at himself. "I should have been more specific with the slave merchant."

"Celts are usually harder to catch," Cailin said, a twinkle in her eyes, "and they do not take well to service, my lord. Nellwyn will suit me admirably. Saxon girls are generally good-natured."

"Then I have pleased you," he replied, smiling at her.

"You always please me, my lord," she answered him softly.

"No," he said sadly, "I do not, Cailin. I wish I could."

"The fault lies with me, Aspar. You know it does! It breaks my heart that I can no longer feel passion when a man is within my woman's passage," Cailin said, tears filling her lovely eyes. "Yet I do gain a different kind of pleasure when we lie together. Your touch is so filled with love for me that it communicates itself to my very heart, and I am filled with happiness and peace. It is enough for me. I could but wish it was enough for you. It hurts me to know that I have failed you in this manner, but I know not what to do to change things. I have not that wisdom, my beloved lord." She lay her head on his shoulder and sighed forlornly. How could she care so for this good man, Cailin wondered, and be unable to completely return his passion?

"I love you for many reasons," he told her, "but your truthfulness in all things pleases me greatly. I would have no whore's tricks from you, Cailin; no simulated cries of passion ringing in my ears. Some day you will cry out for me, but that cry will come from your heart. I will wait until that time. Perhaps not always with patience, but I will wait." He arose from the table and held out his hand to her. "The night is fair, and there is a moon. Let us walk together, my love."

There was no wind, and the night was quiet around them. They walked first through the nearby orchards of almond, peach, and apricot trees with their fragrant pink and white blossoms, some of which were already beginning to drift down to catch in Cailin's myriad auburn curls.

"These trees are far prettier than the olive groves," Cailin said. "I do not like the yellowish flowers upon those trees."

"But the olive is far more practical a fruit," he told her. "The peaches and apricots are quickly gone. The olives, properly prepared, last all year. What is beautiful is not always practical."

"Almonds are beautiful," she countered, "and they last every bit as long as olives, even longer, and they do not have to be salted."

He laughed. "Too intelligent," he teased her. "You are too intelligent for a woman. No wonder you frighten Father Michael."

"Everything frightens Father Michael that is of this world," Cailin told him. As they left the orchards behind and came across a small field to the beach, she cried softly, "Ohh, Aspar! Look at the moon on the sea! Is it not the most beautiful thing you have ever seen?"

It was one of those rare moments when the restless waves were totally stilled. The flat dark surface of the water was silvered, and shimmered like the best silk as it spread itself before them. They stood silently admiring the beauty of it all. It was as if the entire world were at peace with itself and they were the only two creatures inhabiting it. Aspar reached out and took Cailin's hand in his. Together they walked down the little embankment to the beach.

Removing his cloak, he spread it upon the sand for them. Then taking her into his arms, he kissed her softly, lingeringly. When he finally released her, Cailin wordlessly pulled her stola over her head and let the garment drop from her slender fingers. Naked, she stood proudly before him. He responded by removing the long, comfortable tunic he wore within his home, and kicked his sandals off. Then Aspar slipped to his knees before her, drawing her against him, his cheek pressed against her torso.

They embraced quietly for a long moment. Then he began to trace a pattern of warm kisses across her flesh. Cailin sighed softly. His patience and his gentleness always astounded her. How very much she wanted to respond to his loving, but passion, it seemed, was dead, or almost dead within her. The only time she felt the slightest bit of it was when he would tongue her little jewel, but when his manhood lay embedded inside of her, she could feel nothing at all but the thickness of it within her. In an effort to resurrect her passion, she had tried to remember all her times with Wulf Ironfist; but she soon realized that recalling her Saxon husband only seemed to render her body, and soul, colder than before. Several times she had come close to shrieking her frustration and pushing Aspar away because he was not Wulf and could not give her the joy she had once known in her husband's strong arms. Finally she had dismissed Wulf from her conscious mind while her Byzantine lord made love to her. It was easier that way.

Aspar rubbed his face between her breasts, one hand reaching up to fondle her. "They are like perfect little ivory apples," he said, his palm cupping the firm flesh and admiring it. Gently, his other hand pressed upon her back, and when she bent slightly, he lifted his head up to suckle upon the nipple. His teeth teased at the sensitive nub, and then his tongue encircled it enticingly before he suckled hard on it again.

"Ahhhhh," she breathed, her fingers digging lightly into his muscled shoulders. He transferred his attentions to her other breast, his hand kneading and cuddling until she felt as if her breasts would burst with pleasure.

He then pressed the palm of his hand against her Venus mont as he began a leisurely exploration with lips and tongue of her slender torso. Each kiss upon her tingling skin was distinct and individual. His other hand was lightly clasped about her right buttock, the tips of his fingers caressing her. His tongue pushed into her navel, and Cailin murmured softly as it simulated what was to soon come. As if to emphasize the point, he pushed through her nether lips with a single finger and thrust it into her sheath.

Cailin's head whirled and her knees began to buckle. He felt her weakness, and withdrawing the finger, he pulled her to her knees, facing him. Aspar's dark eyes locked onto hers as he offered her his finger, running it sensuously over her lips until she opened her mouth and sucked on it, clutching at his hand until he pulled the finger away and caressed her throat. She lowered her head and bit his hand lightly, surprising him, then kissed his knuckles.

Something is different tonight, Cailin thought, and looking up at him, she realized that he could feel it too. She did not dare speak for fear of breaking the spell that seemed to be enfolding them. He took her by the shoulders, and his lips touched hers in what had been meant to be a tender kiss. The kiss, however, deepened quickly, and her mouth opened to take in his tongue, which danced primitively and hotly with hers. Then he was covering her face with kisses again, and Cailin's head fell back, her neck straining almost desperately as his lips burned their way down the perfumed column of her throat.

She stroked his hot, hard body. Her fingers entwined themselves deep within his thick black hair as she fell back upon his spread cloak. He moved his mouth slowly, almost with reluctance, down her body until his tongue found the delicate and sensitive jewel of her womanhood, rousing it to melting sweetness with a stronger force than she had ever before felt. Then his soldier's body was covering hers, his engorged manhood pressing forward to sheath itself within her. Cailin gasped with surprise as she realized that for the first time in two years her body was anxious, nay, desperate, for a man's possession.

She shuddered with actual pleasure as he filled her. Her arms tightened about him, drawing him as close as she could, reveling in the feeling of him against her. Their eyes met even as he began to move slowly upon her. Cailin could not look away, nor, she realized, could he. Their very souls seemed to blend as the rhythm of his sensuous movement began to communicate the rising passion between them. He said nothing, but she could feel him willing her to wrap her legs about him, and she did. Then she began to match his thrusts with voluptuous, pleasure-seeking motions of her own. The cadence of their deep desire grew almost savage in its intensity, until both Cailin and Aspar were overcome by its tender violence.

She flew. Her spirit seemed to slip from her body and soar out over the still, silvery sea. She was one with the earth, and the sky, and the silken waters below. Nothing mattered but the sweetness enfolding them, cradling them warmly in its embrace. They were one together.

"*Aspar!*" she cried his name softly in his ear as she came slowly to herself once again, and then her vision cleared. She saw his dear face, his cheeks wet with tears. Cailin smiled happily at him, pulling his head down to kiss away those tears, realizing at the same time that she was weeping, too.

Finally they lay together upon his cloak, calm once more, their fingers entwined, and he said with a small attempt at humor, "If I had but known, my love, that making love to you upon the beach in the moonlight would result in such delight, I should have done it months ago. How much time we have wasted in our bed, and in the bath."

"We will waste time no more," she promised him, and when he leaned over to kiss her, her features were radiant. "Whatever prevented me from sharing passion with you before this night is now gone, my dear lord. I am like our mother, the earth, reborn with the springtime!"

If Aspar's love for Cailin had been restrained previously in consideration of her feelings, that love was now plainly visible to all who saw them together. Aspar became more determined than ever that Cailin should be his wife. "We will go to some country priest and have him marry us," he said firmly. "Once the rite is performed, what can they do? You must be my wife!"

"There is no one in the empire who does not know Flavius

Aspar," Cailin said quietly. "And there is no one who does not know of the patriarch's wishes in this matter. Even were I to become one of your Christians, my dear lord, I should not be allowed to become your wife. Those few brief months that I spent at Villa Maxima have destroyed my reputation."

⊰≫⊱

here must be some way in which I can convince the patriarch," Aspar said to Basilicus one afternoon as they came from the palace, where they had been conferring with the emperor. "Flacilla has married Justin Gabras, and the pair of them are the scandal of the city with their orgies and their parties, which rival anything the brothels can create. How can the patriarch justify such a union while denying me the opportunity to marry my Cailin, who is so good?"

"Her goodness does not enter into it, my friend," Basilicus replied. "And it is not just the patriarch. We have a law here in Byzantium that specifically forbids the union of a senator, or other person of high rank, with an actress or a whore, or any woman of lower rank. You would not be allowed to circumvent the law, Aspar. *Not even you.*"

"Cailin is a patrician," Aspar protested angrily.

"She says she is," Basilicus answered, "but who is to prove her truthful, or a liar? Here in Byzantium she was an actress in a brothel, performing sexual acts before an audience. That makes her ineligible to marry with the First Patrician of the empire, Flavius Aspar."

"Then I will leave the empire," Aspar said grimly. "I can no longer be content or useful if I am denied my wish in this matter."

Basilicus did not argue. Aspar would not leave Byzantium. His whole world was here, and he was not a young man. Besides, even based upon his brief acquaintance with Cailin, Basilicus felt she would not allow Aspar to do anything that could endanger his position, or his comfort.

"Casia tells me you have asked her to sit in your box at the games next week," the prince said, changing the subject. "It is kind of you, and I have said she may go, although it will cause a small scandal. Who else will you invite, my friend? Entertainers and artisans, I doubt not."

Aspar laughed. "Ahhh, yes," he said. "How could I, the empire's First Patrician and great general, dare to prefer those who create to those in power? Eh, Basilicus? But I do! And you are correct. Both Bellisarius and Apollodorus, the great classical actor and the masses' favorite comedian, will be in my box on May eleventh. And Anastasius, the singer and poet, as well as John Andronicus, the artist who does those marvelous ivory carvings, and Philippicus Arcadius, the sculptor. I have commissioned him to do a nude of Cailin for our garden. He will spend the summer at the villa. I have built him a studio in which to work, so he will not have to travel back and forth between the country and the city, nor worry about his daily needs, which my servants will see to. Your sister will enjoy that piece of gossip, Basilicus."

"Indeed she will," he admitted, and then he said, "Are not Bellisarius and Apollodorus dreadful rivals? I heard that they despised each other. Is it safe having them in the same box?"

"Their hatred has recently turned to love, or so I hear." Aspar chuckled. "There is another tidbit for our beloved empress Verina to chew upon."

"The gods! They haven't become lovers! But of course they have, or you would not say it," Basilicus exclaimed. They had reached his litter, and he climbed in, settling himself comfortably amid the pillows.

Aspar mounted his stallion, which had been tethered next to the prince's conveyance. "Is your wife coming to the games?"

Basilicus nodded mournfully. "Eudoxia would not miss a chance to seat herself in the imperial box, where she can be seen, admired, and bitterly envied by all of her friends and relations seated in the stands. I will be by her side as convention demands, but afterward when she goes to the palace to enjoy the banquet, I shall join my adorable Casia."

"Will not Eudoxia miss you at the banquet, Basilicus?"

"Nay" the prince replied. "She will be too busy sampling all the delicacies offered the imperial guests; and of course there is that young guardsman who has recently taken her eye. I believe she means to seduce him eventually, and I do want to give her the opportunity. If she is busy with her young man, then she will not wonder if I am busy somewhere else. Eudoxia rarely strays from her marital vows, and so when she does, I like to give her as clear a field as possible. She is an excellent wife, and mother to our children. I might add that her discretion in her little peccadillos is commendable, to say the least. There has never been the tiniest bit of scandal about her, which is certainly more than one can say about most patrician wives these days."

"How fortunate for you both," Aspar said dryly. He did not understand the kind of marriage that most of the nobility had. True, there were exceptions; couples who, like his late wife Anna and himself, kept to their vows of fidelity and loyalty. That was the kind of marriage he would share with Cailin one day.

"I am not needed in town until the games," he said to the prince. "I will see you then." He rode off down the Mese toward the Golden Gate as Basilicus ordered his bearers to take him to the house of his mistress, the fair Casia.

⇜⟐⇝

May *eleventh dawned clear and sunny.* It was a perfect day to celebrate the founding of Constantinople. Cailin dressed carefully, fully aware that she would be the subject of gossip. She wanted to make Aspar proud, and so she chose a stola of pale violet silk which complemented her eye color. The round neckline was low, but not immodestly so. The long sleeves were embroidered with wide gold bands showing flowers and leaves. The stola was belted just below her waist with a girdle of small gold plaques studded with pearls that sat neatly atop her hipbones. A delicate gold and violet shawl of brocatelle, known as a palla, would protect her from the burning rays of the sun. Nellwyn slipped little jeweled kid slippers onto her mistress's feet, and then stood up to view Cailin. Her eyes mirrored her approval.

"You'll look as good as that empress woman, lady," she said.

"Only if she has jewelry to rival Verina's," Aspar said as he came forward with a large ebony box. "These are for you, my love."

Cailin took the box he handed her, set it upon the table and opened it. Within was a beautifully bejeweled collar of gold, small diamonds, amethysts, and pearls. She stood stunned as he lifted it from its case and fastened it about her neck. It lay flat upon her chest, almost covering the skin her neckline revealed, and it made the stola look far richer than it truly was. "I have never seen anything so magnificent," Cailin said. "It is beautiful, my dear lord. Thank you!"

"There is more," he said quietly, and lifting out a pair of large pendant earrings, he handed them to her with a smile.

Cailin smiled tremulously back at him, and affixed the large single teardrop amethysts set in gold filigree to her ears. There were several bracelets in the box as well: two gold bangles set with diamonds and pearls, and a wide gold band with inlaid mosaic that glittered and glistened with the light. Finally there was a filigreed gold headband studded with amethysts and diamonds. Cailin fitted it over the sheer mauve-colored veil covering her hair, which she wore loose in deference to Aspar, who liked it that way.

"I will be the envy of every man in the Hippodrome today," he said sincerely. "You are the most beautiful woman in a city of beauties."

"I wish to be the envy of no one," Cailin told him honestly. "The last time I knew such happiness and contentment, the gods snatched it away from me. I lost everything I held dear. Now that I have found happiness again, I want to keep it, my lord. Do not boast lest the gods hear you and grow jealous of us."

"We will keep it," he said firmly, "and I will keep you safe."

Cailin traveled to the city in her comfortable litter while Aspar rode his big white stallion by her side. He was greeted by many people along the way. Cailin, watching from the security of her conveyance, felt her heart swell with her love for this great and good man. There was no doubt that Flavius Aspar was well-respected by ordinary citizens, not simply feared for his power and wealth.

They entered the city through the Golden Gate. This was Constantinople's ceremonial triumphal gate. Made of pristine white marble set into Theodosius's walls, the gate gained its name from the enormous burnished brass doors with which it was fitted. The elegant severity of the gate's architecture, and its splendid proportions, made it an object of admiration throughout the empire. Passing through the gate, they traveled slowly with the increasing crowds down the Mese to the Hippodrome.

At the Golden Gate they had been met by a troop of cavalry that had come to escort Aspar and his party along the broad main avenue of the city. As they surrounded Cailin's litter, she discreetly closed the silk curtains. She was well aware that she was the object of certain curiosity among the soldiers, but she could not allow them to stare boldly at her as if she were a common prostitute.

The Hippodrome could seat forty thousand people, and was an imitation of Rome's Circus Maximus. However, it had never hosted games quite as cruel as those in Rome, nor had it seen the martyrdom of innocents. It had been first built by the Roman emperor Septimus Severus, but remodeled by the great Byzantine emperor Constantine I. The entertainments it offered were varied. There was everything from animal baiting, theatrical amusements, and gladiators, to chariot racing, religious processions, state ceremonies, and the public torture of famous prisoners. Entry to the Hippodrome was gained by presenting a special token, and tokens were issued free in advance of the games to the populace who came to sit, regardless of class, upon the snowy marble tiers of seats.

In the center of the Hippodrome a line of monuments had been erected, forming what was called a spina. The spina indicated the division between the downward race course and the upward one. Among the monuments was the Serpent Column, which had been brought to Constantinople from the temple of Apollo in Delphi by Constantine I. The ancient column, made up of intertwined bronze snakes, had been given to the temple by thirty-one Greek cities in the year 479 B.C. It commemorated the victory of the Greeks over the Persians, and was presented to the gods with gratitude. Another monument that stood out was the Egyptian obelisk that Theodosius I had placed upon a sculptured base. It was carved on all four sides with scenes of imperial life, including one of Theodosius himself in the imperial box with his family and close friends, watching the games.

Cailin's litter was set down by a private gate to the arena on the eastern side. Aspar dismounted his stallion and proudly handed her from the vehicle. He knew that every man in the cavalry troop was eager to see the woman rumored to have captured his heart. A dainty jewel-encrusted gold sandal was put forth first as she stepped from the litter. Eyes widened. Knowing looks were exchanged by the soldiers, most not a little envious, and as the empire's First Patrician escorted his beautiful young mistress into the Hippodrome, a long, low whistle of admiration echoed behind them.

Aspar grinned, just as any small boy with a new and most admired toy would have, but Cailin scolded him softly.

"Shame on you, my lord! You need not look so delighted with yourself, as if you did something worthy of praise. All those randy young soldiers are wondering about is if it is your power, your wealth, or your skill as a lover that has gained you a young and pretty mistress. It is nothing to be proud of," she finished, looking indignant. "A decent woman would be shamed."

"But you are not considered a decent woman," he teased her. "Those randy young soldiers, as you call them, would envy me even more if they knew the passionate, wildly wanton creature you have recently become. My back is covered with weals that are a testament to your delicious newfound desire, my love. Ahh, yes, you do well to blush!" He chuckled. "But I am content to have you so utterly shameless in my behalf."

She was blushing, but she was also unable to restrain her laughter. His happiness at having been able to overcome the ice in which her soul had been so encased made her happy. "It is you who are shameless, my lord," she countered. "You preen like a peacock in full plumage, and you fully enjoyed displaying me to those young men." She giggled. "They all looked so surprised when they saw me. Is your reputation such that they did not think you capable of attracting a pretty woman? They should but know you as I do."

"If they did, my love, I should be called by a different name, and would have taken Jovian for my lover," he chuckled.

"*My lord!*" Cailin was overcome by another fit of mirth.

He led her up a flight of stairs, explaining as they went that this was the way to the two private boxes allowed in the Hippodrome other than the imperial box. "The patriarch's box is on the emperor's right hand, and the box of the First Patrician of the empire is on the emperor's left hand. I have come early so we will not cause a disturbance with an obvious entry. It would not do to have the crowds hail me before the emperor. We will slip quietly into the box, and then be on hand to greet our guests. The emperor will not come until the races are ready to begin. There will be four races this morning, and four in the afternoon. In between we will see other entertainments, and Zeno will come with our servants to bring us luncheon."

"I have never seen chariot races," Cailin said. "Who will be racing today? There was an amphitheater in Corinium for games, but my father never took us. He said the games were cruel."

"Some are," Aspar admitted, "but there will be no gladiators today, I have been told. There will be actors, and wrestlers, and more gentle amusements that do not take away from the racing. We have four chariot teams here in Constantinople, the Reds, the Whites, the Blues, and the Greens. They will be racing, and the passions they arouse in the collective breast of the populace is ofttimes terrifying. Wagers will be placed, and you are apt to see a fight or two between the adherents of a particular team and their rivals. You are safe in the box."

"Which team to do you favor, my lord?" she asked him.

"The Greens," he said. "They are the best, and the Blues come after them. The Reds and the Whites are nothing, though they try."

"Then I shall favor the Greens as well," Cailin said.

They had reached a small landing where the staircase divided into two sets of stairs, and taking the three steps up to their left, they entered Aspar's box. An awning of cloth of gold striped with purple roofed the box. There were comfortable marble chairs with silken cushions, and benches set about, all with a good view of the arena. The public stands were beginning to fill up, but no one noticed them, and a quick glance showed Cailin that the imperial party and the important religious personages were not yet in their boxes.

"There are no steps going to the emperor's box," she said to Aspar. "How does he enter it?"

"There are stairs directly into the box that lead from a tunnel beneath the palace walls," he told her. "It allows our emperor a quick exit should he find he needs it. I've always thought it an excellent place for an ambush, but there is really nothing one can do should that occur."

"Cailin!" A young woman had entered the box behind them.

Cailin turned and recognized Casia, looking particularly radiant in scarlet and gold silks. Cailin held out her hands in welcome. She had wondered how she would feel seeing Casia again, but the young woman had always been kind to her. "Fortune has smiled on you, I am told," she said, greeting Casia. "I am happy you could come."

"My lady Casia," Aspar said with a smile, and Cailin felt a surge of jealousy race through her. His eyes were too warm and too knowing.

"My lord, it is good to see you once again. I owe you a debt of gratitude for introducing me to my prince. I had not intended to buy my freedom from Villa Maxima until next year, but when the prince offered me his favor, I surprised my masters and purchased myself from them, that I might avail myself of the prince's munificence." Casia smiled warmly at them both, and settled herself comfortably next to Cailin.

Aspar bowed again and replied, "Then you are both happy with the arrangement, and for that I am glad, Casia. You are wise enough still, I trust, to look to your future? Princes are often fickle."

Casia laughed merrily. "I am a frugal woman, my lord. If Jovian and Phocas had had the slightest inkling of what I had saved during my three years with them, they would have set my price higher. They did not, however, and I came away quite comfortably fixed. The house in which I reside is also mine. I insisted. Basilicus understood, and was generous. I will not end my days in the streets like a foolish woman."

"I would be unhappy were it so," he answered her.

There was no time for Cailin to interrogate her lover, for the rest of their guests were entering the box, being introduced, and bowing over the ladies. Bellisarius, the famed classical actor, and his current lover, the ribald comic actor, Apollodorus, were first. Elegantly attired in white and gold dalmaticas, and both quite witty, they awed Cailin at first. She was not used to such men, but Casia chatted easily with them, trading gossip and insults as easily as if she had known them her entire life. Anastasius, the great Byzantine singer, arrived and spoke to them in a bare whisper, which was, Aspar explained to Cailin, his custom. Anastasius spoke little, if at all, saving his glorious voice for song.

John Andronicus, the ivory carver, and Arcadius, the sculptor, arrived almost simultaneously. The former was a shy man, but sweet-natured. He greeted his host and hostess politely. The latter was his opposite, a bold fellow with a bolder eye. "Casia I recognize, so it must be this ethereal beauty you want me to immortalize, my lord." Arcadius stared hard at Cailin. "The body, I can see," he continued, mentally stripping her clothes away, "is obviously every bit as beautiful as the face. You will make my summer a joy, lady, for there is nothing I love better than sculpting a lovely woman."

Aspar smiled, amused, as Cailin blushed again. "I thought her a perfect subject for your classical hands, Arcadius. She is Venus reborn," he said.

"I shall certainly gain more pleasure from the work you have commissioned me to do, my lord, than all the saints I have been sculpting as of late," the sculptor admitted.

Suddenly the crowd roared noisily, and the inhabitants of Aspar's box turned to see the emperor and his party entering their box. Leo had a severe yet serene face, but even in his elegant rich robes, one could not have called him distinguished or regal. It was Cailin's first glimpse of Byzantium's ruler, and she had to remember that Aspar had chosen this former member of his household staff for greatness because of his other qualities. The empress, however, was a different matter. She was a blazing star to her husband's calm moon. The rest of the royal party were made up of men and women among whom only Basilicus's face was familiar. The clergy in their black robes had already taken their place before the imperial party arrived, but Cailin had been too busy with her own guests to notice them before now.

After a few minutes' time Aspar said to Cailin, "Watch!"

Standing on a marble step placed at the front of his box, Emperor Leo raised a fold of his gold and purple robes and made the sign of the cross three times; facing first the center tier of seats, and then those to the right, and finally to the left, he blessed all those in the Hippodrome. Then reaching into his robes, he drew forth a white handkerchief which, Aspar whispered to Cailin, was called a mappa. Dropping the white silk square would signal the beginning of the games. The mappa fluttered from Leo's fingers.

The stable doors of the Hippodrome wall were pulled open, and the first of the four chariots to race drove out onto the course. The audience exploded into cheers. The charioteers, each controlling four spirited horses, were dressed in short, sleeveless leather tunics, which were held firmly in place by crossed leather belts. Around their calves were leather puttees. All were physically well-formed, and many handsome. The women called out to them, waving the colored ribbons of their favorite teams, and the charioteers, laughing with exuberance, grinned and waved back.

"Women should not be allowed at the games," the patriarch was heard to mutter darkly in his box. "It is immodest of them to be here."

"Women attended the games in Rome," a young priest rashly said.

"And look what has happened to Rome," the patriarch replied grimly, while around him the other clerics nodded and agreed.

"Have either of you ever been to the races before?" Arcadius asked Cailin and Casia, and when they replied in the negative, he said, "Then I will explain all to you. In which order the chariots line up is chosen by lot the day before. Each driver must circle the course seven times. See the stand down by the spina where the prefect in the old-fashioned toga is standing? Do you see the seven ostrich eggs upon the stand? They will be removed one by one as each round of the race is run. Usually a small silver palm is awarded the winner of each race, but because today commemorates the founding of our city, a golden crown of laurel leaves will be given the winning drivers of all but the last two races. There will be a fierce competition between the Greens and the Blues to see who takes home the most crowns. *Look!* They're off!"

The chariots thundered off around the race course. Within moments the horses were frothing at the mouth and sweat was flying off their shining flanks. Their drivers drove with a reckless abandon such as Cailin had never seen. At first it appeared that the race course was wide enough to accommodate all four vehicles, but Cailin shortly saw that in order to win, the drivers had to steer their chariots all over the course, this way and that, struggling to get ahead of their competitors. Sparks flew as wheels from opposing chariots clanged together gratingly, and the drivers used their whips not only on their horses, but on the other drivers in their path as well.

The crowd screamed itself hoarse as the Green team's chariot spun around the final turn on one wheel, almost tipping over but quickly righting itself, only to be cut off by the Blue team's chariot, which leapt ahead suddenly, crossing the finish line first by just a nose. Both chariots came to a halt, and the drivers of the Blue and Green teams immediately engaged in a violent fistfight. Pulled apart, they left the track shouting curses at one another as the chariots for the next race queued up and dashed off.

Cailin was delighted by the chariot races. A Celt in her soul, she had always admired good horseflesh; and the horses racing were the finest she had ever seen. "Where do those magnificent animals come from?" she asked Aspar. "I've never seen better. They are finer-boned than the horses in Britain, and they look high-spirited. Their speed and surefootedness is commendable."

"They come from the East," he told her, "and are highly prized."

"Does no one raise them here in Byzantium, my lord?" she wondered.

"Not to my knowledge, my love. Why are you so curious?"

"Could we not take some of your land, and instead of growing grain, put it into pasture in order to raise these horses? If they are so prized here, then certainly these animals would bring you a fine profit. The market for these beasts would be great, as it would be far more accessible to and less risky for the chariot teams than importing animals from the East. If we raised our own horses, they could see them grow from birth, and even choose early those whom they felt showed promise," Cailin concluded. "What think you, my lord?"

"I think she is brilliant!" Arcadius chimed in enthusiastically.

"We would have to find an excellent stallion, or two for breeding purposes, and we would need at least a dozen mares to start," Aspar thought aloud. "I would have to go to Syria myself to find the animals. We should allow no one there to realize our intent. The Syrians pride themselves on their fine horses, and their profitable export market. I can probably obtain young mares here and there by pretending I want them for the ladies in my family, who amuse themselves riding when in the country. Normally," he told Cailin, "women do not ride."

"The Greens have won the second race while you chattered," Casia chimed in. "The Blues are crying collusion, for the Reds and the Whites seemed to have made a decided effort to cut off the Blue team's driver at every turn, and he finished dead last."

Between each of the morning's four races there was a little entertainment as performed by mimes, acrobats, and finally a man with a troupe of amusing little dogs that leapt through hoops, did tumblesaults, and danced upon their hind legs to the music of a flute. These intervals were brief, but a much longer one came between the morning's races and those to be run in the afternoon. Then the emperor's box emptied, as did the patriarch's.

"Where are they going?" Cailin asked of no one in particular.

"To a small banquet that has been prepared for Leo and his invited guests," Aspar told her. "Look about you, my love. Everyone has brought food and is beginning to eat it; and here is Zeno with luncheon for our guests. As always, old friend, you are prompt."

"Aspar positively dotes upon you," Casia said in a low voice to Cailin as their luncheon was being set out. "You are very fortunate, my young friend, to have found such a man. The rumor is he would marry you if he could, but do not count upon it."

"I do not," Cailin said. "I dare not. I have grown to love Aspar, but still something deep within me warns of danger. Sometimes I can ignore that voice within, but at other times it nags, and frightens me so that I cannot sleep. Aspar does not know this. I would not distress him in any way. He loves me, Casia, and is so good to me."

"You are just fearful because the last time you allowed yourself to love a man with all your heart, you were cruelly separated from him, Cailin. It will not happen again." She accepted a goblet of wine offered her by the attending Zeno, and sipped it. "Ahh, Cyprian! Delicious!"

An imperial guardsman entered the box. "My lord general," he said politely. "The emperor requests that you join him at table."

"Thank the emperor," Aspar said, annoyed. Leo knew that he had guests of his own. "Tell him it would be impolite of me to leave my own invited guests, but that if he needs me, I will attend him afterward."

The guardsman bowed and had turned to go when Cailin said, "Wait!" She took Aspar's hands in her own and looked up at him. "Go, my lord, please go, if only for my sake. No matter how gently you couch your refusal, you will insult the emperor. I will entertain our guests until your return." She leaned over and gave him a gentle kiss upon the cheek. "Now go, and you will be pleasant and polite, not irritated."

Aspar arose reluctantly. "For your sake, my love, but only for your sake. You would not have me offend Leo, yet his invitation offends me because it ignores you, and the others with us."

"I do not exist for the emperor, nor does Casia. As for the others, they are artisans and actors. Sometimes invited, sometimes not," Cailin said wisely with a small smile. She was quickly learning the ways of Byzantium's society. "Go, that your return be all the sooner!"

"You have more breeding than most of the court," Arcadius said to her, arching a dark eyebrow. "You are not what you seem, I think."

Cailin smiled serenely. "I am what I am," she answered.

Arcadius chuckled, and seeing he would get no more from her today, turned his attention to the rather excellent ham upon his silver plate. He would learn what he wanted to know this summer when she posed for him.

Shortly after Aspar had departed the box, another imperial guardsman entered it, and bowing to Cailin, said. "Lady, you are to come with me, if you please."

"What is it you want?" she asked him. "And who has sent you?"

The guardsman was young, and he blushed at her frank scrutiny. "Lady," he agonized, "I cannot say. This is a private matter."

Before Cailin might speak again Casia leaned forward, allowing the young man a very good view of her full bosom. "Do you know who I am, young sir?" she purred at him. "My, my, you are such a handsome fellow!"

Arcadius snickered. Casia would have the information she wanted within a very short time by the look on the guardsman's face.

"Nay, lady, I do not know you," the young man replied nervously, unable to tear his eyes from her snowy white breasts. "Should I?"

"I am Prince Basilicus's special friend, young sir, and if you do not tell the lady Cailin who sent you, I shall tell my prince of your rudeness, and of how you violated me with your wicked brown eyes. *Now, speak!*"

The young guardsman guiltily raised his eyes. He reddened, and then he murmured low, "The empress, lady." Then looking anxiously at Cailin, he said, "She means you no harm, lady. She is a fine woman."

Both Casia and Arcadius laughed, causing the other guests in the box to look up from their food with curiosity.

Cailin arose. "Since you all know with whom I shall be, there is little to fear. I will go with you, young sir." Smoothing the wrinkles from her stola, she followed him from the box and down the staircase.

At the foot of the stairs was a small door in the entry wall, so cleverly hidden that Cailin had not noticed it before. The guardsman pressed the wall in a certain spot, and the door opened to reveal a second flight of steps. She hurried down them, following the young soldier. They entered what Cailin realized was the main corridor to the imperial box. The tunnel was well-lit with torches, and several feet down from where they had entered the guardsman stopped, and pressing upon the wall, revealed another door which sprang open at his touch. Before them was a room, and within it a woman who turned at the sound of the door opening.

"Come in," she said in a low, well-modulated voice. "Wait for us outside, John," she ordered the guardsman. "You have done well."

The door shut behind Cailin, who bowed politely to Verina.

"You do not look like a whore," the empress said frankly.

"I am not one," Cailin replied quietly.

"Yet you lived at Villa Maxima for several months, and took part in what I am told was one of the most notorious entertainments ever seen in this or any other city," Verina said. "If you are not a whore, then what exactly are you?"

"My name is Cailin Drusus, and I am a Briton. My family descends from the great Roman family. My ancestor, Flavius Drusus, was a tribune in the Fourteenth Gemina Legion, and came to Britain with the emperor Claudius. My father was Gaius Drusus Corinium. Almost two years ago I was kidnapped and sold into slavery. I was a wife and a mother when this happened. I was brought in a consignment of slaves to this city. Jovian Maxima bought me in the common market for four folles, lady. What he did with me you are obviously aware. My lord Aspar rescued me from that shameful captivity, and freed me," Cailin finished proudly.

Verina was fascinated. "You have the look of a patrician, and you speak well," she said. "You live as Aspar's mistress, don't you, Cailin Drusus? They say he loves you not just with his body, but with his heart as well. I did not think him capable of such a weakness."

"Is love then a weakness, majesty?" Cailin said softly.

"For those in power it is," the empress replied honestly. "Those in power must never have any weakness that can be exploited against them. Yes, love of a woman, of children, of any kind, is a weakness."

"Yet your priests teach that love conquers all," Cailin said.

"You are not a Christian, then?" Verina asked.

"Father Michael, who was sent to me by the patriarch, says that I am not yet ready to be baptized a Christian. He says I ask too many questions, and have not the proper humility for a woman. The apostle Paul, I have been told, said that women should humble themselves before men. I am afraid I am not humble enough," Cailin replied.

Verina laughed. "If most of us were not baptized as infants, we should never be, for we lack humility as well, Cailin Drusus, but you must be baptized if you are to become Aspar's wife. The general of the Eastern Armies cannot have a pagan for a wife. It will not be tolerated. Surely you can deceive this Father Michael into believing you have learned humility."

Aspar's wife? She could not have heard the empress correctly.

Verina saw the startled look on Cailin's beautiful face, and divined immediately what had caused it. "Yes," she told the surprised girl. "You heard me correctly. I said, '*Aspar's wife,*' Cailin Drusus."

"I have been told that it is impossible for me to attain such a status, majesty," Cailin said slowly. She had to think. "I have been told that there is a law in Byzantium forbidding marriages between the nobility and those who are actresses and entertainers. I have been told that the time I spent at Villa Maxima would negate my patrician birth."

"It is important to me," Verina answered her, "that I retain the goodwill and support of General Aspar. It is true that you came here as a slave and served as an entertainer in a brothel, Cailin Drusus, but you are a patrician. I have no doubts as to your lineage. I watched you this morning. Your manner is cultured, and you are obviously well-bred. I believe what you have told me of your background is true. Your time at Villa Maxima was short. Those who know of it will remain silent, *or* I will see that they are silenced when you become Aspar's wife. You do want to be his wife?"

Cailin nodded slowly, and then said, "What do you want of me, majesty? Such a favor will have a high price, I know."

Verina smiled archly. "You are wise to understand that, Cailin Drusus. Very well. I will help overcome the objections voiced to a marriage between you and General Aspar, if you, in return, will guarantee me his aid should I need it. And he must swear to me himself on the relic of the true cross that he is my man should I need him. I know you can convince him to do this in return for my help."

Cailin's heart was hammering. "This is not something that I can broach easily," she said. "I will speak with him in a few days' time, majesty, but how will I be able to communicate my success or failure to you? For now I do not even exist as far as your world is concerned. If I did, you would have invited me to your banquet, not just Aspar, who had to be separated from me so you and I could meet secretly here beneath the walls of the Hippodrome."

"It is so refreshing to have someone speak openly and honestly," the empress said. "Here at Byzantium's court everyone couches their words in hidden meaning; and motives are often so complex as to be unknown. Speak with your lord, and in a few days' time I will come one afternoon by sea, with a few trusted companions, to visit the general's summer villa. If anyone learns of my visit, it will be thought I am merely curious, and it will cause no scandal. Leo is a very righteous man, and I am a most loyal helpmate. If he learns of my excursion, he will naturally assume I have been led astray by my companions; an assumption I will not correct. Such occurrences have happened before." She smiled meaningfully.

"I will do my very best for you, majesty," Cailin said.

The empress laughed. "I have no doubt that you will, my dear. After all, both our future happiness depends on your being successful, and I am a bad enemy to have, I promise you; but we must get back. If I stay too long away from the banquet, my absence will be noted." Verina went to the door and opened it, saying, "John, return this lady to her box, and then take up your post as before. Farewell, Cailin Drusus."

Cailin bowed politely and backed from the room. As she followed the guardsman along the tunnel and up the two flights of stairs, her mind was awhirl with the events of the last few minutes. Reentering her box, she was accosted by an eager Casia.

"What did *she* want?" Casia whispered, and Arcadius leaned over to hear Cailin's answer.

"She was but curious," Cailin said with a smile. "How very dull her life must be that she was that curious about Aspar's mistress."

"Ohh," Casia sighed, disappointed, but Arcadius could see that Cailin simply chose not to tell the other woman all that had transpired. It was obviously going to be a most interesting summer.

Below them half a dozen jugglers were amusing the restless crowds by parading around the raceway balancing various colored balls in the air above them. They were followed by a marvelous procession of exotic animals. Aspar returned to the box and, slipping into the seat next Cailin, put an arm about her. Casia looked to Arcadius with a smug little smile, and he grinned back.

"Ohhhh!" Cailin squealed. "I have never seen beasts like those! What are they? And striped ones, too! There are two kinds!"

"The great gray mammoths with the long noses are called elephants," Aspar told her. "History tells us that the great Carthaginian general Hannibal crossed over the Alps to win many victories on the backs of elephants. The striped cats are called tigers. They come from India, a land far to the east of Byzantium. The striped horses are zebras."

"The tall spotted creatures, my lord, and the funny beasts with humps? What are they?"

"The first are giraffes. They are from Africa originally, but all these creatures live in the imperial zoo now. Foreign countries are always gifting us with rare animals for our zoo. The other animals are camels."

"They are wonderful," she said, her eyes shining, her excitement very much like that of a child. "I have never seen beasts like this before. In Britain we have deer, rabbits, wolves, foxes, badgers, hedgehogs, and other common creatures, but nothing like elephants!"

"Ahhh," Arcadius sighed dramatically. "To see Byzantium afresh through Cailin Drusus's marvelous violet eyes."

"Violent eyes? Who has violent eyes?" demanded Apollodorus, the comedian.

"*Violet*, you shameless comic!" Arcadius snapped. "Cailin Drusus has violet-colored eyes. Look at them! They are beautiful."

"Women's eyes never tell the truth," Apollodorus said wickedly.

"Not so!" Casia cried.

"Do *you* tell the truth when you look into a man's eyes?" the comic demanded. "Courtesans are hardly noted for their veracity."

"*And actors are?*" Casia replied scathingly.

Anastasius, the singer, chuckled softly at her reply. It was the first sound Cailin believed he had made since entering the box.

"The emperor is returning," John Andronicus, the ivory carver, warned the combatants. He, too, had said little since joining them.

Cailin now took the opportunity to speak with him. "We have one of your charming pieces at the villa," she told him. "It is lovely: Venus, surrounded by a group of winged cupids."

"One of my earlier pieces," the carver admitted, smiling shyly. "Nowadays I do mostly religious works for the churches. It is a very lucrative market, and it is my way of returning the gift that God has generously given me, lady. I am doing a nativity for the emperor right now."

"May I join you?" Prince Basilicus said, slipping discreetly into the general's box. "Casia, my love! You look delicious enough to eat! And I shall, *later*." He blew a kiss at her.

"What of your wife Eudoxia, my friend? You should not embarrass her," Aspar reprimanded the prince sternly.

"Her little friend is on duty in the imperial box," Basilicus said with a grin. "She wants time to flirt with him, and can hardly do so with me hovering by her side. Besides, Flacilla and Justin Gabras are also in the emperor's box. See. There they are on the far side. I do not know why Leo allows them in his presence, but probably he did not invite them. My sister undoubtedly did. They are really a dreadful pair, Aspar. Their parties, I am told, are so depraved that the inhabitants of Sodom and Gomorrah would blush. What is worse is that they are so happy. Flacilla has truly found a mate worthy of her. They are awful in their perfection together."

"Very well, you may stay, but be discreet," Aspar warned.

"I am happy to see you, my lord," Cailin said, smiling.

"Lady, you grow more beautiful with each passing minute," the prince gallantly responded. "I can tell you are happy, and he is happy, too." Basilicus then turned to Casia. "How lovely you look today, my pet. Scarlet and gold suits you well. We will have to see how rubies set in gold look against your soft, fair skin, eh?"

The races began anew, the four horse teams kicking the sandy floor of the Hippodrome as they careened and skidded down the course in their quest for victory. In the morning the Greens had taken two races, the Blue one, and the Reds the final race. Now the White team took the first of the afternoon's contests, and then the Blues had a second victory, tying them with the Green team. But the day was to go to the Greens. Victorious in the last two races, they accepted from Leo's own hands an aurigarion, which was a gold emblem, a silver helmet, and a silver belt. The crowds, who had already screamed themselves hoarse, howled their approval anew, and the games were formally concluded as the imperial box emptied of its inhabitants.

Suddenly those people in the seats nearest to Aspar saw the green ribbons he carried and took up the cry. *"Aspar! Aspar! Aspar!"* A small look of annoyance passed quickly over Aspar's face, but it was swiftly gone. Turning, he acknowledged the crowd's cheers with a friendly wave of his hand that was enough to satisfy them, but not enough to encourage further homage or admiration from the citizens of the city.

"How politic you are," Basilicus mocked him. "This little incident will, of course, be reported to Leo, magnified with proper embellishments naturally, and the poor man will be torn between his gratitude to you and his fear that you may one day displace him." The prince laughed.

"Leo knows that I prefer being a private citizen to being an emperor," Aspar said. "Should he ever doubt it, I will reassure him once again on the matter. Frankly, if he would let me, I should retire."

"Not you," Basilicus said with a broad chuckle. "You will die in service to Byzantium. Casia, my angel, have you something delicious for my supper? I am coming with you."

"You are not going to the palace for the celebratory banquet?" Aspar asked his friend. "I know you said earlier you would not, but is not your presence mandatory?"

"I will not be missed, I assure you, my friend," the prince replied. "Besides, the patriarch is invited. He will pray over the food for so long that it will be inedible when he is done, and hardly worth being thankful for at all," he finished with a chuckle.

"I will take better care of him, my lord," Casia said, "and his meal will be precisely to his liking, will it not, my prince?"

Basilicus's eyes glittered wickedly in agreement.

Casia turned to Cailin. "May I come and see you one day? I am so pleased that you included me in your party today. We have both come a distance since our days at Villa Maxima."

"Of course you may come," Cailin said sincerely. "I have been quite alone at Villa Mare when my lord is away, though I have just obtained a young Saxon slave girl who keeps me company. I love to listen to your gossip, Casia. You seem to know everything that is going on in Constantinople. I admit to being happier in the country, however."

"The country is pleasant to visit," Casia responded, "but I was born in Athens, and I prefer the city myself. Basilicus likes to speak Greek with me. He is so very Hellenized for a Byzantine."

Cailin bid all of their guests farewell, and Arcadius promised that he would be arriving at Villa Mare shortly to begin his work. Casia entered her litter along with Basilicus, and they moved off into the crowds leaving the Hippodrome. Cailin climbed into her own conveyance.

"I am required to attend the emperor at the palace," Aspar said, leaning down to speak privately with her. "I will send my cavalry troup to escort you home, and join you as soon as I can."

"I do not need your soldiers beyond the gates, my lord. The road is safe, and busy, and it is daylight. They will aid me in getting through the crowds, but no farther, I pray you."

"Very well, my love. I will send a messenger if I am going to be late. Wait up for me if you can, Cailin."

"What did the emperor want earlier, my lord?" she asked him, curious.

"My presence, and nothing more. It is his way of exercising his authority, and I obey him because it reassures him," Aspar said wisely. "The invitation to the banquet, when he knows I dislike banquets, is but another test. The church is always spilling poison in Leo's ear because I am not Orthodox in my beliefs. By obeying him unquestioningly, I make the patriarch's lies seem foolish. Leo is not a stupid man. He is fearful, yes, but not unintelligent. It is the empress who worries me."

"Why?" Cailin said.

"She is ambitious. Far more so than Leo. Verina would like a son to follow in Leo's footsteps. They have but two daughters. I do not know if she will get that son. Leo prefers prayer to pleasure, it seems."

"If that is a virtue, my lord, and one necessary to an emperor, you will indeed never be emperor," Cailin said with a laugh. "You far prefer pleasure to prayer. I do not think I have ever seen you in prayer to either the Christian god or any god."

In answer, he placed his lips upon hers and kissed her slowly, with passion. She responded warmly, running her tongue mischievously along his fleshy mouth as his hand slipped beneath her gown to fondle a breast. Her nipple immediately hardened and she moaned softly.

Removing his lips from hers, he smiled wickedly into her face. "I will come as soon as I can, my love," he promised, removing his hand from her gown, but not before he gave her nipple a little pinch.

She caught her breath, and then letting it out slowly, promised him, "I will wait, my lord, and be prepared to do your every bidding."

Chapter

12

"D id you see the way he looked at her?" Flacilla Strabo said to her husband, Justin Gabras. "*He loves her!* He actually loves her." Her face was angry.

"Why do you care?" he answered. "You never loved him. It should not matter to you that he loves her."

"That is not the point!" she snapped. "Do not be so stupid, Justin! Can you not see how embarrassing his open passion is? He did not give his love to me, but he has given it to that little whore! I will be a laughingstock among all those who know us. How dare he bring that creature to the games and sit so boldly with her in his box for all to see. Even if no one knew who she was, practically everyone in Constantinople knows Casia, particularly now that she is Prince Basilicus's mistress! How like Aspar to surround himself with artisans, actors, and whores!"

"You are not particularly attractive when you are angry, my dear wife," Justin Gabras softly chided Flacilla. "Your skin becomes quite mottled. You would do well to keep your temper in check, particularly when we are in public." He leaned across the ripe, young body of the slave girl who lay between them, and tipping Flacilla's face up to his, kissed her hard. "I do not choose to discuss this matter any more, Flacilla, my love, *and* further mention of your former husband is apt to rouse my blackest ire. You know what happens when my anger is stoked." He ran a hand down the slave girl's body. "Let us concentrate on far pleasanter diversions, like our charming little Leah. Is she not lovely, my dear, and so eager for our tender attentions? Are you not, Leah?"

"Ohh, yes, my lord," the girl responded dutifully, arching herself toward him teasingly. "I long for your touch."

Justin Gabras smiled lazily at the pretty, compliant creature. Then seeing his wife was still not content, he said harshly, "You will have your revenge, Flacilla, but which would you prefer? A quick strike which will allow Aspar to strike back at us? Or, wait for the right moment, and then destroy them both? I would have you happy, my dear. Make your choice now, and then let us be done with this matter. It begins to bore me mightily."

"Will he suffer?" she demanded. "I want him to suffer for his rejection of me."

"If you will wait for the right moment so I may plan it properly, yes, he will suffer. Aspar's life will become a hell on earth, I promise you, but you must be patient, Flacilla."

"Very well," she responded. "I will bide my time, Justin. As impatient as I am to destroy Aspar, you have a skill for evil such as I have never before witnessed. I will trust in that mastery of wickedness that you possess. Now, which one of us is to have Leah first?" Flacilla looked upon the girl and smiled. "She is indeed lovely, my lord. She is not a virgin, is she?"

"No," he said. "She is not. It would please me if you took her first, Flacilla. I like watching you perform with another woman. You are very good at it, I must admit, and more tender with one of your own sex than you are with those young men you so favor and yet brutalize."

She smiled archly at him. "Men," she said, "are meant to be punished by women; but women should be cherished by lovers of either sex. A woman cherished gives far more than one abused, Justin."

"Then Aspar must truly cherish the fair Cailin," he replied cruelly. "Though he looked at her with eyes of love, his looks were returned by that adorable little beauty tenfold. If he loves her as you so believe, she, I assure you, loves him in return."

"And that knowledge," she told him, strangely calm, "will make our revenge so much sweeter, Justin, my lord, will it not?"

He laughed. "You match me evil for evil, Flacilla. I wonder what your friend the empress would think of you if she knew your true character. Would the beauteous Verina be shocked? One day I shall have her in my bed, I swear! She is ripe for rebellion, you know. Leo virtually ignores her these days, and spends the time he should spend fucking her on his knees in prayer for an heir; or so the court chatter reports to me."

The very next afternoon the subject of Justin Gabras's gossip gathered a small party consisting of her brother and two trusted maids, and set out from the imperial yacht basin to cruise the early summer seas west of the city. It was a perfect afternoon for such sport, and theirs was not the only sailing vessel plying the blue-green waters of the Propontis that afternoon. There was just enough of a breeze to gently propel the boat. The sun shone warmly from a perfectly clear sky. Basilicus had sailed this small inland sea since his boyhood, and he was familiar with its twisting shore and its currents. His skill meant that they needed no boatman, who might later be bribed for information, or carelessly gossip of their destination. The two women who accompanied the empress would have died for her. Their loyalty was such that they could be trusted not to speak even under duress.

Cailin had not known for certain when the empress would come to Villa Mare, but she knew that she would have only a few days after the games before Verina would put in an appearance. She did not like keeping secrets from Aspar, and so she spoke to him the morning following their visit to the Hippodrome. He listened quietly as she told him of Verina's secret summons and its outcome, his face grave.

"Whatever it is she desires of me," he said, "it must be very important to her."

"She agrees to sponsor our marriage if you give it to her," Cailin said to him. "Still, I fear that she might urge you to something unsavory."

"I can do nothing that smacks of treason in the slightest," he responded. "My honor has always been my strongest defense, my love. As much as I love you, and as much as I want you for my wife, I will not compromise my honor, Cailin. You do understand that?"

"I could not love you, Flavius Aspar, if you were not a man of honor," Cailin told him. "Remember that I was raised in the traditions of the old Roman empire. Honor was still paramount when my ancestor came to Britain with Claudius, and it remained so down through the centuries as we became Britons, my lord. I would ask nothing dishonorable of you. Still, it cannot hurt to hear what the empress has to say."

"I will listen," he promised her. "If Verina is to be moved to some foolish action, perhaps I may dissuade her from it."

The empress's mission, however, was not foolish. It stemmed rather from her fears, as she explained to Aspar in the privacy of his garden while Cailin and the maidservants were left behind in the comfort of the atrium, with Basilicus to amuse them. Verina was pale, and she had obviously not been sleeping well. She moved restlessly amid the budding flowers, her fingers plucking nervously at her skirts. Aspar, keeping pace with her, encouraged her to speak.

"Cailin has told me of your meeting on the day of the games," he said. "Do not dissemble with me, lady. What is it you want of me?"

"I need to know that should a *crisis* arise, Flavius Aspar, that you will support my position," the empress said softly.

"I will be frank, lady. Is this treason you speak of?"

Verina paled even more. "No! No!" she gasped. "I do not explain well, I fear. The situation is embarrassing to me. Oh, how shall I say it?"

"Plainly," he told her. "Whatever you say is between us alone, lady. I will grant you the privacy of the confessional this one time. If the e is no treason involved, then you have nothing to fear from me. What is it that troubles you so that you seek my aid in secret?"

"It is certain of the priests who surround my husband," Verina said. "They encourage him to believe I alone am responsible for the fact we do not have a son. *I want a son!* But how can we have one if Leo does not visit my bed? He has never been an overly passionate man, and in recent years he has ceased visiting my bed altogether.

"The priests have become his greatest confidants. They exhort him to greater prayer, and to almsgiving that God will give us a son, but unless my husband binds his body to mine again, there will be no child. I even brought Casia, the courtesan my brother favors, to the palace in secret to teach me her seductive wiles. I wanted to use them to entice my husband, but alas, it was to no avail!" the empress said, her blue eyes filling with tears. "Now there is a movement afoot among those same priests who influence my husband to put me away in a convent for the remainder of my days, that Leo might take a new, young wife who will, the priests assure Leo, give him the son I cannot.

"I am not a girl any longer, my lord," Verina said with dignity, "but I am yet capable of bearing a child given the opportunity to do so. These wicked clerics really seek to give my husband a wife who will be in their debt, and who will spy for them!"

"What is it exactly that you want me to do?" Aspar asked her.

"Leo both fears and respects you, my lord," the empress said. "The respect stems from his many long years in your service, and the fear stems from the fact you put him in his high place. He sometimes wonders if you might not be capable of also removing him from that place. He has quickly grown fond of his position.

"The priests fill his ears with cruel words about you, Flavius Aspar," Verina continued. "They tell him you wish to rule through him, and that if you find you cannot, you will overthrow him and take the throne for yourself."

"I do not wish to be emperor," Aspar said. "In his rational moments Leo must know that. Had I wanted the imperial throne, it would have been mine. I had but to renounce my Arian beliefs for more Orthodox practices, and enough of the clergy would have supported me so that the imperial crown would have rested on my head."

"I realize that, my lord, which is why I have come to you. Your motives are honest, and your loyalty is to Byzantium alone, not to any faction or single man. Help me to retain my place at my husband's side despite the wickedness of those who surround him. If you aid and protect me against my enemies, I will see to it that Leo permits your marriage to Cailin Drusus."

Aspar pretended to consider her offer, although he had already decided to help her. The emperor owed Flavius Aspar his position. If his wife was similarly bound to him, so much the better. His own position would be that much stronger. It was very unlikely that Leo would ever father another child on any woman. He had not the stomach for it. He preferred fasting and prayer to the hot, sweaty tangle of passion. Aspar suspected the emperor would actually be secretly delighted to be relieved of such a duty. Verina had always been a loyal wife to him. He would prefer the old and the familiar to anything new, and nubile.

No, Aspar thought. *I do not want to be emperor. I want my son to be emperor.* With both Leo and Verina in his debt, he would have the power to foster a betrothal between his younger son, Patricius, and the youngest imperial princess, Ariadne, in a few years' time. First the marriage, and then afterward Leo would be convinced to name Patricius his heir.

"I will champion your cause, lady," Aspar finally told the empress, who sagged, visibly relieved, against his arm. "These priests overstep their authority. Their only duty is to the emperor's spiritual welfare. I will personally register my distress at their actions to the patriarch. Once that is done, I know we can trust that he will put an end to the matter. I am truly shocked those chosen to guide Leo spiritually would so abuse their position. It must not be allowed to continue. You were quite right to come to me for help, lady."

Secure now that her cause was just, Verina straightened herself proudly and said, "You will not find me ungrateful, my lord. It will take a little time, you know, but I will see that you and Cailin Drusus are allowed to formalize your relationship within the church. You have my word on it, and you know that word is good."

"I thank you, lady," Aspar said quietly.

"No," she responded, "it is I who must thank you, Flavius Aspar. I could only wish Byzantium had more men like you in its service."

When the empress and her party had departed to return to Constantinople, Aspar walked with Cailin in the gardens, where there was no chance of them being overheard. Quietly he explained to her exactly what it was Verina had sought from him, and how he had agreed to help the empress in exchange for her aid in the matter of their marriage. "You must force yourself to please Father Michael so he will baptize you," Aspar told her. "When the moment comes that the decision is made in our favor, I want no impediment to our marriage. A baptized Orthodox wife can only reflect favorably upon me. There is more at stake than you can know right now, my love."

She did not ask him what it was. Cailin knew that Aspar would share that with her when the time was right. "Very well," she agreed, "I will stop asking difficult questions of Father Michael, and meekly accept all he says with the humility a good Christian woman should possess. If I think the rules and regulations imposed by the church are silly, I must admit to liking the words of this Jesus of Nazareth. They alone make sense to me, even if the rest of it doesn't." She slipped her arms about his neck and pressed her body close to his. "I want to be your wife, Flavius Aspar. I want your children, and I want to walk the streets of Constantinople proudly, the envy of all because I am yours."

They walked together through the gardens and down to the beach, where they removed their garments. They strolled hand in hand into the warm sea. He had just recently taught her to swim, and Cailin loved the freedom of the water. Laughing, she teased him and frolicked in the waves until finally he caught her. Pulling her back up onto the beach, he made passionate love to her upon the very shore where he had first revived her passion. Her cries of pleasure at his possession of her mingled with the mewling cries of the gulls soaring above them. His own cries were drowned by the gentle pounding of the surf on the sand. Afterward they lay sated and contented, the bright sun drying their bodies.

ailin's twentieth birthday had passed. The summer spun itself out in a succession of long, sunny days, and hot passionate nights. She had never imagined a man could be so virile, particularly a man of his age, and yet his desire for her never ceased.

Basilicus came quite regularly with Casia to visit, and when Aspar teased his friend about his sudden liking for the country, Basilicus claimed fussily, "The city is a cesspit in this heat, and I hear rumors of plague. Besides, you have more than enough room for us, and should not keep to yourselves so much." Basilicus also secretly brought them word from Verina.

Aspar had indeed gone directly to the patriarch and expressed his great displeasure at any plan to set the empress aside simply over the matter of a male heir. Another wife would do no good, Aspar bluntly pointed out to Byzantium's chief cleric. The fault lay with Leo, who preferred an uncomplicated, ascetic existence now, which allowed him to rule more wisely than if he were overburdened with carnal matters. There were plenty of men fit to follow Leo, but a wise and godly emperor was a rare blessing upon Byzantium. The empress, Aspar told the patriarch, understood this. She sought to protect her husband from disturbing influences. She was both virtuous and devotedly loyal. To disturb her peace of mind was, Aspar forcefully noted, wicked, unjust, and ungodly.

Basilicus reported that the priests surrounding the emperor had been removed and reassigned to distant places. New priests took their place, and seemed to devote themselves only to the emperor's spiritual life. The empress was both relieved and grateful to have this sword of Damocles removed from over her beautiful blond head. She sent word, through her brother, that she would keep her promise. She had already begun her campaign to influence Leo more favorably in the matter of a marriage between the empire's First Patrician and Cailin Drusus, a young patrician widow from Britain who was soon to be baptized into the Orthodox Christian faith.

In early autumn Aspar was sent to Adrianople, where the governor of the city was having difficulties with two rival factions that threatened anarchy within the city. One of the factions was made up of Orthodox Christians and the other of Arian Christians. Since Aspar, an Arian who served an Orthodox ruler, had the ability to move easily between these two religious worlds, he was the logical choice to make peace. Men of all faiths respected Flavius Aspar.

"I wish I could take you with me," he told Cailin the night before his departure, "but I must be able to move swiftly and without impediment at all times in a matter like this. These fanatics will quarrel with one another over the most foolish things, but unless their anger is stayed, they cause terrible destruction and lives are lost."

"I would be a weakness to you," she said. "Without me you are able to act decisively, and you may have to, my lord. To kill and wreak havoc over a point of religion is pure madness, but it happens far too often."

"You will be such a perfect wife for me," he said admiringly.

"Why?" she teased him. "Because I share your passion, or because I do not complain when you must be away from me?"

"Both," he said with a smile. "You have an inborn skill for understanding people. You know the fine line I must walk between those fanatical factions in Adrianople, and you do not distract me from my duty. Those who have opposed our marriage will soon see that they were wrong, and that Cailin Drusus is the only wife for Aspar."

"*I do not distract you?*" She pretended to be offended, and mounting him suddenly, glared down into his handsome face. Her pointed little tongue snaked over her lips suggestively, slowly. Her eyes darkened with her passion, and cupping her breasts in her hands, she teased her own nipples erect. "Can I not distract you just the tiniest bit, my lord?"

He watched her through slitted eyes as she played, a faint smile upon her lips. He knew her certainty of his love was what made her bold, and it was surely to his benefit. She was so young and so very beautiful, he thought, lazily running both his flattened palms up her torso. Sometimes when he looked at her, he wondered if when he became old she would love him still, and fear gnawed at his vitals. Then she would smile at him and kiss him sweetly and, reassured, he knew she would always love him, for it was her nature to be honest and loyal. His fingers clamped about her waist and he lifted her up slightly, allowing his engorged organ to raise itself up.

"You distract me mightily, my love," he said softly, lowering her slowly, encasing himself fully within the warm sweetness of her hot, wet sheath. Then pulling her forward almost roughly, he kissed her deeply, sensuously, his mouth soft yet firm against hers, turning her quickly over onto her back so that he now held the ascendant position. "And you are hereby sentenced to spend the remainder of your days distracting me, Cailin," he growled lovingly in her ear as he plunged with slow deliberation in and out of her eager body. "I adore you, my love, and soon you will be mine for all eternity! My wife! My very life! The sweet, bright half of my dark, dark soul!"

"I love you, Flavius Aspar," she told him, half sobbing, and then Cailin was lost again in the very special world he seemed to be able to weave about her now. She was warm and cold at the same time. Her heart both raced and soared with his loving. But if her place was in his heart, and in his arms, then why was she afraid? Then, her crisis overwhelming her, Cailin cried out with pleasure, and her fears were quickly forgotten in the security and the safety of his loving arms. Happily she snuggled against him and fell asleep.

When she awoke in the morning, he was already gone. Nellwyn brought her a tray with newly made yogurt, ripe apricots, and fresh bread with a little pot of honey. "Master Arcadius asks if you will pose for him today. He says he is almost finished, and can be gone by week's end if you will but cooperate. I think he is anxious to return to Constantinople. The summer is over. He talks about the autumn games."

"Tell him I will be there in an hour," Cailin told her servant. "I want the statue completed, and mounted upon its pedestal in the garden before my lord returns. It will be my wedding surprise for him."

"I never saw anything like it before," Nellwyn admitted. "It's so beautiful, lady. I thought only the gods were portrayed so."

"The statue represents Venus, the old Goddess of Love," Cailin explained. "I have simply posed in place of the goddess for Arcadius."

Cailin ate, and then having bathed, joined the sculptor in his studio. Nellwyn in attendance, she removed her tunica and took her position. He worked for a time, his eye moving between the smaller clay statue he had originally fashioned from her pose and Cailin herself. When he saw she was growing tired, he stopped, and Cailin put on her tunica before they went to sit outside in the sunshine and drink sweet, freshly squeezed orange juice, and nibble upon sesame cakes that Zeno brought them.

"I shall miss your company," Cailin told Arcadius. "I enjoy all your wicked gossip, and have learned much of those with whom I will have to associate when I am married to Aspar."

"Your life will not be easy," he answered her frankly. "Those at the court with whom you should associate will avoid you until they know you, and even when they know your true worth, some will continue to shun you, Cailin Drusus. Only those of whom you should be wary will be eager to cultivate your friendship due to the influence you have with Aspar, or because they hope to seduce you as they have so many others. Your virtue, in light of the gossip surrounding you, will truly madden them."

"What a paradox you Byzantines are," Cailin said. "You espouse a religion that preaches goodness, and yet there is so much evil among you. I do not really understand your people at all."

"Our society is simple," Arcadius told her. "The rich desire power, and more riches. These things make them feel invincible, and so they behave as other people would not dare to behave. They are crueler, and more carnal, and because their faith promises them forgiveness if they will but repent, they do so every now and then, ridding themselves of their past sins so they may go and sin some more.

"This is not unique to Byzantium alone, Cailin. All civilizations reach this apogee at some point in their development. Those less rich imitate their betters; and the poor are kept in their place by a top-heavy bureaucracy and a beneficent ruler who allows them into the games free. Bread and circuses, my dear girl, keep the poor in check, except for those rare times when plague, or famine, or war interfere with the workings of the government. When those things happen, even emperors are not safe on their thrones." He chuckled. "I am a cynic as you can see."

"All I desire," Cailin replied, "is to marry my dear lord, and if the gods will it, bear him a child. I shall live here in the country, raise my children, and be content. I want no part of Byzantium's intrigues, Arcadius."

"You will not be able to escape them, dear girl," he said. "Aspar is not some unimportant noble with a country estate to which he may retire. This idyll you have been living cannot continue once you are married. You will have to accept your proper place at court as the wife of the empire's First Patrician. Take my advice, dear girl, and do not ally yourself with any faction no matter how seductively they importune you to join them, *and they will*. You must remain neutral, as does Aspar. He has but one loyalty, and that is to Byzantium itself."

"My loyalty is to Aspar," she said quietly, but firmly.

"That is good. Ah, yes, dear girl, I can see you will not be lured by the siren's song sung at the court. You are too sensible. Now let us return to the business of immortalizing you," he said, chuckling. "You have an outrageously lush form for such a practical woman."

"Tell me about these games you are so eager to return to the city for, Arcadius," Cailin said after she had resumed her pose. "I thought there were only games in May on the day of commemoration. I did not know they were held at other times. Will there be chariot races? I did enjoy the races."

"There are games held several times during the year," he answered her, "but these particular games are being sponsored by Justin Gabras to celebrate his marriage to Aspar's former wife, Flacilla Strabo. He was unable to schedule them sooner because in the spring everything is concentrated on the May games. Then the weather grew too hot in the summer. So Justin Gabras planned his games to coincide with the sixth-month anniversary of his marriage to Flacilla. There will be racing in the morning and gladiators in the afternoon. Gabras, I am told, has paid for death matches."

"I have never seen gladiators," Cailin said. "They fight with swords and shields, don't they? What are death matches?"

"Well, dear girl," Arcadius began, "I see that this is another area of your education I shall have to fill in for you. Gladiatorial bouts first began in ancient Campania and Etruria, from whence our ancestors sprang. The first gladiators were slaves, made to battle each other to the death for their masters' amusement. Such matches came to Rome eventually, but were held only during the funeral games for distinguished men. They were rare for many years. Then slowly gladiatorial bouts began being sponsored privately, and the emperor Augustus funded a few of what he called 'extraordinary shows.' Eventually the gladiators were scheduled regularly at the public games in December on the Saturnalia, while politicians, and others wishing the public's support, supplied free gladiatorial combats at other times. The populace loved the excitement and the blood lust of such games.

"In the beginning gladiators were captives taken in war who far preferred death to becoming slaves. They were trained fighters. Soon, however, with the Roman peace imposed over most of the world, the supply of captives dwindled and it became necessary to train men who were not soldiers. Many criminals were sentenced to become gladiators, but even so, there was not enough of a supply to fill the now great demand. Many innocent men were accused of petty offenses and condemned to the ring. Early

Christians were sacrificed because there were not enough criminals or captives to be found. When there were not enough men available, women and, yes, even small children were sent into the ring to fight."

"How awful!" Cailin cried, but Arcadius continued, unmoved.

"There were schools for gladiators in Capua, Praeneste, Rome, and Pompeii, as well as other cities. Some schools were owned by wealthy nobles so they might train their own fighters, but others were the property of men who dealt in gladiators. The schools were strictly run because their purpose was to ensure a steady supply of competent, effective fighters. The teachers were tough, but they trained their charges well, and carefully. Diet was monitored. Each day held a round of gymnastics, and lessons from weapons experts.

"Eventually, however, it became impossible to obtain enough students to train even from among captives and criminals. Today's gladiators are free men who have chosen the life for themselves."

"I cannot imagine why," Cailin replied. "It sounds terrible. But what of the weapons they use, Arcadius? And how do they fight?"

"In pairs, usually," he said, "although in the past gladiatorial combats have pitted masses of men against masses of men. Usually few were left standing. Professional gladiators are divided into three groups: Samnites, who are heavily armed; Thracians, who are lightly armed; and there are net fighters. The net man's weapons are his large net, his daggers, and a spear."

"You still have not told me what a death match is," Cailin said.

"The combatants fight to the death, unless, of course, Gabras grants the loser of each match mercy. Knowing Justin Gabras, I doubt he will. He will be far more popular with the people if he gives them a show of blood."

"How horrible," Cailin said, shuddering. "I do not think I would like these gladiatorial combats, knowing that one of the two men has to die."

"It adds spice to the match knowing it," Arcadius said. "The combatants are always magnificent fighters under such circumstances."

"I am surprised that any free man would agree to fight under such conditions," Cailin noted. "To know that you might be killed is such a frightening prospect." She shuddered.

"But there is always the chance you will not be killed," he answered. "Besides, the fee for a death match is far better than for just the ordinary combat. The little gossip that reaches me here tells me that the current, unbeaten champion, a man known as the Saxon, is to fight in Gabras's games."

"I feel sorry for him," Cailin said. "If he is the unbeaten champion, then all the others will strive harder to bring him down. He faces the most danger."

"True," Arcadius agreed, "but it will make for a far more exciting match. You may step down, Cailin, and clothe yourself. I am finished." He stepped back to admire his handiwork. "It is done, and it is one of my greatest masterpieces, I think," he said, feigning understatement. "Aspar should be well-pleased, and inclined to pay me on time for my efforts."

"What of the base?" she demanded. "I want it set in the garden facing the sea before Aspar returns from Adrianople."

"I have an apprentice in the city working on the pedestal, my dear," he told her. "The marble is most unique, a pink and white mixture. I have no idea where it came from. We found it lying about beneath some old clothes in the rear of my studio, but when I saw it, I knew it was the perfect piece of stone for our Venus. Come and look now."

Cailin had slipped her tunica back on. She came around to view her statue. The young Venus, as Arcadius liked to call it, stood, her body slightly curved, one arm at her side, the other raised, the hand palm outward as if shielding her eyes from the sun. Her hair was piled atop her head, but here and there errant ringlets had escaped and curled about her slender neck and delicate ears. There was just the faintest hint of a smile upon her face. She was both pristine and serene in face and form. "It is beautiful," Cailin finally said. She was frankly awed by the sculptor's skill. She could almost see the pulse at the base of the young Venus' throat. Each fingernail and toenail was perfect in its detail; and there was so much more.

"Your simple homage is more than enough praise," he said quietly. He could see the admiration in her eyes, not for how he had portrayed her, but for his talent, and his art. Her lack of sophistication was refreshing, Arcadius thought. Had this been a woman of the court, she would have complained that he had not really caught her essence, and then tried to cheat him of his fee. Well, it had been a most pleasant interlude. Tomorrow he would return to the city and begin a set of six figures for the altar of a new church being built in Constantinople. "When the pedestal is done, dear girl," he said, "I shall come myself to see the statue installed upon it. I think Flavius Aspar will be most pleased with what we have accomplished together."

After he departed the following day, Cailin found that she missed the scupltor's company. He had been a charming and most amusing companion. Nellwyn was a sweet girl, but a simple one. Cailin could not speak on complicated matters with her. She just did not understand. Still, she was pleasant company, and Cailin was glad for her presence.

The harvest was a good one on Flavius Aspar's estates, and as Cailin walked across the fields with Nellwyn, greeting the workers, she again considered the possibility of Aspar's raising horses for the chariot races. The estate's tenants already raised hay and grain for their cattle and other stock. Much of the pasturage was as suitable for horses as for cattle. If Aspar needed even more land, perhaps he could obtain it from overtaxed landowners whose properties bordered his own. She would bring it up with him again when he returned.

Casia came to visit for a few days' duration, and brought news of the city. "Basilicus swears to me that Leo will give his consent to your marriage when Aspar returns. The general's efforts in Adrianople, it seems, are proving successful. It will cost Leo nothing from his imperial treasury to give his general what he truly desires," she said with a laugh. "Did Arcadius finish your statue?"

"A few weeks ago. He is coming soon with the pedestal to install it in the garden. I want it done before Aspar returns," Cailin answered. "Would you like to see it, Casia?"

"Of course!" the beautiful courtesan said, laughing. "Do you think I mentioned it just merely in passing? I am dying of curiosity."

"Arcadius calls it the young Venus," Cailin explained as she unveiled the statue in the artist's summer studio. "What do you think?"

Casia stood spellbound, and then she finally said, "He has caught you perfectly, Cailin. Your youth, your beauty, that sweet innocence that shows in your face despite all you have been through. Yes, Arcadius has caught your very soul, and were I not truly your friend, I should be very jealous of you." She took Cailin's hand in hers, and squeezing it, said, "Soon we shall no longer be able to pursue our friendship."

"Why?" Cailin demanded. "Because I am to be Aspar's wife, and you are Basilicus's mistress? No, Casia, I will not play their cruel games. We will remain friends no matter the change in my status."

Casia's lovely eyes filled with tears, and she said, "I have never had a friend until you, Cailin Drusus. I hope you are right."

"I have never had a friend, either, Casia. Antonia Porcius pretended to be my friend, though I always knew she was not. Friends do not betray friends. I know we will never betray each other. Now, tell me the gossip from the city. I miss Arcadius's ribald chatter."

They walked from the studio down to the beach, where they sat upon the sand and Casia told her all the latest news of the town.

"Basilicus's wife, Eudoxia, finally seduced her young guardsman. He was the very same fellow who brought you to the empress," Casia began. "His seed is most potent, and poor Eudoxia became pregnant practically immediately, despite her best efforts to avoid it, I am told. Basilicus was furious. She wanted to have an abortion, but he would not allow it. He has sent her to her parents' home outside of Ephesus for her confinement."

"I do not know how he dares to be so righteous, considering the relationship he has with you," Cailin said with a small smile.

"It does seem unfair," Casia agreed, "but you must remember that there are different rules for men and women. Basilicus had been most lenient with Eudoxia because she is a good wife and

mother. She is not at all wanton like Flacilla. That is why he allowed her her little diversion. Becoming pregnant, however, was
very careless on Eudoxia's part, and has proven a great embarrassment to Basilicus. Eudoxia should have considered the conse-
quences when she acted so rashly. The child is due early next
summer, and will be given in adoption to a good family. Poor
Eudoxia will remain in Ephesus until it is born. I do not mind.
Basilicus is now free to spend more time with me. His children are
practically grown and do not need him."

"I wonder what they must think of their mother," Cailin said.

"Basilicus's son knows the truth, and wanted to dash right off
and kill the poor guardsman. Basilicus explained most forcefully to
him that one cannot kill a man for accepting what was freely offered. As for the prince's daughters, they do not know, or at least
he hopes they do not. They have been told their mother has gone
to Ephesus to care for their sick grandparents, and Basilicus sent
them to St. Barbara's Convent to keep them safe until their mother
returns. Left alone, who knows what mischief they might get into.
Girls are most inventive."

"Where do you come from?" Cailin asked her friend as they
gazed at the water. "Athens, I think I once heard you say. Where
is that?"

"It is a city on the Aegean Sea, south of Constantinople. I was
born in a brothel that my mother owned. My father was an official
of the government there. He was not, I remember, well-liked.
When he died, they closed down my mother's business. I was just
ten, but I was sold into slavery immediately. I do not know what
happened to my mother, or little brother. I was brought to Constantinople and bought by Jovian for Villa Maxima. I was very
lucky," Casia said. "You know how well they treat children at Villa
Maxima. They are taught to read and write, and to do simple
sums. They learn manners, and how to please the men and women
who patronize the establishment. When I was thirteen my virginity
was auctioned off to the highest bidder. Jovian and Phocas had
never before nor have they since received such a high price for a
virgin," she said proudly. "Because I had been taught well how to

please a man, and because I seem to have a talent for such work, I became quite popular. Jovian warned me to be choosy about whom I pleasured, for it was my right to refuse any man. It proved to be excellent advice. The more discerning I appeared to be, the more desperate men became to have me, and the more willing to pay the highest price. I managed to garner some magnificent gifts from my appreciative lovers." She smiled. "Then Basilicus came, and after a short time I realized he wanted more than just an occasional visit to my bed. I hinted such a thing might be possible. He offered to give me my own home in a good district, and so I purchased my freedom from Villa Maxima."

"How old are you?" Cailin asked her.

"But a year your senior," Casia replied.

Cailin was surprised. Casia seemed older, but then of course she would. While I was playing with my dolls, Cailin thought, Casia was learning her lessons in a brothel. "How long will you keep the prince as a lover?" she asked her friend. "I mean . . . well . . . you are used to a variety of lovers. Does not having just one bore you?"

Casia laughed. Had the question come from anyone else, she would have been offended, but she knew Cailin meant no offense by it, that she was only curious. "One lover at a time, my friend, is really quite enough," she replied. "As for your other question, I will remain with Basilicus as long as it pleases us both. He and I will never marry as you and Aspar will. I am no patrician like you, Cailin Drusus."

"Being a patrician has not protected me from evil," Cailin said quietly. "Still, though I once complained that fortune did not smile upon me, I was wrong. I may have lost my husband and child, but I have been given Aspar to love. Ohh, Casia! He wants children, and at his age!"

Casia shuddered delicately. "Better you, dear friend, than me," she said. "I am not the maternal sort, I fear. Fortunately my prince is content with his wife's efforts at producing offspring—when they are his own."

They came up from the beach and sat by the fish pond in the atrium, sipping sweet wine and indulging themselves with honey cakes that Zeno's wife, Anna, had made them.

"The city," Casia said, "is agog with excitement over the games that Justin Gabras is sponsoring at the Hippodrome in a few days. He's brought in gladiators for death matches. I can hardly wait!"

"Arcadius told me," Cailin responded. "I am glad I do not have to see such a thing. I think it's horrible!"

"Not really," Casia replied. "You would get used to it. Good gladiators are magnificent to watch, but they are a rare breed now. The church does not approve of them, but I will bet the patriarch and his minions will all be there in their box howling with the same blood lust as the rest of us." She laughed. "They are such hypocrites! I am sorry you are not going. I shall have to sit in the stands, then, but I would not miss these matches for the world.

"The Saxon is fighting. He has never, they say, lost a match. He seems to have no fear of death, and his other appetites are equally insatiable, I am told."

Casia stayed at Villa Mare for three days. The day before she left, Arcadius arrived with a wagon in which sat the pedestal for the young Venus and several beefy helpers who were to move the statue from the studio to its place in the garden. The two young women watched, fascinated, as the work was carried out, hard pressed not to laugh at the sculptor who fussed and fumed at the workmen as they went about their task. Finally the young Venus was settled upon her pink and white marble base, angled so that she was facing the sea. Arcadius heaved a great sigh of relief. "Well?" he demanded. "What think you?"

Casia was visibly impressed, and said so. Cailin simply kissed the sculptor on the cheek, causing him to flush with pleasure.

"It is marvelous," he agreed with them.

"Stay with us tonight," Cailin said.

"Yes," Casia echoed. "You can return to the city in the morning in my litter with me, Arcadius. 'Twill be a far nicer trip than if you ride back in the wagon with your workmen, who smell of onions and sweat."

Arcadius shuddered at her rather graphic but accurate description. "I will remain," he said, and instructed his foreman to take the men and return to Constantinople. Then turning to the women, he told them, "The gladiators arrived yesterday. They paraded through the city in full regalia, as if that were necessary to stimulate interest in the games. The populace is in a frenzy already. I cannot tell you how many women fainted at the sight of the champion. He is frankly the most magnificent piece of male flesh I have ever seen. It would be a pity if he were killed, but then, he has prevailed so far."

Casia and Arcadius, city people to the bone, chattered on throughout the evening, filling Cailin's ears with all manner of gossip. Though it was amusing, she was frankly relieved to be able to seek her quiet bed that night and to bid her guests farewell in the morning. She wondered if she would indeed have to involve herself in the affairs of the court once she and Aspar were married. Perhaps Arcadius was wrong.

In the afternoon, Cailin swam in the still warm sea, and lay naked on the beach, drying in the autumn sun. The peace was wonderful, and she reveled in it. She fell asleep, and when she awoke, she was filled with new energy and was suddenly eager to have Aspar home.

Chapter

13

A *spar returned* to Villa Mare late the next evening and immediately took Cailin to bed. In the early morning, when they had sated themselves of their desire for each other, they lay talking.

"I arrived in Constantinople yesterday afternoon," he told her, "and reported immediately to Leo. The difficulties in Adrianople have been overcome. There is peace in that city once more, although for how long, I cannot say. I have little patience with those who argue over creed and clan. What fools they are!"

"*They* are most of the world," Cailin said, "but I agree with you, my love. Most people like to think life a deep and difficult puzzle, but it is not, I believe. We are bound by one thread—our humanity. If we would but put our differences aside, and weave the cloth of our fate with that one thread, there would be no more differences between us."

"You are too young to be so wise," he teased her, kissing her lightly, and then he said, "Would you like to know my reward for this recent service to Byzantium?" He smiled into her face, his brown eyes twinkling mischievously at her.

Cailin's heart began to race. She didn't even dare to voice the question. She simply nodded.

"You are to be baptized on November first by the patriarch himself in the private chapel of the imperial palace," Aspar told her. "Then the patriarch will marry us. Leo and Verina will stand as our formal witnesses. You will have to choose a Byzantine name, of course."

She gasped. It was true, then. "Anna-Marie," she managed to say. "Anna for your good wife who was the mother of your children, and Marie for the mother of Jesus."

"You have chosen well," he said. "No one can help but approve, but I will never call you anything but Cailin, my love. To the world you will be Anna-Marie, the wife of Flavius Aspar, but it is Cailin with whom I fell in love, and will continue to love for all time."

"I cannot believe that the emperor and the patriarch have at last given their consent," Cailin told him, her eyes wet with tears.

"Neither of them are fools, my love," Aspar told her. "Your introduction into Byzantine society could hardly be called a conventional one," he said with a small smile, "yet both Leo and the church know your behavior since I bought and freed you has been far more circumspect than most of the women at court, especially in light of the current scandal surrounding Basilicus's wife, Eudoxia. As for me, I have given my life for Byzantium, and if in my later years I cannot have what I so deeply desire, what further use will I be to the empire?"

"Did you tell them that?" Cailin asked, surprised that he would have lowered his guard so greatly before the emperor and the patriarch.

"Aye, I did," Aspar admitted, and then chuckled. "The threat was merely implied, my love. I hold a great advantage over the emperor in that there is no other soldier of my standing who can lead the armies of the empire. If I were to retire from public life . . ." He smiled at her again. "I left it to their imaginations. It did not take long for Leo to decide, and he argued the patriarch into acquiescence most convincingly. The emperor has recently learned the value of a loyal and virtuous wife.

"Then having gained my heart's desire, I was forced to sit through a banquet, which is why I was so late in arriving last night. Did you miss me greatly, my love?"

"I missed you terribly," she flattered him, "but I was not too lonely. Arcadius finished the statue. It now stands in the garden, my wedding gift to you, Aspar. He has also counseled me most wisely on the court. I shall remain a party to no faction, I promise you."

"Do you want to go to court?" he asked, surprised.

"Not really," Cailin told him. "Arcadius says it is my duty once I am the wife of the First Patrician of the empire, but I would far prefer to remain here in the country."

"Then you shall," he told her. "Arcadius is just an old gossip. You will, of course, be expected to appear at state functions where I am required to be but, otherwise, if you choose to live a quiet life, you most certainly may. I shall give you children to raise, and my care will naturally be foremost in your duties. Your days will be most full," he teased her gently, running his hand across her shoulder.

"I want to raise chariot horses," she told him. "We have spoken of it before."

"I offer you children to raise, and you ask for horses!" He pretended to be offended, but Cailin knew better.

Pushing him back amid the pillows, she kissed him, sliding her hands across his hard chest. "I am a clever woman, my lord. I can raise both your children, and your horses. The Celts have a way with horses."

"You are a shameless wench to wheedle me so," he said, rolling her beneath him, then sheathing his hardness within her soft body. "How many stallions will you need?" he demanded, moving subtly upon her, pleased to see the look on her face turning to one of passion. *How he had missed her!*

"I but need this stallion, my sweet lord," she told him, molding her body tightly to his as he stoked her pleasure, "but two champions should do for the herd of mares we will assemble. *Ohhhhhh!*" The gods! *She had missed him more than she realized!*

He ceased his movements and lay easily atop her, his hands carressing the sweet small melons of her breasts. He wanted to prolong this interlude. From the first moment he had taken her, he felt like a young man again. The feeling had never diminished in the months that they were together. With Anna there was respect. With Flacilla there was nothing. But Cailin! With Cailin he had found everything! He had never even dreamed that such love between two people was possible, yet here it was. "You are certain you want to do this?" he asked her. "You have seen the chariot races but once."

He throbbed within her, making it almost impossible for her to concentrate on anything else. Her breasts ached with sweetness beneath his tender touch. "I am surprised no one thought of it before," she managed to say. "It is such a logical plan. *Ohh, my love, you are driving me wild!*"

"Surely no wilder than you are driving me," he ground out, and then, unable to contain himself any longer, he bent forward, taking her lips, and thrust with deliberate ferocity into her softness until they both attained their mutual release.

When Aspar was capable of speech once more, he told her, "We will go to the autumn games. Observe the races again, and then if you still desire it, we will make preparations to raise chariot horses."

"But Flacilla's new husband is sponsoring those games," Cailin said, surprised. "Should we be seen there?"

"All of Constantinople will be there," Aspar told her, "including all of Flacilla's former lovers, you may be certain. Flacilla and Justin Gabras will sit in the imperial box with Leo and Verina. At least we will not be subjected to them, my love."

"May I ask Casia? She was disappointed that I was not going to these games, and said she would be forced to sit in the stands with the plebes. I will not desert her because I am to be your wife."

"I would be disappointed in you if you did," he answered. "Yes, you may invite Casia. There will be gossip, but I care not."

"I do not want to see the gladiatorial matches," Cailin told him. "Casia says that they are death matches. I could not bear to see some poor man die because he was not as quick or skilled as his opponent. I think it cruel of Flacilla's husband to require blood."

"Blood pleases the plebes," Aspar said matter-of-factly. "Watch one match, Cailin. You may not be as horrified as you think you will be. If you are truly displeased by it, then you may leave, but it must be done discreetly, my love. We cannot insult our despicable host."

Cailin sent a messenger to Casia that morning, inviting her to join them in their box on the morrow, when the games would officially begin. Casia's reply was a delighted acceptance.

The following day Cailin was up early, for the games would begin at nine o'clock of the morning, the races lasting until noon. She had prepared her costume carefully. Her stola, with its round, low neckline and long, tight sleeves, was of the finest, softest white linen. The lower third of the sleeves, and the wide hemline, as well as a broad stripe extending halfway up the skirt, were woven in pure gold and emerald-green silk threads. The stola was belted tightly at the waist with a wide belt of leather layered with beaten gold, and decorated with emeralds that matched the gold and emerald collar about her neck and her elaborate pendant earrings. Because of the time of year, Cailin had known she would need some sort of outer garment, but she did not want to cover her costume. She had cut a semicircular cloak of bright green silk, which she fastened on her right shoulder with a fibula made from a single oval-shaped emerald set in gold. Gold kid slippers shod her feet, and her costume was nicely completed by a jeweled silken band about her head, from which hung a sheer golden veil.

Aspar, in a purple-and-gold-embroidered ceremonial garment of white silk called a tunica palmata, which he wore with a toga picta of finely spun purple wool embroidered with gold, nodded with pleasure when he saw her. "You will cause many tongues to wag today, my love. You look magnificent."

"As do you, my lord," she replied. "Are you certain we will not inspire imperial jealousy? I have seen the emperor, and you, my lord, are a far more regal figure than he."

"A thought you will not share with anyone else but me," Aspar replied seriously. "Leo is a good administrator. He is precisely the emperor Byzantium needs."

"Leo may be emperor of Byzantium," Cailin said candidly, "but you are the ruler of my heart, Flavius Aspar. 'Tis all I care for, my dear lord." Then she kissed his mouth sweetly, smiling into his eyes.

He laughed. "Oh, Cailin, you will rule not just my heart, I fear, but my soul as well. What a sweet minx you are, my love."

Casia and Basilicus were already awaiting them at the Hippodrome. As they entered the silk-hung box belonging to the empire's First Patrician, the crowds seeing the general began to call his name.

"Aspar! Aspar! Aspar!"

He stepped forward and, saluting them, acknowledged their cheers with a modest smile. Then he retired to the rear of the box, that the populace be allowed to quiet down. To the right of the imperial box the patriarch and his minions sat observing it all.

"He does not encourage them," the patriarch's secretary observed.

"Not yet," the patriarch replied. "Someday, I think, he will. Still, he is a curious man, and may prove me wrong."

The Hippodrome suddenly exploded in a frenzy of cheers as the emperor and empress, along with the games' sponsor and their guests, entered the imperial box. Leo and Verina accepted the homage of the crowd with smiling graciousness, and then presented Justin Gabras to the assembled, who cheered noisily as Gabras waved a languid hand.

At the sound of the trumpets Leo stepped forward and performed the ritual that began the festivities. As the mappa fluttered from his fingers, the stable doors of the Hippodrome burst open to allow the chariots in the first race to dash forth. The crowds screamed their encouragement to the four teams.

"Just look at that," Flacilla fumed. "How dare Aspar and Basilicus bring their whores to our games!"

"The games are for everyone, my dear," Justin Gabras replied, his eyes taking in Cailin avidly. What a magnificent creature, he thought. How I would like to have her in my power, even for just a few minutes.

"I do not think it right that the empire's First Patrician flaunt his mistress so publicly," Flacilla persisted.

"Oh, Flacilla," Verina said with a light laugh, "your jealousy is astounding to behold, particularly given the fact neither you or Aspar could stand one another during your marriage."

"That is not the point," Flacilla replied. "Aspar should not be seen publicly with a woman of loose morals."

"Is that why he was never seen with you, my dear?" her husband inquired drolly, and to Flacilla's mortification, both Leo and Verina laughed.

She began to weep.

"Dear heaven!" Justin Gabras exclaimed. "May I be delivered from the overblown emotions of breeding women." He pulled a white silk square from his robes and handed it to his wife. "Wipe your eyes, Flacilla, and do not make a complete fool of yourself."

"You are expecting a child?" Verina was surprised, but then that would explain Flacilla's expanding girth of late.

Flacilla nodded, and sniffled. "In four more months," she admitted.

Congratulations were offered all around to Justin Gabras.

"It could be worse," her husband pointed out. "What if the girl were Aspar's wife, my dear? She would take precedence over you at court. In her present position she is quite harmless."

Verina could not resist the temptation laid so neatly before her. She smiled with false sweetness. "I'm afraid that that is exactly what is to happen, my lord. The emperor and the patriarch have given their permission for Aspar to marry with Cailin Drusus."

Flacilla paled. "You cannot allow it!" she gasped. "The creature is nothing more than a whore!"

"Oh, Flacilla," Verina said calmly, "you distress yourself over nothing. The girl's introduction to society here was unconventional, I will admit, but she was but a short time at Villa Maxima. Her background is better than either of ours. She conducts herself with a modesty that has even earned the commendation of your cousin, the patriarch. She will make Aspar an excellent wife and, believe me, in time the rest will be forgotten, particularly if you continue to cause such scandals as the one you caused last spring. You are a far bigger whore, and so are half the women in the court, than little Cailin Drusus." The empress smiled and took a cup of wine offered by a servant.

Before Flacilla might reply, her husband pinched her arm sharply. "Be silent, you foolish woman," he hissed at her. "It does not matter."

"Not to you!" Flacilla snapped angrily. "I will never give precedence to that creature. *Never!*"

"Oh, Flacilla," the empress said, "do not distress yourself. Look! The Greens have taken two races in a row this morning." She turned to her husband. "You owe me a new gold necklace, my lord, and a bracelet too!"

"Ohhh, I hate her!" Flacilla murmured low. "How I wish I might wreak vengeance on her for her presumption."

"Well, you cannot now, my dear," her husband replied softly. "As Aspar's mistress, she had a certain vulnerability, but as Aspar's wife, Flacilla, she is inviolate. Look at her! Modest. Beautiful. Soon, I wager, she will become known for her good works. She will be a model mother, I have not a doubt. She has no fault that I can see. If she did, we might find a way to spoil Aspar's happiness, but she does not. You will have to learn to live with the situation. I will not have you upsetting yourself unnecessarily, else you lose my child. If you do that, Flacilla, I will kill you with my bare hands. Do you understand me?"

"The child means that much to you, my lord?"

"Aye! I have never had a legitimate son," he said.

"And me, my lord? Do I mean anything to you at all, other than as the brood mare who will bear your heir?"

"You are the only woman for me, Flacilla. I have told you that often enough, but if it pleases you to hear it again, very well. I never before asked a woman to marry me. It is you I want, but I want the child, too, my dear. Have a care else your bad temper spoil a perfect relationship."

She turned her eyes to the racecourse, knowing that he was right and hating him for it. She did not dare look again toward Aspar's box, for she could not bear the sight of her former husband and Cailin.

The chariot races were finally over. The interval between the races and the games would be a full hour. In the three boxes, servants laid out a light luncheon for their masters. When they had almost finished eating, an imperial guardsman appeared in Aspar's box.

"The emperor and the empress will receive your loyal respects now, my lord, and that of your lady, too," he said, bowing politely.

"You did not warn me," Cailin said to Aspar, signaling Zeno to bring a basin of perfumed water in which to wash her hands. She dried them quickly with the linen towel he handed her.

"I was not aware they would receive us today," he told her. "This is a great honor, my love. They are acknowledging our relationship! There can be no going back now, Cailin!"

"You look beautiful," Casia whispered to her friend. "I have been watching Flacilla. She is consumed with jealousy. It is a great victory for you, my friend. Savor it!"

Aspar and Cailin followed the guardsman into the imperial box, where the couple knelt before the emperor and empress. They are so perfect together, Verina thought, as her husband greeted their guests. I have never before seen a better-matched couple. I am almost jealous of their love for each other. She was brought back to reality by Leo's voice: "And my wife welcomes you also, my lady Cailin, do you not, Verina?"

"Indeed, my lord," the empress replied. "You can but add more luster to our court, lady. You are from the former province of Britain, I am told. It is a dark land, or so I am informed."

"It is a green and fertile land, majesty, but perhaps not as sunny and bright a place as is Byzantium. Your springs come earlier and your autumns later than in Britain."

"And do you miss your green and fertile land, lady?" the empress inquired politely. "Have you family there?"

"Yes," Cailin said, "I sometimes miss Britain, majesty. I was happy there, but," she amended with a sweet smile, "I am happy here with my dear lord Aspar. Wherever he is will be my home."

"Well said, lady!" the emperor approved, smiling at her. "How charming she is," Leo continued after the couple had returned to their own box. "Aspar is a very lucky man, I think."

Justin Gabras squeezed his wife's hand in warning, for he could see she was near to another angry outburst. "Breathe deeply, Flacilla," he instructed her softly, "and rein in your nasty temper. If we are banned from the court because of your ungovernable behavior, you will live to regret it, I swear it!"

The angry color slowly faded from her face and neck, and swallowing hard, she nodded her acquiescence. "I will never be happy again until I can find a way to revenge myself on Aspar," she whispered.

"Let it go, my dear," he told her. "There is no way."

"The fat cow is going to have apoplexy," Casia giggled wickedly in Aspar's box. "She's positively purple with rage. What did the emperor and the empress say to you that has infuriated her so greatly?"

"She has no reason to be angry with us," Cailin said, and then she repeated the conversation she had had with the royal couple.

Suddenly there was a flourish of trumpets, and Casia said excitedly, "Ohh, the games are about to begin! I was visiting with my friend Mara at Villa Maxima yesterday, and I saw the gladiators there. Justin Gabras has taken it over for the entire term of their stay. The public is not allowed. He said he wanted his gladiators to have the very best while they were in Constantinople. Jovian is in his glory with all those beautiful young men about, and Phocas, I am told, is actually smiling, so great a price did Gabras pay him. Wait until you see the champion they call the Saxon! I have never before seen such a beautiful man. Castor, Pollux, and Apollo pale in comparison. Ohhhh!" she squealed. "Here they come now!"

The gladiators marched in procession into the Hippodrome, parading around it until they reached the imperial box, where they stopped. Weapons raised high, they saluted the emperor and their generous patron with a single voice. "Those about to die salute you!"

"There is the Saxon," Casia said, pointing to the tallest man in the group. "Isn't he magnificent?"

"How can you possibly tell?" Cailin teased her friend. "That helmet with its visor virtually renders him invisible."

"True," Casia agreed, "but you will have to take my word for it. He's got golden hair, and blue, blue eyes."

"Many Saxons do," Cailin replied.

Aspar leaned over and said, "The first matches will be fought with blunt weapons, my love. There will be no blood shed for now, and it will give you an idea of the skills involved."

"I think I will prefer it to what must come later," Cailin told him. "Must all these men fight until only one of them survives?"

"No," he told her. "Six specific matches will be fought to the death. That is the number that Gabras purchased from this particular troupe of gladiators. Two death matches will be fought today, two to-morrow, and two on the last day of the games. The Saxon, who is the unbeaten champion, will fight today and on the last day. His main rival is a man called the Hun, who must fight all three days. If he survives the first two days, they will probably pair him with the Saxon on the last day. That should be quite a match."

"I think it horrendous that someone must die," Cailin said. "They are young men. Why, it goes against the very teachings of the church to allow such barbarity, yet there sits the patriarch and all his priests in their box on the other side of the emperor, enjoy-ing this."

Aspar put a gentle hand on hers. "Hush, my love, lest you be overheard," he warned her. "Death is a part of life."

The battle had begun below them. Young men with small shields and blunt weapons fought one another en masse. The crowds loved it, but eventually they began to tire of the mock en-gagement.

"Bring on the Saxon! Bring on the Hun!" they screamed.

The trumpets sounded a recall, and the fighters ran from the arena. The groundskeepers came forth and raked the ground smooth. Then silence descended upon the Hippodrome for what seemed several long minutes. Suddenly the Gladiators Gate in the wall opened and two men stepped forth. The crowds began to scream with their excitement.

"It is the Hun," Aspar said. "He will fight with a Thracian."

"He has no armor," Cailin said.

"He needs none but the leather shoulder pads he wears, my love. He is a net man. Other than his net, he has but a dagger and a spear to fight with, but I think net men the most dangerous of gladiators."

The Thracian, who was helmeted and wore greaves on both legs, carried a small shield and a curved sword. It seemed to Cailin a very unfair match, until the two men began to fight. The Hun tossed his net almost immediately, but the Thracian sidestepped it, and leaping behind his opponent, slashed at him. The wily Hun, obviously anticipating the ploy, moved quickly and was but scratched by the tip of the Thracian's blade. The men fought back and forth for some minutes while the crowds screamed their encouragement to their favorites. Finally, when Cailin had begun to think these combats were vastly overrated for ferocity, the Hun leapt in the air and, with a deft flick of his wrist, swirled his net out gracefully. The Thracian, unable to escape, was enfolded in the web. Desperately, he thrashed at it with his sword, the crowd shrieking with their rising blood lust. The Hun jammed his spear into the ground, drew his dagger out and flung himself down upon the struggling man. It happened so quickly that Cailin wasn't even certain she had seen it, but the sandy floor of the arena was swiftly stained with blood as the Hun cut his opponent's throat and then stood victorious, acknowledging the cheers of the howling mob.

He was a man of medium height, powerfully built, and bald but for a horsetail of dark hair sprouting from his skull and tightly wrapped with a leather thong. He strode around the ring, accepting what he obviously considered his rightful due. While he did so, the groundskeepers ran forth, two of them dragging the lifeless body of the Thracian from the arena, out through the Death Gate; the other two sprinkling fresh sand atop the blood and raking it vigorously.

Cailin was stunned. "It was so quick," she murmured. One moment the Thracian had been valiantly defending himself, and in the next instant he was dead. He had not even cried out.

"Gladiators are not usually cruel to one another," Aspar said gently to her. "They are generally friends or acquaintances, for they live together, eat, sleep, and whore together. Death matches are rare today, and Justin Gabras must have paid well for them. Or perhaps these gladiators are just desperate men who do not care. Some are like that."

"I want to go home," Cailin said quietly.

"You cannot go now!" Casia cried. "The last match of the day is about to begin, and it is the champion himself. The Hun is an amateur compared to the Saxon. If it becomes too bloody, you need not look, and we will just gossip, but you must see him without his helmet. He is a god, I tell you!" Casia enthused.

Aspar laughed, and turning to Basilicus, said, "I think I should be worried about Casia, my old friend, if I were you. She is obviously quite taken, nay, fascinated I think a better word, by this gladiator."

"He is beautiful to look at," Casia replied before the prince might say anything, "but I have usually found that beautiful faces and bodies are all men like the Saxon can offer. There is nothing else, neither wit, nor culture. After one has enjoyed a good romp in Cupid's grove, it is nice to lie back and chatter, is it not, my lord?"

Basilicus nodded silently, but his eyes were twinkling.

"Ohh, look!" Casia said. "Here are the combatants. I should hate to be the poor fellow fighting with the Saxon. He must know he has no chance."

"How sad for him," Cailin answered her friend. "How terrible to know that he is facing his death on this beautiful bright day."

Casia looked discomfited, but then she said brightly, "Well, there is always the chance that he just might get lucky and beat the champion. Wouldn't that be exciting? At any rate, they will put on a good show for us, you may be certain."

The Saxon and his opponent were both armed in the Samnite fashion. Each man wore a helmet with a visor. Each had a thick sleeve on the right arm and a greave on the left leg only. The men's waists were encircled with a belt. They carried long shields and short swords. Their combat would be a very close encounter. Saluting the emperor and their patron, they immediately began to fight. In spite of herself, Cailin was fascinated, for this match seemed more even than the previous one.

Metal clanged upon metal as the two men thrust and parried with their weapons. Cailin soon realized that the battle was not so evenly matched after all. The Saxon's antagonist was not his equal in skill. The champion jumped and twirled in a series of maneuvers deliberately executed to please the crowd. Twice the other man left himself open to attack, but the Saxon feinted to distract attention. Finally the crowd began to catch on, and they screamed with outrage.

"There's few his match," Basilicus noted. "He's but tried to give them a good show, but they want blood. Well, they'll get it now, I think. The Saxon should have been saved for the final day instead of having him fight two days. Gabras obviously wanted his money's worth."

The combat took a different turn now, with the Saxon attacking his opponent vigorously while the other man fought desperately to save his life. The champion, however, refused to draw it out any further. Relentlessly he drove the other Samnite across the ring, his opponent getting few blows in and striving to protect himself with his shield. The Saxon rained blow after blow upon it, until finally the man fell back, exhausted, his defense falling from his hand. The Saxon swiftly and mercifully pierced the other gladiator's heart with his sword. Then he walked across the ring to the cheers of the spectators and saluted the emperor with the bloodied weapon.

"Remove your helmet, Saxon," Justin Gabras said loftily, "that the emperor may see your face when he congratulates you on your victory."

The Saxon removed his helmet and said, "There is no victory against a weaker man, lord. In two days' time, however, I will fight the Hun. I will bring you his head upon a silver salver, and then I will accept your congratulations for a battle well fought."

"You do not fear death?" the emperor said quietly.

"No, majesty," the Saxon replied. "I have already lost everything I ever held dear. What is death but an escape? Yet the gods have willed it that I must live for now."

"You are not a Christian, Saxon?"

"Nay, majesty. I worship Woden and Thor. They are my gods," came the reply, "but the gods, I think, do not concern themselves with little men like myself, else I should have had my heart's desire."

Cailin stared at the Saxon as if mesmerized. She could not hear what was being said, but she knew he was speaking, for his lips were moving. *It could not be.* He looked like Wulf, but it simply could not be. Wulf was in Britain, on their lands, with a new wife and child. This man could not be Wulf Ironfist, and yet . . . She needed to hear his voice, to see him up close.

"I told you he was a glorious creature," Casia purred in smug tones. "Even covered in sweat and dirt he is beautiful, is he not, Cailin? Cailin? *Cailin!*" She tugged at her friend's sleeve.

"What? What is it, Casia? What did you say? I was not listening, I fear. You must forgive me. I was momentarily distracted."

Casia giggled. "I can certainly see you were, and by what."

Cailin smiled. "Yes, he is a beautiful fellow," she replied, regaining control of herself, "but despite it all, I do not like these gladiatorial combats."

"My lord Aspar?" A guardsman had entered the box. "The emperor would speak with you a moment."

Aspar hurried from the box. When he returned several minutes later, he said to Cailin, "There are emissaries here from Adrianople. It seems the peace there grows more fragile with each hour, and fighting is threatening to break out again between the religious factions. I am going to try and mediate this here in the palace with Leo tonight. Do you mind going home alone, my love?"

Cailin shook her head. Actually she was relieved. She needed time to think. The resemblance between the Saxon and Wulf was amazing, though his hair was lighter than Wulf's corn-colored locks had been. "Keep the litter," she told Aspar. "Whatever time you come home, you will need transportation. I will go with Casia to her house, and then her litter will bring me to Villa Mare."

"Of course," Casia agreed. "Cailin is ever practical, my lords. Basilicus, my love, you will join me for supper?"

"I cannot," he said regretfully. "My sister insists I keep her company this evening, for she is entertaining the patriarch. Perhaps I shall come late, my sweet. Would it please you?"

"No," Casia said, "I think not, my lord. If you cannot come to supper, then I shall take the time to catch up on my sleep. I do not seem to get a great deal of it when you are with me," she added suggestively, thus tempering her refusal. Rising, she kissed him lightly on the mouth. "Come, Cailin. It will be difficult enough getting through the crowds, with the arena emptying itself like a full wine cup."

"Good fortune, my lord," Cailin told Aspar.

He bent and, cupping her face in his hand, touched her lips softly with his. "When I look at you, my love," he told her, "I find my devotion to duty growing weaker and weaker."

"You do not fool me," Cailin said with a small smile. "The empire is your first love, and I well know it. I am willing to share you with Byzantium, my dearest love."

He smiled into her face. "You are without peer among all the women I have ever known, Cailin Drusus. I am fortunate to have your love."

"You are fortunate to have his love," Casia told her as they departed the Hippodrome in her large and comfortable litter.

"Why did you refuse to allow the prince to come later?" Cailin asked her friend. "I believe he truly loves you."

"I do not want to cling to Basilicus like some dreadful little vine," Casia said. "Nor do I want Basilicus to ever presume upon my love for him. I am his mistress, not his wife. I will not accept part of an evening at his discretion. I want an entire evening. Surely he knew beforehand that he would be with his sister tonight, but he did not tell me. He presumed that I should be there for him, but I am not, now am I?"

When Cailin did not answer, Casia focused upon her friend and said, "Have you heard a word that I said? What is the matter with you, Cailin? You are suddenly so distracted."

Cailin sighed. She needed to confide in someone, and Casia was the only friend she had. "It is the Saxon," she replied.

"Aye, he is gorgeous!" Casia agreed.

"It is not that," Cailin answered.

"Then what is it?" Casia demanded.

"I think the Saxon is Wulf Ironfist," Cailin told her friend.

"*Your husband in Britain?* Are you certain? The gods!"

"I am not certain, Casia," Cailin said nervously, "but I must know! We wed because he was tired of fighting and he wanted to settle down. My lands were what drew him to me. I have thought Wulf Ironfist to be in Britain, on those lands, these months past. I even decided that he must have taken another wife and had a child by now. I have to know if the man they call the Saxon is he! I must know one way or another."

"Ohhh, Cailin, you are opening a Pandora's box," Casia warned. "What if this man is Wulf Ironfist? What will you do? Do you still love him? What of Aspar?"

"I cannot answer you, Casia. I have no answers. I only know I must learn if it is he, or if my eyes have been playing tricks upon me." She looked so distraught that Casia's heart went out to her. "Ohhh, what am I to do?" Cailin asked, and she began to cry.

"Well," Casia said briskly, "we will simply have to satisfy your curiosity, won't we?" Pulling the curtains of her litter open, she leaned out and called to her head bearer, "Go to Villa Maxima, Peter!"

Cailin gasped. "Oh, Casia, no! 'Tis madness! What if I am seen? Especially now that I am to be married to Aspar."

"Who will see us?" Casia said. "Jovian and Phocas have closed Villa Maxima to their regular clientele while the gladiators are in residence. I will go in while you remain in the litter with the curtains tightly closed. I will seek out Jovian, and he will know how you may learn if the Saxon is your Wulf Ironfist. We will be dis-

creet, and you will be safer than if you were in your mother's
house again," Casia promised. "Then you can go home and feel
foolish, for it is very, very unlikely that this gladiator is your man,
Cailin Drusus."

"But what if it is Wulf?" Cailin fretted.

Casia's face grew serious. "Why then, my friend, you are going
to have to decide just what it is you want—a beautiful but savage
Saxon who is obviously penniless, and willing to risk his life in the
ring; or the cultured and wealthy First Patrician of the empire. If
it were me, Cailin Drusus, I would order this litter to turn back,
and I would return to Villa Mare this instant. If a man like Flavius
Aspar loved me, I would thank God each morning when I awoke
for the rest of my days. I think you are mad to tempt the Fates so.
Let me tell Peter to turn back. I will come home with you and
keep you company this night. The Saxon cannot be Wulf Ironfist."

"I must know, Casia. Seeing him, even from a distance, has
filled my mind with doubts. If I do not resolve these doubts, how
can I ever pledge my faith to Aspar? What if the Saxon is not Wulf,
but someday in the future Wulf does appear upon my doorstep?
What if I still love him?"

"The gods forbid it, you foolish creature!" Casia exclaimed.

The litter made its way down the Mese and then through a series of side streets. The two women had grown quiet. Casia twisted
the rich fabric of her gown with her slender fingers. She was already regretting her impulsiveness. It was not Cailin alone who
was opening Pandora's box. She drew a deep breath. Nothing was
going to come of this. Cailin, having a fit of bridal nerves, was seeing ghosts. The Saxon would turn out to be no one she had ever
known. Still, Casia started nervously as the litter was set down and
her head bearer, Peter, drew back the curtains to reveal that they
were in the courtyard of Villa Maxima. Cailin reached out, touching Casia's arm encouragingly.

Casia nodded. "I will find Jovian. Remain here, and whatever
you do, do not open the curtains. Let them think the litter is
empty." She stepped from her elegant vehicle. "Peter, let no one
be aware that I have a companion with me. I will not be long."

"Yes, lady," he replied.

Casia hurried into the magnificent atrium of the villa. A servant came forward and his eyes widened as he recognized the visitor. "Good afternoon, Michael," Casia said. "Will you fetch Master Jovian to me, please? I will await him here. Were you at the games today?" she inquired brightly. "Was the Saxon not wonderful!"

Michael allowed himself a small grin. Casia had a fine eye for the gentlemen, and it was apparent she had not lost it. He bowed politely. "At once, lady. Shall I have refreshments sent to you while you wait? It is hot for autumn. Some iced wine, perhaps?"

"Thank you, no," Casia returned. "I can stay but long enough to speak with Master Jovian." She sat down upon a marble bench, watching as the servant went off, and wondering how long it would be before Jovian put in an appearance. The gods! Why had she ever suggested coming here?

Jovian came into the atrium, but to her intense distress, he was not alone. She silently cursed herself for a fool.

"Casia, my pet!" Jovian kissed her upon both cheeks. "What brings you here this day? I am quite surprised to see you."

"Indeed, Casia," Justin Gabras purred. "I, too, am surprised. I wonder if Prince Basilicus would be also?"

"No, he would not," Casia replied sweetly, regaining her composure. "I grant the prince certain favors, my lord, but he does not own me. Nor would he presume to interfere with my friendships, many of which are of a long-standing nature." She turned to Jovian. "May we speak alone?"

Before Jovian might answer, however, Gabras said, "Secrets, my pet? I am fascinated. What possible secrets could a whore have? I believed that everything about you was already common knowledge."

Casia felt her temper rising. "I wonder how long it will be, my lord, before you are poisoned with your own venom," she snapped. "Jovian! Where may we speak?"

"No! No!" Gabras persisted, chortling. "I would know your secrets, lady. I really will not leave you to Master Jovian until I do."

Jovian looked helplessly at Casia, and she shrugged. "Ohh, very well! If you must know, my lord, I came to gain a closer look at the gladiators. There! Are you satisfied now?"

Justin Gabras burst out laughing. "You women are all alike," he said. "A look, you say? Is that all, Casia? Perhaps what you really wanted was to sample their passions. Which is it who takes your fancy? The Saxon? The Hun? Were you still a resident of this house, you would have had your pick of them tonight, would you not?"

"Big, sweaty men with big cocks and childish minds do not make particularly good lovers," Casia replied coolly. "Their bodies, however, are beautiful, and I am a lover of beauty, my lord. I could see little from our box in the Hippodrome, which is why I came to Villa Maxima. Perhaps I have chosen a bad time. I can come back in the morning."

Jovian, who was astounded by Casia's speech, finally found his voice. "Yes, my darling, that would really be better," he agreed. "Their day has been long, and they are about to enjoy a fine meal and the kind of entertainment that only Villa Maxima can provide. Come back in the morning and I will introduce you to them all. You may even see them in the baths." What was Casia about? This behavior of hers was quite out of character. "I will escort you to your litter."

"Thank you, dear Jovian," Casia said with a smile.

"And I will come, too," Justin Gabras told them.

"It is not necessary, my lord," Casia said quickly.

"But I insist," Justin Gabras said, smiling toothily at her.

When they had reached the litter, Casia said loudly, "I will come back in the morning, Jovian, and see those beautiful bodies then."

Before she could stop him, Justin Gabras leaned down and pulled the litter's curtains aside. His eyes widened, and reaching in, he pulled a resistant Cailin forth. "Well! Well! Well! And what have we here? Flavius Aspar's bride-to-be come home for a little visit? Did you come to see the gladiators, too, my pet? Or was the purpose of your visit to relive old times?"

Cailin shook his hand off her arm and glared icily at him.

"It's all my fault," Casia burst out. "Aspar was called to the palace after the games today. I said I would take Cailin back to Villa Mare, but I did so want to get a close look at those marvelous men. I detoured my litter here. Cailin did not want to come, and as you see, she has remained in the litter, practically hiding. If Aspar finds out, he will not let us remain friends!"

"If Aspar finds out, the wedding will most likely be off," Justin Gabras said drolly.

"I think not, my lord," Cailin said. "I have done nothing wrong, and my lord Aspar knows I am not a liar. If I but tell him the truth of this matter, he will believe me."

"Probably he will," Justin Gabras admitted, "but will the imperial court? Or the patriarch? They will be all too eager to believe the worst of you, Cailin Drusus." He laughed. "Just today I told my wife that you were now inviolate. It seems that I was wrong."

"Who is to say that we were here today?" Casia demanded. "Given who your wife is, my lord, do you think you will be believed if you tell tales?" She pushed past him, taking Cailin's hand in hers. "Come, I must get you back to Villa Mare before it grows dark and the road cannot be seen. I will stay the night with you."

"No!" Justin Gabras grasped Cailin's other arm in a bruising grip. He had already devised a wicked plan by which he might discredit her.

"*Jovian!*" Casia appealed to the master of the house.

"Jovian cannot help you, my dears," Gabras said. "What do you expect him to do for you? You came here of your own free will. I did not force you to come. Now you will stay, and amuse my guests."

"My lord Gabras," Cailin said pleadingly, "why do you do this thing? What have I ever done that you should hate my lord Aspar so?"

"I do not know Flavius Aspar well enough to hate him," was the cold reply, "but I am tired of hearing my wife Flacilla whine for revenge upon him for their loveless marriage. No, do not tell me that she loved him not. She says it often enough herself, but hate—and hers is very strong toward Aspar—is the other side of the love's coin, Cailin Drusus. Surely you know that. Flacilla's choler is such that I fear for my unborn child. *I want that child!* Until this moment I had not the power to give my wife what she claims to desire so dearly. Your foolishness at coming here has given me an opportunity I never expected to have." He smiled cruelly. "By this time tomorrow, Flacilla will have her revenge, and may rest easy, I think."

"Spare her," Casia said, "and I will personally entertain your guests in any fashion you desire! Just release Cailin, I beg you, my lord Gabras! Jovian, have you no say in any of this?"

"I cannot help you," Jovian said, and his eyes filled with tears. "He would kill me if I tried, would you not, my lord? Even if I dared to send for help, by the time Aspar got here, it would be too late. You should not have come here tonight, Casia, and you most assuredly should not have brought Cailin."

"Michael!" Justin Gabras called to the servant, who came quickly to his side. "Help me take our *guests* and lock them up until we are ready for them." He dragged Cailin into the atrium while she struggled in vain to escape his strong fingers.

"Let us go!" Casia cried as Michael pulled her along in their wake.

"And lock up the whore's litter bearers until we are of a mind to release her," Justin Gabras called out to Jovian.

"Lady, I apologize for this," Michael told Cailin as he pushed her into a sparsely furnished, windowless room behind Casia. He shut the door behind them, and they heard the lock turning noisily.

"Forgive me!" Casia said, flinging herself into Cailin's arms. "I am a fool to have ever suggested coming here! The gods help us both!"

"It is as much my fault as yours," Cailin said generously. "If I had let the matter of the Saxon rest instead of pursuing it, we would not be in this predicament. What do you think they mean to do?"

"It is obvious," Casia replied. "Gabras will give us to his gladiators. It matters not to me. I am a whore and used to taking a variety of men between my thighs, but you, my poor friend!" She began to cry, much to Cailin's astonishment, for Casia was not a woman given to tears.

"Do not cry," Cailin comforted her friend. Strangely, she felt nothing right now. Not even fear.

"Gabras will spread word of this incident all over Constantinople," Casia said, still sobbing. "Basilicus will never forgive me!"

"You love him!" Cailin was again surprised.

Casia nodded. "Aye, the gods help me, I do! He doesn't know, of course. He is not the kind of man one can confide such an emotion in, sadly. He will never accept being embarrassed by me. I will never see him again after tonight, I fear! I have ruined not just your life, but my own as well!"

"Perhaps we can escape," Cailin said hopefully.

Casia, her tears finished, looked at her friend and shook her head. "How? This room has no windows, and but one door, which is locked. They will come for us, and that will be the end of it. There is no escape, Cailin. Make up your mind to that right now."

Chapter

14

he two women did not have long to wait. Four male slaves arrived to escort them to the baths, where they were thoroughly washed and their bodies rubbed with fragrant oils. The bath attendants rubbed Cailin's auburn ringlets and Casia's thick, long blue-black hair until they were dry. Their hair was perfumed, Casia's first being braided into a single plait, and then floral wreaths were set atop their heads. No fresh garments were offered them, and the women realized it would be useless to even ask.

They were then escorted into a large airy room that opened onto the villa's beautiful gardens. Justin Gabras sat, now garbed in a short white tunic, upon a black marble chair. The gladiators were assembled before him. There were no other women in the room. At their entry, the men turned, their eyes avid with interest. The guards forced Casia and Cailin forward, and reaching out, Justin Gabras pulled both women into his lap, balancing them each upon a single knee. His hands reached up to fondle their breasts, pinching at the nipples.

"You have eaten well, my friends," he said to his guests, "and now I have a little treat for you. These two women are the most exclusive whores in Byzantium. They are pretty little rabbits, are they not? We are going to have a little game. We shall release these two little rabbits into the gardens, and then you, as randy a pack of dogs as I've ever seen, will chase after them. They will hide from you, will you not my beauties? But someone will find them, and whoever the lucky men are will have their pleasure of these women for this entire night. There are no losers in this game, however. The rest of you will have your choice of any other woman in the house after our game is over. What think you?"

The gladiators cheered Justin Gabras lustily.

"By the gods," the Hun said loudly, "you give us a difficult choice, my lord. Both of these women are real beauties!"

"Which do you favor?" Gabras asked him.

"I am not certain," the net man replied. He turned to his companion. "What about you, Wulf Ironfist? Which do you prefer?"

"The one I catch," the Saxon replied, and his eyes met Cailin's.

Casia quickly looked to her friend. Cailin was paler than she had ever seen her. Her great violet eyes mirrored both pain and shock. *Is it he?* Casia mouthed silently over the laughter that greeted the Saxon's remark, and Cailin nodded. If anyone catches Cailin, Casia thought, it must be the Saxon. She looked straight at the Hun and smiled her most seductive smile.

"Are you as good out of the ring as you are in it?" she purred suggestively. "If you are, then I shall be happy to be caught in your net."

To Casia's surprise, the Hun turned beet-red as his companions whooped with amusement. So he was shy. But her bold words had certainly made it plain to the others that he was her choice. None of the others would dare to come after her now, for shy though he might be, the Hun would want her. They would not confront him over a woman, she knew. She could see the puzzled way in which the Saxon was looking at Cailin. Now she must make certain of him.

"Cailin Drusus." She said her friend's name loudly. "Do you

have a preference among these fine men? I think the Saxon would suit you admirably."

"I think he would," Cailin replied, having caught on to Casia's little game.

"So you are no better than the rest of them," Justin Gabras sneered. "Why is it that all women are born whores?" He did not see how pale the handsome gladiator had become, nor the tightening of the Saxon's lips and the flash of anger in the Saxon's eyes at his words.

Without waiting for an answer to his question, Justin Gabras dumped the two women from his lap. "Run into the garden and hide yourselves, my beauties. I will count to fifty, and then loose these lusty beasts on you. *Go!*"

The two women ran from the room, through the marble pillars, and out into the early evening twilight. When they had gone a ways together into the dimness, Casia stopped a moment and said, "Hide yourself well, Cailin, and do not come out unless you see the Saxon!" Then she was gone down a grassy path. Cailin fled to the depths of the gardens, finally climbing into the branches of a peach tree. It was unlikely that anyone would think to look for her up there.

"*Fifty!*" she heard Justin Gabras call out.

The gladiators began to thrash through the gardens, noisily seeking the two women. Within a few minutes she heard the rough voice of the Hun crowing triumphantly, "I've caught a little rabbit, lads!" and Casia's coy shriek of false surprise. The hunt for Cailin grew more intense, but she felt safe amid the branches of the tree. She could even see some of the men below, looking under bushes, behind the fountains, and among the decorative statuary for her. They will never find me, she thought smugly, but then what? How could she escape Villa Maxima without her clothes, without a litter? Suddenly the branch upon which she was perched gave way, and Cailin fell with a cry to the grass below. Two men loomed forth from the darkness as she desperately scrambled to her feet. A bolt of pain tore through her right ankle, but she struggled to remain standing.

"Stay back!" she ordered the two men.

"Don't be afraid, lambkin," she heard one say, and then, "She is mine, Greek! Touch her, and I'll kill you!"

"No woman is worth death, Wulf Ironfist," the man called Greek said, and he faded into the darkness.

"Are you really the most exclusive whore in Byzantium, Cailin Drusus?" Wulf asked her solemnly.

"No," she said softly, "but you had best treat me as if I were. Your host is my mortal enemy."

"Can you walk, or is your ankle seriously injured?"

"I twisted it when I fell from the tree," she answered, "but it is not broken. Nonetheless, you will have to carry me, and I will struggle to escape you. Justin Gabras would think it odd if I did not."

"Why?" he demanded.

"We will talk when we have found a private spot. Now quickly! Pick me up before someone else comes along and wonders why we are not already engaged in passion's battle."

He came to stand directly in front of her and reached out to touch her face. "Antonia said you were dead, and our child, too."

"I suspected she might have told you that," Cailin answered.

"I want to know what happened," he said.

"Wulf! *Please!*" she pleaded with him. "Not now! Gabras will soon come after us. He is a terrible and dangerous man."

There were so many questions swirling about in Wulf's head. How was it she was alive? And here in Byzantium? But he saw the genuine look of fear in her eyes. Reaching out, he picked her up and threw her over his shoulder. She immediately began to beat at him with her little fists as he carried her through the garden and back to where the others waited.

"Put me down! Put me down, you great brute!" Cailin shrieked. The blood was going to her head and making her dizzy.

"So, our other little rabbit has been caught at last," she heard Gabras say, and then he came into her line of vision. "You have given us all quite a chase, my dear. Where was she?"

"In a tree," the Saxon answered. "I wouldn't have found her at all, but the branch upon which she was perched gave way."

"I want to see you take her," Justin Gabras said. "Here. *Now!*" A goblet of wine was clutched in his hand.

"My public performances are only in the ring," Wulf Ironfist said quietly.

"I want to see this woman humiliated," Gabras persisted.

He is dangerous, Wulf thought, and so he replied, "By morning I will have taken this woman in every way possible, and in some ways you have never even considered, my lord. If she is not dead, then she will be incapable of even crawling from the room where we will lie this night." He turned to Jovian Maxima. "I want a room with no windows so none may be disturbed by her cries. It is to be furnished with a good mattress, and I will want wine. Also a dog whip. Women frequently need to be schooled in their duties, and this woman is too free, I can tell. It is obvious to me she does not know her place, *but she will learn it!* We Saxons like our females docile, and subservient."

"By the gods!" Justin Gabras said, a genuine smile lighting his handsome features, "you are a man after my own heart. Give him what he wants, Jovian Maxima! The wench is in good hands."

A few moments later they were escorted to the same room where Cailin and Casia had earlier been imprisoned. Now, however, the room was newly furnished with a large, comfortable bed upon a dais, several low tables, a pitcher of wine and two goblets, two oil lamps burning sweet-scented oil, a tall floor lamp, and, set at the foot of the mattress, the whip that Wulf had requested.

Jovian, who had accompanied them personally, looked nervously at it, and Wulf grinned at him wickedly.

"Close the door," the Saxon said softly. "I wish to speak with you."

Jovian complied with the Saxon's request, but he looked distinctly uncomfortable.

"Just tell Gabras that I threatened you if we were not granted absolute privacy," Wulf told the man.

"What is it you want of me, gladiator?" Jovian asked him.

"Tell me the nature of the danger Cailin Drusus faces from Justin Gabras," Wulf demanded.

"He will use what has happened, what will happen this night, to discredit the lady Cailin before the imperial court and the patriarch, who will then forbid her marriage to General Flavius Aspar. This is what Gabras seeks. The rest the lady Cailin must tell you herself, if you are of a mind to listen to her."

"He is Wulf Ironfist, my husband," Cailin said quietly.

"The gods he is!" Jovian Maxima looked thunderstruck, and then he said, "This is the truth, my lady?"

"That is why I came, Jovian," she admitted. "When I saw him today in the ring, I was not certain. I had to be certain before I pledged my faith to Aspar. Wulf Ironfist and I must speak together now, and then I must remain in this room till the morning. When the dawn comes, however, I beg you to help me return to Villa Mare. And help Casia as well. If we are clever, we can keep this from Prince Basilicus. She loves him, you know."

Jovian nodded. "Aye, and the prince loves Casia even as she loves him, but he cannot say it to her. He told me once when he was in his cups. When this night is over, I will tell her. It will give her comfort, I think. Now I must leave you both else Gabras become overly suspicious of why I linger here."

The door closed behind Jovian, and Wulf set the wooden bar into place, which would protect their privacy. Cailin's heart was beating very quickly. *It was really Wulf!* With shaking hands she poured two goblets of wine, sipping nervously at hers as he turned back to her and took up his own goblet.

He drained it swiftly and said bluntly, "So you are to be married. You have the look of a woman who has prospered, and one who is well-loved."

"And you who loved me for my lands left those lands quickly enough. You told me you had tired of fighting, but perhaps a gladiator earns more coin, and certainly he has better privileges than a mere soldier in the legions," Cailin countered. She had been mad to come, and madder still to believe there was anything left between them.

"How came you to Byzantium?" he asked her.

"In the hold of a slave galley out of Massilia, Wulf Ironfist," Cailin said harshly. "I was walked the length of Gaul to get there. Before that my time was spent in a drugged state in a slave pen in Londinium." She gulped at her wine. "I believe our child lives, but what Antonia did with it, I cannot say. Were you even interested enough to find out?"

"She said that both you and the child had perished in the ordeal of childbirth," he defended himself, and then went on to tell her of what had transpired when he had gone to Antonia's villa to bring her home.

"What of our bodies?" Cailin said angrily. "Did you not even ask to see our bodies?"

"She said she had cremated you both, and even gave me a container of ashes. I interred them with your family," he finished helplessly. "I thought you would want it that way."

The macabre humor of it struck Cailin, and she laughed. "I suspect what you interred was a container of wood, or charcoal ashes," she said, draining her cup and pouring herself more wine.

"How is it that you know Jovian Maxima?" he suddenly demanded.

"Because he bought me in the slave marketplace, and brought me here," she told him coolly. "Are you certain you wish to know more?"

She was not the same person, he realized, but then how could she be? He nodded slowly, then listened, his face alternating between anger, pain, and sympathy, as she told her tale. When she had finished, he was silent for a long moment, and then said, "Will we allow Antonia Porcius to destroy the happiness we had, Cailin Drusus?"

"Ohh, Wulf," she replied, "so much time has passed for us. I thought you would stay with the lands that were my family's. I believed you would have taken another wife by now, and had another child of your loins. How could I have ever believed that we would meet again here in Byzantium, or anywhere on this earth?" She sighed, and lowered her head to hide the tears that had sprung into her eyes from nowhere, it seemed.

"So you went on with your life?" he asked her, almost bitterly.

"What else was I to do?" she cried to him. "Aspar rescued me from this silken Hades, and freed me. He sheltered me, and loved me. He has offered me the protection of his name despite incredible odds. I have learned to love him, Wulf Ironfist!"

"And have you forgotten the love that we shared, Cailin Drusus?" he demanded fiercely. Reaching out, he pulled her roughly into his arms. "Have you forgotten what it once was like between us, lambkin?" His lips gently touched her brow. "When Antonia told me you and the child were dead, I was devastated. I could not believe it, and then she was handing me that damned container of ashes. I returned to our hall and buried them. I tried to go on with my life, but you were everywhere. Your very essence permeated the hall, the lands! And without you there was nothing. None of it meant anything to me without you, Cailin. One morning I awoke. I took my helmet, my shield, and my sword, and I left. I didn't know where I was going, but I knew that I must get away from your memory. I wandered the face of Gaul into Italy. In Capua I met some gladiators at a tavern. I enrolled in the school there, and once I began to fight, I quickly became a champion. I had no fear of death, you see. That fear is a gladiator's greatest enemy, but I did not feel it. Why should I? What did I have to lose that I had not already lost except my life, which was now worthless to me."

"And did you escape my memory in your combats, in a wine jug, or in the arms of other women, Wulf Ironfist?" she asked him.

"You have been ever with me, Cailin Drusus. In my thoughts and in my heart, lambkin. I could not escape you, I fear." He held her close, breathing in her scent, rubbing his cheek against her head.

The stone that her heart had become when she saw him again began to crumble. "What do you want of me, Wulf?" she asked him softly.

"We have found one another, my sweet lambkin," he told her. "Could we not begin again? The gods have reunited us."

"To what purpose, I wonder?" she answered.

He tilted her face up to his, and his mouth slowly closed over

326 / To Love Again

hers. His lips were warm, and so very soft, and as the kiss deepened, Cailin's heart almost broke in two. She still loved him! Worse. She loved Aspar, too! What was she to do? Unable to help herself, she let her arms slip up and about his neck.

"I no longer know what is right, or what is wrong," she said helplessly. "Ohh, cease, Wulf! I cannot think."

"Do not!" he said. "Tell me you do not love me, Cailin Drusus, and I will help you to escape Villa Maxima now. I will leave Constantinople, and you will never see me again. Perhaps it would be better that way. Our child is lost to us, and the life you lead here in Byzantium is a better life for you. Civilization suits you, lambkin. You know the rough destiny facing us back in Britain." Yet despite his words, he held her close, as if he could not bear to let her go.

Cailin was silent for what seemed an eternity, and then she said, "The child might yet live, Wulf. I somehow feel it does. What kind of parents are we that we do not even seek to find our child?"

"What of this Flavius Aspar? The man you are to wed?" he asked. "Is there not enough between you that you would remain here with him?"

"There is much between us," she replied quietly. "More than you can possibly know. I give up much to return to Britain with you, Wulf Ironfist; but there is much waiting for us in Britain. There are our lands, which I have no doubt Antonia has appropriated once more; and there is the hope of finding our child. The land has a certain meaning for me. Aspar's love, however, far outweighs it. It is our child that tips the balance of the scales in your favor.

"Once, and it seems so long ago now, we pledged ourselves to each other in wedlock. Our marriage would not be recognized by those in power here in Byzantium should I choose Aspar over you. It was not celebrated within their church. But the vows we made in our own land are sacred, and I will not deny them now that I know you live. I am a Drusus Corinium, and we are raised to honor our promises not simply when they are convenient, but always."

"I am not a duty to be done," he said, offended.

Cailin heard his tone. She smiled up at him. "No, Wulf Ironfist, you are not a duty, but you are my husband unless you choose here and now to renounce the vows we made to one another in my grandfather's hall that autumn night. Remember before you speak, however, that in denying me, you deny our lost child to us as well."

"You are certain of what you are saying, lambkin?" he asked.

"No, I am not, Wulf Ironfist," she told him candidly. "Aspar has been good to me. I love him, and I will hurt him when I leave him; but I love you also, it would seem, and there is our child."

"What if we cannot find it?" he questioned.

"Then there will be others," she said softly.

"Cailin," he whispered, "I want to love you as we once loved."

"It is expected of us," she replied, "is it not? The door is barred, and they will leave us in peace until the morning, but you must take that short tunic off, Wulf Ironfist. The gods! It leaves little to the imagination, and I prefer you without it."

Now they both stood naked in the flickering light of the lamps. Cailin filled her eyes with him. She had forgotten much, but now memory surged strongly through her. Reaching out, she touched a crescent-shaped scar on his chest, just above his left breast. "This is new," she said.

"I got it at the school in Capua," he told her, and then held out his right arm to her, "and this one at the spring games in Ravenna this past year. I was blocking a net man, and thinking he had me, he already had his dagger out. He died well, as I remember."

Cailin leaned forward and kissed the scar upon his arm. "You must never go into the ring again, Wulf. I lost you once, but I will not lose you again!"

"There is no safe place," he told her. "There is always danger lurking somewhere, my beloved." Then his two big hands cupped her face and he pressed kisses on her lips, her eyes, her cheeks. Her skin was so soft. She murmured low, her head falling back, her white throat straining. He licked hotly at the column of perfumed flesh, his lips lingering at the base of her neck, feeling the beating pulse beneath. "I love you, lambkin," he murmured. "I always have."

She suddenly seemed to flame with desire. She devoured him with her kisses; her lips and her tongue kissing, touching, licking at him. She touched the scar on his breastbone with her mouth, and he groaned as if in pain. She straightened herself, and they stared deeply into each other's eyes for what seemed an eternity. They were past words. Reaching out, she touched his manhood, stroking him gently, her fingers slipping around him to softly caress his pouch of life.

"You will unman me, sweet," he grated.

"You are no green boy," she reassured him, "and we may as well put to good use the things I have learned for our mutual pleasure." Slipping to her knees before him, she kissed his belly and thighs, then taking him in her mouth, she loved him until he begged her stop, pulling her to her feet to kiss her hungrily.

He drew her over to the dais, and they lay together upon the mattress, their bodies entwined, kissing more. She was no longer the shy girl he had known. Her hands were bold and touched him knowledgeably. He didn't know whether to be shocked or delighted, but in the end he erred on the side of delight. He had lost a sweet young wife. He had regained a passionate woman. Cradling her in the crook of his arm, he began to stroke her body, and she purred at him like a well-fed feline, encouraging him, crying out softly as her own pleasure began to build.

He cuddled the perfect globes of her breasts tenderly, leaning forward to lick at the nipples with a warm tongue, rousing the rosy tips. The taste of her was exciting, and he began to lick at her warm, silken skin, his tongue sweeping over her flesh; between her breasts, up her throat, back down again to her belly.

Cailin moaned fitfully and half sobbed, "Do you know how to pleasure a woman as I pleasured you?"

"Aye," he rasped, and lowered his head that he might do her bidding, flicking lightly at her little jewel, but then he probed at her more deeply, his tongue pushing into her suggestively.

"Ahhhh!" she cried out, and her body arched to meet him. He

was driving her wild, and she sensed he knew it. Then Wulf pulled himself up, and seeking her woman's passage, slid slowly and sensuously into her. When he had sheathed himself as deeply as he could, he let himself rest a moment, his manhood throbbing its passionate message to her. Then grasping her hips in his hands, he moved rhythmically within her until her whimpering cries rang in his ears. Cailin's lids were heavy, but she forced her eyes open that she might look into his face as he possessed her.

He took her tenderly, kissing her face, murmuring his love and longing into her ear. She was full of him, and yet she longed for more of him. She had forgotten the passion that had once existed between them, but now he stirred the embers of her memory until she was afire, and remained so throughout the night as they made love to one another over and over again, seemingly unable to gain satisfaction for very long.

Finally exhausted, they fell into a light slumber, only to be awakened by a pounding upon the door of the chamber.

Wulf stumbled to his feet. The floor lamp and one of the smaller oil lamps had burned out. Unbarring the door, he opened it to find Casia and Jovian before him. "What do you want?" he growled.

"Justin Gabras has sent to Flavius Aspar," Jovian said. His voice was high-pitched and he appeared frightened.

Cailin scrambled up. "My clothes, Jovian! I must get dressed immediately, and for pity's sake find something respectable for Wulf Ironfist to wear when he meets the general."

Casia, who was already dressed in the garments she had worn yesterday, said, "I have your clothes, Cailin. Come with me!"

"Did you mean what you said last night?" Wulf asked her.

"Aye," Cailin answered him with a smile. "We are going home to Britain to reclaim our lands and find our child. Aye, I meant it!" She pushed past him and, with Casia leading the way, hurried down the corridor.

"You are mad!" Casia told her as she helped Cailin dress. "You would give up becoming Aspar's wife and all that Byzantium has to offer for that Saxon? No man is that wonderful in bed!"

Cailin laughed. "He is, but it isn't just that, Casia. Wulf Ironfist is my husband. We have a child, lost to us right now, to be certain; but we will find our child when we return home!"

" 'Tis madness!" Casia repeated. "How will you get back to Britain? What will you use for money? The chances of finding your child are incredible, Cailin. Have you no thought for Aspar? You will break his heart, I fear."

Cailin sighed deeply. "Do you think I do not know that, Casia? What would you do, caught between the love of two men? I cannot have them both, and so I must decide between them, though it pains me to do so."

The slave woman, Isis, came and told them, "Flavius Aspar and Prince Basilicus await you in the atrium, my ladies."

"Basilicus? Oh, the gods!" Casia sobbed.

When they reached the atrium, they found Justin Gabras was also there, as was Jovian and Wulf Ironfist. *"You see!"* Gabras crowed triumphantly. "What did I tell you, my lords! Once a whore, always a whore. I was shocked when they arrived last evening and then stayed to entertain the gladiators as only they are capable."

"How easily the lie rolls off your tongue, Justin Gabras," Cailin said coldly.

"Do you deny that you spent the night locked in the arms of the brawny Saxon, or that Casia entertained the gladiator known as the Hun?"

"Do you deny that that you forced us to it, stripping us of our garments, and making us play hide and seek in the gardens until we were caught and given as prizes to the gladiators?"

"I did not kidnap you and bring you here, lady," Gabras replied smugly. "You came here of your own free will, and now you would cry rape when your lewd behavior is found out."

"Be silent!" Flavius Aspar thundered, and Cailin drew a sharp breath, for she had never seen him so angry as he was at this minute. He pierced her with a hard look. "Did you come here of your own free will yesterday, lady?"

"Do not blame her, it is my fault!" Casia burst out. She was near to tears, a state that surprised the men who knew her.

Aspar's stern face softened a bit. "Tell me the truth of this, my love," he said, turning to Cailin. "You have never lied to me."

"Nor will I now, my lord Aspar," Cailin said quietly. "Yesterday at the games I thought I recognized one of the gladiators. I confided in Casia, and she felt we should come to Villa Maxima that I might see this man at a closer range in order to determine if I did indeed know him."

"She was reluctant to come," Casia broke in. "She was concerned if someone saw us, it would reflect badly on you, my lord."

"You need not defend me, Casia," Cailin chided her friend gently. "My lord knows my character well."

"And when you saw this gladiator close up, Cailin Drusus, was he indeed the man you thought he was?" Aspar asked her.

"Yes, my lord, he was, I fear. The man who is known as the Saxon is my husband, Wulf Ironfist," Cailin said, and while the two men were absorbing that startling revelation, she went on to explain what had happened to herself and to Casia at the hands of Justin Gabras.

When she had concluded her tale, Casia broke in quickly. "The Hun did not have me, my prince. He has, it seems, a very weak head for wine. My plan was to get him drunk and then hit him upon the head, but three goblets of Jovian's best Cyprian brew, and he was snoring like a wild boar with a bellyful of acorns and roots."

It was obvious that Basilicus wanted very much to believe Casia. Relief spread over his features when Wulf Ironfist said, "She is probably speaking the truth, my lord. I have lived with the Hun these months past, and it is true that he has no head for wine."

"And you, Cailin Drusus," Aspar said. "Did you get the Saxon drunk, too?" She saw the pain in his eyes, which he strove to hide from the others, and vowed silently that Gabras would not have this victory over Flavius Aspar; nor would she hurt him with this particular truth.

"Wulf and I spent the night talking, my lord. There was much for us to talk about, was there not, Wulf?"

The Saxon realized what she was doing, and wondered if

Flavius Aspar would believe the lie that he now gave voice to in her support.

"Cailin speaks the truth, my lord. There was much unresolved between us."

"They are lying!" Justin Gabras shouted. "It is impossible for him to have spent the night with her and not made love to her!"

"Am I some green boy, you snake, that I must poke my sword in every pretty sheath that comes along? To call me a liar, Gabras, is to seek death!"

Justin Gabras paled and took a step backward.

"You've done your mischief, Gabras," Prince Basilicus said. "Now get you gone from here, and if one word of this scandal should reach my ears, I will personally see that you meet a most unpleasant end. You have no real friends in Byzantium, and if you want to see your child born, then you will forget what you have done."

"Is he not to be punished?" Casia demanded, relieved not to be in her lover's bad graces. "Look at the trouble he has caused!"

Basilicus laughed. "He is married to Flacilla Strabo. That is punishment enough, I think."

As Justin Gabras turned to leave, Phocas Maxima stepped from the shadows. "A moment, my lord Gabras. There is the matter of the bill. I think I should be wise to settle it today. You have made powerful enemies here this morning, and the span of your life is no longer certain." He took the man's arm and led him off.

Jovian, looking at the five people in his atrium, wondered what was to come next. He had not long to wait.

Aspar took Cailin's hand in his. "Tell me," he said.

"I must go home to Britain, my lord," she said quietly, but there were tears in her eyes when she said it.

"How easily you leave me, my love," he said bitterly.

"No," Cailin told him. "It is not easy for me to leave you, for I love you, but I have thought long and hard about what I must do. In the eyes of your Orthodox church I am not married, and therefore free to wed you, Aspar. But I know that under the old laws of marriage in Britain, I am Wulf's wife.

"Once the empress told me that love was a weakness for those in power. I did not believe her, my lord, but now I do. What if the Saxon had not been Wulf Ironfist? What would you have done knowing I had been forcibly violated? What if I had been driven mad by the incident? Gabras himself planned to have me, I know. How would you have felt upon learning that the woman you loved and planned to make your wife had been hurt, and shamed so?

"Your value to the empire would have come to an end, my lord, had any of these things come to pass. I am your weakness, Flavius Aspar! Your enemies can reach out and strike at you through me, through the children I would have given you. I was a childish fool to believe that we could live as quiet a life as my parents lived at their country villa. You are important to Byzantium, my love, and your usefulness is not yet at an end. Besides," she smiled at him, "you quite enjoy being an emperor-maker. You would be bored raising horses, hay, and grain.

"I must leave you, my dear lord, if I am to save you from your enemies. There is no other way, and in your heart you know that I am right in this. And what of Wulf Ironfist? He and I have lands in Britain that we must reclaim, and a child who is lost, but whom we will find. I cannot turn my back on any of this, though I am torn between you both! Once I said that Fortuna was not kind to me, but she has been too kind, I think, for what other woman has been so well-loved by two such wonderful men? It is possible, you know, for a woman to love two men.

"Had I ever believed that I should be reunited with Wulf Ironfist again, I should not have allowed you to love me, Flavius Aspar. You do not really need me. I am but a liability to you. Wulf needs me."

"You could not have ever kept me from loving you, Cailin Drusus," Aspar told her sadly, "but if you feel you must leave me, then I will not stand in your way." He wanted to plead with her to stay with him. He wanted to tell her that she was no liability to him; or if it was so, then he would take his chances with his enemies if it meant having her by his side. Instead he said, "You must take Nellwyn with you. Britain is her home, too, and I would not know what to do with her if you left her behind. She would be but a constant reminder of you."

"Yes, I will take Nellwyn."

"I will send word to Zeno to pack your belongings and send them here with the girl. Unless you would like to return to Villa Mare, and oversee this business yourself, my love."

"I can take nothing from you, my lord," Cailin said. "Under the circumstances, it would not be right."

"Do not be a little fool," the practical Casia snapped at her friend. "You need clothing, Cailin! I will go to Villa Mare and pack the garments that will best serve you. It is true that you will not need the more glorious clothing you possess, but you should take a warm cloak, some simple stolas, camisas, and slippers, for you will do a great deal of walking, I suspect, before you get home to your Britain."

Jovian, silent through all of this, now spoke up. "Phocas and I own a small trading vessel that is leaving for Massilia on the afternoon tide. It will not be luxurious, but it will get you to Gaul in just a few weeks. I can arrange passage for you, if you wish it."

"I think that would be an excellent idea," Aspar said. Best to get this over with quickly, he thought. "Do not forget her jewelry, Casia."

"No!" Cailin cried, stricken. "I cannot take it."

"Indeed, it would be dangerous to carry such valuables," Wulf said.

"You will need it to help you start over in Britain, Wulf Ironfist," Aspar said, addressing him for the first time. "Money may not buy happiness as we know it, but it buys a great deal of other things, including cattle and loyalty. Cailin and Nellwyn can sew the jewelry into your cloaks for safekeeping. I will see that you have coin as well."

"My lord . . ." Wulf did not know what to say.

"I want her taken care of, Saxon," Flavius Aspar said harshly. "Do you understand me? She is never to want for anything!"

Wulf nodded, and wondered if Cailin had chosen Aspar over him, would he have been so gallant. He wasn't certain.

Jovian left them to go arrange passage for the trio of travelers. The trading vessel upon which they would travel occasionally took passengers. It had one tiny wooden shed of a cabin upon the deck, which the captain and his mate shared unless there was a paying passenger along. When that happened, the captain and his mate slept in hammocks upon the open deck. The ship would never travel out of sight of land for too long. It was not large enough for an adequate water supply.

Jovian had six barrels of fresh water brought aboard and stored for Cailin and her party. He saw that there was a goat for milk, a pen full of chickens, several boxes of bread, four cheeses, and fruit. The vessel was to carry bolts of cloth woven in Constantinople to Gaul. There were also some expensive luxuries hidden among the cloth in order to escape the custom agent's eyes, although he was well bribed to overlook such infractions of the law.

Casia met them at the boat. She had not only packed the necessary clothing for her friend, but a comb, a pair of boots, and the jewelry as well. Nellwyn was astounded by the turn of events, but excited to actually be returning to Britain. Casia had explained everything to her. Her eyes widened at the sight of Wulf Ironfist.

Wulf's possessions were few and had been easily gathered together. The other gladiators were still sleeping, and would probably not miss the Saxon until the following day, when he did not appear for his match.

"It will be a great disappointment to the populace to find that the great unbeaten champion has disappeared," Jovian noted. "We must see that they hold Gabras responsible. They may riot against him. Perhaps even burn his palace down. Ahh, the possibilities are simply endless. Casia, my dear, I do not think I would go to the games tomorrow."

"I would have only gone to see the Saxon," Casia said with a small smile. Then turning to Cailin, she hugged her. "I will miss your honesty. Go with the gods, dear friend. When the winter winds curse this city, I will think of you back home in your beloved Britain. I still think it a savage place, and you a madwoman to go!" She sniffed audibly.

"And I will miss your irreverent ways," Cailin said softly. "We will not be back to Britain by winter, though. Perhaps in the springtime. Farewell, dear Casia. May the gods favor you always." She turned to Aspar, who stood silently.

Taking his hand, she raised it to her lips and kissed it. "If you regret one moment, I shall never forgive you, Flavius Aspar. Our love is real, and it is true; but the fates have governed that we go in separate directions. I will never forget you, my dear lord."

"The memory of you will have to suffice me," he replied quietly. "I will never forget you, Cailin Drusus. You taught me how to love, and for that I am not certain that I can forgive you. Perhaps it is better not to know how to love than to ache with the loss of it. God go with you, my precious love," he finished, and he tenderly kissed her lips, bringing tears to her eyes.

"Damn you, Aspar," she whispered.

"I was born beneath the sign of the Scorpion, my love. I sting when I am hurt. Now get aboard before I decide I cannot be noble."

The ship sailed out of the walled Phosphorion Harbor, around the point of the city, past the imperial palace. The day was bright, and the water sparkled as they passed the Marble Tower that marked the end of the city's walls. Their vessel skimmed the waves, the fresh breeze sending it onward.

Wulf Ironfist put a hard arm about Cailin and drew her close to him. "I hope that neither of us regrets the bargain between us."

"I do not think so," she told him, and as their ship swept past Villa Mare, she whispered a silent, final good-bye to Flavius Aspar. He would survive, and so would she. She was becoming good at survival, she thought, and then she turned her face to the ship's bow. The wind caught at her long auburn curls and blew them about as she looked west. For the first time in months she knew who she was. She was Cailin Drusus, a Briton, descendant of a Roman tribune and a host of Celtic ancestors, and she was going home. *Home to Britain!*

BRITAIN

A.D. 457

Chapter

15

I*t took forty days* to sail from Byzantium to the city of Massilia in Gaul. The trading vessel exited through the Hellespont and crossed the Mare Thracium past mighty Mount Athos, and on into the Aegean Sea, wending its way along the Greek coast past Delos and the Cyclades. As they reached Methone, the captain came to Cailin and Wulf and said, "Master Jovian wanted you to have this choice. I can either sail north along the Greek coast, and then cross over to Italia at the narrowest point separating the two, or we can sail straight across the Ionian Sea to Sicilia in half the time. The weather is good, and will continue to hold, but we would be out of sight of land for several days. Storms are known to arise suddenly, and you are not sailors; but even should a storm come up, I will get you safely to Massilia." He smiled, explaining, "I get a percentage of the cargo profits."

"Sail straight for Sicilia," Wulf said, making the decision for them. "We are anxious to reach Britain before spring."

For almost seven days they did not see land, but finally the toe of Italia's boot and Sicilia with its rugged mountains rose up on their horizon to their right and left. The ship negotiated the Straits of Messina in the Tyrrhenian Sea. They stopped several times to refill their water barrels, but the ship's captain preferred to anchor along deserted stretches of coast to avoid paying port taxes when all he needed was water.

"The customs men are all thieves. They always claim to have found contraband upon your vessel, particularly if you are just passing through. Then they confiscate the cargo. It's just plain stealing!" he finished indignantly.

They cruised along Italia's coast past Tempsa, Neapolis, Ostia, Pisae, and Genna. At last they had almost reached their destination, and Cailin was vastly relieved. She wanted a bath, and there were certain to be public baths in Massilia.

On their first day aboard she had gone through the clothing that Casia had packed for her, and to her surprise found two small bags of coins. One held twenty gold solidi, and the other was crammed with copper folles. She showed Wulf, and he nodded silently.

"There is a loose board beneath my pallet," she told him softly. "I will hide our hoard beneath it, but there must always be someone in the cabin so that we are not robbed. This, and my jewelry, is all we have to make our way with once we arrive at Massilia, and when we reach home we may need what remains to start again. I trust the captain, but the two mates are another thing. I do not like the way they eye Nellwyn."

"Nellwyn is a foolish little rabbit," he replied. "If she is not careful, she will be eaten by dogs. She is your slave. Speak to her. It is not my place to do so."

"Why are you so irritable?" she asked him. "You are like an old cat with a stiff paw. Are you not happy we have been reunited?"

"I cannot believe our good fortune," he said honestly. "I thought you dead, and then found you alive. You chose to return to Britain with me over marrying a wealthy and powerful man. But we have not been alone since we found each other, and we are not likely to be for months! You are beautiful, Cailin, my wife, and I desire you!"

"You will have to learn patience," she said serenely, then giggled mischievously, "and so will I, Wulf Ironfist!"

When they finally docked at Massilia, the captain was thoughtful enough to tell them that parties of merchants traveled up the Roman roads of Gaul toward the coast facing Britain on a regular basis. Wulf would find the respectable travelers at an inn called the Golden Arrow. "You don't want to try to go it alone, sir. Too many bandits, and you've got the women to consider. A big, strong fellow like you will be welcome in any party. If the women are willing to help with the chores, so much the better."

Wulf thanked the captain for his advice, and their bags of coins and Cailin's jewels safely hidden, the trio departed the ship. Both Cailin and Nellwyn were plainly garbed, and their hoods were pulled well up over their heads. They kept their eyes modestly lowered, following Wulf Ironfist as they made their way through the bustling port's streets to the inn where Wulf inquired about caravans departing for the northern coast of Gaul.

"There are several leaving in a day or two, sir," the innkeeper replied. "How far are you going? Will it just be yourself?"

"We need to get to Gesoriacum," Wulf told him, "and my wife and her servant will be going with me. We have come from Byzantium."

"And are going to Britain, I'll wager," the innkeeper said.

Wulf nodded. "I'm a big fellow, as you can see," he told the innkeeper, "and I have served my time in the legions. I'm a good swordsman, and my wife and servant can cook. We'll be no liability."

"Can you pay?" the innkeeper asked. They didn't look like beggers, but still, one could never tell in these days.

"It must be reasonable," Wulf said slowly. "We've not a great deal left. Our passage from Byzantium was dear. Will not our service be enough? But then if we must pay, I'll expect to receive our food in exchange."

"You're in luck," the innkeeper told him. "There's a large caravan of merchants leaving tomorrow that will go all the way to Gesoriacum. Some of the party will stop at other towns along the way, but the main caravan is going to the northern coast. I know the caravan master. He is the big red-haired fellow drinking in my courtyard right now. He can always use an extra man. Tell him that Paulus recommends you. You must do your own bargaining."

"I thank you, sir," Wulf said. "Can you rent me a room for myself and my wife and servant for tonight? And we need to be directed to the public baths. Then I must buy horses for our journey."

"I have no private rooms, but your women can have pallets in the loft with others of their sex. You will have to sleep down here like all the men do who stop at the Golden Arrow," the innkeeper said.

While Cailin and Nellwyn bathed, Wulf went to the market and purchased two horses for them. One was a fine, strong chestnut-colored gelding, and the other a sturdy black mare strong enough to carry both women upon her back, should it be necessary. He returned to the bathhouse where Cailin and Nellwyn were waiting for him. Their precious hoard and the horses remained in their charge while Wulf washed the forty days at sea from his skin. Then they made their way back to the inn, where Wulf introduced himself to the caravan master, who was named Garhard. The bargain was soon struck between the two men, for Garhard was a man who made quick decisions. Their places would cost them two folles apiece. Wulf would help to protect the caravan, and the two women would be expected to help with the meals. In exchange they would travel in safety and be allowed to eat from the common pot.

"If you want wine, bring it," Garhard said. "You supply your own plates and spoons. I don't want your women whoring for extra coins. It causes too much trouble among the men."

"The women are my wife and her servant," Wulf said quietly. "They do not whore, and if your men look at them askance, or speak to them with disrespect, they will have me to deal with."

"Understood," Garhard replied. "We leave at dawn."

They hurried back to the market, where Cailin purchased newly made wood plates and spoons for them, and a single goblet that they would all share. She found a woman selling freshly stuffed pallets, and bought three along with some blankets.

"We should have a cart," she told her husband. "The mare can pull it, and it will hold our worldly goods. We cannot carry it all. You are used to sleeping upon the ground, but Nellwyn and I are not. And we will need water bags, and a brazier, and charcoal. It is almost winter, Wulf, and the farther north we go, the greater chance there is of snow. A cart will offer us some protection from bad weather and wild animals."

He laughed. "You have been living like a young queen in Byzantium. I would have thought you had forgotten such practical matters, but I see you have not. Come, let us purchase what you think we need."

They left just before dawn the next morning. The two women drove the little cart with its cloth-covered sides and roof. They had carefully packed all their possessions inside, along with extra provisions to supplement the communal pot. The water bags hung from the cart.

The caravan traveled the Roman roads up the spine of Gaul through Arelate, Lugudunum, Augustodunum, and Agedincum, to Durocortorum. They then took the road that turned slightly more north, moving on through Samarobriva, and finally arriving at Gesoriacum, an ancient naval port. It had taken them many weeks to reach their destination. It was already mid-February.

They arranged their next passage with a coastal trader. He would take them across the thirty miles of sea separating Gaul and Britain to the port of Dubris. As the sun rose over Gaul, which now lay behind them, they made landfall in Britain on the morning of February twentieth.

Cailin wept unashamedly. "I did not think I should ever see my native land again," she said, sobbing, as Wulf comforted her.

"We have been traveling for over four months," he said. "Would you not like to rest for a few days now that we are back in Britain?"

Cailin shook her head. "No! I want to go home."

The cart lumbered its way up to Londinium. Cailin looked

about her, remembering little of her last visit. Once this place would have awed her, but now it looked insignificant when compared to Constantinople. She was happy to take Stane Street west to Corinium.

When they reached that town of her family's origin, Cailin was shocked. The once thriving Corinium was almost silent, and deserted. Rubbish littered the streets. The buildings were in poor repair. In the amphitheater there were weeds growing between the stone seats, which were cracked and broken. Many houses were locked and empty. It was not as she remembered it.

"What has happened?" she asked Wulf.

He shook his head. "I do not know, except perhaps without a central government, the town cannot maintain itself. Look about you. Most whom we see in the streets are elderly. They stay, obviously, because there is nowhere else for them to go. The market thrives, however. It seems to be the only thing that does."

"But it is mostly foodstuffs," she noted. "There are few other goods for sale. What has happened to trade? And the pottery works?"

"People must eat," he said. "As for the rest, I do not know." He shrugged. "Come, lambkin, we have two more days of traveling before we reach our lands. Let us not dally. We will have Antonia Porcius to contend with, I am certain. She has undoubtedly annexed our lands for herself once more. At least we will know better than to trust her this time. And your Dobunni family will rejoice to learn you are alive."

Their cart moved up the Fosse Way until finally they turned off on a barely discernible tract. It was raining when they made camp that night. They huddled within the cart, listening to the rain on its canvas roof, the small space nicely warmed, as it had all winter long, by the little brazier Cailin had insisted upon. They had seen virtually no one since leaving Corinium, but Wulf insisted on their keeping watch nonetheless.

"We can't afford to lose everything now," he said. "We'll move out before dawn. With any luck, we should reach our hall by mid-afternoon."

It rained again the next day, and huddled upon the bench in the cart, driving the black mare, Cailin realized she had forgotten how damp and chilly an English spring could be. She almost missed the constantly sunny days she had enjoyed in Byzantium, but still she was content to be home, she decided, shivering. Around her the land was familiar once again. Suddenly they topped a hillock and, stopping, Cailin looked down upon her family's lands for the first time in almost three years.

Wulf swore volubly. "The hall is burned!" he said. "Damn Antonia for an interfering bitch! She'll pay for it, I vow!"

"Why did Bodvoc not stop her, I wonder?" Cailin asked.

"I do not know, but I will soon find out. We will have to begin from the beginning once more, lambkin. I am sorry."

"It is not your fault, Wulf," Cailin soothed him. "We will survive this as we have survived all the rest of our dark destiny."

As they made their way down the hillside, Cailin noticed that the fields lay fallow and the orchards were not pruned. What had happened here? She brought her cart to a halt before what had been their little hall. The damage, to her great relief, did not look as bad now that they could see it close up, as it had appeared from the hillside. Their thatched roof had indeed been burned, but as they walked about, Cailin and Wulf could see the heavy beams of the roof were just scorched. The fire pits were intact, and some of their furnishings, battered but repairable, were still there. Much was gone, however, including the heavy oaken doors of the hall. Still, with a new roof they could salvage it.

"We'll have to thatch the roof first," he said.

"We cannot do it ourselves," Cailin answered him. "Where are our slaves and farm workers?" She sighed. "You know the answer to that as well as I do. We will have to go to her and retake our property. Then, too, there is the matter of our child. Antonia is the only one who has the answer to that puzzle, and I will pry it out of her."

"Let us go to the Dobunni first," Wulf suggested. "They will know what has happened. I think we are wiser learning that before we beard Antonia Porcius over these matters. She has obviously driven Bodvoc and Nuala off, or they would have protected our holding."

"Let us bring the cart into the hall," Cailin said. "Then we can take the horses to my grandfather's village. Should anyone pass by, it will seem as if nothing is different here as long as the cart is hidden."

"Do not leave me here alone," Nellwyn begged them. "I am afraid."

"You and I will ride the mare together," Cailin reassured her servant. "The hall is uninhabitable, but soon we will repair it."

They led the black mare into the hall, unhitched her from the cart and pushed the vehicle into a dark corner, where it was obscured from view even to someone entering the half ruin. Then the two women mounted the beast. Cailin rode in front, holding the reins, and Nellwyn behind her, clutching her mistress about her slender waist. Wulf led the mare from the building, and mounting his own animal, they headed off up the hills, across the meadows, and through the woods, to Berikos's Dobunni village.

They knew immediately as they approached the hill fort that something was very wrong. There were no guards posted, and they were able to enter the village unimpeded. The place was deserted, and upon closer inspection, they could see it had been so for some time.

"What has happened?" Cailin said, not just a little afraid.

Wulf shook his head. "There were other villages, I know. Can you tell me where they were located, lambkin? The Dobunni cannot have simply disappeared from the face of the earth in the two and a half years that we were gone from Britain. They must be here somewhere."

"There were other villages, but I never saw them," she said. "I spent my time here. I know, however, that these villages must be near, for Berikos's territory was not very large. Let us simply ride. We are bound to come upon someone."

"I can think of no better plan," he said, and so they began to ride slowly to the northeast, seeking signs of life.

At first the landscape appeared pristine, and empty, but eventually they began to see signs of habitation, cattle grazing, a flock of sheep in a meadow, and finally a shepherd, whom they hailed.

"Is there a Dobunni village nearby, lad?" Wulf asked him.

"Who be ye?" the shepherd asked, not answering their question.

"I am Wulf Ironfist. This is my wife, Cailin Drusus, the granddaughter of Berikos, the niece of Eppilus, the cousin of Corio. We have been away for some time, and when we returned, we sought out the hill fort of Berikos, only to find it deserted. Where is everyone?"

"You will find our village on the other side of the hill," the shepherd replied, again not answering the question asked. "Eppilus is there."

They rode over the hill, and there, in a small, quiet valley, was the Dobunni village. Guards, strategically placed, watched silently as they passed by and into the center of the village. Wulf dismounted and lifted first his wife and then Nellwyn from the mare's back. They looked about, and when Cailin shrugged back her hood, revealing her face, a woman with two children clinging to her skirts gasped and cried out, *"Cailin!* Is it truly you? They said that you were dead!"

"Nuala!" Cailin ran forward and embraced her cousin. "It is truly me, and I have come home. How is Bodvoc? And Ceara, and Maeve? And what of Berikos? Does the old devil still hold sway despite his illness, or has Eppilus truly become chief of the Dobunni?"

"Bodvoc is dead," Nuala said softly. "He died in the plague epidemic last year that took so many of our people, Ceara, Maeve, and our grandfather among them. We lost almost all our old people, and many children. Corio survived, amazingly, and it never touched me or my children, despite Bodvoc's illness. These are my bairns. Commius, the boy, is the elder. 'Twas he I carried on my wedding day. The girl is Morna. Come, Eppilus will want to see you." She turned away from Cailin a moment and said, "Greetings, Wulf Ironfist."

"Greetings, Nuala. I am sorry to hear of Bodvoc's death. He was a good man. But now I understand why you were not on the lands we gave you. A woman alone with two children could not manage such responsibility."

"We barely had a chance to even settle on those lands, Wulf," she told him. "Antonia Porcius drove us away as soon as you left. She insisted that the Drusus Corinium lands were her late husband's, and now they were hers and her son's. Bodvoc felt we could not fight her."

They followed Nuala into her father's hall. Eppilus, already aware of their arrival, came forward to greet the travelers. "It was told us that you died in childbirth, Cailin," he said, "and then Wulf Ironfist disappeared. What happened to you, my niece? Come, sit by the fire. Bring wine for our guests. Who is this pretty girl with you?" He peppered her with questions.

"This is Nellwyn, Uncle," Cailin said, smiling. "She is my servant, and has traveled all the way from Byzantium with me, for that is where I was." Cailin then went on to narrate her adventures and Wulf's to her assembled kin and the others who had crowded into the hall.

"Our hall has been partly burned," she concluded. "What happened while we were gone, and why is Berikos's hill fort deserted?"

"So many in Berikos's village died of plague," Eppilus explained, "that it was not practical for us to remain there. Antonia Porcius has a new husband. He is neither Celt nor Romano-Briton. He is a Saxon, and his name is Ragnar Strongspear. There are many Saxons now entering this region to settle here. Even this village is no longer completely Dobunni. Saxons live among us, and are intermarrying with our children. Nuala has taken one for a new husband." He invited a pleasant-looking young blond man with mild blue eyes to step forward. "This is Winefrith, my son-in-law. I am happy to have him related to me. He is a good husband to my daughter, and a good father to my grandchildren."

"I greet you, Winefrith, husband of Nuala," Wulf said.

"I greet you, Wulf Ironfist," came the polite reply.

"Tell me about this Ragnar Strongspear," Wulf Ironfist said to Eppilus, leaning forward, his interest apparent in his blue eyes. "What kind of a man is he?"

"From what we have seen and learned," Eppilus said slowly, "he is a bully. He came swaggering across the land some months ago with a troup of bandits like himself. He slaughtered everything in his path, looting and burning as he went along. I expect that is when your hall was damaged. He stumbled upon Antonia's villa. He brought with him two wives, but he made Antonia his wife, too, though the gods know why. Antonia lives with the other women, her father, and the many children who always seem to be underfoot.

"This Saxon is already consolidating his hold on the surrounding countryside, demanding fealty and heavy tribute. He has not yet found our village here in this valley, but we expect he soon will. We will be forced to accept him as our overlord if we are to survive. There is no other choice."

"Aye, there is," Wulf Ironfist said. "You can accept me as your overlord, Eppilus. Nuala says the plague struck down the very old and the very young. That means that most of the men I trained several years ago are still alive. If they will give me their service, we will be able to overcome the threat of Ragnar Strongspear. You will be able to live in peace beneath my protection. We are kin, Eppilus, and I will not abuse those I am sworn to defend.

"The times in which we now live are different than those we once knew. Your village, and the other nearby villages, need a strong man to protect them. You have a choice between either me or Ragnar Strongspear."

"We would choose you, of course, Wulf Ironfist," Eppilus said. "We know you to be a fair and an honest man who will not mistreat us or our families. How can we help you?"

"First I must speak with the men. They must quickly refamiliarize themselves with their fighting skills. Perhaps there are even some new men in this village who would join us."

"I will," said Nuala's husband, Winefrith. "I am a smith, and can make and repair weapons for you. Whatever I can do to make the countryside safe from Ragnar Strongspear, I will do, Wulf Ironfist."

"Good!" Wulf said, smiling at the young man. "Go and speak to

the other Saxons who live in this village. Tell them it is not a matter of Saxon against Celt, but what is right against what is wrong."

Winefrith nodded. "There is no friction between Saxon and Celt
here," he said, and the others agreed. "We are simple people trying to live together in peace."

"I will need the roof of my hall rethatched, and cannot do it
alone," Wulf said, "and I must put a wall about it for better defense."

"We can help," said Eppilus. "I will send to the other two villages left in the area for aid. It is unlikely that Ragnar Strongspear
will know we are repairing the hall. He rarely goes there, for he is
very superstitious, and believes the hall haunted by Cailin's family.
I expect that Antonia told him of the land's history, and he drew
his own conclusions."

"If Antonia told him of the land's history, it was done deliberately and for a purpose," Cailin interjected. "I wonder why she did
it?"

They stayed the night in Eppilus's village. When the morning
came, they were surprised to find that at least a hundred young
men, some of whom they recognized and others they did not, had
arrived. Wulf appointed both Corio and Winefrith his seconds-in-
command. Those who had already had training in martial skills began to train those young men who had not. Another group of
twenty men rode with Wulf, Cailin, and Nellwyn back to their hall.
They carried with them enough thatch for the roof, and began
work almost immediately. Eppilus had sent a wagonload of provisions along. Cailin and Nellwyn cooked simple meals that satisfied
the workers before they fell asleep each night upon the floor in the
hall. When they were not engaged over the cookfires, Cailin and
her servant swept the dirt and the debris from the hall, along with
a young fox vixen who had decided to make her den there, and a
number of field mice who had attracted the fox in the first place.
The furniture that was repairable was set aside.

Each morning the work began anew, until several days later the
hall was reroofed. Winefrith arrived with Nuala and began to repair
the furniture that had been smashed.

Cailin sat outside the hall on a bench with her cousin. "Your father likes your new husband, and he seems a fair man," she remarked.

"He is not Bodvoc," Nuala admitted, "but then there will never be another like Bodvoc. Winefrith loves me totally, and he is so good. If there is no longer excitement in my life, at least I am not unhappy, Cailin. Do you remember the old fortune-teller at the Beltane fair back long ago who said I would have two husbands and many children? Well, she was right. Bodvoc and I spawned two bairns before he died." Her hand went protectively to her belly. "Winefrith and I married last December at the solstice. I am already well gone with our first child."

"You are fortunate," Cailin told her. "I do not know what happened to the child I bore Wulf before I was kidnapped into slavery. I do not even know if it was a son or a daughter."

"You will have others," Nuala said reassuringly.

"Not unless Wulf and I can find some privacy," Cailin admitted with a wry smile. "Our reunion was so swift, and then we escaped Byzantium. We sailed for forty days upon a tiny trading vessel, with no possible opportunity to be alone. Then we traveled through Gaul with Nellwyn always by our side, and all those merchants with us. It has been the three of us on the road here in Britain until we reached home. We have been so busy repairing the damaged caused by that damned Ragnar . . . There is just no time for us, Nuala! I know that there will be, but when? As for the child lost to us, if it lives, we want it. It is our flesh, and has a heritage to be proud of that we would share."

"I can understand exactly how you feel," Nuala replied. "I love little Commius and Morna dearly. If they were stolen from me, I should want to get them back. I would not just let them go."

"Who is that on the hillside?" Cailin suddenly asked her cousin.

Nuala looked hard, then said, "I do not know, but it could be one of Ragnar's men. Yes, I think it may be, for he is turning away and riding off. We had best tell your husband."

Wulf and the others were just refitting new oak doors to the hall when Cailin and Nuala told him of the horseman on the hillside.

"Since we have not yet had time to build the wall, it is good we can at least close off the hall," Wulf said grimly. He turned to Winefrith. "What do you think? Will he come with a large armed party?"

"This man was probably out hunting and just rode past by chance," Winefrith said. "There are enough of us here to make it a standoff for now, I think, my lord. I will warn the men to be on their guard until we see what is to happen. Nuala, go into the hall. I do not want you outside should there be any kind of attack."

"He called you 'my lord,' " Cailin said in a low tone to her husband after Nuala had obeyed her husband's order.

"Several of the men are beginning to do so," Wulf said. "It is only natural. I am their leader, lambkin. I intend to be overlord of these lands, and all the lands to the north and east encompassing the Dobunni territory that once was, if I can hold them. I have the right to do it. The first challenge I face is Ragnar Strongspear. He may have the territory to the south and west, if he chooses, but these lands are mine, and I will fight for them."

"I will be by your side, my lord husband," Cailin said quietly.

He put an arm about her shoulder. "We will survive this new age, lambkin, and we will leave a great holding for our sons and our daughters. We will not be moved from our lands again."

"And we will make Antonia Porcius tell us what happened to our child. I did not deliver a son so large that I was torn apart. There is something I am striving to remember about those last moments, Wulf. I distinctly recall hearing the cry of a healthy infant, but there is something more, if I could but remember it. I know our child is alive!"

"If he is, lambkin, we will find him," Wulf said.

There appeared on the crest of the hill a party of some ten horsemen who began their descent. They were led by a large helmeted man who carried a long spear.

"I remain by your side," Cailin said, forestalling her husband's objection. "I run from no man, and especially not on our own lands."

He said nothing, but he was proud to have her for a wife. She was a strong woman to have survived slavery, and if they could ever find a moment to be together again, they would make strong sons.

The horsemen rode relentlessly onward. Ragnar Strongspear observed the silent couple as he came. The man was a warrior, he was certain, no Saxon farmer to be easily frightened off. The woman was beautiful, but she was not a Saxon woman. A Briton most likely, and a proud wench to boot. She stood unafraid by her man's side, an almost defiant stance to her body. It was a body, he thought, he could enjoy becoming familiar with, and from the look of her, she was a woman who had both met and enjoyed passion.

As the horsemen drew to a halt before Wulf and Cailin, their helmeted leader said in a deep, hard voice, "You are trespassing here."

"Are you the savage who tried to burn my hall?" Wulf demanded coolly in reply. "If you are, then you owe me a forfeit, and I'll have it now."

It was hardly the answer Ragnar Strongspear was expecting. He glared at his antagonist and snarled fiercely, *"Who are you?"*

"I am Wulf Ironfist, and this is my wife, Cailin Drusus. Who are you, and what do you do here on my lands?"

"I am Ragnar Strongspear, and these are *my* lands," was the reply. "I hold them for one of my wives, Antonia Porcius."

"These lands do not belong to Antonia Porcius," Wulf answered, "and they never did, Ragnar Strongspear. You have been misled if she told you so. These lands are the hereditary holdings of the Drusus Corinium family. My wife Cailin is the sole surviving member of that family. These are her lands. I hold them for her. We have been away in Byzantium, and I return to find my hall half destroyed, my belongings either stolen or ravaged, and my slaves disappeared. This is your doing, I assume, or am I mistaken?" Wulf finished, looking hard at the man.

"Do you expect me to just take your word for such a claim?" Ragnar Strongspear said angrily. "I am not a fool. Why should I believe you?"

"Does old Anthony Porcius still live?" Wulf asked.

"Aye, he has a place in my hall," Ragnar Strongspear said.

"And are his wits still with him?"

"Aye, they are. Why do you ask, Wulf Ironfist?"

"Because he can attest to the truth of my words, Ragnar Strongspear. I will come with you now. You will see I speak the truth."

"Very well, I am as eager as you to settle this matter," was the surly reply.

Ragnar Strongspear took in all that had been done to restore the hall. He was impressed by what he saw. He knew in his heart that Wulf Ironfist had not invested his time and effort for naught. He did not appear to be the sort of man who took foolish chances, and the fact that he knew Anthony Porcius by name led Ragnar to believe the warrior spoke the truth. Why had Antonia lied to him?

Wulf and Cailin reappeared now on horseback, surrounded by a group of a dozen armed men. "You will not mind that we are escorted," Wulf said with a straight face. "I cannot know what we may encounter."

Ragnar Strongspear nodded. "You do not offend me, but you have my word, Wulf Ironfist, that no harm will come to you from me or from mine this day. I am an honorable man. Let us go." He turned his horse and moved off with his small party of retainers in his wake. As they rode, Ragnar wondered what else Antonia had told him that wasn't true. He had stormed across her lands well over a year ago. Finding her unprotected, he had claimed both the woman and her property for his own. He had two other wives, Harimann and Perahta, Saxons both. They were devoted to him, and hardworking. Each had given him two children, a son and a daughter apiece. Antonia had two children as well, a boy and a girl. She hadn't wanted to become his wife, but he had raped her before her father and servants in the atrium of her villa, making her further refusal impossible.

She was an odd woman, given to airs, and other than her lands, she had no value he could see, but for one thing: He had never in his life had such an avaricious, hot bedmate. Whereas Harimann and Perahta were complaisant, Antonia was eager, and had the instincts of a skilled whore. He tolerated her for that alone. Now, however, he was beginning to wonder if he had not made a bad bargain of it after all. Were her abilities in their bed worth the trouble she was obviously about to cause him?

Where Antonia's villa had once stood in its pristine glory, there were now ruins. Nearby, a new hall had been raised. About it was a wall of stone. They entered through a pair of open gates, the doors of which had been fashioned from the old bronze doors of the villa.

"Your men are welcome in my hall," Ragnar Strongspear said.

"You have given me your pledge for our safety," Wulf replied. "I will leave them outside but for two to show my good faith. Corio, and Winefrith, you will come with us."

"Yes, my lord!" the two men chorused almost as one, and Ragnar Strongspear was further impressed. Wulf's men were all obviously quite loyal, and not only were there Saxons among them, but Celts as well.

They entered a large aisled hall. There were several fire pits, but the ventilation was poor and it was slightly smoky. Two large, handsome women with long blond braids, little children about their feet, sat weaving and talking together.

"Antonia! Come to me at once!" Ragnar Strongspear called loudly.

"I am here, my lord," came the reply, and she glided forward, a false smile of welcome upon her face. She hated him and everything he stood for.

"Do you know these people, Antonia?" he demanded of her.

Antonia's eyes swung first to Cailin and then to Wulf. Her hand flew to her breast and she paled. Her heart began to increase in its tempo until she thought it would fly from her chest. She couldn't seem to breathe, and she gaped like a fish out of water. She had never in her life been so filled with fear, for before her was her greatest nightmare come to life. How had they survived? But it did not matter. They had survived her revenge, and had now obviously returned to take theirs. She stepped back with a shriek.

"Ohh, villainess!" Cailin cried, surprising the men as she leapt forward at Antonia. "You never thought to see me again in this life, did you? But here I am, Antonia Porcius, alive, and strong! Now, where is my child? I want my child; I know you have my baby!"

"I do not know what you are talking about," Antonia quavered.

"You are lying, Antonia," Wulf said, and his blue eyes were bright with his anger. "Lying as you lied to me when you told me that Cailin was dead in childbirth of a difficult birth, of a son who tore her apart and then died, too. You lied when you told me you cremated their remains. I found my wife in Byzantium by merest chance, preparing to wed another man, damn you! Do you know how very much I want to kill you right now? Do you know all the misery you have caused us? And once again you have tried to steal our lands, Antonia Porcius. You will not succeed now, just as you did not succeed before!"

"Did I hurt you, Wulf?" Antonia suddenly flared. "Did the knowledge that Cailin was dead cause you unbearable pain? I am glad if it did. *I am glad!* Now you know the pain you caused me when you killed my beloved Quintus! I wanted you to suffer! And I wanted Cailin to suffer as well. If she had not returned from her grave that first time, you would not have killed my husband, and I should not have lost my second son! All my misery is due to the two of you, and now here you are again to cause me heartache. A pox upon you! *I hate you both!*"

"Give me my child, you bitch!" Cailin cried out angrily.

"What child?" Antonia said with false sweetness. "You had no child, Cailin Drusus. The child died at birth."

"I do not believe you," Cailin replied. "I heard my child cry strongly before your herbs rendered me unconscious. *Give me my child!*"

"Give her the child, Antonia." Anthony Porcius came forward. He had aged greatly in the last few years. His step was slow and his hair was snow-white, but it was his sad eyes that touched Cailin. Reaching out, he took her hand in his. "She told me that you had died, and that Wulf would not take the child," he said. "She claimed to be raising her out of the goodness of her heart, but there is, I now see, no goodness in my daughter's heart. It is black with bitterness and hatred. The child has your husband's coloring, but in features she is your image. Each day she grows more so, and of late Antonia has begun to hate her for it."

"Her?" Cailin whispered softly, and then suddenly she cried out to her husband, *"That is what she said, Wulf!* I remember it now. The last thing I heard before I fell unconscious on that day our child was born was Antonia's voice saying, 'I always wanted a daughter.' We have a daughter. Give her to me, you viper. *Give me my daughter!"*

Ragnar Strongspear's first wife, Harimann, came forward leading a small girl by the hand. "This is your daughter, lady. She is called Aurora. She is a good child, though the lady Antonia beats her."

Cailin knelt and took the little girl into her arms. She was several months from her third birthday, but she was a tall child. Her tunic dress was ragged, and her blond hair lank. There was a frightened look in her eyes, and upon her cheek was a purple bruise. Cailin looked up at Antonia and said quietly, "You will pay dearly for that, lady." Then she hugged the trembling child, setting her back down finally so they might look at one another. "I am your mother, Aurora. I have come to take you away from the lady Antonia, who stole you from me. Do not be afraid."

The child said nothing. She just stared at Cailin with large eyes.

"Why does she not speak?" Cailin demanded.

"She does sometimes," Harimann said, "but she is always afraid, poor child. We tried to soften the lady Antonia's unreasonable anger toward Aurora, but it only made it worse. She is half starved, though we had sought to feed her when the lady Antonia was not about. Antonia's son, however, follows his mother's direction, and would tell on us. Then Aurora would be beaten. Finally she would take no food from us for fear of being punished. The boy is abusive to her as well."

"Quintus, the younger, is as much of a toad as his father, I see," Cailin said scornfully. "You have reason to be proud, Antonia." She turned to the elderly Anthony Porcius. "Could you do nothing, sir?"

"I tried," he said, "but I am an old man, Cailin Drusus, and my place in this hall depends upon my daughter's goodwill."

"Tell Ragnar Strongspear the land is mine," she said to him.

"I can do that, Cailin Drusus," he replied, and then he turned to his Saxon son-in-law. "The lands she claims are her family's lands and belong to her. Antonia had no right to them at all. She claimed to me that she was holding them for Aurora, but I know that is not true."

Ragnar Strongspear nodded. "Then it is settled," he said.

"It is settled," Wulf Ironfist answered him. Reaching down, he lifted the little girl into his arms. "I am your father, Aurora," he told the child. "Can you say 'Father' to me, little one?"

She nodded, her eyes huge and blue.

He grinned. "I would hear it then, my daughter." He cocked his head to one side, as if listening hard.

"Father," the little girl whispered shyly.

He kissed her cheek. "Aye, sweeting, I am your father, and I will never allow you to be harmed by anyone again." He turned to Cailin and their two companions. "Let us go home now."

"You will not stay the night? I have some fine mead," Ragnar Strongspear said jovially. "And there is a boar roasting on the hearth."

"Thank you, but no," Wulf Ironfist replied. "The last time I left my hall, some damned savage came through and burned it. I will not take any further chances, Ragnar Strongspear."

"There is the matter of our slaves," Cailin prompted her husband.

"I do not know about that," the burly Saxon answered.

"I can separate the Drusus Corinium servants from Antonia's," the elderly Porcius said.

"Then do so, old man," his son-in-law said, "and see that they are sent back with as much haste as possible. I want no quarrel between Wulf Ironfist and myself. We are to be neighbors, after all."

When Wulf and Cailin and their party had departed, Antonia Porcius said angrily to her husband, "You were a fool not to kill him, and Cailin Drusus besides, Ragnar. Wulf is no coward, and he will not let you steal back his lands. You will be fortunate if he does not take ours!"

He slapped her hard, sending her reeling. "Do not ever lie to me again, Antonia," he told her. "I will kill you next time. As for Wulf Ironfist, I will have his lands eventually, *and* I will have his wife as well. She sets my blood afire with her beauty."

Antonia clutched at her aching jaw. "I hate you," she said fiercely. "One day I will kill you, Ragnar!"

He laughed aloud. "You have not the courage, Antonia," he said, "and if you did, what would you do then? Who would protect you, and these lands I took from you? The next man might not care if you lived or you died. You are no beauty, my dear. Your bitterness shows in your face, rendering you less than attractive these days."

"You will regret your cruel words," she warned him.

"Be careful," he responded, "that I do not throw you, your sniveling whelp, and your old father out into the cold, lady. I do not need you, Antonia. I keep you because you amuse me in bed, but eventually even that charm of yours is apt to fade if you remain shrewish."

She glared at him and walked from the hall. Making her way through the courtyard, she moved to the gates and stopped. She could see Wulf Ironfist and his party in the distance, and she cursed them softly beneath her breath. They would pay. They would all pay.

"We are being watched," Cailin said as they rode.

Wulf turned a moment, and then turning back, said, "It is Antonia."

"She hates us so terribly," Cailin said. "To have done what she did, and stolen our child." She kissed the top of Aurora's head. The child was settled before her on the black mare.

"Antonia's venom is not what I fear," he said. "I do not believe Ragnar Strongspear will be content until he has wrested our lands back for his own. He is a fierce man, but I will contain his ambitions."

"He will wait for us to plant the fields and harvest the grain before he attacks us," Winefrith said. "But that will give us the summer months to strengthen our defenses."

"Why would he wait that long?" Cailin asked curiously.

"Because if he attacks after the harvest, he can destroy the grain and hay, thus starving us and our animals over the next winter."

"Is he that strong?" she wondered.

"We do not know yet, lambkin," Wulf said, "but we will. Then, too, there is the chance Ragnar will align himself with another warlord."

"I do not think so," Winefrith interjected. "I think it will be a matter of pride with him that he overcome you himself."

"Perhaps." Wulf smiled wickedly. "We have an advantage our friend Ragnar knows nothing about. We have our villages over the hill. We must decide how we are going to defend it all over the next few days, and then we will implement our plans so that when Ragnar Strongspear comes calling, we will be able to foil him."

"You will have to kill him, and Antonia, too," Cailin said bluntly.

"You know this for certain? The voice within speaks to you?" She nodded. "It does, my lord."

"Then so be it," he said quietly, "but we will wait for Ragnar to make the first move. The defense we make is better if it is of our own choosing and not one we are forced into making. Agreed?"

"Aye, my lord!" his captains answered enthusiastically.

Chapter

16

T*he villages had never* before possessed names. In past times they had simply been known by the name of whoever was in charge, which more often than not led to confusion. Now Wulf decided that each village needed a firm identity, one that would not change with every change in leadership. The Britons were no longer a nomadic people.

Berikos's old hill fort was resettled and called Brand-dun, for since it sat high, it would be the logical place for beacons to be lit. Brand-dun meant Beacon Hill. Eppilus's village became Braleah, which meant Hillslope Meadow, and indeed it had a fine one, as they had discovered the morning of their return. The other two villages were called Denetun, because it now belonged to the estate in the valley; and Orrford, which was set by a stream, whose shallow waters made it a perfect cattle crossing for drovers. The hall itself was named Cadda-wic, which meant Warrior's Estate.

An agreement was forged between Wulf Ironfist and the men in the villages. In return for recognizing him as their overlord, he would lead them, and protect them from all comers. All the lands that had been claimed in the past by the Dobunni Celts were now ceded to Wulf Ironfist and his descendants. The villagers would be given the rights to the common fields, to their kitchen gardens, and to graze their animals in the common pasture.

Their homes were theirs, but the land beneath it was not. They had the right to personally own cattle, horses, pigs, barnyard fowl, cats, and dogs. They would toil three days each week for their overlord at a variety of tasks. They would tend his fields and his livestock. Those with special skills, such as the cooper, the thatchers, and the ironworkers, would also contribute their efforts. They would all spend some time in military training for the defense of the lands.

And if war came, Wulf Ironfist would lead them. He would be father, judge, warrior, and friend to them all. It was a different sort of order than they had ever known, but it seemed to Eppilus and the others to be the best way to live now in their changing world. They needed to be united, and they needed a strong leader whom other ambitious men would respect and fear.

The women, Cailin among them, planted the fields. They tended the growing grain and the animals while the men went about the task of building defenses for the hall as well as for the villages. The hall they had left to last, knowing that Ragnar Strongspear had set a man to spy upon them from the hill above. Antonia's husband was lulled into a false sense of security, as the hall remained undefended by any barriers. Ragnar Strongspear did not know that each of the nearby villages was being prepared to defend itself should he discover them, as he and others eventually would. In midsummer he finally withdrew his spy, deciding the man's time would be better spent elsewhere than lying lazily on the hill. Wulf Ironfist's hall would be his when he chose to take it, Ragnar boasted to his wives.

Antonia, her body bruised by a recent beating her husband had administered, shook her head wearily. She was fairly certain she was with child. That at least should stem Ragnar's irritation with her for the present, and give her time to think. Her Saxon husband was going to lose everything for them if she did not intervene in the matter. Ragnar was not really a clever man. He was more like a marauding bull. And then, too, there was her darling son, Quintus, to consider. These lands Ragnar claimed to have conquered were really Quintus's lands. She could not allow this self-glorifying Saxon oaf to steal from Quintus.

Meanwhile, when Ragnar Strongspear withdrew his spy, Wulf and his men began to build a defense around the hall. It was an earthworks that they topped with a stone wall. Small wooden towers were set atop the wall, allowing for an excellent view of the surrounding valley. Winefrith worked long hours in his smithy producing doors for the walls. They were made of strong, aged oak, a foot in thickness and well-sheathed in forged iron. There had never been doors like them.

The hall was always busy, and always full of Wulf's men. There was so much work to do, and even more to oversee. As mistress here, it was Cailin's duty to provide direction. She seemed to have no time for herself, nor any privacy.

One day, in an effort to escape it all, she climbed the ladder to the solar above the hall. It was not a large room, its wood floor covering only a third of the hall below. There were four bed spaces set into the stone walls. They were bare and empty of bedding, for she and Wulf had been taking their rest below with everyone else.

Cailin sighed wistfully, remembering the early days of her marriage, when he could hardly wait to bed her. Since that wonderful night in Byzantium, they had not found time to couple. Wulf seemed totally absorbed in his task of raising the hall's defenses. He came to bed late, tired, and never woke her. She had tried several times to wait for him, but to no avail. She was exhausted herself, for her days were long and began early.

A ray of sun cut through one of the two narrow windows, partly illuminating the room, and Cailin began to visualize it as she had once planned it. Her loom would be by a window to catch the light. There would be a rectangular oak table and two chairs where they might dine in private. The bed spaces would be empty, but for the one in which they would sleep. Eventually their family would share the solar, but not at first. They would have their privacy for now!

Why not? A determined look came into Cailin's eyes. Why should she not complete the solar? She had her loom, and the furniture was sitting in a distant corner of the hall below, gathering dust. Going over to each of the two narrow windows in the room, Cailin unfastened the small casements, with their panes of animal membrane. Warm sweet air filled the solar, and she was immediately encouraged. Leaving the windows open, she climbed down into the hall again. She saw her cousin Corio at the high board eating bread and cheese, and called to him.

"Corio, come give me your aid."

He arose. "How may I help you, cousin?"

Cailin explained, and before she knew it, Corio, with the help of several young men, had lifted her loom, the table, the chairs, and the bedding to the solar above. "Take the brazier, too," she told him, handing him up the iron heater they had traveled with through Gaul.

He grinned wickedly. "I do not think you will need it, sweeting. Wulf's passion is poorly pent up. He is set to explode with it." He chuckled. "But give him the chance, cousin, and you'll have no need for yon little charcoal burner."

"Is nothing a secret in this hall?" she demanded, her cheeks red with her embarrassment. Did everyone know she and Wulf weren't coupling?

"Very little," Corio answered her dryly. Then he took the brazier from her. "But if you insist, cousin," he said, grinning mischievously.

When the men had gone back to their assigned tasks, Cailin clambered back up the ladder to the solar. Corio, bless him, had had far more sense than she. He had seen that the chests they used to store their personal belongings had been brought up into the room, as well. She fussed with the positioning of her loom and its stool so she would have the proper light. The table was not quite centered, Cailin thought, but she righted its position and straightened the chairs.

She filled their bed space with fresh hay she lugged up the ladder, and mixed it with lavender sprigs, handfuls of rose petals, and sweet herbs. The feather bed, in its practical cotton ticking, she slipped into a cover of sky-blue silk that she had made for it. It was an outrageous luxury, but who would know but them? Fluffing the feather bed, she placed it over the hay, where it settled on the fragrant herbage. Removing the small alabaster lamp from the niche in the bed space, she filled it with scented oil, and putting a wick into it, replaced the lamp in its space. She lay a fox coverlet across the foot of the bedspace. The bedspace was now ready for occupants.

Cailin looked about the solar. Although it needed wall hangings and more pieces of furniture to make it really comfortable, they would manage for the time being. At least it was ready for habitation. Although privacy was not something the Saxons held dear, Cailin was used to it, having been raised with it. Wulf would not find it a burden, she thought, smiling. Then she heard him calling her from the hall below. Cailin scrambled down the ladder from the solar, hurrying to greet her husband.

"We have finished the defenses for the hall," he told her proudly, obviously well-pleased. "The gates have just now been fitted to the entry."

"The barns within the walls are finished also," she told him, "and the harvest is almost all in. I did not go to the fields today, for I was about other business, my lord." She looked askance at his filthy condition. "You need a bath, Wulf Ironfist. You stink of your labor."

"I am too tired to go to the stream and bathe," he told her. "Let it be, lambkin. I will bathe in the morning."

"*Now,*" she said firmly, in a tone he had not heard her use before, "and not in an icy stream, either, my lord. Sit by the fire, and have some ale while I make the preparations. I have spent the better part of this day making the solar fit for our habitation. I will not sleep in the hall another night, Wulf Ironfist. If Aurora is to have a brother, we must have some time to ourselves. There is gossip already! The world will not come to an end because we seek our privacy each night."

"Should not our daughter sleep in the solar, too?" he queried her mischievously, cocking a bushy, tawny eyebrow quizzically.

"For now," Cailin answered him severely, "Aurora will remain in the hall, with Nellwyn to care for her." Then she left him and went to the end of the room, calling instructions to her household servants.

He watched, somewhat astounded, as a large oaken tub was slowly rolled into a corner of the hall. He had never seen it before, and he realized she must have had their cooper make it. She had great foresight, he decided. A hot bath would feel good. A line of male servants began running back and forth with pails of steaming water which they dumped into the great tub. It took fully half of an hour to fill the tub to Cailin's satisfaction. While it was being done, she marshaled soap and other implements necessary to bathing. Then she signaled him, and he arose, walking down the hall to where she waited, tapping an impatient foot.

"Remove your clothing, my lord," she said, then ordered the serving men to place screening about the tub. As he took each item of clothing from his tired body, she gathered it up into a pile. When he was entirely naked, Cailin handed it over the screen to the woman appointed laundress for the hall.

At her command, he climbed sheepishly into the tub. He was astounded when she stripped off her own clothing and joined him. "You mean to make my bath a pleasant experience, I see," he said, grinning lecherously at her.

"I mean to make it a thorough one," she countered sternly. " 'Twill not be easy. A Roman bath is best, but this is better than nothing." She took up her strigil and began to scrape the sweaty dirt from his neck, shoulders, and chest. The water in their tub just barely concealed her breasts, but Wulf's body was exposed from his waist up.

Reaching out, he cupped the twin orbs in his big hands and began to play with them as she worked. "We must begin to bathe again every day," he murmured, leaning forward to kiss her earlobe.

She giggled. "Behave yourself, Wulf Ironfist. How can I do a proper job of bathing you if you distract me so?"

"Am I indeed distracting you, lambkin?" he said softly, his tongue swirling about the shell of her ear. He slipped a hand below the waterline to give her right buttock a gentle squeeze.

Her violet eyes twinkled at him. "You are *very* distracting, my lord," she admitted to him, "and you must not be, or I shall never get done. If I do not, we shall never reach the solar, where our newly prepared bed space is awaiting us. There is food and wine there aplenty, my love. Once we have gained the privacy of that chamber, and drawn the ladder up behind us, no one will be able to reach us." Then she pressed herself against him teasingly. "Do you not wish to be alone with me, Wulf, my husband?" She ran her tongue over his lips and then kissed him quickly.

His aquamarine-blue eyes smoldered at her. Their look was eloquent beyond measure. "Finish your task, lambkin," he ground out. "It is far past time Aurora had a brother, and if you are not finished quickly, we shall begin our endeavor right here in this tub!"

Cailin smiled alluringly at him, and without another word began to smear soft soap over his skin with gentle fingers. She bathed him and then sent him from the tub to dry himself while she washed her own body. A fresh tunic, barely covering his thighs, was set out for him. Cailin, exiting the tub, dried herself under his hot gaze and slipped on a long camisa.

"We must have a special place where we can bathe," she said. "It is too difficult for the servants to have to be constantly moving this great tub. Do you like it, my lord? I had it made."

"Aye, I like it," he said. "It is pleasant to wash with warm water and not cold. There are some things from your old civilization that I enjoy. We will have a bathhouse built next to the hall, where the tub may remain, and there will be a fire to heat the water." He took her hand in his. "Come, lambkin. I would see the solar now."

The hall seemed strangely deserted as they made their way to the ladder leading up into their chamber. Wulf climbed behind Cailin, and having gained the room, he leaned over and drew the ladder up behind him. Then he shut the trapdoor, shoving the iron bolts hard into their casing and laying the ladder across the door. Turning about, he inspected the room. The last of the sunset was coming through the two narrow windows. He could see the stars beginning to speckle the sky.

"Are you hungry?" she said. There was food laid out for them on the table. "You have worked hard."

"Later," he told her. "It will keep," and then he pulled his tunic off, nodding at her to do the same.

Cailin removed the shapeless gown she had put on after her bath. "Your hunger is of another kind," she observed softly.

"I have waited long," he said quietly, "but seeing you like this now, lambkin, I find I cannot wait another moment longer. I fear I am past the niceties."

She could see he was almost trembling, and his male organ was engorged and eager. Reaching out, she caressed him with gentle fingers, and he shuddered. "I will show you a pleasure I learned in Byzantium," she told him. "In a way, it is similar to something we did when I was carrying Aurora." She was surprised to find that she was as eager for him as he for her, despite their lack of foreplay. Taking her husband's hand, she led him to their bed space, but instead of entering it, Cailin knelt upon the bedding and instructed him, "Find my woman's passage, my love. Enter me this way, and see the delights you gain."

She felt him seeking carefully, and then she felt the tip of his weapon touching her wet and pulsing sheath. His big hands grasped her hips firmly, and he rammed himself home, groaning with undisguised pleasure as he realized he was deeper within her than he had ever been. For a moment he simply enjoyed the sensation of warmth and tightness. Then, unable to help himself, he felt his buttocks begin to contract and release, contract and release, as he propelled himself with ever growing urgency and impetus within her feminine channel, actually feeling her expand to accommodate his yet swelling, throbbing member. His fingers dug into her soft flesh, holding her firmly that he might have more of her.

Kneeling upon the bedding, Cailin arched her back, thrusting her hips up at him that he might delve even deeper. She had gasped at his entry, having forgotten how big he was, but then the rhythmic thrust of his weapon began to communicate its passion to her. She whimpered as he filled her passage, the torrid heat of him astounding her. She cried out at the fires he was arousing. The culmination of their combined passions exploded almost as rapidly as it had begun. He collapsed atop her, nearly sobbing with relief.

Cailin was almost smothered in the feather bed by the weight of him, but she somehow managed to squirm from beneath him. Rolling onto her back, she lay quietly, allowing her own heart to cease its frantic pumping. Finally she said softly, "I had almost forgotten how wonderful a lover you can be, Wulf Ironfist. You have restored my memory admirably."

He raised his head up, his blue eyes solemn but his words were humorous. "You will surely not forget again, lambkin."

Reaching over, she gently yanked a lock of his long corn-colored hair. "I will not forget again," she promised him with utmost seriousness, "but in return, you must promise not to let me be stolen away ever again." She righted herself in the bed space and encouraged him to do so as well, taking him into her arms so that his golden head rested upon her bosom.

He nuzzled the soft flesh gently. "I will never let you go, Cailin, my wife," he assured her. *"Never! Ever!"*

They made love again, this time in a more gentle and leisurely manner. She took his face in her hands and kissed him passionately as they reached the peak of their mutual desire. Then they fell asleep, exhausted.

When they awoke in the middle of the starry night, it was to discover that they were both hungry, but this time their hunger was for food. Cailin had brought a roasted capon, bread, cheese, crisp apples, and a heady wine to the solar. Together they shared the feast, returning to their bed space to kiss, and to caress, and to love some more.

The happiness that they had gained in finding each other again quickly communicated itself to all the inhabitants of the hall. Aurora, who had been so withdrawn and frightened, was now a laughing, happy child adored by both of her parents. Her unpleasant memories were fading, thanks to her relatively young age, and her third birthday was celebrated with much festivity, and not just a little excitement. Aurora had not been expected until at least the end of August, but she had chosen to be born on the nineteenth of that month.

The day of her third birthday dawned clear and warm. The grain harvest was all in and stored in the barns within the walls. The workers were preparing to harvest apples to make cider.

The watch upon the walls suddenly called out, "Horsemen upon the hillcrest!" and immediately the gates of Cadda-wic were shut and barred. The horsemen descended the hill slowly as Wulf Ironfist was called from the solar and hurried to a vantage point atop the walls.

Ragnar Strongspear's dark blue eyes narrowed with irritation as he saw the newly built defenses about the hall. Too late, he realized his error in withdrawing his spy. As he drew closer he observed that the wall enclosing Cadda-wic was a very strong one. And the fields about the hall had all been harvested, but where were the grain barns? Within those damned walls, he suspected, and safe from him. Ragnar was not a man of great intellect, but he knew that retaking these lands was not going to be as easy a task as he had earlier anticipated. Looking up, he saw Wulf Ironfist upon the walls, watching his approach.

Ragnar smiled toothily and said in his booming voice, "Good morrow, Wulf Ironfist! Surely you have not closed your gates to me? We are neighbors, and should be friends."

"Friends do not come calling at dawn with a party of heavily armed men," came the reply. "State your business with me, Ragnar Strongspear."

" 'Tis just a friendly visit," the older man declared. "Will you not open your gates and let me in, my friend?"

"We are not friends," Wulf Ironfist replied coldly. "If you wish to enter Cadda-wic, then you may, but you must leave your troop outside my walls. We are a peaceful community and seek no warring."

"Very well," Ragnar said, deciding that he must get a look inside the walls of Cadda-wic if he was to eventually take it. He dismounted and handed the reins of his horse to his second-in-command.

"My lord," the man, whose name was Harald, said, "it is not safe."

"It is safe," his master assured him softly. "If our positions were reversed, 'twould not be so, but Wulf Ironfist is a man of his word."

The gate was opened just enough for Ragnar to squeeze through, and then the strong iron bars were lowered, securing the entry from intruders. He noted that the gates were sheathed in iron. Cadda-wic was well thought out. The well was in the courtyard's center, and there were several grain barns, well away from the walls.

" 'Tis virtually impregnable," Wulf Ironfist said in answer to Ragnar's thoughts as he joined his guest. "Have you eaten? Come into the hall, Ragnar Strongspear."

The hall doors were also thick oak, and bound with bands of iron studded with large iron nails. The two men passed through them into the hall. It was not like his smoky and dirty hall, Ragnar noted. Indeed, the smoke from the fire pits was drawn directly out several smoke holes in the roof. The rushes upon the floor were clean, and filled with sweet herbs that gave off their perfume as they were crushed beneath his feet. Several well-fed, sleek hounds came up to sniff him, and then returned to their places by the fires. The two men seated themselves at the high board. At once a line of quiet, contented-looking servants began to serve them, bringing platters of food and pouring brown ale.

Ragnar's eyes grew wide at the variety of foods offered him. He was certainly not fed like this in his hall. There was a thick pottage, warm, newly baked bread, hard-boiled eggs, broiled trout, ham, sweet butter, hard cheese, and a bowl filled with apples and pears. "Were you expecting guests?" he asked his host.

"No," Wulf said. "My wife keeps a good table, doesn't yours?"

"There is not this variety," Ragnar admitted, and helped himself liberally to everything offered.

There was silence as the two men ate. When they had finished and the table cleared, Wulf said quietly, "If you thought to retake these lands, Ragnar Strongspear, put it from your mind. They belong to me."

"Only as long as you can hold them," the older man said, grinning.

"I will hold them for longer than you have life," was the cool reply. "This hall and the lands to the north and to the east are mine. *I will keep them.* Seek out the lands to the south for yourself and your children. You cannot have my estates."

"You have taken Dobunni lands?" Ragnar was surprised.

"They have given me the fealty," Wulf told him, a small smile upon his lips. "While you spent the summer months plotting and planning, Ragnar Strongspear, I spent those months doing. Go home, and tell Antonia Porcius to cease her greedy thoughts. I cannot imagine why you took her to wife. She is a very evil woman. If you do not know this, be warned. No doubt she wants her lands back for her son Quintus. She will do what she must to gain her desire. She will even destroy you if she can."

"You seem to know my wife well," Ragnar said dryly.

"After Antonia had stolen my daughter and sent my wife into slavery, she told me that they were both dead," Wulf answered. "She offered herself to me, disrobing in the atrium of her villa and pushing her breasts into my face. I found her singularly undesirable."

"She can be at times," Ragnar admitted, "but she is also the best damn fuck I have ever had. I swear it by Woden himself!"

"Then I congratulate you on your good fortune," Wulf said, "but I still advise you to beware her. There is no necessity for us to quarrel, Ragnar Strongspear. There is more than enough land for us all. Stay to the south, and there will be peace between us."

His guest nodded in reply. Then he said, "Where is your wife, Wulf Ironfist? I hope she is not ill."

"Nay, but she is seeing to the preparations for a small celebration of our daughter's natal day. It is the first time since Aurora's birth that we have been able to celebrate it together," he told the other man. "As you know, we did not even realize we had a daughter until several months ago."

Ragnar flushed. "That was not my fault," he said. "I believed Antonia when she said the child was hers. She is fair like Antonia. Why should I have not believed her?"

"We do not hold you responsible," Wulf assured him graciously.

"I must go," Ragnar said, rising. Wulf's manner was beginning to irritate him. "I thank you for the meal. I will certainly consider your words, Wulf Ironfist."

As Ragnar departed Cadda-wic, his thoughts were somewhat confused. Wulf Ironfist had actually given him good advice. The lands to the south of him were rich, and most of the poor souls farming it could not withstand the force of his might. Those lands could be his for the taking, and with little loss of life on his side. He was not afraid of death, nor of battle, but there was something about this Britain that made a man desire peace more than war. He did not understand it, but neither did it make him unhappy.

Antonia, however, did not quite see it that way. "Why would you settle for less than you can have?" she demanded of him scornfully.

To her credit, he thought, she was not afraid of his anger. She knew herself safe as she was growing big with his child. He did not believe in beating a woman who was with child, though the gods knew this particular woman tried him sorely. His two Saxon wives were strong women as well, but they had a sweetness to them. Antonia was bitterly hard of heart, her only softness being that which she showed toward her son. The boy, Ragnar thought, was a cowardly little weasel, always hiding behind his mother's skirts.

"What would you have of me, then?" he demanded irritably. "Why should I war with Wulf Ironfist over his lands, when the lands to the south are as rich, and easier pickings? Perhaps, Antonia, you hope that Wulf Ironfist will vanquish me and you will regain control of these lands for your son. Put such thoughts from your head, *wife*. Soon my brother and his family will join us. If I die an unnatural death, Gunnar will be here to avenge me, and to hold these lands for himself and our sons."

She was astounded. This was the first she had heard of his

brother, but used to deceit, Antonia covered her surprise with a sweet smile. "You did not tell me that you had a brother, Ragnar, or that he would be coming to join us. Has he wives and children? When is he to arrive? We must prepare a proper welcome for our family."

Ragnar's booming laughter filled their bed space. "By Woden, Antonia, you are clever, but I see through you! You were not expecting that I had additional family, but we Saxons are good breeders, as your belly attests to," he told her, patting the place where his child grew within her. "You had some scheme in mind, and now, I have not a doubt, you will form another crafty plot to replace it. Very well, if it amuses you to do so. Breeding women are given to such vagaries, and it is harmless enough, I think." He lowered his dark blond head and kissed her plump shoulder. His shoulder-length hair brushed her breasts.

Reaching up, Antonia thoughtfully stroked his beard. She hated him, but he was the most virile man she had ever known. "Do not be a fool, Ragnar," she finally told him. "Take the lands to the south, for Wulf Ironfist has given you good advice. Even I will admit to that. Lull our enemy into a false sense of security, and when he least expects it, seize his lands as well! Why settle for being a minor lordling when you could be a king?"

At her words, the child within her kicked mightily, and Ragnar Strongspear felt the movement beneath his resting hand. "It is an omen," he said, almost fearfully. "Why else would the child grow so restive in your womb, Antonia? Surely it is a sign of some sort."

"Our son knows that I speak the truth, my husband," she told him. "Or perhaps it is the gods who speak to you through the babe." What a fool he is, she thought to herself. If the gods existed, and frankly Antonia was no longer certain that they did, why would they bother to concern themselves with one as foolish and superstitious as this great bull of a man who lay by her side contemplating the future?

"My brother and his family should be here in a few days' time," he told her finally. "He has just a single wife, as he has never been able to afford more, but now, of course, that will change. He is younger than I am by several years, but he fathered his first child on his wife when he was but fourteen. There are eight living children. Six sons."

"What a fine family," Antonia said dryly, thinking that this horrid hall he had built to replace her beautiful villa—the villa he had destroyed—was already badly overcrowded. The addition of ten more people would but add to the noise and the filth. The gods! She missed her bath with its lovely rejuvenating steam and its delicious hot water. How Ragnar's other wives mocked her when she insisted on washing herself in a little oaken tub filled with warm water. But she didn't care. She would wager that Cailin Drusus had better bathing accommodations, the bitch! "Ragnar," she said to her husband, who was half dozing.

"What?" he grunted.

"If Cadda-wic is truly fortified so well it cannot be taken in battle, then we will have to think of another way to capture it."

He shook his head at her. "There is no way. Wulf Ironfist has built strongly, and he has built well. Even the water supply is safely within his walls. I am not a man to easily admit defeat, Antonia, but Cadda-wic cannot be taken. It simply cannot be!"

"Let me tell you a tale of ancient times, Ragnar," Antonia said patiently, but he silenced her with a wave of his hand.

"Another time, woman," he said, and rolled her onto her side. "I have other things in mind for you, and then I must sleep. In the morning you may tell me your fable, but now I want to fuck you."

"Your needs are so simple," she taunted him, hissing softly as he penetrated her expertly. "If you are as good a warrior as you are a lover, my husband, you will have no difficulty in taking Cadda-wic once I have shown you how. Ahhh, yess, Ragnar! Yesss!"

Cadda-wic. He thought about it as he methodically pumped her. The lands were good, the hall sound, and Cailin would be an extra bonus. He had seen her several times, but he could not dismiss her from his mind. What fire and spirit she had! He imagined she would be as strong and sweet as his Saxon wives, and as lustful as Antonia. It was a perfect combination, and he meant to have her. There was time, however. Neither she nor Wulf Ironfist were going anywhere. They had made it abundantly clear that the land meant everything to them. He would have more than enough time to take the lands to the south. To settle his brother and his family on a nearby holding. To find Gunnar a second wife with a good dowry. Oh, yes, there was plenty of time.

⋘⋙

*T*he *autumn came*, and Nuala bore Winefrith a fine, big son, who was called Barre. It meant a gateway between two places. Nuala thought it appropriate, for Barre was indeed a bridge between the Britain of old and the new Britain. Cailin was present at the birth, and afterward marveled at the child's size and how strongly he tugged upon his mother's breast when he was put there to nurse.

"You'll have a son of your own soon enough," Nuala teased her. "Surely you and Wulf do not spend all that time in the solar just talking, cousin." She giggled. "I know I wouldn't!"

"Fresh from childbirth, and totally shameless," Cailin said, pretending to be scandalized. "For your information, Wulf enjoys watching me at my loom, Nuala. And then, of course, we sing together."

Nuala looked thunderstruck. "You jest!" she said.

"I assure you it is quite true," Cailin replied sweetly.

"Indeed it is," Wulf said, agreeing with his wife, whom he had overheard spinning her mischievous tale. "Cailin weaves a most marvelous spell about me when we are in the solar together, and sings passion's song far better than any I have ever known."

Nuala burst out laughing, realizing that they were teasing her. The infant at her breast hiccuped, and began to wail. "Ohh, see what you have done to Barre!" she scolded them, suddenly all maternal concern and caring. "There, my little sweetheart. Do not fuss."

By the Winterfest, the lady of Cadda-wic was beginning to swell with another child, much to everyone's delight. It would be born, Cailin told them, after Beltane.

"And it is a son, I am certain," she assured Wulf.

"How can you tell?" he asked her, smiling.

She shrugged. "I just can," she said. "A woman senses such things. Is that not so?" She turned to the other women in the hall for support, and they all nodded in agreement. *"You see!"*

The winter set in, and the land around them grew white and silent. The days were short, and quick. In the long nights the wolves could be heard howling about Cadda-wic, their eerie cries answered by the mournful howls of the hounds in the hall who grew restless at the knowledge of the predators prowling beyond the strong iron and oak gates.

Wulf and Cailin were alone, for the others had returned to their own villages after the Winterfest. Cailin missed Nuala. Nellwyn, though sweet and loyal, was not particularly interesting to chat with by the fire. Aurora, however, adored her, and without anything being said, Cailin's former slave became the child's nursemaid. It was just as well, for Cailin did not need a personal servant. Her mother had raised her to be a useful person who could do for herself. Now, as mistress of Cadda-wic, Cailin found herself responsible for the well-being of all those in her charge.

Finally the days began to grow discernibly longer. The air felt milder. Patches of earth became visible, and the snow cover shrank rapidly as the earth began to grow warmer with the coming spring. Snowdrops, narcissi, and violets began to make their appearance. Cailin was pleased to find several large clumps growing near the graves of her family. The marble marker had never been finished, and it was now unlikely that it ever would be. It simply read: *The Family of Gaius Drusus Corinium.* Looking down at it, Cailin sighed, her hand moving to her swollen belly in a protective gesture. How her family would have spoiled her children!

"This child I carry is a son," she assured them aloud. "How I wish you could be here to see him when he is born. He is to be called Royse. Aurora is very excited about the new baby. Ohh!" Cailin looked up as an arm went about her shoulders. "Wulf, how you startled me!"

"You miss your family, don't you?" he replied. "I cannot even remember my mother. I often wonder what she was like."

"Until they were murdered," Cailin answered him, "they were my whole life. I cannot help but wonder what it would have been like if they had not died. My parents, of course, would not be much changed, but my brothers would. They would truly be men now, with families. How my grandmother would have enjoyed those great-grandchildren. I think, perhaps, it is Brenna I miss the most. How strange that must sound to you."

"I am sorry that I did not know them," he told her. Then together they returned to the hall, where their daughter ran to greet them.

The spring was well under way and the plowing started when the gates were opened one morning to reveal a young girl crumpled upon the earth before them. Wulf and Cailin were summoned from the hall.

"The gods!" Cailin exclaimed. "The child has been beaten cruelly! Is she dead? How came she here to Cadda-wic?"

The girl moaned as if in answer, and rolled over just enough to reveal a form more mature than they had thought. She was small and slender, but obviously older than they had originally believed.

Cailin knelt and gently touched the maiden's arm. "Can you hear me, lass?" she asked her. "What has happened to you?"

The girl opened her eyes slowly. They were a pale green in color, and the look in them was one of total confusion. "Where am I?" she whispered so low that Cailin had to bend closer to hear her.

"You are at Cadda-wic, the holding of Wulf Ironfist," she replied. "Who are you? Where have you come from, and who has mistreated you so cruelly?" She shifted herself, uncomfortable in this position, as she was within a month of bearing her child.

The girl looked uncertain as to what to answer, and her eyes filled with tears that spilled down her very pretty face.

"What is your name?" Cailin gently pressed her.

The girl appeared to think a moment, and then she said, "Aelfa. Aelfa is my name! I remember! I am called Aelfa!"

"Where have you come from?" Cailin asked.

Again the girl appeared to consider, and then said, "I do not know, lady." The tears slipped silently down her face again.

"Poor little thing," Wulf said. "The beating she has received has obviously addled her wits. She will remember in time."

"I will carry her into the hall," said Corio, who had come but the day before from Braleah. Gently, he lifted the girl into his arms, and when her head fell against his shoulder, a strange look crossed the young man's face. No woman had yet captured Corio's heart.

The girl was brought to the hall, where Cailin carefully examined her. Other than her bruises, she seemed fine, but for her loss of memory. Cailin had the tub brought and bathed the girl herself. Aelfa's hair was like cornsilk, a pale, almost silvery gold in color. A tunica and camisa were quickly found to fit her dainty stature. As she was brought to the high board, everyone in the hall could see that Aelfa was not simply a pretty girl. She was a beautiful one. Corio appeared besotted as he watched her eating, picking sparingly at the food.

"He is bewitched," Cailin whispered to her husband.

"As I would be had I not found you, lambkin," he answered.

Cailin was discomfited by his reply, to her great surprise. She had not thought herself capable of such silly jealousy. She gazed from beneath her lashes at the girl. I am just as lovely when I do not look like a sow ready to birth her piglets, she decided. Why are men such fools over a beautiful, helpless female? I should far rather be strong.

When Aelfa had finished eating, Wulf gently asked her, "Have you remembered anything else about yourself that might help us to find to whom you belong? Surely your family is worried."

"Perhaps she is a slave, a runaway," Cailin suggested.

"She wears no collar," Wulf replied. "Did you see any mark of ownership upon her when you bathed her, lambkin?"

Cailin shook her head. "Nay, I did not."

"I can remember nothing of myself," Aelfa said in a sweet, almost musical voice. "Oh, I am afraid! Why can I not remember?"

"You will remember in time," Cailin said briskly, seeing that

Aelfa was preparing to weep once more. The men were being fool-ish enough without being subjected to that. "Have you not work in the fields?" Cailin asked her husband. "Do not worry about Aelfa. She will stay with me, and I will keep her safe. Corio, will your father not want you at home to help? We are so pleased you came to visit, but go, and do not come back until the Beltane fires, cousin!"

"Are all women so impatient when they are close to delivering their young?" Corio asked Wulf as they exited the hall. "I have never seen Cailin so short of temper." Then, dismissing his cousin, he said, "Is not Aelfa the most exquisite creature you have ever seen? I think I am in love with her already. Is such a thing possi-ble, Wulf Ironfist?"

Wulf laughed. "Aye, it is," he admitted, "and I can see you are certainly taken with our waif-child. If we learn anything of import about her, like a husband languishing somewhere, I will send word to you."

Aelfa, however, could not seem to remember anything of her life before they had found her, apart from her name. Wulf felt that all evidence pointed to a gentle birth, and had wanted to house her in the solar, not the hall. Cailin had, with strangely uncharitable feelings, refused.

"The solar is for the lord and his family," she said sharply to her husband. "Aelfa is not family. She is safe in the hall, and to house her with us would say otherwise, causing unpleasant talk."

Among whom? he had wanted to ask, but Cailin's expression was so forbidding he dared not. He put her irritation down to the fact the child's birth was near and that she was anxious for it to be born. "You are mistress of this hall," he soothed her, and was sur-prised when she glared up at him. He had never seen her like this. Certainly she had not been so easily angered when she had carried Aurora.

"The girl must stay," Cailin said. "It goes against all the laws of hospitality for us to expel her from Cadda-wic due to the mysterious circumstances surrounding her arrival. Nonetheless she is not family, and I will not have her treated as such, lest it be misunderstood."

He was forced to agree, and Aelfa settled into the routine of their lives. She was courteous and pleasant to all, but Cailin thought she seemed more so to the men. Cailin did not know what it was that made her suspicious of Aelfa, but her voice within was strong. She had long ago learned not to deny it even when she did not fully understand the warning. Cailin knew from her past experiences that all would be revealed in time. Until then she would be vigilant and on her guard. Her family and all she held dear were once again being threatened. Would there never come a time when they would know real peace? she despaired silently.

Across the hall, Aelfa sat upon the floor with Nellwyn, giggling as they played with Aurora. They made a most charming picture, even if that was precisely what Aelfa had intended, Cailin thought angrily, wondering why the others could not see the girl for the schemer she was. In time, that little voice counseled her wisely. *In time.*

Chapter

17

There would never be a Beltane celebration, Cailin thought pensively, when she would not remember the tragedy that had struck her family. The merriment of the festival would always be tinged with sadness for her. When she and Wulf had returned to Britain last year, the holiday had been a subdued one for them because they were too involved with rebuilding their lives. This year, however, it was different. The fields were already green with new grain. There was an air of new hope about them that she could not remember having felt in all her life.

The weather was perfect, and despite the impending birth of her child, Cailin arose early to gather flowering branches for the hall. She took Aurora with her, and upon their return, Cailin noticed Nellwyn and Aelfa loitering about the hall's gates, flirting with the men on duty. She called sharply to Nellwyn to come and take Aurora, and scolded Aelfa for her idleness. Then she hurried into the hall, hearing laughter behind her and knowing that Aelfa had probably said something rude.

Cailin could not understand why the girl's memory had not returned. She had not been that badly injured when they had found her. In fact neither her head nor her face had been touched, it seemed. She had been treated with great kindness in the weeks she was with them. Cailin suspected that the girl knew full well who her people were and where she had come from, but would say nothing lest she be dislodged from her comfortable place at Cadda-wic, which was obviously better than anything she had ever known. Cailin realized that she did not want Aelfa at Cadda-wic much longer. If the girl could or would not remember, then a husband must be found for her in one of the villages by summer's end. Cailin was perfectly willing to supply the dowry, but Aelfa must go.

"Mama! Mama! See fire!" Aurora, who was snuggled into her mother's arms, pointed with fat little fingers at the Beltane fires leaping up across the hillsides as the sun set.

"Aye, Aurora, I see," Cailin answered her daughter.

"Pretty," Aurora said. "Look at Papa!"

Cailin smiled as Wulf leapt the fire, laughing, and then other men and women both began to follow him.

"Mama jump!" Aurora commanded her mother.

"Nay, precious, not this year," Cailin laughed. "I am too fat with the new baby. Next year," she promised.

Aelfa leapt over the flames, her pale gold hair flying. She was laughing, and Cailin had to admit, even grudgingly, that she was beautiful. The men clustered about her like bees to a honey pot. Corio had come from Braleah village just to see her, but Aelfa did not seem to favor him, to his great disappointment. Her two favorite swains were men-at-arms, Albert and Bran-hard, who vied mightily for her attention. It was just as well, Cailin thought. She was sorry to see the look of hurt on Corio's face, but she also knew he could do better than Aelfa if he really desired a wife. She watched, half amused, half annoyed, as Aelfa disappeared into the darkness, first with one of her admirers, and then returned with him to shortly go off with the other.

"She has the morals of a mink," Cailin said to Wulf. "She will have those two at each other's throats before the night is out."

"She is young, and it is Beltane," he answered mildly.

"We must find her a husband, and the sooner the better, from what I have observed here tonight, my lord," Cailin told him severely. The gods! She sounded like an old woman! What was the matter with her?

"I suspect you are right, lambkin," he answered, to her great surprise. "She is far too lovely a maid to be allowed to run freely much longer. I cannot have dissension among my men over a pretty girl. Discord is a weakness we can ill afford. Ragnar Strongspear has taken my advice and is expanding his territory to the south. He has been joined by his brother Gunnar. I have no doubt that, egged on by Antonia, he will be foolish enough to turn his eyes toward our lands sometime in the future. We must remain strong."

Aurora, half asleep, was heavy in Cailin's arms. "Nellwyn," she called to the nursemaid, "take Aurora and put her to bed." Then she turned back to her husband. "Make inquiries in Orrford to see if any young men need wives. If you make Aelfa choose between Albert and Bran-hard, there will be hard feelings between those two. She is in love with neither, but rather plays with each like a cat with a mouse. Corio is taken with her, but she is not the right woman for him. Best we send her as far from Cadda-wic and Braleah as we can. That way, none of her admirers here is apt to see her again for a long time, *if ever*. By summer's end, Aelfa must be wed."

"I must make a tour of all the villages soon to see how it goes with them," Wulf told his wife. "I but wait for the son you have promised me before leaving you, lambkin. I will personally seek out and find the right young man for Aelfa to wed in Orrford."

"Good!" Cailin said, but despite their agreement in the matter, her voice within nagged her yet. She remained on her guard, but for what, she was unable to tell.

Royse Wulfsone was born on the nineteenth day of May. Unlike his sister's hard birth, his entry into the world was a swift and easy one. Cailin awoke in the hour of the false dawn to realize her waters had broken. Within minutes she was being racked with labor, and in the hour that the sky began to lighten with the new day, the baby was born, howling lustily, his face red, his small arms flailing. Nellwyn had assisted her mistress with the birth, but Aelfa swooned at the sight of the blood involved and had to be carried from the solar.

Cailin and Wulf's son was strong and healthy from the moment of his birth. He suckled eagerly at his mother's breasts, and always seemed hungry. Denied her daughter's infancy, Cailin reveled in her motherhood. Sensitive, however, to Aurora's feelings, she involved the little girl in her brother's care as much as she could so that Aurora would not feel neglected. As a big sister, Aurora, who would be four in the late summer, did admirably, running to fetch her mother at her baby brother's least cry; helping to dress him; watching over him with Nellwyn.

"She is so patient with him," Cailin observed. "He is going to be very spoiled, I fear. He already recognizes her."

"Do you see how strong he is?" Wulf said proudly. "He will be a big man someday. Perhaps even bigger than I am."

When Royse was six weeks old, and Cailin fully recovered from the birth, Wulf Ironfist set off to visit his villages. Before he left, he called Aelfa into his and Cailin's presence. She came meekly, looking particularly pretty in a pale blue tunica she had made from a length of fabric Cailin had given her on Beltane.

"How may I serve you, lord?" she inquired politely.

"Has your memory returned yet, even in part, maiden?" he asked her quietly, his voice both gentle and encouraging.

Aelfa's light green eyes grew visibly misty. "Alas, my lord, no," she answered him. "I have tried to remember something of myself, but I cannot. Ohh, what will become of me?"

"It is time that you were wed," Wulf answered her.

"*Wed?*" Aelfa looked startled. This was obviously not something that she had even considered. "You would marry me?"

Cailin hissed angrily. The nerve of the wench!

"Not I," he said, somewhat startled himself by her words. "I go tomorrow to tour the villages belonging to my holding. Since you can remember nothing of yourself, and we have heard of no lost lasses in the time you have been with us, then it is time for you to begin a new life. As lord of this land, your welfare is my responsibility. I will therefore seek out a good husband for you, and you will be wed as soon as it is possible. Before the summer's end, I think."

"But I do not think I want a husband," Aelfa said nervously. "Perhaps I already have a husband, my lord. What if that is so?"

"Is it, Aelfa? Do you have a husband?" He pierced her with a sharp look. "Perhaps you have run away from a husband who caught you with a lover and then beat you for your faithlessness."

"I cannot remember, my lord," she stubbornly insisted.

"Then," Wulf said, smiling benignly, "I think it best we find you a good man and resettle you, maiden. Is it agreed?"

For a very long moment Aelfa was silent, and then finally she said, "Yes, my lord, but could you not marry me yourself?"

"One wife is more than enough for me," he replied with a chuckle. "Eh, lambkin?" He swept a loving look at Cailin by his side.

"You will never need another," she said quietly.

When Nellwyn learned of the other girl's fate, she complained to her mistress, "Why is it that Aelfa is to have a husband and I am not? Have I not served you well, my lady?"

"More than well, Nellwyn," Cailin assured her. "You may have a husband whenever you choose him, unless, of course, you would prefer that my lord and I select a good man for you. Aelfa is alone in the world and needs our aid; but you, Nellwyn, have always had me, and whatever you desire within reason I will give you for your faithful service."

"When Aelfa first came," Nellwyn told her mistress, "I thought her nice, but she is not, my lady. She teases the men to distraction."

"I know," Cailin replied. "That is why I suggested to my lord that he find her a husband—in Orrford, if possible."

"Orrford?" Nellwyn giggled. "It is far, my lady, and not very big, and there are so many cows. More than people, I think."

"Indeed?" Cailin said, a single eyebrow cocked.

"She will have to work very hard," Nellwyn continued. "Life is harsh is Orrford, and once she is married, she cannot flirt with others."

"No," Cailin answered solemnly. "Husbands will take umbrage if a wife flirts with other men, Nellwyn. Aelfa will have to become a very good and most proper wife, won't she?" She grinned at her servant.

Nellwyn giggled. "I do not think Aelfa will like either that or Orrford, my lady. She pretends to be meek and modest before you and my lord, but her tongue is sharp, and sometimes foul. She is not, I think, what she pretends to be, yet never has she spoken to me of her past. She does not even talk in her sleep, for I have listened."

"Soon Aelfa will not be our worry any longer," Cailin said soothingly to Nellwyn. "By summer's end she will be gone from us to a husband."

"Good riddance!" Nellwyn said feelingly. "I shall not be sorry to see the back of that one, my lady."

Cailin suddenly had a flash of intuition. "Is it Albert or Bran-hard you favor, Nellwyn, my lass?" she asked the girl.

Nellwyn blushed to the roots of her yellow hair. "Ohh, my lady! How did you know? 'Tis Albert, the fool, but he cannot see me for his eyes are too full of Aelfa, though she toys with him, first favoring him and then Bran-hard. Both are confused by her wicked behavior, but 'tis Albert I love."

"He will have forgotten her by Samain, I promise," Cailin said to the girl. "Then we will see if he favors a marriage with you."

Nellwyn's blue eyes filled with tears. "Oh, my lady, thank you! I would make Albert a good wife. I would. The fool!"

Yes, Cailin thought after her revealing discussion with Nellwyn, the sooner Aelfa was gone from Cadda-wic, the better. Still her conscience nagged at her. Was she being fair, foisting the wench off on some poor unsuspecting young man? Wulf, however, was fully aware of Aelfa's shortcomings. He would choose the right man. It would be up to the bridegroom to correct Aelfa's behavior. Cailin hoped he would be strong enough.

Wulf had been gone for over a week when Aelfa disappeared

one afternoon. "Has she run away, perhaps?" Cailin wondered aloud.

Aelfa, however, reappeared before the gates were closed that evening. When questioned about her whereabouts, she claimed to have been out berrying.

"You brought no berries back," Cailin noted sharply.

"I could find none, my lady," was the meek reply.

"She lies," Nellwyn said as she and her mistress made their rounds to see that the fires were banked for the night, that the door was bolted, and everything else in the hall was secure. "She had no basket with her, my lady. How could she berry without a basket?"

"She could not," Cailin answered. "More than likely she was out meeting a lover upon the hillside, the bold wench."

"Albert and Bran-hard were looking something fierce at each other in the hall at supper, my lady," Nellwyn reported.

"There is our answer," Cailin said. "She is setting those two against one another again, but for what purpose I do not know."

Cailin climbed to the solar where Aurora and Royse were already long asleep. Lifting the baby from his cradle, she fed the half-sleeping infant before finding her own rest. She could not imagine a better life than the one she had. *Wulf. Their children. Cadda-wic.* Sometimes she would glimpse the old marble floor of what had once been her childhood home, and the memories would flood her being. Lately when that happened, she found she was no longer sad. Most of her memories were good ones, and whatever happened, those memories could not be taken from her. She would always have them, and in having them, she would always have her family with her.

Cailin slept, not hearing the bolt to the hall door being drawn softly. The door opened, and then it closed as silently as Aelfa could make it. She stood outside the entry a long minute, listening to the sounds of the night, and then she ran on bare feet across the courtyard to the gatehouse. The waning moon silvered her naked form. She carried a small skin of wine in her hand. Gaining her destination, Aelfa quickly entered the small gatehouse, shutting the door quietly. A smile of derision crossed her face at the sight of the dozing man on the stool in the corner. What a weakling he was, and his sense of duty was certainly lacking.

Kneeling down next to him, Aelfa kissed Bran-hard's mouth, startling the man awake. "Did you not want to see me?" she murmured seductively at him, and his eyes widened at her nudity. "I have brought you some fine wine from the lord's own barrel. It will not ever be missed," she reassured him, and handed him the full skin. "Have some." She kissed him quickly a second time.

"Aelfa," he said in a strangled voice. "You should not be here. Where is your clothing? What if someone should come?"

"Albert would not be so faint of heart," Aelfa taunted him. "He met me on the hillside today and tried to have his way with me. I fought him off and refused him, for it is you, Bran-hard, that I really want. Let Albert have Nellwyn, who is so cow-eyed over him." Her small hands reached down and fumbled beneath his tunic. "You are a *real* man! I know you are!" Then she kissed him hard. "Do you not want me, Bran-hard, my big, strong warrior?" Aelfa ran her tongue over her lips seductively.

Bran-hard found, to his surprise, that he was holding his breath. He let it out with a slow hiss as her hands found his manhood and began to play with it. She was skilled beyond any he had ever known. His eyes closed, and pure pleasure such as he had never experienced filled his being. Her little fingers stroked him slowly, lingeringly at first. Then pushing the covering from his battering ram, she worked him swiftly. He began to ache with his great need. "Aelfa," he groaned hungrily, catching his hand in her hair and drawing her closer to him. "I want you, Aelfa!"

Giggling, she took his cloak and spread it upon the narrow floor of the tiny gatehouse. Laying down upon it, she opened her legs wide and said huskily, "Come, stuff me with that great pole of yours, Bran-hard! You want me every bit as much as I want you! No one will come and find us. All are abed, and we may take our pleasure. As much of it as we like!"

He could not have stopped himself if he had wanted to. She was beautiful, and she was hot for him. No man in his right mind would refuse Aelfa's plea. With a low cry he fell upon her, pushing his engorged organ into her hot, wet sheath; humping her almost violently while she encouraged him onward, murmuring a soft stream of foul yet madly exciting obscenities into his ear as she writhed wildly beneath him. He was astounded that she would know such words, for she looked so pure, but it lessened his guilt at using her so enthusiastically.

She seemed to fill him with incredible strength, and his lust knew no bounds. He pumped and pumped and pumped himself into her, while Aelfa twisted and moaned beneath him, her little cries arousing him even further. Finally he could no longer contain himself and his passions burst violently within her throbbing body. He collapsed upon her with a groan of satisfaction. "By Woden, wench, you are the best! I have never had better, I swear it!" His oniony breath assailed her.

"Get off me, you oaf," she said, "you are crushing me."

He rolled away from her. "Where's that wine you brought?" he demanded, feeling relaxed now and more in control of the situation. "Let's have a drink together, and then I'll give you another bit of a poke if you're of a mind. You will be, won't you?" he said with a leering grin. "I've never known such a woman as you, Aelfa. You be one of those girls who cannot get enough, aren't you?" He sat himself back down upon his stool, pulling his garments into some semblance of order again. Then reaching out for her, he drew her near, tweaking the rosy nipples of her full, fat breasts. Her clothing had never given him any indication that she had such fine teats, but they were magnificent.

Rutting fool, Aelfa thought as she smiled up at him. She lifted up the skin of wine and pretended to drink before handing it on to him. "Hmmmm, 'tis good," she said as he swilled away, some of the purple-red liquid drizzling down into his thick blond beard.

Bran-hard let the sweet, cool liquid run down his throat. It was the best drink he had ever tasted. Wulf Ironfist lived well. He handed her back the wineskin and began to fondle Aelfa's big breasts. "You've the best pair I've ever seen, wench," he said by way of a compliment, "and your cunt is the tightest of any I've ever reamed. I swear it! You really know how to give a man his pleasure, Aelfa. I can hardly believe it, but I'm ready to have at you again. On your back, my girl," he said, as loosing his organ from his clothing once more, he pushed her down to the floor.

What he lacked in subtlety he more than made up for in endurance and brute strength, Aelfa thought, as she pretended to be overcome with passion. She had taken her own pleasure with him the first time, but now she could not allow herself the luxury. When his lust exploded again and he rolled away from her, she offered him the wineskin once more, smiling encouragingly as he gulped down the potent liquid. This time, within moments, Branhard fell into unconsciousness. Aelfa sighed with her relief. She was actually sore with his enthusiastic attentions. A third bout with him would have certainly rendered her raw.

She rose from the floor of the gatehouse, and after much effort, managed to drag Bran-hard's limp, heavy body back onto his stool. His shaggy head lay upon his chest. He appeared to be dozing. She slipped from the building and ran quickly back across the courtyard to the hall. Letting herself in, she hurried to her bed space. The hall was quite silent, the contented snores of its inhabitants the only sounds she heard.

Aelfa put on her clothes and then returned to the gatehouse where Bran-hard sat, unconscious. Seating herself upon the floor, where she would not be seen, she waited for the predawn. When it finally came, Aelfa stood up, stretched, and then leaving the gatehouse went directly to the great gates of Cadda-wic. Slowly and with great difficulty, she pushed the heavy bar that lay across one of the gates to one side. Above her the sky was quickly lightening. Perspiration, half due to exertion, half to fear of discovery, rolled down her back as she struggled with the bar. When at last she succeeded, the single door swung open to reveal a large party of armed men.

"Uncle," Aelfa said archly. "Welcome to Cadda-wic."

"You have done well, niece," Ragnar Strongspear said, and then led his men quietly through the gates into the courtyard. "Where is the mistress of the hall? And how long before Wulf Ironfist's return?"

"Cailin sleeps in the solar with her children," Aelfa replied. "As for her husband, he should return in a few days' time, I expect."

"Secure this place," Ragnar said to his second-in-command, Harald, and then he turned back to Aelfa. "Fetch the lady Cailin to me, girl, and her children, too. I will want food also."

"Yes, Uncle," Aelfa said. She hurried off back into the hall to do his bidding, only realizing too late that Cailin always drew the ladder to the solar up each night. There was no other way into the room but through the trapdoor. As Ragnar strode into the hall, she ran back to him and explained the dilemma.

"No matter," he said. "She must come down eventually, and I will be waiting for her. The lady Cailin is a most toothsome wench."

"You desire her?" Aelfa was surprised. She thought Cailin far too prim and proper for her lusty uncle. She was also too old, being past twenty.

"Do not be fooled by her dignity and manners, girl," he told her. "Beneath it all she is a woman, and a fiery woman, I will wager."

The sleepy and surprised inhabitants of Cadda-wic were roused and brought before Ragnar Strongspear. Outside, the men-at-arms were rounded up, subdued, and marched into the hall, including the half-conscious Bran-hard.

"This place is now mine by right of conquest," Ragnar said in a sonorous voice. "No harm will come to you if you obey my wishes. If you try to rebel, you will be killed. Now start your day as you normally would, and someone bring me some food. I am fair starved!"

For a moment they looked at him, still but half awake, and totally unaware of what they should do. How had this happened? How had Ragnar Strongspear gained entry to Cadda-wic? It was a common thought.

"You will obey Ragnar Strongspear for now," Cailin said as she came into their midst. "I want none of you harmed." She was very beautiful in a dark green tunic dress decorated with gold threads. Cailin turned to Ragnar and demanded in proud tones, "How came you here?"

His eyes devoured her. By Woden, she was a beauty, and he would have her this night beneath him! "By means of a Trojan horse," he answered her. "Do you know the story? Antonia told it me."

Cailin nodded. "I know the tale well," she said, and then a light of understanding dawned in her eyes. Her gaze swept the room and found what it was seeking. "Aelfa," she said. "Aelfa was your Trojan horse, was she not, Ragnar Strongspear? Who is she?"

"My brother Gunnar's eldest daughter. She is fifteen, and very wily," he said, chuckling.

"The girl, Aelfa, has betrayed us," Cailin told the gathering of her people. "She is Ragnar Strongspear's niece."

A terrible groan arose from Bran-hard. "Bitch!" he cried, and then flung himself before Cailin. "Lady, you must forgive me! I desired her, and she knew it. She came to me last night as I kept watch and offered herself to me. Then she fed me drugged wine to render me unconscious. It is my fault that the hall is taken! Forgive me!"

"You are a fool, Bran-hard, but get up and go about your duties. What is done is done, although you are not likely to escape some punishment from my husband when he returns," Cailin told him.

Bran-hard scrambled to his feet. His complexion had a decidedly yellow-green tinge to it. He looked as if he would be sick at any moment. "Thank you, lady," he managed to gasp.

Cailin realized now that the reason Aelfa had fixed her attentions on poor Bran-hard and the hapless Albert was that they were the two men assigned to the gatehouse. Each took his turn in rotation, keeping the watch through the night. Aelfa did not care for either of them, and poor Albert could have just as easily been her victim had he been on duty last night. It was only bad luck for Bran-hard that it had been his turn.

"How did Aelfa communicate with you?" Cailin asked Ragnar as they seated themselves at the high board and the hall regained some semblance of normalcy. "I sensed something wrong, but did not know what."

He looked eagerly toward the end of the hall for the servants

394 / To Love Again

who would soon be coming from the cook house with the morning meal. Ragnar well remembered the good table Cailin kept. "I had a man on the hill watching from the day you found her at your gates," he told Cailin, and then he gulped down the good brown ale poured into his cup. "I've never tasted better," he complimented her with a grin.

"Yesterday," Cailin said slowly. "She contacted the man yesterday afternoon when she slipped out, ostensibly to berry, but she took no basket with her. I knew it a lie, but not the reason for the lie."

The food was now beginning to arrive. Ragnar took his knife from his belt and cut himself two thick slabs of ham. He helped himself to several hard-boiled eggs and a small loaf of bread. "More ale!" he commanded the attending servant, then he asked Cailin, "Where are your children, lady? I hear you had a son but a few weeks back. That bitch Antonia lost my child after the solstice. It was a son, too. She is a bad breeder, but you will be a good breeder for me. Did you know that I am going to make you my wife, Cailin? The first time I ever laid eyes on you, I knew that I wanted you. My Saxon women are good creatures, loyal and hardworking, like milk cows. Antonia is a viper, but sometimes a little poison is sweet. You, however, my little fox vixen with your russet curls, will give me the greatest pleasure of all."

"I have a husband," Cailin said quietly. She was not afraid of this braggart. He could not have taken Cadda-wic without treachery, and he would be driven out.

"I will kill Wulf Ironfist," Ragnar bragged.

"I think rather he will kill you," Cailin replied quietly.

"Your children?" he demanded again. "Where are they?"

"They are gone," she said with a small smile.

"That cannot be!" he roared angrily, furious, for her children were the weapon he intended to use against her. "How can they be gone?" The veins in his thick neck stood out clearly, and they were throbbing.

"You gained entry to Cadda-wic by means of a ruse, Ragnar Strongspear," she said. "I was already awake when you entered the hall. At first I believed my husband had returned. I opened the door to look down, and saw you. My son was newly fed, and so I awoke my daughter. I dressed both children, and while you were bragging and bellowing and attempting to put the fear of the gods into my people, I brought my children down into the hall, gave them into the keeping of my servant, Nellwyn, and watched while she walked through the gates with them. Your men were so busy trying to bully mine that they never even noticed Nellwyn pass them by. She is now well on her way to Braleah. You will not catch her, I think," Cailin concluded, laughing lightly.

"*Braleah?* What is that place?" he growled.

"One of the villages belonging to Cadda-wic," she told him. "Surely you did not think we were alone but for a few of my Dobunni kin? Cadda-wic has four villages belonging to it. You will be unable to hold them, if you can even find them. Nellwyn will raise the alarm against you, and Wulf Ironfist will come with many men to drive you out. If I were you, I should finish my meal and hurry home."

"What a woman you are!" he answered her, grinning. "Even if I were to take your advice, I should take you with me, Cailin. You are not simply strong and beautiful, you think like a warrior. I do not believe I should like such a trait in any other woman, but it becomes you, my fox vixen. By Woden, it becomes you well!"

Cailin sipped her watered wine and ate heartily of bread, ham, and hard cheese. She had nothing more to say to Ragnar Strongspear. Finally she stood up and strode from the high board.

"Should I stop her, lord?" Harald asked nervously.

"Are the gates *now* secured?" Ragnar demanded sarcastically.

"Aye, lord!" Harald said.

"Then let her be, you fool. Where will she go that I cannot find her? She is, I suspect, about her daily duties, and nothing more."

Cailin was, but she also made the rounds of Cadda-wic reassuring each and every member of the household with her calm manner.

"What shall we do, my lady?" Albert asked her nervously. He was more than well aware how close to disaster he himself had come.

"Do not resist," she told him, as she had the others, "unless, of course, your very life is threatened. Go about your daily duties as you normally do. Wulf Ironfist will come soon, and he will drive Ragnar Strongspear back to his own lands. Do not fear. Nellwyn will raise the alarm, and Ragnar Strongspear's only advantage was in surprise. He no longer has that advantage."

Cailin moved on. In early afternoon she gathered the women about her, telling them, "I will not allow anyone to abuse you. Hide yourselves in the cellar beneath the largest grain barn. Do it as soon as you can, and remember to bring water skins. Do not come out until morning, when I shall come to fetch you. Hurry now!"

"But what of you, lady?" one of the serving women asked.

"I will not be harmed," Cailin assured them. She had already decided what she must do. If she could not deter Ragnar Strongspear from his lustful intent, then she must kill him.

Her breasts were beginning to ache dreadfully, and looking down, she grimaced with irritation. Her milk was beginning to leak through her nipples and stain her tunic dress. Royse last nursed in the early morning. Nellwyn would have found a nursing mother for him at Braleah, and Cailin knew she would have to do something to rid herself of her milk.

Cailin took bread from the bake house and a small cheese from the dairy. The servants would have put several pitchers of water in the solar, as was the usual practice. Entering the hall, Cailin saw that Ragnar Strongspear was not there. With a chuckle she climbed up to the solar and, pulling the ladder behind her, bolted the door fast. There was no other ladder available that would reach the chamber. She would be safe for a time. Removing her tunic dress, she sighed at the sight of her soaked camisa. She pulled it off, too, and then expressed the milk from her swollen breasts into an empty basin. Immediately she felt better, and washing herself off, she put on clean garments.

She could hear fresh activity in the hall below. She had given her menservants orders to serve the evening meal as usual, and deny the intruders nothing in the way of food and drink. She had to keep Ragnar Strongspear and his men as content as possible until Wulf Ironfist returned. Cailin had absolutely no doubt that her husband would come, and when he did, he would regain Caddawic. No one was going to take this land from her, *from them*. She had been born here, as had ten generations of her family. They would live on through her children. *No one would take these lands from her again!* Not Ragnar Strongspear. Not Antonia Porcius. *No one.*

"Lady? Are you in the solar?" She heard Ragnar Strongspear calling up to her. "Lady, I would have you join us at table. Come down."

"I am ill," Cailin answered him. "The excitement of today has been too much for me, Ragnar Strongspear. I must rest. It has been but a short time since I gave birth to my son. I am yet weak."

"You would feel better, lady, if you ate. It will help to build your strength up. Come down, my little fox vixen. I will feed you dainty morsels of meat from my own plate, and give you sweet wine to ease your distress," he told her in dulcet tones.

Cailin smothered her giggles. "I think not, Ragnar Strongspear. I am best left alone," she replied, and then made a series of rather convincing noises to give the impression that she was retching, and quite close to vomiting. "Ohhhh," she moaned, sounding quite desperate.

"Perhaps you are better alone," he agreed nervously, and she heard him hastily moving away from below the solar door. "I will see you tomorrow, lady."

Nothing, Cailin thought with a mischievous grin, discouraged a lustful man from his chosen path more than a woman threatening to disgorge the contents of her stomach in his lap. She tore a chunk of bread from the loaf and sliced a wedge of cheese off the piece she had taken. She washed them down with cool water from a pitcher, and then sat down to work her tapestry.

When the light had faded from the sky, so that she could no longer see what she was doing, Cailin sat quietly listening to the sounds from the hall below. The men were growing drunk. She could tell by the high hilarity, the laughter, and the singing. Occasionally she heard the sound of breaking crockery and was angered. It was difficult obtaining good Samienware now. Eventually, however, the din lessened, and finally the hall grew silent.

Satisfied that the intruders were sleeping a drunken sleep, Cailin arose and stretched. She was exhausted with the tension involved in keeping a step ahead of Ragnar Strongspear. With her very last bit of strength, she shoved two storage chests over the solar door for extra protection. The windows were much too narrow for anyone to get through. She wondered what had happened to Aelfa. The bitch would have been the only woman in evidence tonight. Cailin removed her tunic dress and lay down in her bed space. How long would it take Wulf to return? she wondered, and then fell into an uneasy sleep.

She awoke automatically, as she always did and, arising, went to the window to look out. The sky was already growing light, and she could see smoke coming from the bake house. Her breasts were full again, and she once more expressed her milk. Cailin splashed water on her face, relieved herself, and quickly dressed. Pushing the chests away from the solar door, she slipped the bolt silently. Opening the door, she lowered the ladder to climb down into the hall.

About her she observed Ragnar Strongspear and his men sprawled in their drunken slumber. There was absolutely no sign of Aelfa, but then the wench was no longer her concern. The hall was a shambles of overturned benches and tables, broken pottery and vomit. Cailin wrinkled her nose distastefully. The rushes would have to be changed immediately. The hall door had not been bolted, and so she slipped out into the courtyard. Although the gates were barred, she could see no one on duty.

Hurrying to the bake house, she entered and asked the baker, "Where are the men? There is no one in the yard."

"I do not know, lady," the baker replied nervously. "I have not left the bake house since the intruders came. I am safest here, I think."

"Aye," Cailin agreed, "you are. Do not fear, Wulf Ironfist will come soon, and then these men will be driven from Cadda-wic."

Cailin left the bake house and hurried to the storage barn. "Come out," she called to the women servants. "It is morning, and the invaders lie drunk in the hall. It is safe now."

The women climbed up from the cellar beneath the barn and stood before their mistress. She viewed them carefully. Two were young and very pretty. They were still apt to be in danger, but the others, older and plainer, would not be unless the men were very drunk and very randy. She sent the two pretty maids to the bake house.

"Tell the baker you are to remain with him. You should be safe if you stay there. If any of Ragnar Strongspear's men come in, keep your heads down, your eyes lowered, and if you must look up, twist your faces to look ugly. It may be your only protection. Go now. The yard is safe and empty. Our men seem to have disappeared."

The two girls ran off, and Cailin then told the remaining women, "Go about your duties as you normally would. If Wulf Ironfist does not come today, then you must hide here again tonight. I will not be able to come for you when the time is right. You must help yourselves. It is all I can do to stay out of Ragnar Strongspear's clutches."

The trespasser and his men finally awoke and stumbled from the hall to relieve themselves. Cailin and her women swept the hall free of debris and all signs of sickness. Fresh rushes were laid, mixed with fragrant herbs. The morning meal was served, but eaten by few before being cleared away.

Ragnar sat at the high board, a large goblet of wine gripped in his fist. "Where are your men?" he demanded of Cailin.

"I do not know," she said. "I thought, perhaps, that you had locked them up somewhere. When I awoke this morning, they were gone. If they knew a means of escape, I am angry at them that they did not take me with them," she concluded, and her irritated tone convinced him more than her words that she was speaking the truth.

He nodded. "Very well. I see your women have returned."

"I sent them into safe keeping for the night," Cailin answered tartly. "I will have no rape or abuse of the women in my charge. Where is Aelfa? I have not seen your niece all morning."

"She is to marry Harald at Lugh. They are probably somewhere making the beast with two backs. Aelfa is a very passionate girl."

"She has the morals of a mink," Cailin observed dryly.

"Aye, she does," Ragnar said with a hearty laugh. "I have warned Harald that she will make him a very bad wife, but he is determined to have her, so what can I do? My brother has given his permission for the marriage. I could not withhold mine."

The remainder of the day seemed to pass more slowly than any day she could remember. As the sun began to set, Cailin was pleased to see that the women had all disappeared once again. She hurried to reach the solar before Ragnar Strongspear could find and stop her. Her breasts were near to bursting with her milk, and it was already leaking through her clothing once more. Quickly climbing the ladder, she pulled it up behind her, closing and bolting the door. She shoved the clothing chests atop the door and sighed, relieved. Stripping off her garments, she reached for the basin and began to relieve herself of the pressure that was making her breasts ache so unbearably. Where was Wulf? If he didn't come soon, her milk would finally run dry. Then she would have to give her precious Royse to some other woman to nurse.

"What are you doing?"

The sound of Ragnar Strongspear's voice rendered her icy with fear. Her eyes widened as he climbed from her bed space. "How did you get in here?" she demanded. Her heart was beating wildly.

"I climbed the ladder," he said simply, and she silently cursed her stupidity that she had not hidden it. "What are you doing?" he repeated, his dark blue eyes sweeping admiringly over her lush form.

It was then Cailin recalled her state. She was naked before this man's eyes, but it was done and there was no helping it. "I must express the milk from my breasts," she said, "as my son is not here to take its nourishment." Her voice was cold and emotionless.

A slow smile lit his face, and moving to stand before her, he clamped his big hands about her waist. Lifting her up, he positioned her so that her breasts hung over his face. Then lowering her slightly, he began to suckle upon her.

It was to Cailin's mind as great a violation of her body as if he had raped her, which she knew he fully intended to do next. *"Don't!"* she cried out, anguished, but it was as if she had never spoken. She writhed desperately, but the mouth on her breast could not be dislodged.

When he had drained the first breast, he looked into her eyes with a smile. "I like the taste," he told her. "It is said that if a man takes the milk of his lover's breasts, he is rendered potent beyond any other man." Then his greedy mouth grasped her other breast and he began suckling hard on it. When he had taken every drop she had to give, he carried her to the bed space and threw her roughly upon the feather bed. She watched horrified as he pulled his clothing off to match her state. "I've never had a completely naked woman," he said.

Cailin attempted to escape the bed space. She was in a total panic. Ragnar laughed uproariously at her efforts. Holding her down with one hand, he climbed atop her, positioning himself upon her breasts. "Open your mouth," he commanded her, and when she shook her head, refusing, he pinched her nose tightly until, unable to breathe and starting to lose consciousness, Cailin gasped for air. As she did so, he thrust his organ into her mouth. "If you bite," he warned her, "I will have every tooth in your head pulled out," and she believed him. "Suckle me, my little fox vixen, as nicely as I suckled you," he ordered her.

She shook her head in the negative, but he only smiled, and reaching back, found her little jewel with his fingers and began to pinch it cruelly. Cailin cried out with the pain, and beaten, began to comply with his desire.

"Ahh, yes, my little fox vixen," he groaned as she stirred up his lust. "You're skilled beyond any I've ever known!" His eyes closed with his pleasure.

Cailin stealthily moved her arms back over her head even as she continued to tease her captor with her tongue. One hand began to surreptitiously feel beneath the feather bed in the straw. She moved carefully, slowly, terrified that she might attract his attention to what she was doing. *Where was it? Had he found it himself?*

"Enough!" roared Ragnar Strongspear, drawing his engorged organ from her mouth. "This randy fellow wants to seek his proper place!" He began to slide himself down her body so he might couple with her.

She couldn't find it! Cailin's fingers sought desperately. *It had to be there!* She must delay him in his intent. "Ohhh, my lord," she pleaded prettily with him, "Will you not give me a bit of the same pleasure I have given you? Ohh, please! I must have it!"

Laughter rumbled up from his chest. "Then you shall have your desire, my russet-haired little fox vixen! I will not disappoint you!" Yanking her legs apart, he almost dove between them.

Cailin attempted to block the feel of his wet tongue on her flesh. Frantic, she dug into the straw beneath the feather bed, and just when she was certain that he must have found it and removed it earlier, her hand was sliced slightly by the blade she sought. Relief pouring through her, Cailin grasped the weapon, ignoring the pain of her wound. "Ohhh! Ohhh!" she cried, remembering he would expect something of her for his obscene efforts. "Oh, it is good! I am ready for you, my lord!"

Wordless, Ragnar Strongspear positioned himself.

"Ohh, kiss me!" Cailin cried to him, and when he leaned forward to cover her mouth with his, she plunged her knife several times into his back. With a surprised grunt, he rolled off of her onto his back. He was wounded, but not mortally so, she saw. "Bitch!" he growled at her. "You'll pay for that!"

Cailin quickly straddled him, grasped his head by the hair, and yanking it back, swiftly cut Ragnar Strongspear's throat. The look of total amazement in his eyes faded so rapidly that she wasn't even certain she had actually seen it. She scrambled off of him and stood shivering, staring down at the dead man, not even sure he was really dead. She was afraid for a long moment that he would jump up, but no. He was dead. Very dead. She had killed Ragnar Strongspear. *She had killed a man.*

Cailin began to weep softly with relief. When at last her sobs subsided, she became aware of the fact that she was covered in blood. *His blood.* She shuddered with distaste, and forcing herself to function, moved across the solar, poured water into a basin and washed, washed, washed, until finally she was clean again. Being clean and having fresh garments seemed to help a little. She avoided looking across the room to the bed space where Ragnar Strongspear lay sprawled in a widening pool of his own blood. Instead she sat down by her loom, eventually dozing with exhaustion, until the birds, twittering excitedly in the predawn, roused her. Starting awake, Cailin remembered what had happened the previous night.

What was she going to do? When Ragnar's men discovered that she had killed their master, and they certainly would, they would kill her. She would never see Wulf and their children again. Nervous tears began to slide down her pale cheeks. *No!* She would not allow herself to be slaughtered like a frightened rabbit.

Perhaps she could escape Cadda-wic before Ragnar's body was discovered. It was very early, and no one was stirring in the hall. She could climb down, and then she would hide the ladder to the solar. Everyone would assume Ragnar was sleeping off the excesses of his night's sport. She would rouse the other women, and together they would all slip through the gates on one pretext or another.

No! It simply wouldn't work. There were too many of them not to seem suspicious. She couldn't leave the other women behind to face the violent wrath of Ragnar Strongspear's men. She would go and fetch the two girls hidden in the bake house. They would join the other women beneath the grain storage barn. Yes! That was a far better plan. No one would find them there, and surely Wulf would come soon.

Cailin pushed the chests from atop the door and, sliding the bolt, opened it, and lowered the ladder before her. Drawing the door softly shut after her, she swiftly descended into the hall. Where would she hide the ladder? Cailin wondered. She would throw it down the well! She could never go back into the solar again. Not after what had happened to her there last night. A hand fell heavily upon her shoulder, and unable to help herself, Cailin screamed softly with her terror.

"*Lambkin!* It is I."

She whirled, heart pounding, and Wulf Ironfist stood before her. Beyond them in the hall, Ragnar Strongspear's men stood shackled and surrounded by their own people. "Ohh, Wulf," she sobbed, collapsing with relief into his arms. After a moment she stiffened and, pulling away from him, she queried, "How did you get into Cadda-wic? Were the walls not manned by Ragnar Strongspear's men?"

"We got in the same way our men got out the other night. There is a small trapdoor in one of the gatehouses. It leads to a narrow tunnel beneath our defenses, lambkin. I sent Corio back for the men. They departed the other night by means of that tunnel. Then they told me in detail of Ragnar Strongspear's defenses. We returned this dawning the same way and took back Cadda-wic."

"Why did I not know of this tunnel?" Cailin demanded, outraged. "I had to hide our women in the cellar beneath the grain barns to keep them safe from these intruders. Why was I not told of it?"

"Corio sent Albert to look for you, lambkin, but you had disappeared. Albert had no choice but to go with the others," Wulf explained, but Cailin would not have any of it.

"He might have told one of the women," she insisted, forgetting that she herself had hidden the women away for safety's sake. "I had to barricade myself in the solar to escape the unpleasant attentions of Ragnar Strongspear. Would you have had me wandering the hall, playing the gracious hostess to that savage pig?" She was furious.

"But you did not escape my uncle last night," Aelfa said meanly, coming forward, a nasty smile upon her beautiful face. "You look quite well, considering the active night you must have had beneath my uncle."

"I will kill him if he has touched you!" Wulf Ironfist said angrily.

"I already have," Cailin told him bluntly, and Aelfa grew pale at her words. "He did not rape me, my lord, though he sought to do so."

"How could you have killed so large a man, lambkin?" her husband gently inquired. Was she truly all right? he wondered.

"I slit his throat," Cailin said tonelessly.

"With what?" he asked. The gods! She was so pale.

"The voice within would not stop nagging at me," she began. "I do not know why I did it, but when you departed to visit our villages, I put a knife beneath the feather bed in our bed space. When he climbed atop me, I found it and I killed him. There was so much blood, Wulf! I can never sleep in that solar again. *Ever!*" She began to weep.

He comforted her as best he could, and when she had ceased to sob, he told her, "I have much news, lambkin, and it is good." Then seeing the darkling stain spreading across her tunic dress, he cried out, "Lambkin, are you injured?"

Cailin looked down and laughed weakly. "I need Royse," she said. "My breasts are overflowing with my milk."

"Nellwyn will have him here shortly," he promised her, and put a loving arm about her. "Aurora too."

"How devoted you are to each other," Aelfa sneered, "but what is to become of us, I should like to know?"

"Her memory has returned, I take it," Wulf said with a small attempt at humor. They walked into the hall and seated themselves at the high board. Aelfa followed, but positioned herself next to Harald.

"She never lost her memory," Cailin told him. "Let me tell you a story that I learned as a child. In ancient times a Grecian king named Menelaeus had a beautiful queen who was called Helen. The king was old, but he loved his wife. The queen, however, was young, and she fell in love with a handsome youth, Paris. They fled to his father's city of Troy. A war between Troy and several powerful Grecian states erupted over the insult to Menelaeus and his efforts to regain Helen, the beauteous queen.

"Troy, however, was considered impregnable. Enormous high walls surrounded it. There was a goodly supply of fresh water and food. For many years the Greeks besieged it, but they could not take the city. Finally they agreed to cease their war with Troy, and as a gesture of peace, the departing Greek armies left a magnificent large, carved, and decorated horse on wheels behind for the Trojans. The citizens of Troy opened their gates and brought the horse into the city. All day they celebrated their victory over Menelaeus and his allies.

"In the dark of the night, when all lay sleeping, the Greek army, which had secreted itself within the belly of the Trojan horse, came forth and took the city of Troy, showing no mercy. All were killed, and the city destroyed.

"Aelfa was Ragnar Strongspear's Trojan horse. She allowed herself to be beaten, and she pretended to have no knowledge of herself but her name, so that she might gain our sympathies. Then she set about to fascinate and lure both our gatekeepers because she could not be certain which one of them would be on duty the night she intended to let her uncle and his men into Cadda-wic."

"Albert and Bran-hard told me what happened," Wulf said. "I have forgiven them both. They have learned a valuable lesson by this." He looked out over the hall at Ragnar's men. "Now I must decide what to do with these men. Shall I kill them, or show mercy?"

"Mercy, lord!" the men cried with one voice. *"Mercy!"*

Cailin leaned over and whispered to her husband. "Ragnar's brother, Gunnar, will think to profit from his brother's death; but his daughter, Aelfa, is, I think, ambitious. She will want her uncle's lands for Harald, who is to be her husband. Is there not some way in which we might set these men against each other? If they are busy battling one another, they will not have time to bother with us, my lord. And let us not forget our old friend Antonia Porcius. Those lands were hers before Ragnar Strongspear stormed across them. I do not think Antonia is ready to let go of her dreams for Quintus, the younger, yet."

Wulf grinned at his wife. "Truly Flavius Aspar and Byzantium lost a valuable strategist in you, lambkin." Then he turned to his prisoners, his look fierce. "Ragnar Strongspear is dead," he told them. "Harald Swiftsword, will you swear fealty to me? If you do, I will not oppose your taking of Ragnar Strongspear's lands. You are, I think, your master's natural heir. His sons are too young to be strong neighbors."

"What of my father?" Aelfa demanded. "He is Ragnar's brother. Should he not inherit my uncle's lands?"

"Why would you want your father to have what your husband could have, Aelfa Gunnarsdottar? If Harald does not claim Ragnar Strongspear's lands for himself, he will never have anything of his own. If he is strong enough to hold them against your father, why should you mind? Do you not desire to be a great lady?"

"I am strong enough to hold those lands for myself," Harald bragged loudly, and turned to the other men. "Are you with me?" he demanded, and they cried their assent. Harald turned back to Wulf Ironfist. "Then I will swear to be your man, my lord, and keep the peace between us. Aelfa, what say you?"

"Yes!" she said. "It was decided long ago between us, Harald, and if I would take you landless, I would certainly not reject you when you are about to become a great and propertied lord."

"Then," said Wulf Ironfist, "I will free you all!" and they cheered him loudly.

Ale was brought, and a toast drunk to the peace between Wulf Ironfist and Harald Swiftsword. Then they prepared to march from the hall, but Wulf took Harald aside and told him, "Beware of the lady Antonia. The lands you now claim were her family's lands for many generations. Perhaps you might take her as a second wife to keep her from another man who might attempt to gain those lands through the woman."

"I thank you for the advice," Harald replied. "It might not be such a bad idea. Ragnar always said she was bad-tempered, but the best fuck he had ever had in his life. Under the circumstances I must either wed her or kill her. I'll think on it."

"Best to marry her," Wulf said. "She and Aelfa will battle each other constantly, and consequently keep out of your business."

Harald laughed. "Perhaps you are right," he said slowly. "Yes! I know you are!"

When they were gone, and the morning was beginning to take on a more normal tone, Wulf took his wife by the hand and led her out into the summer sunlight. They strolled together amid the ripening grain.

"This incident has made me realize that we cannot remain at Cadda-wic," he told her. "It is too prone to attack here in its narrow valley. The hills press too closely about us. We cannot see our enemy until they are almost upon us. I have ordered a new hall to be built at Brand-dun for us. It sits upon a hill, and we cannot be taken unawares by an enemy. We will continue to farm these fields and tend to the orchards that once belonged to your family, but we will no longer live here, lambkin. Will you mind very much?"

Cailin shook her head. "No," she told him. "Though I have many happy memories of the house in which I grew up, it is gone. The earth is drenched with my family's blood, and now the blood of Ragnar Strongspear as well. I do not think I could remain here even if you wanted me to, my lord."

He nodded with understanding, and she continued, "In my childhood the roads that the Romans built to connect the towns they erected in Britain became unsafe. There was a time, not in my memory, but surely in my father's memory, when those roads were safe; but then the legions left, and with them the way of life we had known for centuries departed as well. No one would have dared to attack the estate of Gaius Drusus Corinium or Anthony Porcius in that faded past. Times are different now, Wulf, and your people are a different people. To survive we must change, and I think we can do so without sacrificing the values that we hold dear. You are not like Ragnar Strongspear or Harald Swiftsword. You are a different kind of Saxon. Your feet, like mine, are not mired in the intractable past. You, too, dream of a future that cannot even be imagined by most. I will gladly go with you to Brand-dun! There is nothing left for us here at Cadda-wic but memories. I will discard the bad ones and leave them behind. The good ones I will carry in my heart always. Ohh Wulf! We almost lost each other once, but the gods ruled that we should be reunited to love again. I am so happy!"

"Mama! Mama!" Aurora came running through the fields toward them, her silky golden hair flying, her little legs pumping for all they were worth. "Mama!" Behind her Nellwyn came, carrying Royse.

Cailin swept her daughter up into her arms and covered the child's face with kisses. "I missed you, my darling," she told her daughter. "Did you miss Mama?"

"Are the bad men gone, Mama?" Aurora asked nervously.

"They are gone forever, and will never come back, I promise you, my daughter," Cailin answered the child, hugging her.

"When shall we leave for Brand-dun?" Wulf asked his wife, his heart full with his love for this brave woman who was his mate.

"Today!" Cailin said. "Have our men take our things from the hall. We will burn what we can of it, and tear down what is left. It is finished."

"Where are we going?" Nellwyn asked as she came abreast of them.

Cailin took Royse from her servant, praising her bravery. Then as she sat down upon the ground and put her son to her aching breasts, Wulf explained to Nellwyn what had been decided. When he had finished, and while Royse suckled greedily, Cailin said to her husband, "Nellwyn must have a husband. She desires Albert. Will you arrange it, my lord?"

"I will," he said, "and gladly! Your loyalty saved our children's lives, Nellwyn. It is little enough repayment. Albert is a very lucky fellow, and I shall tell him so."

Wulf gave the order to empty the hall of their possessions, and as it was being done, he climbed to the solar. Ragnar Strongspear lay spread upon his back, naked, and as white as a fish's belly. There seemed to be blood everywhere. Gingerly, Wulf pulled the man's head back, for it had fallen upon his chest. His eyes were wide and sightless, and there was a look of surprise on his face. The gaping wound shocked him. Ragnar Strongspear's throat was deeply slashed from ear to ear. *How had she done it?* His delicate lambkin did not seem capable of such a savage act, but he could not deny the evidence of his own eyes. It was certainly a most

410 / To Love Again

mortal wound, and hardly the sort of death a man would want to face. At best, a man died in battle. At worst, of old age in his bed. To die at the hands of a frail woman was shameful. There would be no Valhalla for Ragnar Strongspear. He would likely haunt this place forever. Cailin had been correct. They could hardly sleep and make love in the place where Ragnar had attempted to rape her, and where she had killed him.

"Is the hall cleared yet?" he called down.

"Aye, my lord," a voice answered him. "We are ready to fire it."

"Hand me up a torch," Wulf Ironside said. "We will start here." When the torch was given to him, he set fire to the bed space where Ragnar Strongspear lay. Then tossing the torch aside, he climbed down into the hall and directed his men to set the rest of the building alight.

He exited the burning hall, to find Cailin awaiting him, already mounted upon her mare. Aurora was seated before her mother, and Nellwyn was settled in the cart, Royse in her arms. He looked at his wife, and their eyes met in silent understanding. He looked at his children and smiled. Aurora and Royse and the children who would come after them were a bright future. He no longer feared a dark destiny. Whatever happened, the years ahead would be golden with their love and the hope of a better world to come.

Mounting his stallion, Wulf Ironfist smiled at his wife, and Cailin smiled back at him. With his love to sustain her, she thought, she could face any obstacle and overcome it. "I love you," she said softly, and was thrilled when he responded, "I love you, too, lamb-kin." Together they rode away from the bleak past and into a shining tomorrow.

A u t h o r 's N o t e

The Celtic tribes of Britain faded into history as they intermingled their blood with that of the newcomers. Only in Cornwall and Wales could any strong evidence of them be found again in Britain.

The Saxons, the Jutes and the Angles poured into Britain in increasing numbers seeking land and a decent future for their peoples. For the next six centuries their combined cultures spawned kingdoms with names like Northumbria (which combined Bernicia and Deira); East Anglia, Mercia, Kent, Essex, Sussex and Wessex. Kings with names like Albert, Ethelred, Edward, Aethelswith, and Edwin ruled. Britain became *England*, the land of the Angles.

Then in 1066 the Normans arrived to take England by conquest. Once more another culture combined, and mingled itself and the blood of its people with that of those who had come before them. This is the way of the world even today. Nothing remains the same . . . *ever.*

I hope you have enjoyed *To Love Again.* Next year Ballantine and I will bring you *Love, Remember Me*, the story of Nyssa Wyndham, the daughter of Blaze; and her many adventures in the court of Henry VIII, and two of his queens, the clever and witty Anne of Cleves, and the charming, but foolish, Catherine Howard. Until then I wish you much Good Reading!

Bertrice W. Small
Southold, NY, and, soon, Tryon, NC